My Brother's Daughter

A Chronicles of Warfare Novel #10

Written By:

Melinda Michelle

Published By:

GMME

This book is a work of fiction. Names, characters, places, and incidents are either the product of the author's imagination or used fictitiously. Any resemblance to actual persons, living or dead, or to actual events or locales is entirely coincidental.

Global Multi Media Enterprises (GMME)
P.O. Box 3763
Tallahassee, FL 32315-3763
850.694.2165

GMME Results...GMME Purpose...GMME Destiny!

Visit our website at www.gwendolynevans.wix.com/gmme

Email us at: gwendolynevans21@yahoo.com

ISBN: 9781092116305
LCCN: 2019938070

Cover Design: GMME
Cover Photo: Bigstock Photo

Acknowledgments

I would like to acknowledge the Great I AM. This book is an ode to God's grace, mercy and most of all, His sovereignty. I'm in awe at how He continues to order my steps on this journey. Every *yes* to God ensures my protection on this path of obedience as it also delivers me to the next set of ordered steps. It is a privilege and an honor to do what I do. Always grateful. Always humbled.

I'd like to thank my faithful betas – **Ileana Guerrero, Ashley Croft** and **Angela Y. Hodge**. Thank you for always being willing to take the first dive into my wild imagination. To my editor **Brittany Mirvil**, you my dear are an exquisite human being. Thank you!

Shout out to my family, friends, and church members (Fdub!) who continue to support me in all I do.

A special shout out to **Teleshia Lewinson** for her contribution to the name of the cemetery.

To my awesome, loyal, supportive, and sometimes CRAZY readers: Thank you for all the laughs, gifs, and threats y'all have given me on this journey waiting for the release of this highly anticipated book. Your shenanigans kept me motivated to press through the process and finish this story. I sincerely hope it is worth the wait! I love you all and am so humbled that y'all have chosen to take this journey with me. Thank you! Forever grateful.

Dedication

Honestly, I dedicate this book to myself. This three-year process was not without its obstacles. The warfare I went through to birth this book was by far the hardest I have *ever* endured. From lies to depression to witchcraft and some other shenanigans in between. I now understand that I couldn't write this book had I not endured the trials and tests that came with it. I am sincerely proud of myself for finishing this book in the midst of everything else I had going on. God definitely revealed a more resilient version of myself during this process. I now understand that no matter what I can do anything I put my mind to. In other words, *"I can do all things through Christ who strengthens me."*

Praise for "Saturday Showdown"

Whew! This was an epic finish to an outstanding series. I do feel some kind of way now that it's over because well...it's over. Melinda Michelle did an excellent job of closing the gaps and still delivered a few plot twists and revelations in the process. Saturday Showdown was a definite spiritual awakening. It's apparent that God's hand was in every aspect of this book and even the entire series. There is a message for every reader. Simply open your heart to receive what lies in the pages of this book just for you.

I couldn't get enough of this series. I have been obsessed from Sunday to Saturday and never disappointed. I recommend every single page of all 7 books. It has everything, but most of all, I appreciate the faith journey and the inspiration to seek [a] relationship with God. I would give the whole series 10 stars if I could.

Wow! This is a good read for everyone out there. Saturday Showdown is by far the best of the series. Must read. Saturday Showdown is "Nothing but the truth". Looking forward to reading more of Melinda Michelle books. My sister continue to keep it real!

Man, oh man! What a ride. We have lived with these characters for some years and the battles were epic! Truly love and war! Can't wait to see what God does next through author Melinda Michelle!

This book is the business. The last of the Chronicles of Warfare series was everything I expected and more. Melinda Michelle created scenes that we often dream of in the spirit realm. To see the word of God come to life on the pages of this book was phenomenal. I recommend it 100%! Oh, it left me wanting more. Looking forward to what's to come!

Special Note to the Reader

There is an appendix in the back of the book to refresh your memory of the characters from previous novels. There is also a list of all the angelic and some demonic beings to help you keep track. Please be advised there are some <u>SPOILERS</u>!!!

"My Brother's Daughter" begins the "new war" in the *Chronicles of Warfare* saga. If you finished the seven days in the series, but have not read previous "bonus" books, you may not be up to speed on this storyline. I have included two chapters from "The Unexpected Gift" (Book 8) and one chapter from "Deleted Scenes" (Book 9). If you are all caught up, feel free to skip. If not, this will bring you up to date on MOST of what you missed in Nigel and Kadijah's story.

Continuity of Storyline

Even though the Chronicles of Warfare (COW) and the Divine Love Story (DLS) series share characters, keep in mind that DLS is a current story (2018), while COW is still in 2015. Therefore, Dylan has not yet met the crew from DLS.

The Unexpected Gift

Chapter 1: A Divine Union

The garden tub in the honeymoon suite was humungous. It was surrounded on each side by two marble steps that led to the deep bowl-shaped tub. Nigel's six-foot-two lean frame was appreciative of the roominess.

Kadijah sat with her back against her husband's chest. He placed a soft kiss on her cheek. She couldn't stop the grin that spread across her face. Never had she been happier or felt this loved and adored. She was so blessed. Her heart was grateful it waited for the man God had for her.

Nigel wrapped his arms around his wife. *Wife.* That word was powerful. The warm water was soothing as they enjoyed an intimate conversation.

He said, "I promise, when we get out of this tub, we're going to have a do-over and I'm going to take my time."

"I look forward to it, but you should know I'm not in the least bit mad about earlier."

He chuckled. "That just makes you nasty."

She laughed. "I'm glad we waited until our wedding night. Are you?"

"Yeah, I am. You were definitely worth the wait."

"You were too, handsome."

"Girl, you don't know how hard I prayed for God to keep me. The struggle was real!"

She laughed. "You know that brings up a thought we never addressed. It was hard to resist your sexy behind for so long. I know we steered away from a lot of sexual conversations, but maybe we should have discussed some things."

He could sense her hesitation.

"Go ahead, love. I'm an open book to you. Feel free to be open and honest with your concerns," he assured her.

She turned slightly to look up at him. The minute she looked into his eyes; butterflies bombarded her stomach. This man was beautiful. His skin was light, what they referred to as "yella." His hair was closely cropped with deep waves and his facial hair was a neatly trimmed mustache and goatee. His father's hypnotic light brown eyes watched her with intensity. His exotic eyes changed color depending on his mood.

"I know we both had a past before each other, but have you dealt with your soul ties? I'm so very much in love with you and I know marriage will have its challenges, but I just want to make sure we have dealt with the heavy ones up front. I dealt with mine after Elliott. I had to fast because it freaked me out knowing his demonic background. I guess my main concern is your soul tie to Lauren."

He nodded understanding her concern. He knew she wasn't finished with her thought.

"We never really talked about how many people were in our past. I will tell you mine if you want to know. I *think* I can handle yours."

He chuckled at the look on her face. She frowned. "I don't mean to laugh baby, but how many people do you think I've slept with?"

"I don't know," she shrugged.

"But the look on your face tells me you have a working theory, and it seems like you might be scared to hear it."

"Well... I don't want to assume so..."

He laughed. "My number is 15 including you." She stared with a blank expression. He frowned slightly, "I'm not proud of it or embarrassed by it. It's just my past. I can't change it now." She continued to stare. "Okay, I can't quite interpret that face."

"Whew... I thought it was like at least double that."

He laughed and pinched her. "What's your number?"

"You make five." He nodded. "So, have you dealt with the soul ties?" she asked again.

"I have. Grey and I talked about it, actually. She broke it down for me. I did, a lot of self-inventory after I had the encounter with God in my brother's kitchen. It's like the more you tap into God the more truth you get. His presence illuminates every dark thing in your life."

He stared down at his beautiful wife. Her makeup was still flawless, from their wedding, but he was grateful she didn't need it. Her luxurious natural mane was tamed for the moment. She had it up in an elegant bun. Her skin was fair. She had a naturally beautiful face. Her body was perfect for him. She had just enough in all the right places which he planned to explore much more thoroughly when they finished their bath. He ran his thumb over her tempting lips.

He said, "I wanted to make sure my heart was completely open for you, but also completely healed from anything in the past. I want to build a life, legacy, and family with you. Nothing and no one in the past is going to stand in the way of that."

She placed her wet hand on his cheek. The love that was on his face as he stared into her soft brown eyes gently squeezed her heart.

"I love you sweet pea."

He leaned down to softly put his lips on hers. It was the sweetest kiss she had ever known. Something stirred deep within her soul as his passion for her poured out through his kiss. Reluctantly, he pulled away. Her breath hitched as her eyes popped open to stare at him. His eyes were a vivid green. They were greener than she'd ever seen them before.

He trailed kisses up her neck until he reached her ear. He whispered, "Let me show me how much I love you."

Her body shivered. All she could do was nod.

Once they were out of the tub, Nigel carried his bride to the still untouched California king-sized bed. The plush, white down comforter had red rose petals in the shape of a heart on top of it. He placed her in the middle of the heart. She reached up and pulled his mouth towards hers.

He said, "Wait."

She frowned, "What is it, love?"

"I want to pray with you first."

"You want to what?" she asked confused by what she heard.

He smiled. "I know it's strange, but it's something I feel I need to do."

"Are you gonna ask God to make it good?"

He laughed hard. "No, crazy. I'm going to ask God to bless the child we will eventually conceive. We may even conceive her tonight."

"Oh," was all she could manage. This man completely undid her.

"When I talked to Neil about you, he told me something that has remained with me and always will. I believe it also applies to our daughter. He said, if I wanted to protect you, it was spiritual first, then natural. I love you and I'm excited about our journey as husband and wife, but truth be told, God brought us together for something so much greater. Knowing everything we know now about our bloodline; I have to protect my daughter by any means necessary. I want to cover you because you're the one that has to carry them. You now have my last name, that makes you and our children my responsibility. Like I said, I know it's strange, but it's just something I feel the need to do."

She nodded with tears in her eyes. Her heart was overwhelmed at the moment.

"I really meant to do it before we consummated our marriage, but..."

She laughed.

"Let's pray, baby," she told him. The four angels that guarded them lit up the room in their brilliant majestic white light. Bomani, one of his naval warriors smiled. He said, "He is truly ready for the mantle given." Lajos, his other naval warrior nodded. "Indeed. He understands his dominion and he's exercising it." Her warriors, Cheveyo and Quan, nodded in agreement.

Nigel linked their fingers and pulled his wife into his chest. Kadijah wrapped her arms around her husband.

He began, "Father, thank you so much for the blessings that you have given us. We are truly grateful, humbled and honored to be a part of your master plan. Father, I pray right now for the protection of our daughter. We know her arrival is in your time, but I cover her now from dangers seen and unseen. I plead the blood of Jesus over her now before she even gets here. She is your vessel that you entrusted to us." He placed a firm hand on Kadijah's stomach. She placed her hand on top of his and linked their fingers again. "I cover my wife's womb. I know that this is the only womb you authorized to carry my seeds so now I decree that it is a place of safety for my children. Lord, make her womb a place of protection for them until we meet them no matter what the enemy may try to throw our way. I cancel every tactic, assignment and fiery dart that may try to come against my wife. Now father bless the love between us and bless the fruit of our loins to be used in the earth as weapons against the Kingdom of Darkness. Equip us with whatever we need to teach them, guide them and protect them. Let them be healthy, whole, intelligent and have the heart to serve you from the day they take their first breath. In Jesus name, I pray, amen."

"Amen," Kadijah agreed as tears ran down her face.

He looked down at his wife. She said, "Well that was different."

He laughed and said, "Weren't you about to kiss me or something."

She grinned and pulled his mouth to hers.

Nigel's heart was overwhelmed at the love he felt for his *good thing*. He thought back to their ceremony and how they both shed silent tears as they exchanged their vows. He felt favored by God to have this woman by his side. It's when he realized he held God's best for him in his arms and he got to have, hold, and cherish her for the rest of their lives.

As he gently explored her, he thought about the first night he saw her so frightened and how her eyes captured his heart. He never had a chance. She had his heart at that moment and neither of them knew it. He knew what a tremendous effort it took for her to give him her heart. He was honored to hold it and grateful that she was the one holding his.

Kadijah trembled beneath his expert touch. This man took her places she didn't even know existed. Knowing that they were still enjoying the appetizer, she didn't know if she could handle the entrée without her heart bursting. She felt safe with this man. She felt treasured by this man. She felt blessed to have this man in her heart, in her life and she wanted more than anything to carry his seed in her womb.

He stared down into the soft brown eyes that had him spellbound. She reached up and stroked his face.

"You ready?" he whispered.

She nodded.

With the next kiss, they became one.

Their dance was slow, deliberate, patient, and majestic. As he loved her, he reached up and grabbed her hand. Their fingers locked as their passion soared. He found no shame in the tears that ran down his cheeks. What she gave him, he had never experienced before.

There were many women before his wife, but he never could find what he was searching for with any of them. The chance for a deeper connection that he knew existed, but one that continued to elude him. His promiscuity was him searching in ignorance for something only his wife could provide.

He was grateful that God had intervened, and they decided to choose to wait for each other. He felt that if they had experienced each other before their appointed time, it would have cheapened the experience. Loving her now he understood not only was this authorized by God himself but favored. He knew their union had a special blessing on it because he'd waited to know her in this way at this appointed time and for God's glory.

When he opened his eyes, he saw her tears as well. He kissed them away as he watched the pleasure bloom on her face. They cherished every kiss, every caress, every whisper, every sigh. After a while, he gave in to the inevitable. She held on tight and whispered his name in his ear, sending a shiver down his spine.

They were silent for a long while. She lay her head on his chest and listened to his heartbeat. He listened to her smooth breathing. He would never forget how she made him feel at this moment as long as he lived. He was trying to figure out how to describe what he felt. He didn't have the words.

He scooped her up in his arms as he pulled the comforter from beneath them. Kadijah snuggled into her husband's chest as she inhaled his intoxicating scent. Nigel wrapped his brand-new wife securely in his arms as their satisfied silence eventually led them to satisfied sleep.

Epilogue: Full Circle

Kadijah regurgitated again. She had no idea how there was still anything left in her to come up. The nausea she felt had plagued her all day long. No matter what she tried, her stomach just wouldn't settle. Finally, she had the common sense to take a pregnancy test.

The moment she saw the positive sign on the stick, the morning sickness that arrived late in the afternoon, made its way up and out. Now she was sitting in the corner of their bathroom in a ball with her head on her knees. She didn't know how long she had been sitting there, but she knew it was a while. She was afraid to move. Every time she did the nausea assaulted her again.

She heard Nigel enter their apartment. He called out to her. She didn't even have the energy to answer. Nigel walked through the house looking for his wife. He knew she was home because her car was outside. He thought maybe she might be sleeping. He went into their bedroom and didn't see any evidence of her.

He frowned. "Dij, babe. You in here?"

He heard her cough and followed the sound to their bathroom. He opened the door to see her balled up in a corner of the bathroom. A look of puzzlement spread across his face.

"Now, this looks familiar." She looked up at him. He frowned. "What's wrong?"

Uneasiness struck him. Her eyes were red, it looked like she had been crying.

Pointing to the pregnancy test on the sink, she said, "Your kid decided to announce herself in a grand way."

"My what?" He questioned as he blinked in surprise. He walked over to the sink and picked up the pregnancy test. He stared at her. "Are you serious?"

She nodded. The grin that spread across his face made her heart dance, but it was followed by another wave of nausea. She quickly scrambled to the toilet. She was sick again. Embarrassed, she waved Nigel away. He rolled his eyes and held her hair away from her face.

When she was done, he let down the toilet and flushed then led her over to the sink. She rinsed her mouth out then gargled with mouth wash. She washed her face. He handed her a towel to dry off.

He said, "I'm sorry you're sick, baby, but I can't stop smiling."

She gave him a small smile. "I'm happy too baby, but I got a feeling this isn't going to be a cakewalk."

"Well, you won't be doing it alone. I'm right here." He kissed her forehead. "I am going to run you a warm bath and find out what I can get for you to eat that will settle your stomach. I'm taking you to the doctor first thing in the morning."

She nodded. "I just want to lay down right now sweet pea."

He led her to their bed. Pulling back the covers, he fluffed the pillows for her. She sat down on the bed. He removed her shoes. He went to get a nightshirt for her, then helped her out of her clothes. She lay back on the cool, comfortable sheets. She looked miserable. Nigel felt so bad for his wife, but there was nothing he could do except try to make her as comfortable as possible.

She said, "There's ginger ale in the fridge."

"Okay, I'll be right back."

Minutes later he returned with a glass of ginger ale. He put the straw to her lips. As she sipped, he put his hand on her forehead. She felt a little warm, but not enough to alarm him. He'd make sure to monitor it throughout the night. After a few sips, she finally managed to burp.

He asked, "You feel better?"

"A little," she nodded.

"So, tell me what happened today?"

"I went to go visit Julian today. I hadn't seen him since we've been back. We were catching up when this wave of nausea hit me so hard. We concluded that a pregnancy test was likely in order. So, I left there and went and picked up one along with some ginger ale. I got back here and took it. From the minute the results showed up I've been sick."

Nigel frowned. "How long were you on the bathroom floor?"

"Probably a couple of hours."

"A couple of hours! Why didn't you call me?"

"Sweet pea, I couldn't move. Every time I did, I was sick again."

He frowned. He felt so bad for her.

"I'm sorry love."

"It's okay. It's not your fault... well, actually it kinda is."

He chuckled. "Yeah, I guess it is."

He kicked off his dress shoes and came out of his suit jacket. Loosening his tie, he lay down next to her. He reached for her and pulled her in close burying his face in her hair.

He began to rub her belly and said, "We're going to be parents."

"Are you ready?" she asked.

"Nope!" He laughed. "You?"

"I think I'm ready to be a mother, but I don't think I'm ready to be pregnant. I've only known for two hours and I'm like, nope, this ain't for me."

He laughed. "Good luck with that." He kissed her cheek. "It's going to be okay."

The minute the words left his mouth a feeling rushed over him. He recognized it as his discernment. Bomani touched his shoulder to confirm what his gift was trying to tell him. Instinctually Nigel knew his child was about to be under attack. He didn't know by who, how or when, but he knew the attack was imminent. He pulled his wife a little closer as he continued to rub her belly. He was grateful he'd been obedient to the instructions in his spirit to cover their daughter even before she was conceived. He began to silently pray.

Kadijah leaned her head on his chest and linked her fingers with the hand on her belly. Everything in her now understood what Angela and Grey were trying to tell her. She was carrying something powerful and the opposition was waiting with open arms to test her faith to see if she had what it took to carry it to fruition. All of a sudden, Nigel's need to cover them in prayer before they conceived didn't feel so foolish anymore.

Cheveyo and Quan, her angelic warriors stood watch over her. They knew her battle had just begun...

Deleted Scenes

Sunday Dinner: A Faith-Filled Prayer

Bellies were full, and itis was settling in. Jeremiah had outdone himself today. The close-knit group feasted on barbecue ribs, chicken and brisket which were complemented by his homemade barbecue sauces, both red and yellow. He also cooked collard greens, corn on the cob, macaroni and cheese, potato salad, peach cobbler, and a pound cake. They were deliriously full and practically comatose.

In attendance were the owners of the cozy home, Jeremiah and Mia along with their three children, Jeremiah Junior, Madison, and Isaiah. Seth, a pregnant Sheridan, Daniel, Grey, Neil, Hunter, Nigel, Kadijah, Nathaniel, David, Genevieve, Lindsey, Jamal, Hope, and Jacob rounded out the makeshift family.

Uncharacteristically Nigel interjected. "Hey, guys. Before everyone passes out. I have an announcement to make."

"Please tell me it's something that will give me an opportunity to clown, Grey," Jeremiah interjected.

Everyone laughed while Grey launched a pillow at Jeremiah's head from the sofa she and Neil were on.

Jeremiah caught the pillow and laughed.

"Um, no. Not quite," Nigel said as he reached for Kadijah's hand.

She looked up at him shocked and realized he was about to announce her pregnancy. It was still pretty early; she was only eight weeks. A slight panic hit her because she recalled that was the stage at which Grey lost their first child. Nigel kissed her hand to calm the nerves he saw on her face. He was confident that the curse had been abolished and his baby girl would be born full term and healthy.

"Kadijah and I are expecting our first child, our baby girl."

"You negroes ain't waste no time, I see. What's the due date, let me calculate to see if y'all was creeping before the wedding," Jeremiah said mischievously?

Everybody fell out laughing then followed up with their congratulatory remarks.

"I'm so excited for you guys," Sheridan said smiling as she rubbed her belly.

"Well, Grey, Lindsey, Genevieve, y'all might as well come on and join the party," Seth told them.

Lindsey grinned. "We're trying."

Jamal showed all his teeth and puffed out his chest. They laughed.

"Your pastor is on it," David said as Genevieve hid her face from embarrassment.

"Heck nol. It took me 22 hours to push out Neil's big head son. I think not. I currently suffer from PTSD from that experience and am not anxious to repeat it," Grey said as Neil fell out laughing.

"Sis, you said, you were going to give my brother a house full of babies," Nigel called her out.

"Whatever, that was before I realized that y'all seeds were nine months of spiritual drama."

Everyone laughed.

"Aye, she got a point," Jeremiah said.

"Oh, Lord, Jeremiah is on my side. I might get knocked up just to be contrary," Grey said dryly as everyone laughed.

"You better get knocked up, that's the only time I'm willing to be nice to you," Jeremiah quipped. Grey rolled her eyes. "But as I was saying, you negroes do seem to have a lot of drama that follows your seeds. I'm not in the mood for no kidnapping, no witches, no warlocks, no voodoo, no hoodoo, no Beetlejuice, and no violence."

Everybody fell out laughing.

"So, let's pray right now against all types of foolishness and shut this mess down now!"

Only Jeremiah could start out clowning and find a way to be spiritually deep in the same breath.

"Agreed."

"Amen."

"I'm with you bro."

"I hear you."

"Let's do it," Nathanial rounded out the agreements.

"Let's cover this baby girl, in the blood of Jesus Christ."

Every warring and ministering angel in the room glorified. Unseen to the human eye, they bathed the living room in opulent white and sapphire light. Their eyes flamed as they made a circle to surround these prayer warriors. Their wings snapped in unison forming a canopy. These believers were now under the *Shadow of the Almighty*.

Death, in all his black diamond beauty, cast his massive shadow over the entire house to protect it as he took flight to hover above the home. His scythe appeared in his hand as his diamond eyes sparkled with every color of the rainbow twinkling whenever he blinked. He duplicated himself as many times as needed to reach from this house to the gates of Heaven. If any demonic force tried to block this prayer, they would face off with him.

Neil shared a glance with Jeremiah and nodded his appreciation. Choked up, Nigel had to clear his throat. Tears ran down Kadijah's face. She was so overwhelmed at God's love for her. She woke up today starting week eight of pregnancy and wanted to panic knowing what she knew of their family history. God had heard her silent prayer.

"Let's pray," Jeremiah said.

They all stood up and joined hands after David led Nigel and Kadijah to stand in the middle of the circle.

Jeremiah began, "Lord, I do not believe this moment is coincidence. It is my sincere belief that this moment in time, this prayer is divine. So, Father, we come before Your throne of grace full of faith, full of hope and full of love for the blessing that You sent to this family. Lord, we cover their baby girl from this day until the day she is held safely in her parents' arms. We know that You sent this voice into the earth to be used for Your glory. Therefore, we declare that no scheme, no plot, no curse, no distraction, no person, no disease, no attack can stand against the promise that proceeded from Your mouth. This little girl is healthy. She is whole. She is the promised child You sent to do Your will. Now, Father, have your way."

Jeremiah laid his hands on both Kadijah and Nigel. Mia and Grey clasped hands to close the gap he left behind. Nigel had one hand on his wife's stomach as tears ran down her face. As their praying voices elevated, the children ran out to see what was going on. Jeremiah Jr., being the oldest whispered for the others to grab hands when he saw his father laying hands and praying. They stood in the hallway holding hands with their heads bowed as his father continued to pray.

"Strengthen their bond, strengthen their faith, strengthen their love, strengthen their fortitude to stand against any wiles of the devil. We declare they will be victorious, and the enemy will be defeated on all fronts. Lord, I even pray now for the medical staff that will be assigned to them. Lord, let them be believers that will look beyond what they learned in school and see Your hand in the life of this baby. Surround this pregnancy on every side with faith-filled warriors that will make this a personal fight to see this weapon birthed in the earth. We thank You, we praise You, we love You. I seal this prayer in the matchless blood of Your precious son, Jesus. Amen!"

There was a chorus of amens that followed. They all felt the presence of the Most High God enter the room and wrap Nigel and Kadijah in His loving embrace.

Jeremiah wiped a tear. He took Nigel and Kadijah each by the hand. As much of a clown as he was, when it came to the things of the Lord, Jeremiah's anointing always shined through.

"This is not a test of your faith, but your *trust* in God. Understand, there is a battle on the horizon, and it will not be easy, but the battle is not yours, it's the Lord's! We're in this fight with you."

Sheridan, Grey, Lindsey, and Genevieve broke out into a praise. A mighty move of God swept through the living room and all the believers rejoiced including the children because they knew the Great I AM had just stepped into the room.

My Brother's Daughter

Prologue: The Escape

Her eyes remained alert as she studied everything around her. This was her only opportunity to get away and she wasn't about to squander it. To some, it might seem suicidal, but she was a calculating woman and decided that the odds were in her favor. It didn't matter that she was cruising at an altitude of 30,000 feet in the air flying across the country. All that mattered was getting out of there.

She'd been locked up for months, but she used that time wisely to plot and plan a way of escape. This turned out to be her best option. There was one thing fueling her beyond her fears and common sense - *revenge*. Those two brothers would pay for what they cost her. She could not rest until she extracted unimaginable pain from them. While death was the ultimate goal, it was too easy.

First, she'd go after what was most precious to them. They would suffer and then beg her for mercy she would never grant them. She smiled wickedly. She felt the plane level off. There were four federal agents on the plane. She knew the pilot and copilot were of no concern to her. She was shackled, hands and feet, in the ugly orange jumpsuit.

One of the first things she was going to do when she escaped was to indulge herself in a proper wardrobe. She was far too sexy to be in such hideous attire. She heard the agents talking. Two were in front of her - and two behind. She eyed the closet near the cockpit. It was her saving grace.

She began to choke and gag. Her body began to convulse, her eyes rolled into the back of her head. The four agents jumped into action.

"She's having a seizure," one of them announced.

"Where are the keys?"

"Don't unlock her!"

"We have to unlock her to help her."

She continued to convulse as slobber began to come out of her mouth.

"Oh, for goodness sakes," one of them said and headed over to unlock her wrists.

Once she heard the satisfying sound of her hands being released, she made her head lull only to swing it back up with a vengeance. She heard a satisfying crunch as he screamed. Hands free, she grabbed the weapon on his right hip. She had her arm around his throat and the gun to his temple before any of them knew what happened.

Their guns were drawn and aimed at her.

The agent with the gun to his head said, "You don't have to do this."

"Shut up!" she hissed. "Guns down gentlemen."

"That's not going to happen," one of the agents said.

She spoke what they were all thinking.

"Neither of you can get off a shot without hitting your man or blowing out a window and killing us all."

"What's your plan? We're thirty thousand feet in the air."

She smiled. "That is my plan."

Quick as lightning she turned the gun and shot the window on the exit door. The agents screamed, but it was too late. The door began to cave in from the pressure and then it was ripped away. She slung the agent down and held on. The alarms began to go off as oxygen masks fell from the overhead compartments. The force of rushing air whipping through the plane sucked one of the officers out right away.

The one she held at gunpoint was next. His fate was sealed as the pressure snatched him out into the night sky. The remaining two officers were trying to hold on. Their screams were drowned out by the strong force of the wind.

She got down on her knees, her shackles benefitting her at this moment. She shot off her restraints then secured the gun as she continued to hold on. She heard a scream and knew another officer had been snatched away. She carefully used her legs and arms to lock on to each seat as she made her way to the closet by the cockpit.

The wind was howling as she used every ounce of strength and grit to hold on. She looked back and saw the last agent coming for her. She smiled and continued on her way. When she got to the closet, she pulled the latch and smiled. Grabbing the edge of the closet she pulled her legs inside.

The force of the pressure building was strong, but her will was stronger. Using her legs to keep her braced in the closet she stood up and held on to the bar. She pulled down one of the parachutes. After some effort, she put the chute on her back and strapped herself in. She was about to reach for the goggles but saw the agent was gaining on her. She smiled and folded herself into a ball.

The pressure pulled her out of the plane. She was sucked out in a flash. She kept her eyes closed as she spread her arms and legs to slow down her speed. She pulled the cord and opened her parachute.

First Trimester (May, June, July) 2015

Chapter 1: Frenemies

For the time being, all was quiet in the Lawson home. There had been no spiritual drama or emergencies looming over their heads. Neil was at work, while Grey decided to catch a much-needed nap now that her baby boy had finally decided to take his.

Grey lay on the plush sofa knocked out with a book on her chest as Barrington Scottsdale, the feline she loved to hate, sat curled up at her feet getting in his afternoon nap as well. The baby monitor was right next to her head.

Hunter was in his crib, which is why Barry was in the living room. Still jealous of the new addition to their family, he avoided Hunter like the plague and made no qualms about letting them know he didn't like their little bundle of joy. It tickled Grey to no end. Neil, on the other hand, remained ready to evict the tabby cat the first instance his jealousy got out of control.

Suddenly, the tan fur on Barry's chubby body began to stand up on end. His low purring stopped as he opened one of his green eyes. Something wasn't right. Both eyes opened now, the cat stood up to see what was amiss. He looked up at the two angels that guarded Grey, Savas, and Bojan. He knew them, but they wouldn't create this feeling of evil.

Apprehensive, Barry watched as the angels glorified. They drew their weapons as their eyes and artillery lit up with blue flames. Barry sat back on his haunches and watched as they headed outside the house. He stared waiting to see what was about to unfold.

Outside and invisible to the human eye, Insidious casually strolled to the edge of the Lawson's yard, careful not to cross the threshold. He was an ancient, menacing demon that stood 7-feet tall with a long and lean frame. His skin was smoke gray and reptilian. A darted tip, that could whip out and snatch enemies in a heartbeat, adorned the end of his long tail. He had a canine face and jet-black eyes that held a mysterious glow. His fanged teeth glinted in the sunlight.

Righteous indignation flooded Grey's warriors as they could not believe the audacity of this vile creature.

"State your cause or see the pit this day!" Savas, a Turkish warrior, said with conviction as his two broadswords flamed brighter at his sides.

Insidious grinned. He raised both of his oyster-colored clawed palms in a sign of surrender.

"My brother, I come in peace," he smoothly replied. "If you know nothing about me, you know I respect protocol. I'm more civilized than that. Besides, I'm alone. Why would I engage the four of you without back-up?"

Savas' eyes narrowed. "You stopped being my brother when you chose to follow Lucifer in his plot against Father."

In his smooth silky voice, Insidious responded.

"That was eons ago. Surely, we're past that, brother. Let's move on, shall we?"

Bojan, a Serbian warrior, was over it. He demanded, "State your cause, now!"

Insidious chuckled. "I'm here to see *him*, of course."

Bojan's long sword flamed even more as he took a step towards Insidious. "I see insanity has captured you in your old age."

"Careful brother," Insidious said in a warning tone without flinching. "I didn't come here to start a war. Now, I could alert his mother to my presence, but we all know that's not wise. If she detects my level of power all sorts of bells and whistles will go off in her spirit."

Bojan and Savas glanced at each other.

Insidious continued, "If she's alerted to my presence and feels that I am a threat to her son, surely she will go into warrior mode. Neither of us wants that. We know she's more dangerous than his father could ever be, which is why her womb was chosen to carry him. I want no parts of an unnecessary war with that seer."

Again, Savas and Bojan looked at each other knowingly.

"Furthermore, if she's concerned with the safety of her son, even though he's behind a hedge, she won't be able to focus on protecting her niece. She's her watchman. We all know Nigel's daughter is the only reason I'm in this abysmal region in the first place. Let's try and stay focused shall we brother?"

Savas and Bojan eyed each other again. They knew Insidious was one hundred percent correct. Grey would lose it. Her love for her son would unleash everything inside of her that was capable of protecting him. Even she didn't know just how powerful she was. It wasn't yet time to reveal it.

Finally, Savas asked the obvious question.

"Why?"

"Why else?" Insidious replied with a nonchalant shrug. "I'm curious. He has been talked about for decades. I just want to lay my eyes on this promised child. You know I've always had an appreciation for Father's work, especially the uniquely gifted ones. Rest assured I *will* alert her to my presence and make her believe I am a threat to her child if you deny me the chance to satisfy my curiosity."

"Curiosity? That would be laughable if you weren't so dangerous," Bojan snapped. "I'm curious to know why you care seeing as how you and your cowardly comrades tried to take him out."

"*I* did no such thing. They did. You know I don't insert myself in the promises of God. It's a frivolous fight for which I don't have time. I excel at what I do because I'm not greedy nor do I let my ego dictate my actions."

Again, Savas and Bojan looked at each other. Insidious was indeed a different type of demon. He never tried to work outside of the will of God, but his subtle manipulations within the boundaries set by God and His *permissive* will were legendary in the spirit realm. They considered their options, as a bemused Insidious watched them ponder his request. He had no doubts how this would go.

After a few intense moments, Savas reluctantly said, "We will allow this one time. You cannot touch him, and we will shield your presence from his mother. Those are the conditions. Accept them or walk away."

Insidious nodded.

Bojan warned, "If this is a trick of any kind, we have no problem inciting this war and taking you out to protect this charge."

"You have my word, brothers," Insidious said with sincerity.

He took two steps onto their property. The Light responded!

Hunter's two naval warriors, Alvise and Ranj, arrived first along with Captain Valter, Lieutenant Nero and the Angel of Death in all his black diamond beauty. They stood between the house and Insidious, weapons drawn and eyes aflame.

"What is the meaning of this breach?" the Scandinavian Captain's voice demanded with a boom.

Insidious smiled, "Well, if it isn't my favorite Captain of the Hosts."

In a flash, Valter drew his blue-flamed saber and pressed it to Insidious' throat.

"I'm not playing games with you."

Insidious didn't flinch because he knew the captain wouldn't strike without sufficient cause. He did eye Nero carefully though because he just might.

"As I told Savas and Bojan, I'm curious about the promised child and I wanted to meet him. I mean him no harm. We all know he isn't the reason I'm here. I do not have permission to attack him and you know that I do not step outside of the boundaries set by Father."

One of Death's golden chains shot out and yoked Insidious by the throat. The move caught everyone by surprise especially Insidious as he had never known Death to engage in warfare. Death lifted him off the ground.

"No!" Savas screamed. "Your glorified presence will alert Grey."

Death immediately dropped him as they all turned to see Grey stirring in her sleep and Barry climbing down off the sofa heading towards the front door.

Insidious coughed as he rubbed his clawed hands over his throat.

"I see I've missed a lot since I've been to this region." No one responded as he got up and dusted himself off. "As I said, I am only here out of sheer curiosity. When I chose to follow our brother Lucifer, I gave up many privileges. I'm simply asking for this one dispensation, brother. His mother is still stirring, let's not move her focus from where it needs to be."

Captain Valter turned to face Savas and Bojan. Before he could give instructions, Death walked up to the Captain and touched his temple to share something only he knew. The information caused Captain Valter's eyes to de-flame and stare at the Angel of Death wide-eyed.

Death whispered to the Captain, "Sometimes we must pick our battles in order to ensure we win the war. He's right. We don't want to stir the warrior in Grey or remove her focus from the assignment the Almighty has given her. There is a reason she was chosen to be the watchman for Nigel's firstborn. Only she can see the truth behind this war and fight accordingly."

Valter nodded. He looked at his comrades and said, "Escort him to the child."

The angels obeyed their Captain's order without hesitation, even they had to admit they were interested to know what changed his mind. Insidious was gracious because he knew this was indeed a privilege.

All the spiritual beings walked into the house. Barry watched in stunned astonishment as all the angels crowded into the Lawson living room, but the minute Insidious strolled through, he broke out into a full-on fit. The Angel of Death cast his shadow over Grey to keep her from detecting this demon in her home as well as Barrington's reaction.

They walked to the nursery where Hunter was still sleeping peacefully. Barrington was fit to be tied. He hissed at Insidious. The demon spared him one glance and a chuckle.

"That's cute," he said as he headed to the baby's room.

Transcendent blue light surrounded the baby boy. Every angel stood around him with their weapons drawn, just in case Insidious tried to pull a fast one. Since they all had something to lose, they decided the risk was enough to make everyone involved trustworthy – at least for the moment.

Insidious looked down at the sleeping chubby caramel bundle.

"Wow," he said. "This is really something."

All the angels, save for Death, smiled despite the situation. He was indeed a special child.

"So, he's a shield. Even as a baby, he's already activated," Insidious said with genuine reverence in his voice.

Valter nodded. "Yes."

Death asked Insidious, "Does it make you regret your choice to serve darkness?"

Insidious sighed, "Regret is too much of a burden to bear for as long as I have lived. I accept my fate, but that doesn't mean I can't wreak havoc while I'm here. And I plan to be around until the bitter end."

Insidious looked up and flashed a wicked grin at his former angelic comrades.

"My brothers, I bid you adieu. Thank you for the opportunity. We can go back to despising each other now."

With that, Insidious walked out. Even though his words were sincere, his motives were not. He wanted to know just how special Hunter was to try and gauge what Nigel's child could possibly possess beyond what they had already heard. They thought Neil was the only shield that existed, but clearly, the Light was up to something. Now there were two, and they weren't even trying to keep it a secret. That was indeed very interesting. He couldn't calculate his next move without this information. He was grateful his brethren were more wise than ferocious. Using Grey as a bargaining chip had been the perfect manipulation to get what he'd truly wanted - insight!

Death's shadow was still covering Grey as Insidious made his exit. In the baby's room, they all looked at each other.

Nero, an Italian warrior, was the first to break the silence.

"Captain...," he began.

Valter shook his head, cutting Nero off.

"My reasons will remain hidden until the truth is revealed. Believe me, when it is, you'll understand my decision. Come, we must go and plan for Insidious' attack. He's going to come for Nigel's daughter with everything he's got. Insidious is a formidable adversary and the most strategic demon I know. His decision to come here was a calculated risk - one he deemed worth the price he may have to pay. This bold move was more than what he alluded it to be that I am confident of."

They all nodded as Death, Nero and Valter took off in a tangle of white and navy-blue splendor.

When Death's shadow lifted, Grey heard Barrington hissing. She got up trying to figure out what was going on. She hoped some rodent or worse, a snake, hadn't gotten into the house. She followed Barry's hissing to the nursery, and the sight she saw once inside left her flabbergasted. There was the fat tan cat marching back and forth in front of Hunter's crib wearing the meanest look she'd ever seen on his face. She understood by his demeanor he was being protective of her son.

"What in the world has gotten into you, Barry?" she inquired chuckling.

The cat relaxed when he saw Grey and sat on his haunches at full attention. He still didn't like the baby, but no evil was going to just walk in and mess with him either. Grey and Neil would never understand what prompted Barry's change of heart, but he had officially just assigned himself as Hunter's guardian.

Chapter 2: Freefall

Agent Michelle Fuller
Natchez, Mississippi

I was grateful that the cover of a starless sky aided in my concealment as I touched down with a thud in some bushes. Thank goodness this awful orange jumper was long-sleeved because the small trees I landed in were unkind and unyielding. I managed not to scream as I didn't want to draw attention.

As I descended upon the earth, I noticed not many people were out and about which meant it was likely the wee hours of the morning. I needed to figure out where the heck I was, get a change of clothes and make my way to the Black Mecca, better known as Atlanta. Surely, I could hide in plain sight there with my fellow melanin rich brothers and sisters.

I tried to navigate myself somewhere obscure, but I was left at the mercy of the wind and she was being a certified beast. I sat still for a few moments listening for barking dogs. They would definitely give away my position. When I heard silence, I gathered up the parachute then unhooked myself from it. I had to get out of this federally mandated romper as soon as possible.

I folded the parachute into the smallest wad I could then stuffed it in the bushes. I climbed out of the bushes and looked around. To my utter shock when I looked up, I saw a white water tower. *Well that's awfully convenient*, I thought. I listened again. No cars were out, and no dogs were barking. I ran to get a look at the water tower to see where the heck I was. Then I saw it and my stomach turned.

The water tower read: Natchez. Clearly the universe was out to punish me. I was in Mississippi. Not just any town in Mississippi, but home to the Devil's Punchbowl. I sighed and quickly scrambled back to my bushes. My quick scan of the streets revealed I was on North Baxter and Simmons Street. The other intersection was North Flag Street.

At the corner of Flag and Baxter Street was a funeral home. Dead bodies didn't bother me, but surely, I could find something to change into. I mean it's not like anyone there had anywhere to be.

I also needed a phone. Google maps would help me navigate my way out of here as soon as possible. I could find places to hide as I planned my escape out of this city. I didn't know anyone in this city, but I did have a contact in Jackson, which I didn't think was too far from here.

I tried to stop my mind from drifting, but it was pointless because I kept thinking about the infamous Devil's Punchbowl. The story I heard made me shiver with rage. I hope it's not true, however, knowing America's original sin makes it very plausible. America is full of dirty little secrets they conveniently left out of the history books. Google has the receipts and anybody with a mouse could click their way through some piping hot tea.

When slaves were emancipated, they had to go through the soldiers to get to freedom. Of course, they began recapturing slaves and putting them in concentration camps. Yes, America had concentration camps and Natchez was the most notorious.

The influx swelled the town's population from 10,000 to over 100,000 practically overnight. The freed slave men were recaptured and forced to work, while the women and children were locked behind walls made of concrete left to starve and die of disease. The benevolent white folks were kind enough to give them shovels to bury their dead, instead of removing the bodies.

It is said that over 20,000 freed slaves died in one year's time. Their bodies buried in the cavern like pit surrounded by trees on the bluffs, hence the moniker, the Devil's Punchbowl due to its shape. Interestingly enough, the bluffs are now known for their peach groves which the locals supposedly won't touch because they know how they were fertilized. I heard the Mississippi River participates in snitching on America's dirty little past as bones have been known to wash up when the river floods.

Yeah, the sooner I got out of here, the better. True or not, I wanted out of this state expeditiously. I opted to remove the orange jumper and parade around in my underwear. If I ran into anyone, they'd be distracted by my body long enough for me to get the drop. I ran across Baxter Street and then down to Flag.

Again, the streets were quiet. Barking dogs would do me in so I hoped, they were either sleep or didn't exist in this neighborhood. The area looked quaint, the homes and lawns were well kept. Which meant these were the type of folks to immediately dial 911 at the first sign of trouble.

I ran to the back of the funeral home and knocked on the door. Surely, there was a night guard or something. I knocked again. I heard a gruff voice laced with sleep ask who it is.

"I need help, please," I whined in my most seductive voice.

Thank God for small town manners because like an idiot, he opened the door. He stared so hard at me wearing nothing but my bra, panties, and these awful shoes. He stood with his mouth agape and never saw the brick I found lying outside coming for his face.

I struggled to catch him from hitting the ground just in case he wasn't alone. I slipped inside, checked to see if anyone was coming, then closed the door behind me.

I searched his pockets for his cell phone. I grabbed his hand and used his finger to unlock the phone then immediately reset the screen's timeout to the max amount of ten minutes. I knew I couldn't change the way the phone was unlocked without the code either pin or pattern. He better hope I found what I was looking for and quickly, otherwise I'd have to take that finger with me.

I cautiously moved through the funeral home searching for any more of the living, thankfully I found none. So, I searched for something to wear. I found two female bodies, thankfully one had a pantsuit that was hanging up to be dressed the next day as her viewing was on the calendar.

I looked down at the woman on the slab and said, "Sorry, sis, I need this more than you."

I quickly dressed. It was a little bulky on me, but it would work. I checked on my admirer and found him knocked out cold. I checked his pockets for car keys. I couldn't very well drive out of here with a funeral vehicle. Talk about conspicuous. But I could take his vehicle and switch the plates with one of the cars in the neighborhood.

I used his finger again to unlock the phone and headed straight for Google maps. I had the beginnings of a plan. Now I just needed to figure out how to get to Jackson before the sun came up. From there, I'd be home free. I knew it would take the Feds a few more hours to figure out where to even begin looking for me.

Chapter 3: The Grapevine

Back at the Lawson home, Grey strode into the office carrying Hunter on her hip. Her skin was caramel. She had big brown eyes and full lips. Her hair was pulled back in a tail. Standing at five-feet-five-inches, she wore her well-defined curves very well.

Her shirt and chest were covered in baby puke, and her son, as sweet and lovable as he could be, was getting on her very last nerve. It was time to tag her husband because she desperately needed a minute to herself. Sixty full seconds sans baby because she was just one more spit-up, outburst or dirty diaper away from throwing her kid in a crib and leaving him to fend for himself. Grey adored her son and loved being a mother, but some days, she just wasn't feeling it.

Neil looked at his wife, taking in her dirty shirt and annoyed face. He wanted to laugh, and probably would have, but currently, he was on the phone with the FBI. He stood six-feet-four inches and was mahogany brown like his deceased father. He wore his hair close-cropped with waves that were always smooth with a full beard and mustache.

He held up his finger, silently asking her to give him a minute. Grey sighed as she stood and waited impatiently for him to get off the phone.

"Yes, this is Neil Lawson." Neil's brow furrowed as he listened intently to what Special Agent in Charge Tom Phillips was telling him. When his mouth dropped open, Grey frowned. "No, yeah... uh, thank you for letting me know. Please keep me informed on her recapture." Grey's brow raised at that.

Recapture? Whose recapture? She thought. This phone conversation had now piqued her curiosity. Grey watched her husband for additional clues, but he gave nothing else away as he continued to listen silently. After a few more quiet moments, he spoke.

"Yes, of course, I'll definitely let you know if I hear from her. Thanks again for the heads up."

With that, Neil ended the call and stared at his wife. He reached for his son, Grey gladly handed him over. Neil grabbed a wipe from the stash he kept on his desk and attempted to clean his baby boy's face as Hunter attempted to eat the wipe. He handed a few to his wife, who began to try to clean her shirt and chest.

"What was that about Neil?" Grey asked, as she vigorously wiped at the puke stains on her shirt.

"Babe, you will never believe this. Fuller escaped from FBI custody!"

Grey paused mid-wipe. "How the hell did she do that?"

"From 30,000 feet in the air apparently," Neil responded. "The FBI was transporting her by plane to another facility, and somehow, she managed to get loose and jumped out."

Grey stared at her husband in disbelief.

"What?" she asked incredulously. Neil simply nodded in affirmation.

This was insane. Grey hoped Neil was joking, but she also knew he would never kid about something like this, and definitely not about anything involving Fuller.

"Only the pilot, co-pilot and one of the four agents transporting her survived," Neil continued. "The other three are missing. They got sucked out of the plane when she shot open the exit door."

Grey stood there with her mouth wide open as she processed all her husband was telling her. After a long moment, she let out a low whistle.

"She's a bad girl."

Neil let out a half-hearted chuckle and nodded.

"Yeah, and one that should not be underestimated," he agreed as he shook his head. "I gotta call Nigel."

Neil picked up his phone to video chat his brother, deftly maneuvering the device from his son's grasp just as he tried to reach for it. Hunter had already cost him one phone screen - he wasn't trying to repair another. Neil smiled at Hunter's pouting face and planted a kiss to the top of his son's head.

Nigel answered on the fourth ring. An image of him still lounging in bed with Kadijah lying on his chest appeared on Neil's phone. Neil rolled his eyes.

"Come on man, block video or something."

"What? We ain't naked," Nigel said laughing. Neil just shook his head.

"Hi Neil," Kadijah said smiling.

"Hey, sis."

"What's up, bro?" Nigel asked. "And it better be important, I was just about to get some."

Grey laughed in the background, prompting Kadijah to pull the cover over her head. Nigel turned to his wife; a look of pure amusement plastered on his face.

"What you embarrassed for? You already carrying my child - clearly, we did something."

Neil heard Kadijah moan in embarrassment as he laughed. They were a trip, and their banter was always entertaining, but right now, they had bigger issues to discuss.

"Bro, focus! I am calling to tell you something important."

Nigel put on a serious face that made Neil chuckle.

"What's up?"

"Just got off the phone with the FBI. Apparently, your girl pulled a fast one and escaped their custody. She's in the wind. They think she bailed somewhere over the Texas, Mississippi, Louisiana area, but can't be for sure."

Nigel sat up and stared back at his brother, wide-eyed.

"Oh snap! Are you serious?"

Neil nodded.

"Yeah. They wanted to put me on alert just in case she tried to come for me."

Nigel frowned. Kadijah, who had emerged from the covers, looked at her brother-in-law's sober expression through the phone with her mouth wide open.

"You worried bro?" Nigel inquired.

"Not especially," Neil replied calmly. "I think she wants her freedom more than she wants revenge. If she does still want to come for me, it's gon be a minute. She has to get herself together - reestablish herself you know."

Nigel nodded. "True."

"Their organization is scattered."

Again, Nigel nodded. His brother's logic about Fuller's likely strategy made sense, but he knew better than to believe it meant they could let their guard down. In fact, it meant just the opposite.

"Let me know if you want a security detail for Grey or whatever you need," Nigel said. "I got you."

Neil smiled at his baby brother.

"I know you do, but I got it."

Nigel nodded, then frowned as a thought came to him. "Hey. Speaking of re-establishing herself, you need to put your boy on alert about those vials. If she's making moves like that to escape federal custody, they could be trying to regroup. We don't know who she had access to and who she's been in contact with. Those vials need to be under heavy guard. I personally think they should just destroy them, but they won't because it's evidence."

"You're right," Neil agreed. "Good thinking, I'll let him know."

A beat passed between them, and Nigel studied his older brother for a moment.

"You good, bro?" he asked. "I remember our last encounter with her." Nigel knew his big brother, arguably just as well as Grey did. Neil was being calm about this. Still, Nigel couldn't help but worry a little.

Neil nodded. "I'm good, bro."

Nigel observed his brother for a second more before deciding he was satisfied with Neil's answer.

"A'ight, well like I said, you interrupted my Saturday morning plans and I need to get back to them," Nigel said, grinning widely at his brother.

Neil laughed and shook his head as he hung up the phone. He looked up and met his wife's questioning eyes. Grey stared at her husband.

"Do we need to be concerned?" she asked.

"Nah," Neil said with assurance. "If it comes to that, you know I'll handle it. I don't want you worrying about it."

"Okay, baby. I'm gonna go clean up."

Neil kissed Hunter's cheek as his baby boy giggled. The way that little boy tugged on his heart never failed to amaze him. If Fuller thought he was dangerous before, she had no idea how lethal he was now that he had a child to be around for. No one and nothing was going to take him from his child.

The shrill ring of his cell phone interrupted Neil's thoughts of his son. He frowned when he saw it was Eva. He picked up.

"Hey," he answered cautiously.

"Neil, listen... I need to tell you what I just found out." He could tell by her voice she was distressed.

"Okay, calm down. What's wrong?"

"The woman you were undercover with - the one that killed my sister... She's escaped from FBI custody," she said hurriedly.

Neil frowned.

"Yeah, I know. I just got the call from the FBI."

"Oh, okay," Eva said baffled. "Well, I guess that makes sense they would tell you."

"And how do you know?"

"I can't get into that right now. I gotta watch my six Neil -you're not around to do that anymore."

Neil frowned. That wasn't his fault, and he had half a mind to remind her of that, but he bit his tongue.

Eva continued, "To be honest, I've gathered as much information as I could about her because she took my sister from me. I'm trying to let it go, but I can't."

"Eva, revenge is a hollow pursuit, and you can't exactly afford to have any more illegal activity on your record while we're looking into how to bring you out of hiding," Neil warned.

"I know that Neil, but you don't understand." She paused for a second as Neil listened intently. "There's more to my connection to her."

"Connection?" he asked. "What do you mean? How the heck are you connected to Fuller?"

"She's my sister."

Neil dropped the phone in shock. *Sister? This has to be a joke.* Dumbfounded, he picked up the phone to hear Eva repeatedly screaming, "Hello!" into the receiver.

He shook off his shock and spoke in a voice that displayed a calm he didn't actually feel.

"Say that again..."

"You heard me right."

"How is that possible?"

"She's an Untouchable, remember? The same woman that carried me and my sister, carried her. We have different fathers though. I was looking through the files that my sister left, and I found one she kept from me. I don't know why she didn't tell me. I don't know if Fuller knows we are sisters or not."

"Were you and your twin raised with your parents?" Neil inquired.

"Yes, we were, but she wasn't. She was sent off for special training apparently. She's older than us. Remember, she wasn't born an Untouchable, she was made."

Neil was quiet for a moment as he attempted to absorb everything Eva had just told him. This, on top of the news of Fuller's escape, was officially "team too much."

"Eva, I need a minute to process this."

"Okay, I get it," she responded. "But Neil you be careful. She could have an agenda for you and me. We don't know what she knows, but whatever it is it compelled her to escape federal custody. I was calling to warn you to watch your back since I can't anymore."

Neill nodded. "Yeah, you too."

"Love you."

"Love you," Neil replied then hung up the phone.

He stared dumbfounded as he absently rubbed his son's head. Grey came back into the office wearing a new shirt and immediately frowned as she took in her husband's face.

"Babe, you look like you saw a ghost. What happened?"

"That was Eva," he told her pointing to his phone.

"Is she okay?" Grey asked grabbing her chest.

Neil shook his head trying to scramble all the information he'd just received in the last ten minutes. Grey frowned even harder.

"Are the girls okay?"

Neil ignored her question. "She was calling to tell me about Fuller escaping. Apparently, she's been keeping track of her somehow."

"Okay, that's weird, why?"

"Because Fuller is Eva's half-sister." Grey's mouth fell open. "Yeah, that's exactly where I am with this."

"What in the... How in the... Where did...," Grey stuttered. Neil simply shook his head, as his wife stared at him with wide eyes.

"This is too much."

Grey took their son from her husband's grasp and cradled him. "I need a minute," she replied quietly and walked out of the room, clutching Hunter to her chest.

Neil let out a heavy sigh and rubbed his temples in a vain attempt to alleviate his budding headache.

"Lord, what in the world is going on?"

Chapter 4: Sunday Dinner: Revelations

Bellies were full, children were passed out and the adults were deciding whether or not to surrender to the "itis" or strike up another thought-provoking discussion. Jeremiah had filled their bellies with a delicious spread of soul food for their Sunday Dinner tradition. In attendance were Jeremiah, Mia, their three kids - Jeremiah, Jr., Madison, and Isaiah. Their guests included Grey, Neil, Hunter, Nigel, Kadijah, David, Genevieve, Jamal, Lindsey, Hope and Jacob along with Sheridan, Seth, and Daniel.

David had claimed the infamous recliner, with his wife, Genevieve, sprawled across his lap.

She looked around the room and said, "Hey y'all are we going to have a big discussion? Because if not, I am about to pass out."

Smatterings of laughter and utterings of agreements filled the room.

Uncharacteristically, Nigel spoke up. Something had been gnawing at him and he wanted to see what everyone else thought.

"There's something that I've been thinking about."

Everyone perked up to listen. Lindsey had to hit Jamal because his snoring pierced the silence when Nigel took a pause to lean forward in his seat.

"Huh, what?" he asked bewildered.

Everybody fell out laughing as Lindsey just shook her head. Jamal snuggled up against his wife as he tried to wake up. Sober now after Jamal's comedic interruption, the group turned its attention back to Nigel.

"By now, y'all know all the crazy stuff we discovered in California when we went to get Grey," Nigel continued.

There were nods of agreements and confirming words.

"Oh, here y'all go with that spooky stuff," Jeremiah interjected. "Don't you bring that voodoo in my house!"

Everybody laughed except for Mia who gave her husband a playful shove.

"Baby, hush!" she scolded. "Go ahead, Nigel."

"It just got me to thinking about some stuff. It's 2015 and the world around us is just straight crazy. Racism, injustice, oppression, especially for black men and black youth, is center stage every time you turn on the news. And you wonder how can so much of this be going on when so many people are supposedly "woke." He emphasized the last work with air quotes. "How do you accomplish systematic oppression that lasts for centuries?"

Everyone looked at him waiting for him to answer his own question.

"Witchcraft," he said. The room erupted in collective agreements. "Y'all follow me," he said now using his hands. "Think about Hitler - he was into some weird mess. The U.S. Government even created a section just to study the occult. Think of the similarities to what we found in Pasadena to what we continue to find even after all these years from slavery days. The mass graves, the sex trafficking rings are basically prisons aka concentration camps. So many similarities. But how did they have so much power to maintain this evil for so long?"

"Witchcraft," Grey said.

"Exactly. So, I'm not a spiritual warfare aficionado, but it seems to me like throughout history anytime evil reigned at massive levels for long periods of time demonic power was at the root."

"Correct," Grey agreed. "Anything dealing with systematic oppression has to have its source of power in something demonic. The third of the angelic contingent that fell from heaven fell with their power intact and those are the principalities, powers and spiritual wickedness referred to in Ephesians."

Nigel nodded before continuing, "Think about all the blood that was shed during slavery. All the bodies and what not. If the KKK used witchcraft to sustain their power, they had access to lots and lots and lots of blood. And if systematic racism is still being felt around this country, they could still be operating in it. Think of all the blood we found from the Untouchables. That organization had only been around for 30 years. The killing of millions over centuries would have produced a lot of blood and I'm sure they didn't use it all. And I'm also sure, like the Untouchables, those at the top of the organization, like the grand wizards and what not, used the blood of slaves to give their witchcraft power. And if that's the case, it makes sense why white supremacy is still running rampant in 2015 and black people are still oppressed."

"Whoa."

"Um..."

"That's crazy."

"That makes sense."

"Yikes."

"Ooh, I just got goosebumps," Mia said rounding up the reactions.

Grey sat up.

"According to your line of thinking that would mean they have access to the bloodlines of everyone who descended from slaves in this country," she told them.

"Exactly!" Nigel exclaimed. "Just like the Untouchables used it to get access to all the bloodlines they had to recruit."

"But where would you store that much blood for that many years?" David inquired thoughtfully.

Neil chimed in. "Well, strategically, I would store it in the most unassuming places. The small towns that are charming, endearing, and non-threatening. The last place you'd expect."

"Like Thomasville, Georgia," Sheridan suggested.

"Exactly," Neil said.

"Learning what we have about the Marine Kingdom, I'd also say some place near water," Grey interjected. "Since the demonic forces are stronger in those regions, they would likely be better protected. I mean there has to be more than one place. It's just stupid to keep it all in one place."

"True," Jeremiah replied.

Neil, Grey and Nigel all looked at each other.

"It wasn't all in one place," Grey said with horror on her face.

"What are you talking about, Grey?" Sheridan asked confused.

"The vials we found. It wasn't the only place!"

"That's right," Neil began. "It couldn't have been. Didn't Tiara say the symbol of her tattoo was somewhere else?"

"Yeah, she did, but we found her files," Nigel stated.

"But we went looking for files, not blood," Neil stated resolutely. "There could have been another room, or someplace hidden in that location," Neil said.

"We gotta find that other location before they do. That is if they haven't already," Nigel told them.

"No need to panic. We removed Niles' blood. There's no more access to our bloodline. We'll find it though," Neil said confidently.

Suddenly, something struck Grey hard in the gut. She grabbed Neil's hand as she locked eyes with Nigel. Nigel frowned.

"That's not true," she stated somberly. "Your brother's daughter is still out there, and she could give it willingly or unwillingly. Either way, they can gain access through her."

Fear hit Nigel and Kadijah in the belly. The blood was discovered to protect their child, and now it seemed there was a tiny loophole they needed to close to ensure her safety.

"That means she was never a physical threat to your daughter, but a spiritual one," Neil told his brother.

"That might be true, but the bottom line is, she's still a threat."

Neil frowned but nodded his understanding.

"Oh, lawd, y'all trippin'," Jeremiah said as he fell out on the floor. "Next time let's let the itis take over and we all fall asleep!"

Everyone but Neil, Grey, Nigel, and Kadijah fell out laughing.

"I told y'all I wasn't in the mood for this," Jeremiah said.

He noticed there was laughter, but not from the four people involved. He'd intended to lighten the mood with his wise crack but realized this was indeed a serious matter.

"Hold up, y'all. Remember what God said at that Sunday dinner we had where I prayed for your daughter? It's all good. The battle is not yours - it's the Lord's!"

They all nodded in agreement, remembering that Sunday dinner turned prayer covering and praise session for Nigel and Kadijah's unborn daughter.

The angels that guarded them looked at each other grateful they had finally put the information together. Insidious would definitely be doing his best to get to the rest of the vials. Even if he beat them to it, forewarned was forearmed.

Chapter 5: The Watchman

Nigel and Kadijah arrived at Shula's Restaurant in downtown Tallahassee, Florida. As always, he was impeccably dressed, and heads turned as he charmingly strolled to the hostess station with his arm linked to his beautiful wife's.

Kadijah wore her big, beautiful afro straightened today. Her thick hair cascaded down her back and complimented the simple black dress she adorned with pearls that contrasted her fair skin. Her brown eyes were bashful, her frame medium.

Nigel stood six-feet-two inches with a slender build and skin that was "high yella." He wore his hair closely cropped that sported deep waves. His mustache and goatee were perfectly groomed. He and his brother inherited their hypnotic eyes from their father. They were light brown but could change to gray or green depending on their mood.

They were a striking couple, and the hostess made sure to mention so before she directed them to the table where their party was waiting.

Their angelic contingent of four - Cheveyo, Quan, Bomani, and Lajos, surrounded them. As Nigel and Kadijah approached, reaching the table, an older man, in his late forties, stood up and extended his hand.

"So nice to see you and your wife, Nigel. Thank you for agreeing to meet with us."

Kadijah nodded as Nigel shook the man's hand.

"I look forward to the evening and getting to know you, Stewart. I'm sure this will be beneficial for *you.*"

Stewart smiled cockily as if he knew it was already a done deal. He turned to introduce his wife.

"This is my wife, Selena."

She extended a dainty hand with freshly manicured fake nails. Nigel, always the gentleman, grabbed her hand and kissed it.

"It's nice to meet you."

He took note of all the diamonds the woman had dripping from her hands, wrist, neck, and ears. He was a man that enjoyed the finer things, and his wife wasn't short on diamonds, but he wasn't pretentious about it. He thought she was doing the most for dinner on a Tuesday night.

"This is my wife, Kadijah."

Kadijah extended her hand to both and then they took their seats. Stewart and his wife were already drinking cocktails.

"Would you and your wife care for a drink?" Stewart asked.

Nigel raised a brow. "No thank you, my wife is expecting."

Stewart caught the look on Nigel's face. He smiled sheepishly. Nigel had already informed him they had a baby on the way. From what he knew of this man, he only worked with those who were highly skilled in all things security, but especially those who paid stark attention to detail. Selena, oblivious to the silent conversation between the two men, chimed in.

"Oh, congratulations. I admire people who have children, but it's not for me. Wherever would I find the time to give to such needy creatures?"

She cackled with an ostentatious laugh.

Kadijah tilted her head slightly to the side. Nigel gently squeezed her knee to discourage the lashing that was certainly about to exit her pretty mouth.

Instead, he said flatly, "It's not for everybody."

Stewart shot his wife a look. She was oblivious.

He cleared his throat and said, "The steaks here are superb."

"I think I'll have one," Kadijah interjected.

Selena waved over a waitress.

"We're ready to order."

"Certainly, let me go grab your waiter," she said and scurried off.

Nigel continued to observe without saying much. His decision to work with this man had already been made. The answer was emphatically no. But he knew Stewart's ego wouldn't allow him to take a simple no. Nigel had only decided to attend dinner, so he could personally hand the man his own ego on a rejected platter.

The waiter finally made it to their table, and they ordered. Nigel kept the table discussion to small talk and consistently steered the conversation away from business every time Stewart tried to bring it up.

Kadijah could tell the man was getting frustrated with Nigel's evasive maneuvers. She knew her husband. There was always a method to his madness. She trusted in that single fact even when she didn't understand what he was doing. Either way, she was going to enjoy him putting these awful people in their place.

This lady had one more time to talk down to her husband or make an off-hand comment about their child being a creature. Nigel kept squeezing her knee to keep her from going off. Then she noticed that as the lady continued to ramble on about nothing with substance that she had red lipstick staining her teeth. She wondered how long it had been there.

Unconsciously her hand reached up to her mouth. She was about to tell the lady to clean her teeth when Nigel squeezed a little harder. She glanced over at him and caught the faint shake of his head. This time she sat back and sipped her Arnold Palmer. Clearly, he was up to something.

Finally, the waitress arrived with their food. She quickly refreshed their drinks and asked if they needed anything else. They declined, and she quickly walked away, leaving them to enjoy their meal.

"Do you mind if I bless the food?" Nigel inquired.

Selena frowned. She was about to say something flip when her husband spoke up.

"Not at all, please go ahead."

Nigel quickly blessed the food. The other couple began to dig in. Nigel pushed his plate aside and grabbed Kadijah's. He cut her steak in half and then began to cut up one half into quarter inch squares. He knew she wouldn't finish the whole thing. Selena's mouth fell open. Stewart was a little puzzled too, but also intrigued.

Selena couldn't help herself. These people were ridiculous. She knew the deal Stewart was trying to make was lucrative, and she loved more money, but these people were absurd.

"Is he going to chew it for you too?" she asked sarcastically. "Are you capable of doing anything for yourself?"

Kadijah didn't even bother answering even though she didn't get the squeeze warning her not to say anything. The fact that Nigel was willing to let her go off meant he'd surpassed his level of patience.

As Nigel continued to cut up his wife's steak, he didn't even acknowledge Selena by looking at her. He simply began speaking in his strong, no non-sense voice.

"A good steak should be cut in quarter inches. Big enough to enjoy the flavor, but small enough not to choke on. By your sarcasm, you imply that my wife is somehow incapable. I assure you, she's quite the opposite. That's why I married her. However, I don't believe women should open their own doors, pump their own gas or cut their own meat. My father did it for my mother and I do it for my wife. While you're judging her about having a husband who controls her, which couldn't be farther from the truth, your husband's eyes have watched every skirt that has passed by this table with no regard for you."

His eyes shifted to Stewart; whose mouth was now opened.

"That last one that made you lick your lips - was a man."

Stewart began to choke on his steak.

Nigel chuckled and said, "I bet you wish they were cut into quarter inch squares now, huh?"

Ignoring the choking man, his eyes focused back on Selena whose mouth was scrunched up in embarrassment and anger.

"And not only is he blatantly disrespecting you in front of strangers, but he also has let you sit here for the past 20 minutes with lipstick on your teeth."

Kadijah handed her a napkin and said, "I'll see your disrespect and raise you chivalry."

Selena gawked at the napkin but didn't take it. She rolled her eyes at Kadijah.

Once Stewart got his bearings, he said, "Nigel, I don't..."

"Appreciate you wasting my time," Nigel cut him off.

He stood up and smoothly pulled four one hundred dollar bills out of his pocket to put on the table. He reached for Kadijah's hand. She backed up her chair, reached for his hand and stood up.

"Enjoy the rest of your evening," Nigel told them. "Don't ever contact me again."

Kadijah smiled and waved, "Good night."

They heard the argument erupt as Nigel led them out of the restaurant. Once outside, Kadijah turned to her husband, a slight pout on her face.

“Baby, I really wanted that steak. I’m hungry,” she wined as she subtly patted her belly.

Nigel chuckled. “Let’s go to Marie Livingston’s. I like hers better.”

She grinned and said, “You knew you weren’t going to work with him the moment he gave you that weak handshake.”

“I knew I wasn’t going to work with him after speaking with him on the phone earlier.”

Kadijah raised an eyebrow.

“So why did you subject me to those insufferable people?”

He shrugged, “Because he was rude to Cynthia, so I had to get him.”

Kadijah laughed as they continued to walk hand-in-hand to the car.

Chapter 6: A Father's Embrace

Sarah had dealt with her fair share of challenges in life, but none seemed to test her more than the one she was facing right now. Currently, she was staring at her 16-year-old son and contemplating how she was going to keep herself from strangling him. Nothing had challenged her resolve more. She took in his sullen face and defiant posture. Something was definitely going on with him, and she was sick of it.

"Marcus, what's really going on with you?" she asked, voicing her silent thoughts. "It's like every few months, we are back here. You're acting up. Your mouth has you two seconds away from being popped in it. Your grades and behavior at school start suffering."

Marcus rolled his eyes.

"Ma, I'm cool, just back off," he snapped, cutting her off.

"Back off?" Sarah stared at him incredulously. She was up in a flash and in his face. Marcus quickly stepped back. She now had to look up to her 16-year-old son, but that did not phase her one bit.

"Little boy, I will drag your behind all through this house, do you hear me? Who do you think you are talking to? Now, I don't know which one of your little raggedy friends got you smelling yourself, but I ain't the one. I will not tolerate disrespect in my house. You are not grown and as long as I pay for the clothes on your back, the roof over your head and food you eat, you will show me the respect I demand. Do you hear me?"

Marcus stared down at his mother. Her fair skin was tinted red. He knew she was hot with him and he had gone too far.

"Boy, I asked you a question."

"Yes, I hear you," he replied.

"Yes," she frowned.

She grabbed him by his shirt collar and snatched him so they were face to face.

"Yes ma'am," he said quickly.

Sarah released him and put her hands up in surrender.

"I'm done. You are about to see a side of me, you really don't want to."

Before he could respond, the doorbell rang. Sarah continued to fume and stare. Marcus didn't know if it was okay to open the door. He honestly was scared to walk past his mother, not knowing if she would indeed drag him. Yeah, his mouth had been unruly lately, but he'd never put his hands on his mother. It was clear, however, that she was ready to put her hands on him.

The doorbell rang again.

"Open the door, Marcus!" she yelled.

He quickly sidestepped his mother and went to open the door.

"Who is it?" he inquired.

"It's Neil."

Marcus turned to stare at his mother, aggravated that she'd called him.

"Little boy, open the door."

Marcus sucked his teeth and opened the door.

"What's up?" he asked defensively.

Neil frowned as he observed Marcus' body language. He could see Sarah standing behind him and the look on her face told him Marcus was very close to meeting his maker.

"Let's take a walk," he told Marcus.

Marcus rolled his eyes but headed out the door, slamming it behind him. Neil stared at him like he was crazy. He popped him on the back of his head.

"Ow!" Marcus exclaimed.

"That's why your mama is ready to jump on your little disrespectful behind now," Neil chastised. "You better act like you got some home training and quick."

He gave Marcus a stern glare, then stalked off in the direction of the walking trails situated behind the townhomes where Sarah and Marcus now lived.

Marcus didn't dare say anything, just simply followed Neil with his head down, quietly falling in step with him.

It was a beautiful May spring day, pleasantly warm thanks to a gentle breeze that kept the typically stifling Florida heat at bay. As the two continued to walk in silence along the trail path, Neil glanced over at Marcus.

The young boy he'd met stealing from a Southside corner store all those years ago was growing up. A smart, handsome young man had taken the place of the charming little boy who'd captured Neil's heart that day.

Neil knew Marcus was entering some of the most challenging and confusing years of his young life, and the decisions he made now could make or break his future. It's why Neil had rearranged his schedule to make time to talk to Marcus when Sarah had called, fuming about his recent behavior. Even though Neil had a son of his own now, his role as a father figure in Marcus' life still took priority.

They had been walking for about 10 minutes when finally, Neil spoke.

"You know Marcus, it's my job to observe, investigate and draw conclusions. I've been in your life a while and though we don't get to hang out as much as we use to, I still know you pretty well. When you get like this, all defiant and macho, it's usually because you're hurting inside."

Marcus winced inwardly at Neil's appraisal of him but did his best to keep his face neutral. The older man's ability to read him like a book was one of the things Marcus loved and loathed about him. He loved it because it meant Neil cared enough to try and understand him, but he loathed it because it meant he couldn't hide squat.

Neil continued. "From your mom's view, it's not that she doesn't care enough to see your pain, but she has a lot on her plate, and she can only ask you so many ways to tell her what's going on, before she has to move on and address your behavior rather than the actual issue at hand. Your behavior leaves her no choice. She called me and asked me to come and talk to you. So, I'm not leaving until you tell me what's up."

Neil stopped walking and turned to face Marcus. He immediately went on the defensive.

"Nothing's up, I'm fine," Marcus said, attempting to brush past Neil. "I just wish everyone would leave me alone."

Neil side-eyed him.

"Well, that's a lie and we both know it. Just so you know, I am going to call you out on all your crap because I am neither in the mood nor do I have the time to waste on this merry go round."

Marcus sucked his teeth, and Neil fought the urge to thump the teen in his chest. Instead, he took a step closer to Marcus and looked him dead in the eye.

"Let me explain something to you. You're at that age where you swear you're smarter than everyone around you, which is nowhere near the truth. You don't have enough life experiences to walk around being that arrogant. If you would take the stick out of your behind, stop being a victim and use your common sense, you would realize that whatever it is you are facing, you aren't the first person to go through it. If you would actually communicate with the people who care about you, they could help you navigate what you're going through. Now, I'm going to ask you this one time and you better tell me the truth, because if you don't and continue to behave like this, your mom is going to kill you and I'm going to let her."

Marcus stared wide-eyed at Neil. Neil shrugged his shoulders and took a seat on a bench.

"You're almost a grown man Marcus, there is no more coddling from me. It's time to grow up and be a responsible human being."

Reluctantly, Marcus sat too. He kicked around an obscure rock near his feet as he prepared to unburden his heart.

"What's up Marcus? What's got you in your feelings?"

"Jessica," he finally said.

Neil nodded. He should've known.

"What happened?"

"She doesn't want to be my girl," Marcus stated sadly. The kid looked utterly heartbroken. Neil placed a comforting hand on his shoulder.

"Well, I'm sorry to hear that," he replied sincerely.

Marcus sighed and looked up at the man who had become the greatest role model in his life.

"And the worst part of it is I lost my best friend." He sighed again and gave the rock he'd been playing with a strong kick.

"How?" Neil asked frowning.

"Man, I can't be around her like that," Marcus replied sullenly. "I can't watch her be with other guys or be the one to listen to all her escapades with guys she's hanging out with."

Neil studied Marcus. He felt bad for him, but such was life.

"Let me ask you this son," Neil began. Marcus looked up at him. "How many times did you share stuff about other girls with Jessica?"

Marcus frowned. "I mean..."

"Exactly," Neil cut him off.

"Now all of a sudden because the shoe is on the other foot, you're not capable of being the kind of friend she's been to you."

Marcus looked away from Neil. He really didn't want to hear this right now, but Neil pressed on anyway.

"I'm not saying I don't get that you're hurt. You have feelings for her. Heartbreak isn't easy, but what I am saying to you is it's not Jessica that's stopping you from being her friend. It's your pride and your ego."

Marcus frowned harder and slumped a bit on the bench.

"Did she tell you why she doesn't want to pursue a relationship with you?"

Marcus sighed. "She said that she doesn't trust herself around me because we're so close. So, she thinks it would be best if we remained friends only."

Neil nodded. "Did she say she liked you as more than a friend?"

"She skirted around answering the question, but I always catch her rolling her eyes when she sees me talking to other girls."

Neil chuckled. *Ahh, young love,* he thought. He understood the pain of heartbreak more than the kid knew.

"Son listen, at the end of the day, you need to grow up. Life is full of adversity and not just in relationships, but also in your career, in every other area of your life. What you can't do is break down and start throwing a tantrum because life isn't working out the way you want. I don't know if you'll ever get over your feelings for Jessica, but I do know it's your choice on how you move forward with the weight of those feelings or without. Your mother has sacrificed too much for you to give her grief every six months just because life happened. You have got to find a better way of dealing with the tough situations life brings. You also need to open your mouth and talk to me, your mom or even your dad about what's going on in your world instead of putting on this disrespectful macho attitude."

Neil turned to look Marcus squarely in the face.

"Do you hear me?"

Marcus nodded.

Neil stared at him.

"Yes, sir, I hear you."

Neil nodded, then continued, "Now, you need to decide how important Jessica is to your life. Do you want her in your life in whatever way she's available or do you want her in your life on your terms only?"

Marcus frowned. When Neil put it like that, he realized just how selfish he was being. Jessica meant the world to him. Removing her from his life simply because she didn't want a relationship with him would be unfair.

"In whatever way she's available. She's my best friend. She knows all my secrets and we just have so much fun together."

"Then you have to meet her where she's at," Neil told him.

Marcus sighed.

"But how do I be around her with all these feelings?" he asked earnestly. He didn't want to lose Jessica, but he couldn't lie - the sting of her rejection hurt worse than he had expected.

"You process heartbreak one day at a time, sometimes minute by minute and other times, second by second. It's a process and eventually, it becomes bearable if you do the work to move past it. Maybe you guys can take a little break from each other, while you sort through your disappointment. Tell her you need space to get yourself together. I'm sure she'll understand. If you feel like your life is great without her, then cool. Let it be that - a girl you're cool with, who used to be your best friend. However, if you find out that life just isn't right without her being there, swallow your pride, put aside your ego and figure out the new friendship."

Marcus nodded.

"You owe your mother an apology."

"I know," Marcus said.

"Speaking of apologies, did you ever apologize to Candace?"

Marcus looked at the ground and shook his head. Neil frowned.

"Why not?"

Marcus shrugged still looking at the ground. Neil bumped his shoulder, forcing Marcus to look up at him.

"Clean up the mess you made Marcus. Don't be the guy that leaves a mess and never takes responsibility to clean it up. Be a man of character and integrity." Marcus held Neil's gaze and nodded. "I love you, Marcus."

"I love you too, Neil. Thanks," he responded giving Neil a small smile.

"I'm always here for you. Don't let your mom call me again and tell me you're acting out instead of dealing with whatever is going on in your life."

Marcus nodded. "I will do better."

"And remember, nothing you face is exclusive to you. Somebody in the world has healed battle scars from everything you will face. Open your mouth, get their wisdom, and face adversity head-on. Do not pout, do not throw a tantrum and for goodness sakes, do not tuck your tail and run from it."

"You're right. I promise I'll do better."

Neil stood up. Marcus did too then suddenly, he grabbed Neil and hugged him. Neil squeezed him back and kissed the top of his head.

From her bedroom window, Sarah watched the exchange and smiled. She was so grateful Marcus had Neil, because sometimes her son drove her to her wit's end. The phone rang interrupting her thoughts. She looked down at the number, recognizing it was a collect call from Alonzo. She smiled as she answered.

"Hey baby, how are you?"

"I've been better," Alonzo replied. "Just counting down the days until I can hold you in my arms again."

She grinned. "I'm counting with you."

"How's Marcus?"

Sarah sighed, then told him about the way their son had been acting for the past few weeks.

"Bring him out here to see me," Alonzo responded when Sarah finished. "I'll talk to him."

"Oh, it's fine. Neil came over today. They went for a walk and I just saw them hugging so I know they dealt with whatever was goin on."

There was a long pause on the other end. Sarah pulled the phone away from her ear, checking to make sure the call hadn't dropped.

"Hello?" Sarah asked. "You still there?"

"Yeah, I'm here," Alonzo replied with an obvious attitude. Sarah frowned.

"What's wrong?" she asked, puzzled by the annoyance in his voice.

"So, you mean to tell me, this Neil character knew about and had a chance to deal with my son before I even knew there was an issue?"

Sarah bit back the choice words that danced on the tip of her tongue.

"First of all, watch your tone," she said with a warning. "And yes, why are you acting like that. You know Neil has been a part of Marcus' life for years. He's the only father figure he's known, Alonzo."

"And now he has an actual father who can be in his life."

Sarah rolled her eyes. He couldn't possibly be serious right now. The man was sitting in a federal prison – definitely not a situation conducive to fostering a parental relationship with a teenage son who barely knew him.

"Um, don't even go there," Sarah scoffed. You're being ridiculous. The choices you made, got you in the situation you're in. It's not Neil's fault and Marcus shouldn't have to suffer for it."

"I didn't even know I had a son," Alonzo snapped.

"No, but you knew what you were doing was wrong and still chose to do it," she fired back. "You won't use my decision to protect myself and my son from your psychotic parents as an excuse to justify your jealousy. You and Marcus aren't even that close. He didn't even tell me what was going on, but he told Neil. I'm not going to cause a problem with my son's confidant because you're jealous."

Alonzo fumed on the other end of the phone in silence. As much as he hated to admit it, he couldn't really argue with her. He was continually realizing the weight of his actions carried consequences he wasn't sure he could handle. Alonzo simmered in his anger as Sarah continued to berate him

"You can't even be a father to him because you're incarcerated. I get that you missed time with him, I do. I get that you feel some type of way about Neil, I truly, do. However, this isn't about you. It's about our son and what's best for him. Neil knows you want to be in his life, and he encourages Marcus to talk to you all the time.

You have to let your relationship with Marcus blossom organically. Forcing it will only push him away."

An uncomfortable silence stretched between them for several moments. Sarah hated to be so harsh with him, but he needed to hear the truth. He was in no position to criticize her parenting decisions, no matter how much he thought so.

"You know what, I'll talk to you later," Alonzo told her.

"Wait, are you serious right now?" Sarah asked incredulously.

"Very," he replied, then hung up.

Sarah stared at the phone in disbelief. She shook her head. She knew when Alonzo got out, there was going to be some definite tension between him and Neil. She shook it off as she heard Marcus and Neil returning. Placing her phone on her nightstand, she headed to the living room.

Marcus walked up to her and scooped her up into a bear hug.

She squealed. "Boy put me down."

Marcus put her down and kissed her cheek.

"I'm sorry, ma. I'm going to clean up my act and find better ways of dealing with whatever I'm going through."

She smiled up at him. "I love you, baby."

"I love you too, ma," he said.

Marcus gave Neil a fist bump then headed to his room.

"I cannot thank you enough," Sarah told Neil.

"I'm always going to be here for Marcus. Don't ever hesitate to call me."

Sarah nodded. Neil gave her a hug then headed out. Sarah closed the door behind him, then leaned against the it and sighed.

Chapter 7: Newly Weds

"You're irritating me," Kadijah sniped at her husband.

"By doing what? Breathing?" Nigel asked sarcastically.

She rolled her eyes. "No, by popping your ankles. Must you do that?"

"Must you leave the cabinet doors open every time you use one?"

Kadijah rolled her eyes again in sincere annoyance. "You could go in the other room with all that, I'm trying to read."

"You could go in another room to read also. This is my morning stretch routine, you know this," he replied from his spot on the floor, barely giving her a sideways glance.

She sighed exasperated and threw the covers off her as she got up from the bed. Just breathing the same air as him was irritating her to no end. She headed towards the master bathroom, making sure to bump him ever-so-slightly as he continued to stretch on the floor.

Nigel glared up at her. She was working his last nerve - nagging him about insignificant matters and doing it on purpose. He was sick of it. He had no idea what he'd done to aggravate her so much, but he was getting to the point where he really didn't care, especially as Kadijah continued to rant.

"While we're on the subject, can you please remember to move the shower head back when you finish. Water sprays everywhere."

Nigel rolled his eyes and answered in a voice that did little to betray his utter annoyance.

"I'm sorry that I'm tall and I need the water to cover my body. How about this? Just like I close the cabinets, why don't you adjust the shower head *before* you turn on the water. It's just a simple as looking at the toilet seat *before* you sit down."

Her eyes narrowed. "You know what..."

She leveled a finger in her husband's direction - a sure sign that she had reached peak level of irritation and was about to go off. Nigel frowned.

"Okay, stop," he said as he put his hand up. He walked over to her. "We've been snapping on each other for two days over petty stuff. This isn't us. What's up?"

Kadijah realized he was right, but she couldn't back down yet. Not when she finally had an opportunity to unleash the tongue lashing she had been practicing in her head for the past two days. She folded her arms over her chest and let out an exasperated huff.

Nigel recognized her resistance but refused to give into it. Instead, he pulled her into him and whispered in a low voice against her ear.

"When's the last time we made love?"

The feel of his warm breath and deep voice so close to her made her shiver. She hated that he could do that. Melt her in an instant. It was emotional extortion! She thought about his question.

"Like two weeks," she answered after a moment. The past several days had been a whirlwind for the couple. Between Nigel's long hours at work, and Kadijah's seemingly constant bouts of morning sickness and prenatal exhaustion, sleep had managed to take priority over intimacy.

Nigel pulled back and stared at his wife, then grinned. She laughed. Suddenly, all of the bickering made perfect sense.

"We're sexually frustrated," she admitted.

He laughed and pulled his wife even closer.

"A sure sign of our frustration is when we start being petty."

"Let's fix it then," she grinned. She looped her lean arms around his neck and placed a soft, lingering kiss on her husband's lips.

"Girl, you gon make me late for work."

"I'll make it worth your while," she smirked as she ran her hand down his bare chest.

That's all the push Nigel needed. He grabbed her face and kissed her hard and desperately. She responded in kind, pouring out all of the pent-up passion that had been building between them for the past two weeks.

When they were done, they lay contentedly beside each other, completely spent. It took them a full five minutes to get their breathing under control. Kadijah rolled towards her husband and looped a leg over his waist.

"So, was it worth being late?" she asked smugly.

"Absolutely," he said.

She kissed his shoulder. "You need to shower and get dressed," she told him.

"I will as soon as the feeling returns to my legs."

She snickered and kissed him. They were so ridiculous. When he stood up ten minutes later, he looked down at his beautiful wife. The glow of satisfaction on her skin made him want to climb back into bed and tell Darryl to run the company for the day.

Her large afro was wild and sexy against her fair skin. Her face was starting to get fuller as were other parts of her. He loved his wife's medium build but couldn't deny his appreciation for her new "assets."

"Trust and believe, I am going to make it home to you as soon as possible today," he told her.

She laughed. "Good thing, I'm already pregnant because you got that look in your eyes."

He laughed then leaned down to kiss her. Reluctantly, he pulled away.

"I gotta get ready. Can you text Darryl and Cynthia for me and let them know, I'll be in soon?"

"I got you bae, seeing as how it was kinda my fault."

He chuckled and headed into the bathroom. Kadijah grabbed her cell phone off the nightstand and did as her husband asked, then dove right back into her book.

Fifteen minutes later, Nigel emerged from the shower with a towel wrapped around his waist. Kadijah bit her lip as she watched her husband go through his morning routine. The man and the meticulous way he went about getting ready each day was so sexy to her. In fact, it was the only reason she had opted to read some more instead of immediately going back to sleep. She did not want to miss it.

Nigel sauntered into their walk-in closet and reappeared ten minutes later, wearing a tank top and the pants to a suit that had been tailor-made for his six-foot-two slender frame. Today's choice was dark charcoal, not quite black, but equally flattering against his "high yella" skin tone. He lay the jacket, shirt, and tie across the bed.

Back in the mirror, he brushed his hair revealing the deep waves of his Caesar cut that boasted black hair excellence. He rubbed his hand over his brows and stroked his goatee. He also had a neatly trimmed mustache. Grabbing the bottle of blessed olive oil off the dresser, he dabbed a small amount in the palm of his hands then rubbed them together. He prayed the prayer he recited every morning over himself.

First, he touched his eyes.

"Father anoint my eyes to see what I need to see. Let me see beyond the surface." Next, he touched his lips.

"Anoint my mouth to speak life and not death today." After that, he moved to his ears.

"Anoint my ears to hear your voice no matter what's going on in my world." He placed his hand over his heart.

"Keep my heart pure Father, no matter what madness I see today." Finally, he rubbed his hands together and used the excess oil, to moisturize his arms.

"Give me divine strength today Father, in Jesus name, I pray, amen."

When he was finished, he grabbed the white towel that he always kept on the corner of his dresser and wiped off his hands. He slipped into his shirt, then the jacket and lastly added the tie. He picked up his firearm and holster then attached it to the 5:30 position on his back.

Kadijah hated guns but had to admit, the element of danger her husband possessed thoroughly added to his sexy swag. Nigel grabbed his wallet, loose cash, and phone off the dresser. He walked over to his wife.

"I love you."

"I love you, too," she said. "Stay safe today."

"That's the plan," he said as he leaned down and kissed her.

Kadijah smiled as she watched his bowlegged stride lead him out of their bedroom. Satisfied with her morning, she put her book down, rolled over and finally gave in to sleep.

†††

Later that afternoon, Nigel sat in his office as Darryl, his most-trusted employee and second in command, briefed him on the status of their current clients. Darryl had been a trusted associate of Nigel's for years now. He was one of the few people Nigel trusted implicitly, which was saying a lot. In their line of work, loyal people were hard to come by, but Darryl was an exception. He had earned Nigel's respect, both as a colleague and a friend, which was why, on occasion Nigel and Darryl would lay aside their professionalism to engage in brotherly small talk.

"So, did you take her out or what?" Nigel asked.

"Yeah, I did," Darryl replied in a noncommittal tone. He shrugged. "She was cool, but I don't know if I'm ready for the dating circus again. We see the most ratchet behavior in our line of work. I spent more time analyzing her body language to see if she was lying or being deceitful than I did appreciating how fine the sista was."

Nigel chuckled. He understood all too well what Darryl meant.

"Par for the course in this business. But do not let ratchet people keep you from being happy."

Darryl nodded.

"I know man, it's just hard to trust. But she's clear."

"Clear?" Nigel asked. "Wait, did you do a background check on that woman?"

Darryl simply shrugged again, refusing to give his boss an affirmative answer. Nigel shook his head.

"You did one on Kadijah," Darryl defended himself.

"Um, that's because I met her while she was doing something shady in the building I had been hired to secure."

Darryl gave Nigel a blank stare.

"That's semantics," he replied simply making Nigel chuckle. "And I'm just trying to make sure there isn't anything shady about her before I get my emotions involved."

Nigel was saved from responding when his phone signaled a video call. He checked the caller ID and smiled when he saw Kadijah's face. He put up a finger to let Darryl know he was going to take the call. Darryl grabbed his coffee and took a sip.

"Hey beautiful, what's up?" Nigel asked when the call connected.

He saw she was outside and dressed in a brightly colored flowy maxi dress.

"Hey, sweet pea. I'm on my way to meet Grey for a late lunch, but I had to call you because I am having such a good boob day!"

Darryl choked on his coffee, then got up to excuse himself. He gave the "deuces" sign, letting his boss know he was out.

Nigel fell out laughing. "What?"

"I mean, I had to call and thank you for them. I never had any before, but since I'm carrying your baby girl, a sister is getting thick."

Nigel laughed again. His wife was in rare form. Looked like their morning rendezvous had definitely lifted her mood.

"You are out of control," he said still laughing. Kadijah gave him a flirtatious smirk.

"Don't act like you don't appreciate my new thickness," she said saucily.

He shook his head. "I do appreciate it and congrats on your great boob day. Enjoy the fruits of my labor."

Kadijah threw her head back and laughed then blew him a kiss and disconnected the call. Nigel chuckled as he stood up from his desk and walked across the hall to Darryl's office. His wife's antics had interrupted their conversation.

"My bad dawg, I didn't know the call would be so animated."

"It's cool," Darryl said laughing.

"Seriously though bro, give the woman a chance. She seems nice. God will show you everything you need to know, trust me."

"A'ight, I'm going to call her and invite her out tonight."

"If you ever need it, we'll double date with you."

Darryl nodded. "I might take y'all up on that."

Nigel nodded and headed to the lobby to check in with Cynthia.

Chapter 8: Because We're Happy

Hope and Jacob laughed to their hearts content as they watched their favorite movie *Minions* for the thousandth time. It was a lazy Saturday morning in the Parker household, and the kids had taken residence in their parents' bed. Much to their parents' chagrin, that meant taking over the television too.

Lindsey looked over at her husband and grinned at Jamal as he rolled his brown eyes and ran a hand absentmindedly through his curly black hair.

"I'm kicking them out," he said. Lindsey snickered.

"No, you're not. Punk!"

Jamal laughed. He was indeed a punk. He absolutely adored his children. He loved looking at Jacob and seeing a miniature version of himself. Hope with her mixed heritage was a blend of both of them. She had her mother's haunting green eyes with an explosion of fat brown curls.

Being around them in moments like this filled his heart with so much joy he often wondered how it didn't burst. He was so grateful these days.

His family was whole and healthy. He and Lindsey were getting along great, and to his heart's content, Lindsey and Jacob had formed a true bond. He still had moments where he missed his mother, but they were finding ways to cope with that.

Jamal made sure to let Jacob spend time with his grandparents once a week. His uncle was slowly but surely coming around too. For the moment they were in good health and once again, he was thankful.

"I've been thinking," Lindsey began.

"About what?"

"Taking a trip with the kids."

"To where?"

"Disney." Jamal raised his brows as he glanced over at his wife.

"Yeah? That would be fun," he replied thoughtfully as he mulled over his wife's suggestion. It really would be nice to get away as a family.

"Let's make it a big deal and go for a week," she continued.

"A whole week, huh?"

Lindsey nodded enthusiastically.

"We've earned it don't you think?"

She knew it would cost them a nice chunk of change, but she felt like they deserved it after all they had been through and overcome. Lindsey stared at her husband expectantly as he thought it over. After a long moment, he turned to her and smiled.

"Let's do it," he told her.

"Really?" she squealed her strawberry blonde hair falling in her face.

He nodded, then chuckled as she leaned over to grab his face and give him an exaggerated smack on the lips.

"Ewww Mommy," Hope said.

"Ewww Hope," Jamal teased as he snatched her up to place kisses all over her face.

Hope giggled at her dad's antics and tried to escape to no avail.

Not wanting to be left out, Jacob looked up at his father. Lindsey began to tickle him as he squealed. She scooped him up and pulled him to her bosom as she continued to tickle and kiss him.

Jamal looked over at his wife holding his son and his heart melted. He kissed Hope one more time for good measure then leaned over and tickled his son making sure to cover his face with kisses too. Jacob giggled in pure glee. The sound of laughter in their home was music to both their ears.

Their angels valiantly watched over them. Hope's constant Guardian stood in all his black beauty keeping watch over his little charge.

Chapter 9: A Miracle Indeed

Across town, Neil and Grey were enjoying a leisurely day, hanging out on the couch with their 9-month-old son. Their life had been so simple lately, the normalcy of it all honestly freaked them out at times. However, they knew better than to look a gift horse in the mouth, so they made sure to enjoy every drama-free minute to the fullest.

Neil relaxed into the plush sofa; his long legs propped up on the equally plush matching ottoman. Grey sat facing him, her feet in his lap, as she balanced a squirming Hunter on her legs.

"Watch this," she said. Neil looked over at her as Grey blew a zerbert on their son's belly. The sound of pure glee filled their living room, as Hunter laughed and could hardly breathe. His contagious giggles made Neil laugh until he had tears in his eyes. For the next several minutes, he and Grey took turns making their baby boy laugh. There was nothing sweeter than the sound of a baby's laughter.

A few minutes later, they were interrupted by a video call on Neil's phone.

He dug it out of his pocket and said, "Oh my God, it's Aliaksana."

Grey grinned. "Answer it! Answer it!" she urged him.

He laughed at his wife and connected the call. Aliaksana's smiling face appeared on the video.

"Hi!" she waved at them grinning broadly.

Neil and Grey both observed her. Those big brown eyes were vibrant and clear. Her brunette hair looked shiny and was now cut in a tapered bob that framed her pretty face. She'd even put on a little weight.

"Hey there!" Grey said.

"How are you?" Neil asked.

"I'm great. Is that the baby?" she asked pointing to Hunter.

"It is," Grey grinned as she turned him to face the camera.

"Oh, he is so yummy," Aliaksana gushed.

"Thank you," Grey said and kissed her son's cheek.

"Are those teeth?" she asked smiling.

"Yep, he's got three pegs now," Neil said.

"Is he walking?" she asked.

"With assistance, but he won't just let go and take the plunge," Grey said rolling her eyes. Aliaksana laughed.

"How's your mom and dad?" Neil asked.

"They are doing well considering. They have their moments as do I."

"That's understandable," Neil told her. "Do you guys need anything?"

"No, we're fine," she responded. "But I am calling for two things. I just missed you guys and wanted to say hi. I pray every day for God to bless you all for what you did for us."

Neil and Grey smiled. "We were just being obedient," he told her.

Aliaksana smiled.

"I knew you'd say that - which brings me to my second reason for calling. I am being obedient too," she smiled.

Neil and Grey exchanged a look.

"What's up?" Grey asked.

"Well, those two Psalms you gave me changed my life. They made my ordinary life extraordinary and helped me to take down a great evil. I want to tell others about how powerful the Word of God is."

"That's great, Aliaksana," Neil said. "How do you plan to do it?"

"YouTube. I have started a channel and I am going to do a weekly Bible study about a new verse or chapter I have memorized over the course of a week and whatever it manifests in my life. So sorta like a scripture documentary," she said excitedly.

Grey wiped a tear that ran down her cheek. She was simply overwhelmed by the display of God's providence in this young woman's life. The power of His Word had freed her from the clutches of pure evil, and now, it was manifesting in her life in such a way that she was sharing God's truth with the world. Grey glanced at Neil, who also seemed a little choked up by Aliaksana's confession. He had to clear his throat to speak.

"I am so incredibly proud of you. You have one of the brightest lights I have ever seen, and I know that after everything you have been through and survived, nothing will dim it. We support you a thousand percent. Let us know anything you need and it's yours."

Grey, still too emotional to speak, simply blew a kiss at the screen. Aliaksana grinned.

"Well, I need you guys to subscribe to my channel."

They laughed. Grey pulled out her phone.

"What's the handle?" She told them as Grey searched. "Just subscribed and hit the bell so I can receive notifications."

They laughed. "I will subscribe when we hang up," Neil told her.

"I'm so excited and a little nervous."

"Obedience can be scary, and it will definitely push you out of your comfort zone, but that same God who brought you out of darkness, will be with you as you proclaim His Word," Grey told her.

"He will never leave you, nor forsake you," Neil added.

Aliaksana nodded.

"I know that now. I know He was there with me in that hell hole. And as crazy as it sounds it's pretty amazing that He, this supreme and Holy being, was willing to be down in the trenches with me, a soul who didn't even really know anything about Him. To me that says a lot about Him. Now, I understand why in the Bible it says, Abba Father. He's like a parent who's always there to guide you, teach you and most importantly, love you. I know that not everyone can survive what I experienced and that He sent me there to be a support for other girls who make it out."

"Are you still keeping in touch?" Grey asked.

"Yes, we have a GroupMe where we encourage each other, and I keep in touch with the parents or guardians of the girls who are too young to be able to communicate. I want to meet up with them soon, but I'm still not ready to come back to America and definitely not by myself," she said as she cast her eyes downward.

"There's no shame in that," Grey told her. "You experienced unfathomable trauma. You have a right to your specific healing process. Are you still going to therapy?"

"Yes, I love my therapist," Aliaksana answered. "She's great. My parents have gone with me a few times too."

"That's beautiful love. Stick to the process, it works if you keep at it."

"She's right," Neil interjected. "And when you're ready, wherever you want to go, just let me know and I'll get you a security detail."

Aliaksana stared at him. "Are you serious?"

"Very much," he nodded.

"Well, some people at an organization that fights for survivors of sex trafficking asked me to be a keynote speaker at their benefit in a few months. I was thinking about it, but I'm very hesitant. If I go, would you send security with me?"

"If I can't be there myself, I will send someone I would trust with my own family," Neil answered. "As a matter of fact, email me the information on the event and organization so I can vet them just in case you decide you want to do it."

Her eyes got huge, "Not the big guy that's always with Miss Grey. He's scary."

They laughed.

Grey waved a hand, "Beau is harmless unless you mess with whomever he's responsible for protecting."

Aliaksana chuckled.

"Okay, I'll forward the info."

"Keep in mind, we can always send a woman if that makes you more comfortable."

She nodded. "Okay, I'll pray about it and talk it over with my parents."

"We're here if you need us," Grey told her.

Aliaksana smiled in sincere thanks.

"I love you guys," she said and waved bye.

Neil replied, "We love you, too," then ended the call.

He turned to look at his wife.

"Well, that was something."

"Wasn't it?" Grey marveled. "What a remarkable young lady. Her testimony will change lives, I'm sure of it."

"You're right," Neil agreed.

"Don't forget to subscribe to her channel."

"Oh right."

Neil did as he promised he would do then scooped up his son who had been playing with his shirt to make him laugh again.

Chapter 10: All in a Day's Work

Monday morning brought the start of a new week at Sheridan's Christian Counseling practice. She took a sip of her coffee as she walked inside her office. She was a slender woman with skin the color of butterscotch and brown bedroom eyes.

Her mother greeted her from the receptionist's counter. Sheridan smiled and walked over placing her purse on the counter and taking another sip of her coffee. Emma Lee had smooth honey brown skin that hardly sported a wrinkle and big dark eyes. She wore her salt and pepper hair in a short, texturized, precisely cut coif that complimented her flawless, slender face.

"Hey, ma!" Sheridan greeted enthusiastically, a bright smile gracing her face.

"Um, that is unprofessional Dr. Richard's," her mother scolded playfully.

Sheridan rolled her eyes and made an exaggerated show of clearing her throat.

"Good morning Ms. Ellis. What's on my agenda today?"

Her mom grinned. "Well, your usual Wednesday roll call with the exception of a new one for your first appointment."

Sheridan nodded and reached for the file on the new patient.

"What's the name again?" she asked.

"Deborah."

Sheridan viewed the first page of the folder as she rubbed her 4-month pregnant belly.

"She'll be here at nine."

Sheridan nodded as she looked at her watch. She had thirty minutes.

"Okay, let me go in here and pray to get my mind right."

"Okay baby, I'll hold it down."

"Oh, and ma, I'm already hungry so please find something amazing for lunch and have it here exactly at noon!"

Emma Lee fell out laughing as she responded.

"I will have something great waiting for you and my grandbaby."

"God is gon bless you because you're out here doing the work of the Lord," Sheridan yelled back as she headed to her office.

When she entered, Sheridan immediately sat down her bags and took off her shoes. She went to the cushy chair in the corner behind the desk she'd recently added to her office for the sole purpose of being a place of communing with God.

She began to seek God, asking him to guide her and give her wisdom, insight, and protection as she took on this day of dealing with the mental health of others. The golden key she earned for her part in the battle for Simone's soul began to glow releasing her gift of deliverance. After years of managing this practice, she'd learned the necessity of safeguarding her own mental health, and she understood she could not be an empty vessel trying to pour into others. Her angels, Tero and Wayland stood guard to indeed protect her.

After she prayed, she sat still for several moments and just let God do His thing. Five minutes before her client arrived, she heard the buzz of her phone alarm letting her know it was time to get ready for the day. She slipped her shoes back on and went to sit behind her desk.

Six minutes later, her mother, who was her acting receptionist, knocked on the door.

"Come in," she said.

The door opened to reveal a petite woman who seemed to give off a shy vibe.

"Dr. Richards, this is Deborah Smith, your first appointment."

Sheridan stood up and briskly walked over to extend her hand. The woman had a chocolate complexion, average height, and a slender build.

"Nice to meet you Deborah," Sheridan greeted. Please, have a seat."

Emma Lee nodded and closed the door behind her. Deborah sat down and looked around the spacious office. This was her first time in therapy, and she had no idea what to expect.

The warm colors of deep orange, brown and beige were comforting. They gave off some vibrancy, but also made the introvert in her not feel overwhelmed by too much too soon. The love seat she sat on was plush and cozy. There was a longer matching sofa on a different wall. Obviously, the doctor had put some thought into making her office feel as comforting as it looked.

She observed Sheridan's degrees that were neatly displayed on the wall behind her desk. If those degrees were to be believed, then this Dr. Richards woman knew her stuff. Curious about the plush chair she saw in the corner behind her desk, she wondered if Sheridan used it to take cat naps during the day.

Finally, Deborah turned her attention to the doctor herself. This woman exuded competence and compassion; two qualities Deborah desperately needed right now. She hoped she had the courage to bare her soul to this stranger, but at this point, she was willing to take whatever help she could get.

Sheridan smoothed her skirt as she took the orange chair that sat near the corner of her desk.

"So, Deborah tell me. What brings you in today?"

"I had a panic attack last week at work and it really freaked me out."

"Have you been stressed about anything lately?" Sheridan asked as she took a sip of her coffee.

"Oh, just the fact that I caught my mother in bed with my husband."

Sheridan spit out her coffee, earning a look of surprise from her patient.

"Oh, Jesus. I'm so sorry."

Sheridan said as she reached for a tissue to wipe her mouth. She was used to hearing all sorts of dramatic confessions. So much so, she thought she couldn't be surprised anymore. Obviously, she'd been wrong.

Deborah stared at Sheridan for a moment, then did the last thing she expected - laughed. Sheridan watched in disbelief as her new patient fell into complete hysterics. Deborah laughed and laughed, until she was nearly doubled over. Sheridan continued to watch quietly, until suddenly, Deborah's hiccups of laughter dissolved into gut-wrenching sobs. Sheridan got up and handed the woman some tissue. Deborah took the tissue and wiped her face. She hadn't expected to break down like that, but apparently, she'd finally reached her breaking point.

Once Deborah was calm, and her own initial shock over the situation had worn off, Sheridan pressed forward.

"Do you have more background information?"

"My mother has always been jealous of me. I generally ignored her and tolerated her because she was my mother, but this is new territory."

"Are you still with your husband?"

"No, I'm not, he's shacking up with my mother."

Sheridan coughed awkwardly. "Oh my, they out here living reckless I see."

"Listen Doc, I need you to help me deal with this and find a new normal. These evil people cannot take my sanity too. They broke my heart. Took my dignity and now it's threatening to take my mind. I can't have that."

Sheridan nodded. "God can bring you back from anything if you're willing to do the work."

"I'm willing."

"Okay, let's unpack this," Sheridan said as she picked up her pen again. "When was the first time you realized you were in competition with your mother?"

"The day I got breasts and an older man made a comment."

Sheridan sighed and whispered, "Help me Holy Ghost."

This patient was far from witchcraft and demonic possessions, but still, crazy was crazy.

Chapter 11: The Gentle Giant

Neil drove through Downtown Tallahassee on his way to meet up with Beau. He'd been thoroughly intrigued by the random phone call, but Beau had been there for him and his family more times than he could count. Whatever the man asked of him, he would do his very best to make sure to answer the call.

A few minutes later, Neil arrived at Cascades Park. He parked near the amphitheater and spotted Beau's large frame sitting down close to the front. Neil locked his pickup truck after he hopped out.

Cascades always had people roaming about no matter what time you came. It was a beautiful park that had an amphitheater where concerts were held, a small waterpark for the children to play, long walking and bike trails, a waterfall, facilities for event rental space and monuments that spoke of Florida's history. The lush trees, perfectly coordinated flowers and layout made for beautiful summer scenery.

Dressed in jeans, boots, and a black t-shirt, despite the June heat, Neil tucked his detective's badge inside his shirt as he made his way down to where Beau was seated. The big man tended to draw attention just by his size, he wanted to blend in as much as possible.

Beau turned to look up when Neil was two rows from him. He nodded and waved as if Neil had trouble spotting him. Beau was nearly seven-feet tall; his skin was the color of a Hershey Bar. His almond shaped eyes were dark brown with a clean-shaven face. He wore his hair in a fade.

When Neil reached him, Beau stood up and extended a hand. Neil grasped it and they greeted each other with a shake and one arm-hugged hug. Leaving an empty seat between them, Neil sat down.

"What's up, man. You sounded a little nervous on the phone."

Beau smiled, exposing the small gap in his smile that gave it character. If Neil didn't know better, he would swear the man was blushing, well as much as he could with chocolate skin.

Beau smiled and pulled something out of his pocket. His hands were so large, Neil didn't know what it was. Beau extended his hand and Neil reached for it. When he let go, Neil saw a small black velvet box in his hand.

He whistled. "Oh, yeah, that will make a man nervous."

Beau let out a chuckle. Neil opened the box. The ring was simple; however, it was exquisite. It was a single diamond solitaire, but it was easily three karats. A whistle escaped Neil's full lips again.

"Well, I see you ain't playing the radio."

Beau laughed. "She's worth every penny."

Neil admired the ring once more before closing the box and returning it to Beau. Instead of putting it back in his pocket, Beau absent-mindedly turned the box between his fingers.

"So, what's up?"

Too nervous to make eye contact, Beau stared at the ring he manipulated with his large fingers as he talked.

"I never thought this would be me. A man trying to settle down and marry somebody's daughter."

"Don't take this the wrong way, big man, but you don't seem like the player type."

Beau laughed as some of his nervousness fell away. He shook his head.

"Nah, that's never been me either. I'm more the loner type. My life has always been plagued by violence, so I never wanted to bring anyone into it. Once I got out of the gang life, I was also afraid of Karma you know. I never gave my heart to anything because I knew one day Karma would come knocking. I just assumed it would snatch what was most precious to me."

The words coming from his friend were heavy and sobering. Neil understood his hesitation.

"So, what made you decide to take this step?"

"You know Neisha, she's a good church girl. I gotta come correct with her. Besides, I want that. I want to make vows to her. I want to let my mama see me walk down the aisle of somebody's church and promise to love and protect her."

Neil nodded. "I understand that," he replied. And in all honesty, he truly did. At one point, he too hadn't been sure he could actually have the life he enjoyed now, but he'd always desired it. Thank God for Grey. He continued to listen quietly as Beau poured out his heart.

"I see your lil man and it pulls on my heartstrings. I want to bring a child into this world with the woman I love, but I am so *scared.*"

Beau turned to look at Neil, who for the first instance in all the time he had known the big man, recognized a very real fear in his eyes.

Neil asked the Holy Spirit to help him talk to his friend. Everyone had a past and Neil firmly believed that if you had reconciled with the it, and repented before the Creator of all things, then it was in the past. Yes, it was true a man reaped what he had sowed, but nothing could top God's grace, mercy, and favor.

"Beau, you're a very different man than the one I first met to protect my wife when I was undercover. Have you prayed about taking this next step in life?"

Beau nodded firmly. "Of course. Because if I didn't your wife would fuss me out."

Neil laughed. "She definitely would."

"I pray about everything now, which still shocks me," Beau admitted laughing.

"So, where do you feel God is leading you on the matter."

Beau held up the ring.

"Well, after I prayed about it, I felt so much peace surrounding me and then two days later, I found myself in the mall shopping for this ring."

"So, what happened to the peace?" Neil inquired.

"It's still there, but sometimes you need something more than that spiritual feeling you know. I'm new to this relationship with God, but I just wanted to talk to someone here on earth, if that makes sense."

Neil chuckled. "It makes complete sense. Faith is hard, and its very definition goes against what's natural to us as humans. The tangible. You've already made up your mind that you are going to marry her, you just want to talk it out and get some perspective."

Beau nodded. Neil had always been intuitive.

"Yes, yours is the only marriage I've ever seen up close. Miss Grey is the only Christian I've ever seen up close and personal. She's taught me a lot about my walk with God but being her security detail has taught me that being a Christian doesn't stop the attacks on your life. In her case, they seem to be amplified."

Neil chuckled. "You have no idea. My God that woman is like a magnet for spiritual drama."

"I'm a protector by nature and I love my woman with my whole heart. I feel like if anyone or anything came to harm my family, I might lose my salvation."

Neil laughed. He didn't mean to, but Beau was such a genuine spirit.

"You can't lose your salvation. Once you believe you believe. You can give yourself over to sin and bring separation between you and God, but the Bible says, God is married to the backslider. You were called to be the priest, provider, and protector of your home. It's your job to keep your family safe."

"I've always wanted to know. Why are you so protective of Miss Grey? I mean, I know it's natural to protect what you love, but you be on some other stuff."

This time Neil laughed hard as he bent forward to let the laugh out. Beau smiled; it was rare Neil lost his composure unless he was around his silly brother.

Neil sat back and gave it some thought. Finally, he spoke as the realization hit him for the first time, "The life I live, doing what I do, carrying the weights that I carry, have been plagued by ugliness and constant anxiety. I used to walk around with this tightness in my chest. There's a certain paranoia that comes with the territory. The women before her could never soothe it. I didn't even know they were supposed to. When I first met Grey, she made me laugh. She's silly and so not like me, but the first time I held that woman the tightness in my chest left. I was surrounded by peace. I'll never forget, she tried to pull away after a few moments and I said, 'not yet.' I had never felt that before and I didn't want to let it go. It was the longest hug ever."

Beau laughed, and Neil smiled at the memory of one his earlier encounters with his wife. Thinking about it now made him realize just how grateful he was to still have her. He continued.

"I knew she was special. My mind was always racing because of what I do. I meet murderers, rapists, and criminals quite often. I lock people up, it's my job. Any of them or their family could be looking out to get me. I see the worst in people on a daily basis. That weighs on you. The first time I slept next to her, I dropped into sleep, immediately. The reason I used to work so hard is I needed to exhaust myself to sleep at night and block out all the ugliness I saw day in and day out. Her touch relaxes me. All she has to do is scratch my head and she soothes that beast inside me that's needed to do what I do. It's like her spirit is always interceding for mine. It's crazy when she's silently praying for me, my spirit recognizes it. She doesn't know this and probably wouldn't believe it, but I need her more than she's ever needed me. I'm able to be her protector but only because she's my peace. She is who God sent to ease the weight of the cross I was born to bear."

Beau let out an expletive. Neil burst out laughing.

"My bad, God still working on me," Beau confessed.

"You good, man. Her presence calms me down, so, I think I protect her the way I do because doing so is also guarding my sanity if that makes sense. I waited a long time to find that and I'll be doggone if anybody takes away my light in all this darkness."

"Do you ever feel conflicted being a Christian and loving her like that? I mean to the point of...," Beau hesitated at looked at Neil, the unspoken question evident in his eyes.

"Eliminating a threat?" Neil finished.

Beau nodded.

Neil sighed. "I'm gon tell you like this. If it's preemptive, that's you taking matters from God and putting them in your own hands. If it's a defense of what's been entrusted to you, that's you exercising the authority given to you by God. I can be honest; my first thought is to remove any threat to my wife and family. There are times where God has stayed my hand made it crystal clear that vengeance belonged to Him and then there are times when He didn't. Beau, God is never going to leave you. His voice, His hand, it will be there in those dark moments as well as the good ones. I no longer doubt God's ability to keep my wife and son safe, however, the method in which He chooses to do it may be through my hands and I'm okay with that. You can't not live your life because you're afraid. Our days on this earth are numbered. No one knows the day, the hour or exit plan, but life is worth living. So, live it, man. You find your piece of happiness, snatch it up and enjoy it while you can."

Beau nodded. "Thanks for this."

"No problem," Neil said. He clapped a hand on Beau's shoulder and gave it a friendly squeeze.

They sat in companionable silence for a few more minutes thinking about the matters of their hearts.

Chapter 12: The Call

Darcy walked through her home letting the peaceful stillness envelop her. Jessica was gone for the moment hanging out with friends, so Darcy had the place all to herself. The gentle but steady pound of the summer rain outside prompted the need for purposeful solitude.

Darcy turned off her cell phone. She wasn't in the mood for vibrate or silence, she wanted it off. No distractions. No phone calls. No texts and no notifications from the hundreds of apps Jessica had installed on her mobile device. She found technology convenient for the generation she lived in, but also often irritating by the separation of human contact it prompted.

Darcy had no reason for her actions but followed them nonetheless because for some reason her spirit craved the solitude. Her maternal instincts never far from her conscious mind, reminded her that Jessica could reach her on the house phone in case of an emergency. The only people who called that line was her mother and Jessica. Her mother only called once a month, so she had a good three weeks before she was graced with her self-absorbed, self-imposed required check-in.

As Darcy walked through the empty house her longing spirit drew her to the back porch. She stepped out of the sliding glass door and inhaled the beautiful scent of rain.

She thought, *how can people believe there isn't a God when nature is this amazing?* Every time she experienced nature, she felt closer to her Creator.

She took a seat on one of the plush rocking chairs she and Josiah had picked out. She let the cushions envelop her as she closed her eyes and rocked. She smiled at the memory of the day they bought the chairs, grateful that it didn't incite tears but a smile.

Losing him no longer, stung, but his loss remained a gentle ache she'd learned to embrace because it meant that he lived on through her. She saw his face every day as she stared at their beautiful baby girl. That comforted her in ways she couldn't explain.

Her mind drifted to the nine-month anniversary of his death. That day she had felt something stirring in her spirit that she just couldn't describe. She'd literally felt something leap in her belly. That day, she'd known she had been carrying purpose through her grieving process, but God had yet to reveal what it all meant. Little did she know, He was about to do just that.

As Darcy continued to rock, she opened her eyes and stared at their beautiful backyard. She watched as the trees, plants, bushes, and shrubs consumed the water from Heaven that God sent to keep them beautiful, nourished and cared for. She was reminded of the scripture in Luke that said, *"Consider how the wildflowers grow. They do not labor or spin. Yet I tell you, not even Solomon in all his splendor was dressed like one of these."*

It reminded her once again that she had no need to worry because the God she served would take care of her. Suddenly, there was a press in her spirit. She had never felt anything like it. She looked down at her arms as the goosebumps began to saturate her skin. She knew the presence of the Most High God had just enveloped her.

Tears began to roll down her cheeks and blur her vision. Then she heard... no felt... no sensed... she couldn't adequately describe the words that were being downloaded into her spirit.

"My beloved daughter, the time has come for me to reveal your calling. You are a gatekeeper of this city. It's no coincidence that your son is the governor of this state and you all reside in the capital city. It's no coincidence that your daughter is gifted as a spiritual amplifier. This was all by My design. Each of you must embrace who you are. Nothing shall happen in this city without your knowledge. Some things you can stop and some you cannot. Your job is to pray My will be done and sound the alarm when I tell you to. It's no coincidence that your house is on a hill on the north side of town. I positioned you there as the North Gatekeeper. Watch for the other three gatekeepers. You will join together to keep this city, but your position is the greatest. Your obedience is vital. If you keep my city with all diligence, I will deny you nothing. When you're ready I will send you a great love, not to replace Josiah, but to be a tangible reminder of my love for you."

Darcy shivered as the words softly reverberated through her. She was in awe. She was overwhelmed. She was speechless. As she stared out into her yard, she could swear she saw the outline of a large figure walking away from her through the rain. She fell to her knees and began to worship.

As she worshipped the lighting began to strike and the thunder rolled. The heavens opened up. Unseen to the human eye, four flashes of fire descended from the heavenly realms. They dropped down onto the porch to surround Darcy on the north, south, east, and west. Each landed on one knee as their massive white wings tipped in gold covered them. They each stood to their full height of 13-feet as their wings spread tip-to-tip to cover Darcy.

These naval warriors had been summoned from their position in the Gulf of Mexico. They had just received their commission from the throne room to guard the city's North Gatekeeper.

Andronicus, the Latin Captain, nodded at his fellow comrades and said in a voice that shook the spirit realm, "It is time!"

Chapter 13: Peek-A-Boo

Thailand

Remote, simple, and serene, the monastery sat alone amongst the mountain scenery. It was the perfect hiding place for someone who wanted to disappear from the rest of the world. It was always a struggle to play this role, but it was the safest place he could think of to lay low, from both natural and spiritual predators.

Lucca sat Indian style on a cliff overlooking lush greenery with his eyes closed and his hands laying on his thighs. It had taken him months, but he was finally at peace. True enough he'd be in hiding for the rest of his life, but at least he still had a life.

His family, the Untouchables was in shambles and rumors had gotten around that the four puppet masters had been found dead. Because of the nature in which the bodies were found, autopsies had been performed revealing the true identities of the gang leaders who'd presumably faked their deaths decades ago.

The connection to the house in California, as well as the sex trafficking brothels, had been connected. Currently, federal investigators were conducting a massive investigation to connect all the breadcrumbs left behind.

Lucca knew it was best he stayed as far away from the fray as possible. He trusted no one. Because of his decision to run, he no longer had demonic help or access. He accepted that part of his life was over. He longed for the power he'd held when he belonged to the dark side. He had no desire to go to the light, so he was just stuck on earth as a regular human.

He had been reduced to a silent monk. While he had been a great actor in convincing the monks, he wanted to live a life of solitude and service, it couldn't be farther from the truth. Lucca sighed. He missed his money, his women, and his power.

Suddenly, a familiar sensation pricked his skin. Evil was very near. Lucca's eyes popped open as he stared into Insidious' face. He scrambled back in fear for his life. He looked around bewildered, thankful he was alone and away from the watchful eyes of his fellow monks.

Insidious looked at him unimpressed.

"You can't be here. This place is holy," Lucca said his voice trembling slightly.

Insidious scoffed, "No, this place may be sacred, but it isn't holy because the power of the one true living God does not reside here. You should have learned much more about your adversary. Clearly, you don't have a clue."

Lucca frowned, "Why are you here?"

"Because, pretty boy, you have finally become useful." Lucca eyed Insidious suspiciously. "You've been a coward long enough - it's time to get back to work."

Calmer, Lucca asked, "Who are you?"

"The fact that you don't know who I am tells me you weren't as powerful as they let you believe."

Lucca's temper flashed. He shot a glare in Insidious' direction. Despite his less than desirable life, his arrogance remained intact, and he definitely didn't appreciate his ego being challenged.

"Enough! Get to the point or leave," he demanded.

"Careful," Insidious warned. "Learn to stay in your place or get expedited to your fiery eternal destination."

Lucca's hand trembled. "Now that I have your attention...," Lucca glared at Insidious. "It's time you stopped playing charades and redeem yourself."

"How?" Lucca asked.

"By doing what you do best - seduction," Insidious said with a grin.

"And who might I ask am I seducing?" Lucca inquired with disgust.

"Oh, let's not act like you have standards."

Lucca scowled.

Insidious continued ignoring Lucca's facial tantrum. "Your nemesis' granddaughter."

"And why would I do that?"

Insidious raised a brow. "Oh, just you know, so you could keep breathing and so she can exact revenge on *his* sons and grandchildren."

Lucca's face lit up with sheer joy. "Are you welcoming me back into the fold?"

"If you can prove you belong..."

"And I only answer to you?"

"Just me."

Lucca considered.

Impatiently, Insidious said, "The only other option you have to keep breathing is to turn to the light, and we both know that is something you will never do, which is frankly why I'm making this deal. Hesitate any longer and you die right here, right now."

"I accept," Lucca said through clenched teeth. "What about Naamah?" he asked skeptically.

"She was taken out. You no longer have to worry about her or those who were loyal to her. I was personally invited by Lucifer to handle this."

"So, who are you?"

"Insidious," he said smugly.

Lucca shivered just a bit when he recognized the name.

Insidious grinned fiercely.

"Oh, before I forget. When you seduce her, watch your back. She's more than likely to take you out afterward."

Lucca frowned. Cockily he said, "They usually want a repeat performance, so I doubt I need to be concerned."

Insidious gave him a blank stare.

"Your ego will always be a problem. Get it under control. Trust me when I say, you need to be careful with this one. Her codename is Black Widow. Like I said, when she's done with you, watch your back."

Lucca scowled his ego struggling to accept the warning.

"Drop the act, get out of here and be ready when I give you the green light. I will have demonic sentries to give you safe passage back to America. Don't worry, you'll be concealed from the authorities."

Lucca nodded. "How am I supposed to get out of here and hide until you call?"

"You're a resourceful man. Figure it out."

Insidious smiled as he disappeared from Lucca's sight.

Chapter 14: Thinking Ahead

When Neil arrived back at the precinct, he was shocked to see his brother sitting in his visitor's chair. Nigel stood up when his brother walked in. They embraced.

"Bro, what are you doing here? Why didn't you just call me?" Neil asked. "Have you been waiting long?"

Nigel shook his head. "It's all good. I used the time to iron out some details. Is there somewhere we can go and talk?"

Neil frowned. "Everything alright?"

Nigel simply stared at his brother. Neil asked no more questions and led him through the homicide bullpen then through the rest of the precinct and out of the building. Nigel looked at him trying to figure out what he was doing.

"Let's take a ride," Neil suggested as he unlocked his truck with the keyless entry. Nigel climbed in without objection. Once they pulled out of the parking lot, Neil asked, "What's on your mind, bro?"

Nigel rubbed his hand over his forehead. Neil frowned. It wasn't like his brother to show signs of stress or anxiety.

"I've been praying about how to keep my child and Kadijah safe in lieu of all this crazy. I mean we need to find our niece, but I can't shake the feeling that she is a foe and not a friend." Neil nodded but didn't interrupt. Nigel eyed his brother. "I mean, have you thought about that?"

Neil gave a noncommittal gesture with his hand.

"I mean, have you seriously thought about what that moment will be like? Coming face to face with her and instead of a beautiful family reunion, it's like who's got the quickest draw? And don't think I haven't noticed you haven't brought up telling mama about her."

Neil briefly dropped his head but continued to look at the road, again not committing an opinion to anything his brother was saying.

"Exactly," Nigel said knowingly. "We gotta tell Mama and she's going to be a problem because you know she's going to want to meet her, pray for her and get her saved, sanctified and delivered."

"And you are thinking about the most effective way to take her out if she poses a threat to your daughter," Neil interjected.

"You already know. She's got to go." Nigel emphasized his point by swiping his hand in front of his neck in a slicing motion.

Neil sighed. He should have known Nigel would recommend taking her out, and honestly, he couldn't blame him. But Neil had enough blood on his hands, and the prospect of making them bloodier made him more than a little apprehensive.

"Why does it have to be death?" he asked, voicing his private concerns aloud. "Jail is a possibility. I'm sure she's got a criminal record. After all, she has to be affiliated with the Untouchables in some kind of way."

"If she's alive, she will always be a threat," Nigel countered.

"I'm just saying bro, she *is* our niece." Neil spared a glance at his brother as he weaved through traffic, driving nowhere in particular.

"Listen, I get it, I really do," Nigel responded. "But like it or not, you may have to choose between your nieces, and I may have to choose between my daughter and my dead brother's daughter. I'm okay with the choice I have to make. I need to know that you can handle the choice you'll need to make. *My* daughter is the only innocent one in this."

"How do we know she's not innocent, Nigel? She could be a victim. There's just as much of a chance of her needing us to save her as there is of her being evil."

Nigel turned to look at his brother.

"Tell me what your gut says."

Neil met his brother's challenge with silence.

"Exactly!" Nigel exclaimed matter-of-factly. "I need to know that you won't hesitate, because let's face it if she's got our blood, she's going to be a formidable opponent. Think of how Eva was trained."

Neil nodded. After a moment of silence, he responded.

"I won't hesitate."

And he wouldn't. He didn't doubt his ability to do the right thing in the moment, but Neil couldn't shake the feeling that this decision would come at a heavy cost.

He sighed. The two brothers rode in silence for a few blocks as Neil worked to finally get his emotions in check. He hated that, once again, drama was rearing its ugly head in their lives. After a few more pensive moments, Neil broke the silence.

"That's not why you were waiting at my job," he said, cautiously eyeing his brother. "What's up?"

Nigel sighed, then spoke.

"I've been thinking, this might get a lot worse before it gets better," he began. "I feel like I need contingency plans. I know you had some for Grey, but I have something a little different in mind."

"Okay, what is it?" Neil asked.

Nigel hesitated and wrung his hands together. Neil glanced at him sideways as realization hit him.

"Hell nol, bro. The answer is no!"

"You don't even know what I'm going to ask," Nigel argued.

"Yes, I do, and she's not going. Grey and Hunter are not going to be separated from me!"

"I need you to hear me out..."

"I need *you* to read my lips. Hell no!" Neil said in a stern tone that made Nigel roll his eyes. He stared nonchalantly at his older brother, visibly unfazed by his tantrum.

"Are you done?" Neil sighed in frustration. "Hear me out. We know Grey is assigned to cover my baby girl. Wherever I send Kadijah, she's going to need spiritual as well as natural protection. I only trust Grey like that - plus she can see in the spirit."

Nigel spared a glance at his brother. Jaw set and eyes narrowed; Neil was a picture of pure tension.

"Now, I know she'd have to take Hunter with her and essentially, I'm asking you to put your whole family in danger to protect mine, but just listen. Hunter is gifted the way you are, so Grey is safe. We know he's kept her safe before when you weren't around. We also know that my daughter is a promised child and God is going to watch over His word. It's really not that big of a risk."

Neil squeezed the steering wheel in frustration. He was not trying to get back into any crazy spiritual drama, especially at the risk of his family. But he also couldn't deny the truth of Nigel's words. For his brother to be relatively new to this scene, his strategy made sense.

Neil sighed. "Let me think about it."

Nigel nodded.

Changing the subject, Neil asked, "What's your contingency plan for her?"

Nigel began to layout the contingencies he had in mind as his brother listened and helped him strategize any holes he detected in his plans. After all, if his family was going to be there, he didn't want any issues in the strategy.

Their angels glorified protecting Neil's truck and its passengers from spiritual eavesdroppers. As Neil drove through the city with no specific destination, they went back and forth ironing out details of the ideas that Nigel presented him.

"You hungry?" Neil asked.

"Nah," Nigel told him.

"Well, I am. I haven't had anything today except for coffee."

He saw a Jimmy John's coming up and decided to swoop in and get a Bootlegger Club sandwich. After Neil got his sandwich, he pulled into traffic.

"You awfully quiet over there, bro. And you never turn down food, so what's really up?"

Nigel decided to go ahead and get this off his chest.

"When and how are we going to tell mama?"

Neil sighed.

"Man, I don't know."

"You know, she's not going to listen to reason if ol' girl is foul," Nigel continued.

Neil nodded.

"All she's going to see is she has a piece of Niles back," he replied wearily.

"Exactly," Nigel agreed. "I'm not trying to get caught in the middle, but you already know how I feel about it," the younger brother stated matter-of-factly. "It's really simple for me."

Neil simply shook his head at his brother's response. He couldn't say he hadn't expected it, but he also knew they would have to approach this situation with intentional delicacy.

"No need to get worked up until we have the conversation with her," Neil replied.

"So, when are we going to have it?"

"Sooner rather than later. We need to give her as much time as possible to digest it."

They were sitting on a ticking emotional time bomb - one they knew would rock their mother to her very core. Their deceased brother had always been and always would be a touchy subject for her.

"Okay," Nigel said. He spared an apprehensive glance at his older brother and saw the same concern reflected right back at him.

"My stomach is in knots," Nigel confessed.

"Tell me about it," Neil responded in kind. "I don't even want my sandwich anymore."

Chapter 15: Blindsided

Angela Lawson trudged through her front door, feeling more burdened than she had in quite some time. She'd just returned home from a long day of checking on her sons' properties and tending to any management issues. She didn't know the cause of it or what she needed to do about it. She walked in, slipped out of her shoes and put her purse on the sofa. The burden she felt had plagued her for most of the day. She couldn't shake the feeling of dread that had coated her belly all day.

Angela Lawson was a petite woman who had managed to defy time in her face as well as her body. She was light skinned with a pleasant face and a body that would put women half her age to shame. Her face held traces of Nigel, her baby boy, but mostly her face resembled that of her first-born, Niles. Neil was every bit of his father. He looked like she hadn't even participated in the process. She wore her hair in a short haircut that complimented her high cheekbones.

She enjoyed the feel of her plush burgundy carpet on her bare feet as she headed to the kitchen. The coolness of the tile floor gave her a little chill, but she ignored it as she went to the refrigerator to pour a cup of her coveted pineapple tea.

"Lord, something's not right," she said out loud as she placed a hand on her belly and took a seat at the kitchen table. Her spirit was warning her of something, but she didn't know what. She also wasn't in the mood to find out. However, she knew this was a moot point. Life moved at its own pace, and it did not request permission to do so.

As she sat contemplating what could be wrong, an idea came to her. She got up to grab the letter that Etienne had delivered to her the day of Nigel's wedding. She kept it in her Bible, which was always on her nightstand. Taking a seat on the edge of her meticulously made bed, she pulled out the letter. Angela marveled at his impeccable handwriting, just as she had the first time, she'd read the letter. She began to reread the words she could practically recite from memory. She'd actually lost count of how many times she'd read them.

My Dearest Angel,

I know today your heart is overwhelmed. You could not have asked God for two better women to love your sons. I extend my congratulations to you and Neville on getting Nigel married. We didn't think we would ever see this day. Even his shenanigans weren't enough to trump God's plan for his life. You know better than anybody else what it means to be the carrier of a powerful seed. You carried three of them. Today as you reflect back over your life, I don't want you to spend any time on regret. The past is the past. What's done is done. Keep your eyes on what's ahead. Learn from the mistakes of your past. Do not let pride, arrogance or shame keep you from equipping your daughters with what they need to continue carrying this spiritual legacy. Help them understand who they are and what they've been called to do. You are a woman of great strength. Not many could have survived all you have, but that's because God's hand was on your life. You are now the matriarch of this family. It's up to you to keep them covered spiritually. There are still battles ahead. Some that will shake your faith to its core.

She paused as those last two sentences sounded off in her spirit. What battles lay ahead and how was her faith going to be shaken? She felt it in her spirit; she was about to get answers to the question she didn't even want to ask. She took a deep breath and continued reading.

You must keep your eyes on God and know that He's already given you the victory if you just stand. Stand as a watchman on the wall for your sons, your daughters, and your grandchildren. If you remain obedient, it will be well with your children. Equip your daughters to know what they've been assigned to carry. They will need your wisdom, your patience, and your understanding. There is nothing like the faith of a true witness. Kadijah doesn't have a mother and Grey's mother won't be able to get to her as quickly as you can. Well, I think you've got my point, so I won't beat a dead horse. Now, let me be obedient. I know there has been a stirring in your spirit. A call to greatness. I know it's there because I saw it the first time I met you. I wanted to tell you then, but of course, Jehovah kept me silent. All things are in His time. Your life hasn't been easy, but you must understand everything you've gone through was meant to strengthen you and train you for what you were created to do. It's no coincidence that you were married to a police officer and that his seed followed in his footsteps. You carry a unique burden for the law and order of the city you reside in. You are a gatekeeper for the Capital City of Tallahassee. It's no coincidence your sons are both there with you now. Think of them as your guardians. They will cover you as you cover this city. Nigel is your sword and Neil is your shield. Your post is the Southern Gate of the city. There are other gatekeepers. Watch for them, Jehovah will bring you together once each one has been made aware of her assignment. Each of you are a powerful force to be reckoned with in your own right, but together you can prevail against the gates of hell. Do not fear this assignment but embrace it. Remember, whether YOU perceive the battle as lost or won, God's sovereignty will always remain in effect. Trust in His omnipotence more than your emotions. You'll know when your assignment begins. Let me warn you now – the devastation you feel will be your indication. This new assignment of yours will not be birthed in victory, but in pain. I'll leave you with this. Let this be what you stand on as you go about your assignment. "Trust in the Lord with all your heart and lean not to your own understanding."

Eternally,
Etienne

Angela sighed. Every time she read the letter there was the dichotomy of feeling empowered and burdened. She understood this was not something to shy away from. She had a personal vested interest in this city's safety. Her son was one of many who guarded it and put his life on the line every single day to keep it safe. Mostly, she wondered what Etienne meant by Nigel being the sword and Neil being the shield.

She sighed as her heart began to ache. Something deep inside was telling her; something was not right. Just then she heard her front door opening, which could only mean one or both of her sons was paying her an unexpected visit. She folded the letter and put it back in her Bible.

"Ma! "Where you at?" she heard. It was Nigel.

"I'm in my bedroom," she answered. "I'm coming."

Angela walked into the living room to see her two handsome boys. Neil sat on the sofa, dressed in jeans, boots and a button-down shirt with his gold badge hanging from his neck. Nigel, the complete opposite, wore a tailored blue suit with a crisp white shirt. He wasn't wearing a tie and the collar was undone.

She stopped when she saw the looks on their faces. Plopping down in the seat nearest to her, she said, "What's wrong? Just tell me. I've had dread in my spirit all day."

Neil and Nigel looked at each other. They both moved to sit on either side of their mother. Each one grabbed a hand. Angela closed her eyes and braced herself for whatever news they were about to deliver.

"Is everybody okay?" she asked with fear coating her voice. Neil squeezed the hand he held reassuringly.

"As far as we know, Ma, everyone is fine." She let out the breath she was holding. "But we do have some news and it's not going to be easy to take," Neil told her.

Angela turned to look at her oldest son. His face bore a serious, almost somber, expression. What they were about to tell her was going to tear her apart -- she just knew it. She glanced at Nigel. His face mirrored Neil's. Angela sighed deeply.

"Just tell me."

Nigel turned to face their mother. He took a deep breath and released it.

"Ma, we have strong reason to believe that Niles had a child."

Angela snatched her hands away from her sons and stood to look at them like they were insane.

"What? How do you know this?" she questioned, her voice getting loud. She stared at them wide-eyed. Of all the things she was expecting them to reveal, this wasn't anywhere on the list.

"Ma calm down...," Neil started, holding out his hands in an effort to calm her. Angela cut him off.

"Don't you tell me to calm down, Neil! I have a grandchild out there. My dead son's seed is out there with no family!"

Nigel looked at his brother, his eyes communicating what his mouth knew better than to speak: "Do something."

Neil stood and grabbed his mother by her shoulders.

"Ma, I need you to calm down and I need you to listen." He kept his tone respectful, but stern enough to get the point across.

Angela closed her eyes, took a breath, and willed herself to calm down. She took her seat again and waited for Neil to explain.

"You remember when dad asked to speak to me just before he died?" Neil asked. She nodded. "Well, that's when he told me about a pregnant girl who was nearly due at Niles' funeral. He said he tried to find her, but she disappeared before he could get to her. He talked to the Matthews about it, but they told him they didn't know anything about anyone being pregnant. He even talked to the girl Niles had been involved with down there, but she wasn't pregnant. He told me to look into it because he couldn't stand the thought of his seed out there in need of anything. I looked, but I never found anything."

Angela's mouth hung wide open. She gaped at her son. "He never said anything to me about this, ever."

"He probably didn't want to get your hopes up without any evidence, ma," Nigel told her as he squeezed her hand.

"Continue," she said shaking her head. Her sons glanced at each other. They could tell she was shaken by the revelation her husband had kept something so vital from her.

"Last year, when all this craziness went down, Grey was told by someone who had been involved in the organization that there was more to our brother's story, and that it was only a matter of time before it was revealed. She was instructed to prepare his brothers because it was no coincidence, and we wouldn't see it coming."

Angela frowned, as Neil continued.

"That's why we believe Niles had a child and we believe it's a girl. Well, she would be a woman now, likely my age or one year older, making her 38," Neil told her.

Angela couldn't believe what she was hearing. Her firstborn had a child. A child who'd likely grown up alone, separated from her family. The very thought broke her heart.

"Well, you have to find her," she stated. "She's our blood, our family. I get to have a piece of my child back. You boys find her!" Angela looked at her boys imploringly.

Nigel looked at his brother. Neil nodded for him to go ahead. This was his part to do.

"Ma, that's the thing," Nigel began. "There is a possibility that she is a threat to my daughter. There is a possibility she's not who we think she is."

"I don't care who she is," she stated matter-of-factly. "She is my flesh and blood. She's Niles' daughter, that's all I need to know."

Nigel blew out a frustrated breath.

"Ma, it isn't that simple. If she's a threat to my daughter, I'm not going to risk my child's safety for anybody or anything, and I need you and everybody else to understand that."

Angela drew back as if she had been slapped. She stared into her son's now gray eyes. She looked at Neil. His eyes were green and looked as if they held unshed tears. She stood up and paced as she clutched her heart.

"This is what Etienne warned me about," she muttered softly. Neil's ears perked up at that.

"Huh, when did you talk to Etienne?" Neil asked.

"He had a letter delivered to me the day of Nigel's wedding."

"What?" Nigel questioned.

"Wow," Neil said as he shook his head.

That prophet was an eternal hot mess.

Angela nodded. "He said, there are still battles ahead. Some that will shake my faith to its core. I know this is what he meant." She stopped her pacing and leaned against the armchair. "I was reading the letter just before you two got here and that part just stood out. I've had this sick feeling in the pit of my stomach for most of the day. It's like I could sense it was coming."

She turned to her baby boy and took in his hardened face.

"Nigel, I love you and I understand all that our family went through was to ensure the safety and survival of your little girl..."

She paused and sighed deeply before continuing.

"But you cannot ask my heart to choose between the two. You just *can't*," she pleaded.

"Ma, I don't want to be at odds with you about this, but my mind is made up."

"My heart can't choose son. I'm not built that way."

Neil saw the hurt look on his brother's face. Nigel stared at his mother incredulously.

"You don't even know this woman, ma."

Angela shook her head.

"That doesn't matter. She is flesh of my flesh and blood of my blood."

"So, am I. So is my daughter," he defended.

"Why do you automatically assume she's a threat to your child?" Angela exclaimed exasperatedly. "I can't just throw her away without knowing her and giving her the benefit of the doubt."

Nigel pinched the bridge of his nose in order to keep his anger at bay. He took a deep breath and let it out slowly before speaking again. No matter how frustrated he was, he knew blowing up at his mother would only make things worse.

"Ma, Niles was killed by the organization that tried to take out this family. You do understand that she is likely one of them, right?"

"Yes, I do," Angela said calmly. "But she was a part of us, first."

Neil saw his brother's temper spike. He took that moment to intervene.

He stood up and said, "Listen, we have to find her first, and then we'll figure out what to do next. I have a feeling the revelation of who she is will be a hard pill to swallow based on what Grey was told."

Angela eyed the older of her two boys carefully. Neil had always been the more even-tempered of the two, but there wasn't much her sons didn't agree on.

"Where do you stand on this, Neil?" Angela asked.

Neil swallowed thickly, as he looked at his mother's face. His eyes held sincere pain when he answered.

"Though it breaks my heart to do Ma, I have to stand with Nigel on this one."

Again, Angela reared back as if someone had slapped her. She stared at Neil, disappointed and dumbfounded.

"You gotta understand," Neil explained. "I already lost my daughter to this madness. I feel your pain, I really do, but if I can stop Nigel from having to feel the same pain we did, then that's what I'm going to do."

Neil crossed the room to stand in front of his mother. He took her hand and sighed deeply.

"This is bigger than us, ma. You need to understand; Nigel's daughter has a promise on her life. So, any opposition that comes for her is going to have to deal with the wrath of God. You know He's going to watch over His word. You need to prepare your heart and mind for whatever happens."

Angela's heart broke with the conviction of her son's words. The tears spilled out. Neil looked away. He couldn't stand to see his mother cry. Nigel walked over to where his mother and brother stood, reached out and pulled his mother into his chest.

"I'm sorry, mama. I am truly sorry."

Angela cried for several moments in her son's embrace. This was all so overwhelming. Her head was spinning, and her heart was breaking - both for the sons she loved more than anything in the world, and the long-lost granddaughter she didn't know but felt obligated to protect. Her heart felt literally split in two, tugged between loving the family she knew and the family she didn't. Etienne had told her she was made to handle this, but at the moment, she wasn't so sure.

Nigel continued to hold his mother close. He felt bad for her, he really did. But he'd meant what he said. Protecting his family came first, at all costs and against all threats, even ones from within. He only wished doing so didn't have to mean hurting their mother.

Eventually, Angela's tears slowed, and she pulled away from Nigel's arms. With her back turned to her children, she quietly spoke.

"I need to be by myself right now if y'all don't mind."

Nigel and Neil exchanged a look. Neither of them liked the idea of leaving her alone right now, but they also knew arguing with her about it was futile. Neil strode over to where she stood with her back still turned to them and kissed his mother's cheek.

"We'll see you later, ma."

Angela nodded but didn't say anything, waiting silently until she heard the front door shut behind them.

When they were gone, she fell to her knees and wept loudly. "God, I need you right now!" she cried out, the rush of hot tears fell down her face.

Little did she know, help had already been in route. The infinite wisdom of the Ancient of Days knew this moment would be a difficult challenge. The moment her desperate plea left her lips, help arrived. Four massive Naval warrior angels, from the Gulf of Mexico, descended upon Angela Lawson's living room. Adorned in gold battle regalia, the angels crowded the space, each standing at a towering 13-feet, their wings were white tipped in gold and their eyes glowed brightly with a majestic golden flame.

The four of them stood valiantly around Angela and they glorified to comfort and prepare her for the assignment given. Not only did she have to guard one of the gates of the city, but she also had to guard the gate of her family, and there was nothing more torturous than an enemy from within.

Cathal, the Gaelic warrior, watched over her as she continued to pray for God's help and declared in a booming voice, "It is time."

Second Trimester (Aug., Sept., Oct.)

Chapter 16: Marital Bliss

David turned the key into the front door of their apartment. He stood six feet with smooth chocolate skin and a medium build. His brown eyes were sincere and heavily lashed. Coming out of his shoes, he dropped his messenger bag by the door. He could smell the aroma of something tasty, but he had a taste for something else.

He appreciated that on her days off, Genevieve went all out for dinner and she dressed just for him. They hadn't been married long, but he was already spoiled. He did some spoiling of his own too, which is why he had a gift for her that he'd gotten on his lunch break. He placed the box behind his back as he crossed the living area and headed into the kitchen.

S He was greeted by the sight of his wife dancing around the room, as R&B music from her favorite Pandora Radio station pumped through a Bluetooth speaker. He smiled as he watched her move sensually to the music. He almost lost his composure as she continued to dance wearing just a t-shirt that read: "I Sleep with The Pastor."

Her feet were bare, but her toes were freshly done with a sexy bright red color. He had a thing for pretty feet. It only fanned the flame that had been ignited in him all day. Her honey-colored skin was glowing, and he could tell she was definitely a woman in love. A constant boost to his pride. Those big brown eyes always looked at him with such adoration. Her curly black hair was short and closely cropped. She had a button nose and heart shaped lips.

He was going to make that shirt the gospel truth in the very near future. He couldn't get his wife out of his head all day and found himself grinning and whistling anticipating this very moment.

She had yet to notice him. She turned the pot off and pulled the bread out of the oven. The cheese on the garlic bread bubbled up, the aroma tickling David's sense of smell. Genevieve went to the refrigerator and pulled out a bottle of water. Standing with the door still open, she twisted the cap off and took a satisfying sip then replaced the cap.

When she turned around, she smiled.

"Hey, you," she grinned at her handsome husband. His heavily lashed brown eyes never left hers. In lieu of returning her greeting, he quickly closed the gap between them placing the box he had for her on the table. He grabbed his wife and backed her into the refrigerator after he closed it.

"Oh my," she managed before his lips covered hers.

David let all of his pent-up anticipations flow out of him through his kiss. Genevieve dropped the bottle of water and wrapped her hands around her husband's neck. She gave as good as she was getting. He trailed kisses down her face and neck lingering in the spot on her neck he knew drove her to madness.

Almost breathless, she asked, "And what's gotten into you?"

"You," he said and covered her mouth again. She had no objections as she began to tug at his shirt, tie, and pants. Wrapping her legs around him, David exercised his privilege to *know* his wife.

When they were done, they collapsed on the kitchen floor. David reached for her discarded bottle of water and took a sip before handing it to her. She stared at him as she sipped slowly.

"Why you looking at me like that?" he asked.

"Cause you nasty," she said.

He laughed and leaned over to place a sweet kiss on her lips. She grinned and kissed him back. He helped her up then fixed his clothes. She eyed the box on the table.

"If those are what I think they are, you are wasting your time with them clothes, bruh."

David laughed. His wife was a mess.

"Girl don't play with my emotions, 'cause we can make that happen!"

She laughed and went to the table to remove the lid off the Aldo shoe box, one of her favorite stores. The leopard print stilettos managed to be both sexy and classy. Genevieve squealed. She was always impressed with his ability to accurately dress her. David grinned at her reaction. He loved to see her face light up when he gave her gifts.

"Maybe you can rock those with the skinny jeans I bought you last month," he suggested.

"Or, maybe, I can wear them right now," she said wickedly.

David's brow winged up as she took the paper out of the shoes, placed them on the floor and then stepped into them. David eyed his wife up and down and grinned.

"I am one lucky man."

"Yes, you are," she said and pulled him by the tie that hung loosely around his neck. Like a puppy, David followed his wife into the living room. She pushed him down on the sofa. Genevieve made sure to show her husband how much she appreciated his thoughtfulness.

When they were done, they lay on the sofa intimately entwined. David stroked his wife's belly as they enjoyed the post-coital bliss. He placed soft kisses on it.

"One day there is going to be a baby in there."

Genevieve smiled as she stroked the waves of his low-cut Caesar.

"I know. I can't wait to have your baby."

He looked up at his wife. The glow her skin held continued to stir him. He leaned up and kissed her.

When he broke the kiss, she eyed him.

"What's gotten into you?"

"You complaining?" he countered.

"Not at all, I'm just curious."

"I don't know," David said honestly. "I've been craving you all day. When I tell you, I couldn't wait to get home to you today..." He planted soft kisses along her collarbone, slowly trailing his way up her neck. She giggled.

"Well, I'm so glad you did. That was, um... one of the memory books."

David smiled into her neck, then shifted to face his wife. He looked directly into the eyes of the woman who owned his heart.

"I love you, Vie," he said sincerely. Genevieve placed a hand on his cheek and softly smiled at her husband.

"I love you too, King."

He kissed her again, stirring her in ways she wasn't prepared for.

"Again?" she inquired.

"All night. You down?"

All she could do was grin as she looped her arms around her husband's neck and pulled him in close for another kiss.

"Wait," he said, his lips just inches from hers. "This time, let's set the mood." He leaned to grab his phone from his pocket. He set the Pandora app to the Dru Hill station. Genevieve raised a brow at her husband.

"Oh, so we going old school this time, huh?" Genevieve asked in jest.

"Girl, I gotta get my groove on to all the songs I couldn't back in the day 'cause God just wouldn't let me." She giggled. "We doing this for nine-nine and two thousands."

Genevieve hollered! She laughed until she had tears in her eyes. He grinned but was eager to switch her focus back to where it needed to be. The speakers blasted "These Are the Times" by Dru Hill followed by classic R&B music from the epic music era of the nineties and two-thousands.

When they finished round three, they were exhausted. Some kind of way they ended up on the floor. David grabbed the fleece blanket they kept on the sofa to pull down over them. He didn't want her to get sick with the air conditioning blowing on her. She caressed his face. He was so thoughtful. She absolutely adored her husband.

"I know you said all night baby, but I need a nap," she confessed.

David's eyes were closed when he responded. "I'm with you when you right cutie."

He pulled a pillow off the sofa and slid it under his head then pulled his wife onto his chest. She snuggled up next to her man. They were out in minutes.

†††

About two hours later they resurfaced from their pleasure induced siesta.

"You woke cutie," David whispered in his wife's ear.

She squirmed. "I am now. If we gon' do another round, you gotta feed me first," she told him.

He chuckled. "Yeah, I'm hungry too."

"We definitely need to reheat since you had your dessert before dinner."

He grinned against her neck as he continued to place kisses on that one spot that managed to always make her melt. She shivered.

"You need to stop. I am going to be useless at work tomorrow."

"Well, you betta eat your Wheaties for breakfast because I am not done with you. This is just intermission."

She laughed. He got up and put on his dress slacks. He reached down to help her up. She scooped up his dress shirt and slipped into it. He closed the gap between them and placed kisses on her face as he buttoned just a few of the buttons in the middle. He bit his lip as he eyed her up and down.

"Always keep it sexy."

She grinned and ran her hand down his broad chocolate chest. He grabbed her hand and pulled her behind him into the kitchen.

"You cooked so I'll fix our plates."

She took a seat as she watched him move about the kitchen getting plates, utensils, and glasses. He fixed their plates of shrimp and shitake mushroom fettuccine alfredo.

After he warmed them up, she said, "Oh there is salad mix in the fridge. Do you want a salad? I can make it right quick?"

"Nah, I'm good."

"Okay," she said as he placed her food in front of her.

He poured juice in their glasses and sat them on the table. Finally, he joined her with his plate. After blessing their food, they causally discussed their day as they enjoyed each other's company.

When they were done, they did the dishes together, a common nightly routine for them. David dried the last dish as Genevieve drained the sink and rinsed out all the suds. He dried his hands then dried hers. Their eyes met.

She grinned. "How do you turn washing dishes into something sexy?"

"That can happen when you do it half dressed."

"Oh, good point," she smiled.

David scooped her up and sat her on the edge of the sink.

"Oh, okay," she managed before he placed a demanding kiss on her heart-shaped lips.

Eventually, they made it to their bedroom, where David remembered there was something important he needed to discuss with his wife. They were both pretty spent, but he'd been hearing it in his spirit for about a week and they needed to discuss it. Genevieve lay on her husband's chest as she stroked the fine hairs.

"What you thinkin' 'bout King?"

"How do you know I'm thinking about something?"

"Because I know my man. Now, spill it."

David sighed.

"I've actually been playing around with this for the last week."

She leaned up to look at him. "You okay?"

"Yeah, but I believe God is telling me to quit my job and become a pastor full-time."

"Oh," was all she managed. After a few beats of silence, she asked, "How do you feel about that?"

"I'm not sure. I really love my job and I've been thinking about our finances. You know buying a house, having kids."

"Well, you know God will provide," she told him.

"Yeah, I do, but I like being able to afford what I want when I want it."

"Well, you knew this path wasn't going to be easy." He nodded. "Obedience is key baby. We know this."

"I know."

"I'm thinking about just not returning after the end of this school year."

"Whew, that's soon," she said.

"Yeah, it is. But like you said obedience."

She could tell he was struggling with this. She kissed him.

"I promise to still give you some on a pastor's salary."

David hollered. "Girl, you are crazy!"

She laughed; grateful she'd lightened the mood. She leaned down to kiss him.

"It's going to be okay, baby. I told you, I got your back. You got my support."

"Do you know how amazing that feels to hear you say that cutie?"

She smiled and kissed him again.

He asked, "You got one more round in you?"

She looked at the clock. It was after one in the morning. She had to be to work at 7 AM.

"I know I'm going to regret this," she grinned.

He grinned too, then kissed her.

Chapter 17: Black Widow

Agent Michelle Fuller
Atlanta, Georgia

I was on the prowl. My life was more complicated than a solution to the current racial divide of these here United States. I needed a release quick, fast and in a hurry. My body was coiled up like a snake ready to attack just about anything of the opposite gender. I knew I needed to keep a low profile, but the way my anxiety was set up, this little inconvenience needed to be addressed quickly. If not, the frustration could throw me off my game.

Besides, when I took him out afterward, it would give me a chance to brush up on my assassin skills. I hadn't taken anybody out since I'd sent that traitorous wench to an early grave in the warehouse. I sashayed through the club letting the reggae music pulse through me. Months in jail had deprived me of my freedom and my dignity. Tonight, I was taking back both with a vengeance, the same way these racists were out here trying to take back the White House.

The music was intoxicating. The sensual island rhythms stirred something primal in me. The club was littered with people like the subways in Harlem. I moved through the crowd looking for some space to strut all this goodness to disarm my next victim.

As I continued to search for my prey for the night, the locals were ogling the goodies I had wrapped up in black leather. The short leather dress hugged my statuesque frame like it was created with me in mind. I couldn't blame them. Before I left, I spent five minutes in the mirror looking at my dern self.

I smiled at the gentleman who was heading straight for me. I liked them bold. He was sexy. Fair skinned, light eyes and a mouth I could put to good use. He approached me smelling like my next conquest. He groped my backside like I belonged to him. Perhaps the look of desire on my face inspired him to nibble my ear as he whispered what he wanted to do to me.

When he pulled away to stare at me with his light eyes, mine dropped down to his crotch. He saw the knife I had holding his family jewels hostage. The fear that rose in his sensual eyes actually turned me on. Unfortunately, I'd have to pass. His aggressiveness caused a scene and I needed to keep a low profile.

"Always ask permission first. Got it?"

He nodded, still speechless as I closed my blade and disappeared into the crowd. I hated men who thought my consent was optional and not required. Didn't he know silence meant no. "No" was a full sentence, and only an unintoxicated, uncoerced yes constituted indisputable consent. The music continued to fill the open space. The smoke from weed, cigarettes, and cigars created clouds that mimicked the smog in LA.

A disharmony of scents filled the air. Perfume, cologne, drugs, alcohol, and lust all clashed with each other like they were ratchet housewives performing for reality fandom. Ironically, it made me feel alive for the first time since I'd hopped out of that plane. I wanted to put my agenda on pause just for a minute and enjoy the moment. My inner bad girl was dying to get out.

I wanted to spend the night with a man and take out all my frustrations on him until I'd had my fill. I'd slit his throat and be gone before the east was lit up by the sun. It was just that simple. Making my way to the bar, I smiled at the young man drooling over me.

His face lit up like the sky on the Fourth of July when I smiled at him and used my ample chest to brush up against him. Within five minutes I had a drink at his expense, then I dismissed him to browse the crowd for someone worth wasting a bullet. Two more drinks were paid for and the buyers met with dismissal. I slow grinded to the music as I let the alcohol work its magic.

When I spotted him, I almost dropped my drink. A unicorn. He was just that beautiful, he had to be a magical creature. Either that or I had suddenly become a lightweight and the drinks had my mind playing tricks on me.

Tall, dark, and wickedly handsome he stood with confidence and mesmerizing eyes. His skin tone gave no clue to his ethnicity. His eyes and silky black hair only further complicated the mystery of his cultural roots.

Dressed trendily, he looked like he was heading straight for me. I looked around to be sure it was me he had his eyes on.

It had been ages since I'd reacted to a man like this. He was so beautiful; I wasn't even sure he was just a man. He had demigod written all over him. All I could think as he walked toward me with the gait of a black panther, the face of a fallen angel and the mouth of a sinner is it would be such a waste to kill him after. I may have to ride this ride a few times before I execute him then apologize to God for wasting the beauty of such a well-designed creation.

He strolled to the bar and stood next to me. His cologne assaulted every sense I had. I literally had to close my eyes to keep them from crossing. He ordered a drink then turned to me. Our eyes locked. His hypnotic gaze was throwing me off my game.

"You're beautiful," he said.

"As are you," I spoke my truth.

He grinned. "Are you here alone?" he asked.

"Are you?" I countered. I was mesmerized, but I wasn't stupid and wanted him to know that up front.

"Yeah, I am. But I don't plan to leave alone."

"Aren't we cocky," I chuckled.

He grinned.

"No, just honest. I spotted you from across the room and I was hoping you're the one I'd leave with."

"Stalk much?"

He chuckled, and I swear my spine shivered.

"No, I just recognize what I want, and I go after it. Interested?"

I smirked. "Stranger danger."

He laughed. Even his laugh was sexy. "Somehow I feel like you're more dangerous than I'd ever be."

I smirked. He had no idea how true his flirtatious words were. "Why do you say that?" I asked pursing my naturally pink lips that I accentuated with a nude gloss.

"Oh, you have *black widow* written all over you."

That made me pause. That was my codename. Was this coincidence or a setup? I dismissed it. Only people in the organization knew about the organization. I think I would have remembered if he was one of us.

"Oh, I didn't mean to offend you, just keeping the conversation interesting," he said trying to ease my sudden rigidness.

I raised my brow. "If I was a black widow, shouldn't you be afraid?"

His dark eyes sparkled. "Nah, I'm the one that makes things go bump in the night," he countered.

"Maybe we can make some things bump tonight," I suggested, raising my eyes in a flirtatious challenge. He grinned. "Name?"

"Lucca," he said so seductively it made me shiver. "Yours?"

"Black Widow."

He smirked. "Well, Miss Widow, my car is right outside," he said licking his full lips.

"So, is mine."

"Follow me?"

"Lead the way," I said and pointed.

He tossed his drink back and winked at me as he led the way. I watched his perfectly sculpted body stride through the club. The women nearly passed out as he passed by.

He was exotic.

His eyes hypnotic.

His scent toxic.

His voice melodic.

Maybe it was the alcohol, but I felt a little spellbound. Sure, this is what I wanted, but I felt like he got it too easy. If I didn't know better, I'd swear he hypnotized me, but I couldn't quite figure out how. I shrugged, he wouldn't live to tell anyone about it, so what difference did it make? His sports car was just as sexy as he was. It was sleek, black, and reminded me of a stallion.

"Stay here," I told him. "I'll pull up and then I can follow you."

He nodded.

Five minutes later, I was speeding down the highway following the sexiest man I had ever seen in real life. As he pulled up to the hotel, I was a little aggravated. Oh well, I guess I couldn't enjoy him as many times as I wanted to. I'd need to put him down early to make sure I had time to get far away before housekeeping found my handiwork. He was too sexy to pass up, so I would improvise.

When I got out of the car, I pulled my black hoodie out of the trunk along with my black Louis Vuitton book bag. His brow winged up as he came to stand near me.

"You don't come off as the modest type. What's with the cover-up?"

“I have a husband, and he has friends. You picked this conspicuous hotel.” He frowned. “Are the vows I took going to be a problem?” I asked as I licked the side of his neck.

“Not at all,” he said shivering from my touch.

I smiled. “When you get the room have the bartender slip me the key and room number.”

“Paranoid much?”

“Careful much. Prenup,” I said winking. “If you can’t handle the cloak and dagger, just say your goodbyes right now. Go home and regret me.”

He smirked. “As you wish Ms. Widow.”

He strolled off. I headed to the hotel bar and ordered a club soda. I needed to sober up because this man was capable of throwing me off my game. Fifteen minutes later I was sliding the key into his room door.

When I entered the spacious suite, there was champagne and two glasses chilling in the living area. I slipped off my hoodie, poured myself a glass of champagne and sipped. The bathroom door opened to reveal tonight’s lover clad in only a towel looking like he wanted me to devour him.

He glided up to me and placed his lips on mine. He licked the champagne off my soft lips as he nibbled the bottom one. With one touch he set my entire body aflame. I was truly going to regret returning this fine specimen back to dust.

He took his time undressing me. He carefully perused my body as if he were looking for something. Good luck with that. I only allowed my prey to see what I wanted them to see. What he saw was a flawless body covered in well-hydrated butterscotch skin. I took advantage of all the butters Mother Earth offered to make sure my melanin stayed in top notch form. Toned muscles, a flat belly, well-sculpted arms, and legs greeted his highly skilled caress.

I felt his touch pause as he got to my tramp stamp. I had to suppress a chuckle. Just above my perfectly toned derriere was a deep red hourglass tattoo. That’s right, just like the spider I was named after, it was a sign to warn my predators that I was toxic. If you entered my web and ignored my warning, what happened to you next was your fault, not mine. Forewarned is forearmed. I also had a web of silk that I used to trap my prey. Once they were caught up in this powerful web, there was no getting out. Well, at least not alive.

I wrapped my arms around his neck and took what he willingly gave. We christened the wall, the bed, the shower, the floor, and the couch. Five times in one night was a new personal record for me. Guess I was trying to stock up, not knowing when I'd be able to get my next fix.

As he slept, I jumped in the shower and washed his DNA off me. When I came out, he was still knocked out. I contemplated getting in one more round. The regret of taking this option from my fellow species hit me again, but I had to resist it. It wasn't worth the risk.

I put my knife in the pocket of the plush robe I wore. I climbed on the bed and seductively ran my fingers down his back. He stirred.

"Hey sexy, got another round in you?"

He purred as he turned on his back. I smiled as I climbed on top of him and looked down. He pulled the string on the robe. I continued to smile as I reached in my pocket. I whipped my blade out but before I could slash his throat, he grabbed my wrist with one hand and had his other hand around my throat.

My eyes widened in shock as I stared at his now evil eyes. There was nothing exotic about the dark orbs that stared back at me. With a freakishly strong grip, he flipped me on the bed and squeezed my wrist until he made me release the blade. I grabbed at his hands to get him to release me. I continued to gag as my eyes began to water.

"Where's your mark?" he demanded. I stared in disbelief. "Answer me!"

My eyes widened. "Who are you?" I managed to strain out the question.

"Your mark! This is the last time I'm going to ask you."

"The bottom of my foot," I managed. His eyes narrowed. "It's the truth, I just cover it in makeup, now let me go."

He released his grip. I rubbed my aching throat.

"They warned me about your penchant for post-coital kills," he told me.

I continued to cough as I tried to get my breath back and figure out who the hell was *they*. If he knew about my mark, he had to know about the organization. He was definitely going to die, but first I needed answers.

"Who are you and what do you want with me?"

"The question isn't about my true identity, but yours," he countered.

I frowned. "What the hell do you mean?"

"It's time you started to shake out the secrets hanging on your family tree."

Now, he had my undivided attention.

Chapter 18: The Family Tree

Agent Michelle Fuller
Atlanta, Georgia

As I sat there listening to the mystery man of the hour telling me about a family, I never knew I had, I got mad. Not just regular mad, but big mad, like Plies says. This could not be real. There was no way what he was saying was true. Then it got even worse. I stared at him as my stomach began to turn.

"The man you were undercover with, Neil Lawson." He paused to ensure I was still listening. "He's your uncle. He and his brother are highly trained and very dangerous individuals for reasons that you can't even fathom."

A wave of nausea ran through me.

"Did they know that?" I managed. "Did the organization know that before they sent me in to seduce and kill him?"

"Of course, they knew," he said laughing which only served to piss me off more. "Why do you think you were chosen?"

I used all 43 muscles in my face to frown at him. Right now, I was wishing my spirit animal was the chimpanzee, so I could throw my feces right at his pretty face because this was one big pile of disgusting mess. The murderous thoughts that were running through my head were even scaring me.

"Why would they do something so viciously sadistic. That's repulsive."

He shrugged. Like, he *actually* shrugged as if this wasn't the most twisted war tactic I had been given.

"You're an assassin for one of the most notorious criminal organizations to ever exist. You've seduced more men to their death than the world's population of actual black widows. What's the big deal?"

"There are some things that should just be off limits," I said viciously.

"Look, their father - your grandfather - knew your father's murder was more than what we made it appear to be. When Neil and Nigel came along, he made sure to train them because he knew they would also be targets."

I couldn't hold back the bile rising up in my throat. I hated my weakness, but there was no amount of training or willpower I had to keep this at bay. I scrambled out of the tangled sheets and ran towards the bathroom. I did manage to slam the door before I was violently ill.

I was so in love with him. How could they do this to me? I still dreamed about him. I could still feel his lips on mine when I closed my eyes and thought of him. It's true - he was at the top of my list of people to take out, but what I felt for him was genuine and to be honest he was the first and only man I had ever had those feelings for.

And on top of that the gang I had pledged my loyalty to had murdered my father. I cringed as my thoughts bombarded my heart and emotions. I continued to empty the contents of my stomach.

When my vomiting took a break, I got up to lock the door. I looked around for some kind of weapon because as emotionally tortured as I was, I wasn't stupid. I grabbed the toothbrush Lucca had left on the sink. If I put enough force behind it and aimed for something with soft tissue, it could give me a chance to get out and get to a weapon that was capable of doing more permanent damage.

I sat on the floor and leaned against the tub and wept. The sobs that racked my body came from deep within my soul. There was not only anger and disgust but a profound sadness that I could not quite place. I don't know how long I sat on the floor as my emotions left my eyes like an angry river, but I heard him tapping on the door.

"I don't mean to be insensitive. I know this is a lot to take in, but we're just getting started. Get yourself together and get out here now!" he demanded.

I narrowed my swollen eyes at the closed door. I slipped the toothbrush in my robe pocket. I was going to invent new ways to inflict pain on this man before I snatched his breath from him. He would definitely be added to my kill count soon and very soon. The minute he proved to be useless is the day he would cease to exist.

I cleaned my face and blew my nose. My reflection showed swollen eyes, a red nose, and flushed cheeks. I needed to get myself together and fast.

Slowly, I opened the door, he was sitting on the bed fully dressed and completely unbothered. I had to reassess this situation. The way he grabbed me, the strength he had, the way I felt spellbound, something wasn't right. There was something much more sinister here at work that I could no longer ignore.

I did have a burning question that my crying fit induced. "Why did they kill my father?"

"He wouldn't join the gang, no matter what we tried. He was a cop's kid through and through. As a matter of fact, because of the bloodline, your family carries, yours was the only sanctioned birth that was approved by a nonmember of the organization. We had to have his seed, by any means necessary."

"What's so important about my bloodline?" I asked confused.

"I should tell you this as I'm sure you'll find out when you go behind me to do your own research. I was one of the masterminds that orchestrated the plot against your father. It would be wise for you to accept the sacrifices we all had to make for the survival of our organization and not take anything personally. Don't let my pretty face fool you into thinking I'm not capable of great violence."

I sat there stewing in my rage for a full minute. I wasn't oblivious to the fact he ignored my question, but he was right, I would be independently verifying all this information, so I would choose my battles wisely because winning the war was now my sole focus.

I took a breath and said, "Continue," as I stood there with my arms folded across my chest.

"Would you like to sit?"

"Would you like to die?" I clapped back.

He chuckled and shrugged, then continued. "Of course, you weren't the only soldier with the trained skills to combat either one of the brothers, but you had an advantage the other soldiers did not."

"My DNA," I said.

He nodded. "When your father came to Miami, he was immediately put under watch. The darkness was adamant about getting him away from the protection of his father's hedge. Once your mother seduced him, he opened the door for us to walk right through."

I frowned. "What do you mean, the darkness? Opened what door?"

He stared at me baffled. "You're kidding right?"

"About what?"

He shook his head. "You do know that the only reason we were successful in this organization was because we had demonic powers orchestrating everything in the background, right?"

I stared at him then fell out laughing. When I composed myself, he was staring at me with a straight face.

"You're serious?" I asked flabbergasted.

"How the hell could you be in the organization this long and not know these things?"

"I was a soldier. I followed orders."

"Well, let me enlighten you. There's a war going on between good and evil. We are merely pawns in their celestial chess match."

"I've read all the sacred books. You're telling me this stuff is real?" I asked incredulously.

"Well, I can't speak for all of them, I'm not versed. But the only one I *am* versed in is the Bible."

"Why that one?"

"That one's an actual weapon. You don't get involved in spiritual dimensions without a manual. If you were wise, you'd study it because your family is deep into the Light and they will use that weapon against you."

I continued to frown. "You're talking God and his resurrected Son, the fallen, Satan aka Lucifer, Michael, and Gabriel."

He nodded. "You don't believe me, do you?"

"Hell no, it's fiction! Fanfare. Propaganda. A way to control the masses. A way for colonizers to justify their rape and pillage of others."

He gave a humorless chuckle. "Remember a weapon can be used to protect or terrorize. It's never the manufacturer's fault on how it's used, but simply to provide it. I think Insidious made a mistake by choosing you to take out Nigel's daughter. Your defeat is imminent because you lack faith and imagination."

I narrowed my eyes at him. "If you believe why are you on Team Darkness?"

He shrugged, "I like the instant gratification, power, influence and no restrictions."

"And that's worth your eternity in the lake of fire?"

He chuckled, ignored my question, and countered with a question of his own. "Why submerge yourself in the information and not believe?"

"I'm an assassin. I'm well-versed in all of history. It's what makes me good at what I do. The Bible has some great warfare tactics to be honest."

"You missed the most important target of your career."

My eyes dropped. "I was distracted by my emotions with Neil."

His brow winged up. "You're in love with him?"

I didn't answer. I swore I saw anger pass over his face at that revelation. How odd.

"What do you mean take out Nigel's daughter? He doesn't have any children."

"He has a baby girl on the way."

"You sick bastard. I am not going to take out an innocent baby!"

"You don't have to. I just need a vile of your blood and we'll handle the rest."

"My what?"

He stood to walk toward me, "Your blood."

"Don't take another step." He put his hands up in surrender and stopped moving. "All of this is about a baby?"

"All of this is about a weapon. One that will be very dangerous for the Kingdom of Darkness and we just can't have that."

"How can a baby do that much damage?"

"Jesus started off as a baby too. Don't let the package fool you. This is war and your cousin is a weapon that needs to be dismantled before she can mature. If you refuse to take her out, they will send someone else. They will never stop coming for her."

"The reason I escaped prison is to kill Neil, his annoying wife, and his sharp-tongued brother. Once I put them in the ground I am out, do you hear me? Out!"

"There is no out," he said with complete conviction.

"I'll make a way out of no way. Trust and believe. There is no way I am going to continue in this organization that murdered my father, stole his child, lied about it and used me to take out my own flesh and blood. We're supposed to be a family. Family doesn't treat each other like this. The loyalty I've given my entire life has meant nothing to you people. So, once I complete the assignment I failed with bonus bodies for good measure, I'll disappear. Anyone and I mean anyone that comes looking for me will get a first-hand glimpse of how and why I earned my moniker."

Again, he raised his hand in surrender though his face held unmistakable arrogance.

"I'm going to tell you this, because I have a vested interest in your success. This chess match you've been a pawn in was designed to make you your family's enemy. There will be no welcome home party for you. While your uncles and their wives and their children may look like regular people, they're not. They are highly gifted, highly skilled, and well-protected. Like I said, you lack imagination and faith and that will be your undoing. Don't let their salvation fool you into thinking they are pacifists. Nothing is stronger than a parent's love for their offspring. They know you are a threat to Nigel's first born and they will stop at nothing to keep her safe including putting you in the ground. The power they have on their side is not available to you. If you're smart, you better embrace all of the dark side and fast, it's your only chance at survival. Your sudden development of morals manages to be admirable and stupid at the same time. You may not have the guts to take out a baby, but I guarantee you, she's more than capable of rendering you useless. The sheer lengths the Light was willing to go to just to keep her safe speaks volumes. They took down the entire Untouchable Organization just to invalidate the curse that was sent to all the first-born in the family. Just think about the implication of that."

That caught me off guard.

"How am I here, if the curse took out all the firstborn until her?"

He smirked. "My dear naïve soldier. You weren't the firstborn of your father's. Your twin didn't make it. And you're not the only born to your mother. You already took out one of your own sisters. There's a reason you were raised as an orphan and not allowed to be with your siblings."

I couldn't hide the shock that sprung into my eyes.

"Eva? His partner was my sister?" I asked incredulously.

He chuckled.

"She was raised to be connected to him which meant, she had to be kept from you. And I heard you took her out mercilessly, bravo," he said with an air of pettiness.

I slapped the piss out of him. The look he gave me as his dark eyes narrowed put a fear deep in my soul, but I would never let him see that. He rubbed his cheek then got in my face. I didn't flinch. My pride and ego, my constant companions, wouldn't let me.

He continued his voice extremely dangerous.

"Now, I asked for your blood politely. If you continue to refuse to do your part for our side in this war you'll find yourself all alone fighting both good and evil and sweetheart as skilled as you are, you're no match for both sides to be coming at you with everything they've got. Do your part to take her out or we'll take you out. Your usefulness to the organization is the blood that runs through your veins. Other than that, you have no value to us."

He took a cautious stroll towards me. He gently kissed my cheek. I swear it felt like the kiss of death.

"You've been warned. I'll see you soon," he whispered seductively in my ear.

I hated that I couldn't suppress the shudder. Sidestepping me, he casually strolled out of the hotel room leaving me with my head in an absolute tailspin.

Chapter 19: Decompression

Agent Michelle Fuller
Atlanta, Georgia

I knew I was off my game when I opened my eyes to the sun interrupting me watching the back of my eyelids in the same soiled sheets of the man that destroyed my life. I've never been a depressed person. I just take what life gives and roll with it, but real talk, this had me sick – like for real, for real sick to my stomach.

I'm a stone-cold-hearted killer every day of the week. I don't take breaks on anybody's sabbath, Saturday or Sunday. I rest on the eighth day, you feel me? So why were my emotions choking the life out of me?

I wiped the tears from my eyes that appeared out of nowhere. This hurt was deep. It was severe. It was painful. I needed to pinpoint my pain because if I didn't, I could lose my life simply from being distracted.

One of the reasons why I never entertained a man longer than my climax was because I couldn't afford any distractions. As a young girl, I was well educated and trained to kill. I grew up with other orphans, though we all knew we were Untouchables. We were told our isolation was forced upon us to make us better assassins. It was the detachment that made us good at what we do.

Now, I feel like that may have been a lie. Of course, I bought into the lie because I have leveraged many a loved one on a target, but they say it's always different when it hits your front doorstep. I've been pissed at myself, because I couldn't shake my feelings for Neil up until I found out he was my uncle.

That emotion made me weak and sloppy. It caused me to walk right in trusting him, and my ego and pride did me in the way they always do. I was pissed about that, but I wasn't sad. They wanted me to help them take my niece out. I mean, they weren't asking me to physically kill a child, but they wanted my blood for some demonic ish that I couldn't even wrap my head around. I mean seriously. Angels and demons, bruh.

I think your opposition should be able to fight back even if they are guaranteed to lose. I was aggravated about that, but I wasn't sad. Then there's the whole family thing. Like, I have a whole family. They seem to be great people, but there's bad blood between us. Like black blood between us. No, they probably wouldn't welcome me, but truth be told I didn't want their welcome.

My moral compass has never pointed due North and though I was hesitant in the murder of a defenseless baby, my position on the adults that surrounded her hadn't changed. Again, I was angry, but I wasn't sad.

What is it? What is hurting my heart? It's bleeding out and I don't know how to stop it. I continued to lay there as the tears continued to spill out. I knew my edges were going to need to be dealt with because my tears were washing away this good silk press.

I sighed, and the ache intensified. There was this pressure on my chest as if an anvil were sitting on me. Then it hit. The thing I wanted most in the world, they had deprived me of. It's the reason I was so emotionally damaged I couldn't have a normal life if I wanted one.

My.

Father.

They took my father from me. I will never get a chance to know him. I will never know what it feels like to be loved by the man who seeded me. And the sad part is, I know he would have loved me unconditionally. The same way Neil loved his unborn child, he had been taught how to love that way, so surely my father had been too. There it was. The source of my ache. The longing and sadness were for my daddy. Niles Lawson.

The floodgates opened.

I cried.

I screamed.

I wept.

I sobbed.

I released all the pain that kept shooting through my heart trying to get a handle on my emotions. My head drummed as if mercy was never created.

I willed myself to get up and found my way to the shower. I turned the water on as hot as it would go. I stood in the mirror and watched my swollen, tear-stained face blur as the steam filled the bathroom. I let the robe drop to the floor. I heard the faint sound of the plastic toothbrush falling out of the pocket and hitting the tile floor.

I slipped into the tub and let the water pummel me. I sat down in the tub and let the water wash away all my pain. As I sat in the water, I realized what I needed. I need to grieve for my father. I needed to properly deal with these emotions in order to remove them as a distraction.

Once I had a focal point, I felt better. It gave me enough strength to bathe, wash my hair and scrub my face. The water had just begun to cool when I finished my face. I turned off the water and stepped out.

Out of sheer habit, I went to grab my Louis Vuitton bookbag to dig out my coconut oil. Something I never left home without. I applied the oil to my wet skin then dried off. Turning on the blow dryer, I began to dry the steam off the mirror.

Within a minute, I had a clear picture of myself. I shook my head at my face. Not my best day. I needed some green tea ice cubes to rub on this emotionally stained canvas of sorrow. I sighed. That's what makeup was for.

Twenty minutes later, I was dressed in light denim severely distressed jeans, a sassy tank top that read "cool vibes only" with my wet jet-black hair piled on top of my head. I slid into my red chuck's, grabbed my bag and my hoodie and I was out.

†††

I let the top down on my ride and let the breeze take me away from here. I drove and drove and drove, trying to decide how to grieve my father and to strategize how to deal with enemies past and present.

It's true I had a plan B in case anything ever went crazy in the organization, but it wasn't to cut ties. This was a cease and desist. Once I took out Neil, Grey and Nigel, I would need to disappear.

I had a couple of storage units around these here United States with cash and IDs, but I didn't know who knew about them at this point. I was so paranoid. I couldn't trust anyone. I was angry at myself because I let my libido dictate my actions, and now I had Satan on my scent.

Lucca was the devil himself, of that I was sure. His sudden strength and the darkness in his eyes were seared into my mind. Maybe there was something to his rhetoric. Even if God was real, I couldn't get down with a supreme being that would allow so much suffering and injustice in the world.

Yeah, some people deserved to be taking a dirt nap, but innocent children suffering for basic necessities like food and clean water - nah. I wanted no parts of him, her, or that. It was time to get my ducks in a row.

Neil and Nigel were likely looking for me. I couldn't let them find me like this. I also needed to have mastered my fear of snakes by the time I saw them. I shuddered at the thought but knew it was essential. That weakness is what took me down.

I rubbed my shoulder as a phantom ache hit at that moment as I remembered where Neil shot me. Nigel was the more dangerous one in theory, but I knew that Neil wanted my blood on his hands. I hurt him, deeply. I finally understood his pain.

Nigel is fueled by the need to protect his daughter. I'm not really pressed about Grey - she's just intentional collateral damage. She gets taken out on principle. He said they were gifted. *What does that mean?* He said I lacked faith and imagination. Could I acquire both before we met on the battlefield?

I felt some type of way about taking out a sister I didn't know I had, but she was a traitor, and I can make my peace with that. Besides, she wasn't my father's seed. I am the only one of my kind and that matters.

I could try and talk some common sense into myself, but it wasn't going to happen. It was absolutely necessary to take out whatever was left of the organization because they had to pay for taking my daddy away from me.

Lucca was a dead man walking; he just didn't know. He was pure evil. There might not be enough good in me to battle it out with him, but I'd find a way to improvise. I needed information. I couldn't make my next move without it. When I got to the light, I took a left and headed for the interstate.

Chapter 20: Hungover

The next day at work, Genevieve fumbled to her desk, sipping on her second cup of coffee. She yawned again. Her coworker, Melissa, walked up to the nurse's station and plopped a file down on the counter.

"Girl, you are dragging today," she said.

"Yeah, I know. I was up late last night."

"Doing what?"

"Minding my business."

Melissa smirked. "Okay, be coy. I should let you walk around all day with that hickey showing," she said pointing to the side of her own throat.

Genevieve gasped. She slapped her hand on her neck in embarrassment.

"I do not have a hickey."

"Yeah you do," said her coworker, Sharon, as she sauntered over to the nurse's station, a sly grin plastered on her face.

"Why didn't y'all tell me?" she whined, as she dug through her purse for a mirror.

"Why would we tell you about something you were obviously participatory in?" Melissa countered back playfully. "You don't recall getting it? I mean, it's not like you're too dark for it to show up."

Genevieve narrowed her eyes at Melissa.

"Y'all wrong for that."

The two women laughed.

"Wait - aren't you married to a pastor and y'all carrying on like that?" Sharon asked.

"I'm married to a *man* who happens to be a pastor. He's no different than any other man, except that he's all mine," Genevieve replied with a smirk.

She held up her hands in playful surrender.

"Well alright Ms. Thang," she responded with a laugh. "Enjoy your freaky pastor, but please go put some coverup on that mess before our boss sees it."

"How old are we again?" Melissa asked.

Genevieve rolled her eyes and pulled out her makeup bag to find coverup.

"I am going to kill my husband," she muttered.

Her two co-workers laughed as Genevieve gathered her makeup bag and disappeared to the bathroom.

After she'd momentarily erased her passion mark, she pulled out her phone to fuss at David. She sent him a text:

KING!!!! *angry emoji*

What's up, cutie? *heart face emoji*

Really with the passion mark?!

I mean, I'm passionate about my wife... *laughing emoji*

Well, can you be passionate on parts of my body that aren't on display at work?! *eye roll emoji*

Nah, this way is more fun. *crying laughing emoji*

Punishment.

The devil is a lie.

Not this time.

Girl, bye!

laughing emojis You scared?

Nah, you ain't about to give up this good lovin'. You done with your tantrum? I can give you a matching one tonight?!

Boy, bye!

laughing emoji Luv u.

Love you.

Genevieve rolled her eyes as she checked to make sure you couldn't see the evidence of her escapades from last night. She had to be dern near comatose to miss that deep red mark on her fair skin. She shook her head and headed back to her shift.

As soon as she was able to take a break, she was going to her car to get in a much-needed power nap. She had to give it to her husband though, love's hangover rivaled anything alcohol had ever given her - back in her party days.

Chapter 21: Due Diligence

The restaurant was abuzz with the lunch crowd. Kool Beanz Café, a favorite of Sheridan's, was a common lunch and dinner niche serving an eclectic American menu in a colorful, peculiar setting. The dessert was what kept her coming back for more. When Dylan said he wanted to meet with her to discuss something very important that didn't have to do with his personal therapy, she decided to show him one of Tallahassee's hidden treasures.

The waitress had just brought her a glass of cool ice water. She often sat outside when she dined there. The atmosphere was so serene and therapeutic. She took a sip of her water as she closed her eyes when she felt the rare Florida summer breeze caress her face and hair. It was the middle of the summer, and the July weather was living up to its tortuous hype. The restaurants had fans blowing to keep their outdoor customers comfortable.

A few minutes passed before she spotted Dylan coming through the doorway looking around for her. Sheridan stuck her hand up and waved. Dylan Smith was average height with an average build. His blonde hair was neatly combed back, and his gray eyes lit up when he spotted her.

Dylan smiled and walked over. Sheridan stood and leaned in as he kissed her cheek.

"Wow, you look amazing. That pregnancy glow suits you well," Dylan said. Sheridan smiled at the compliment as she rubbed her belly. "It's great to see you. Thanks so much for agreeing to meet me."

"Thank you, you're so sweet. It's no problem," she told him. "I have to admit when you called, I was intrigued. Your session was anything but boring."

Dylan laughed. "Yeah, I guess not."

They took their seats. The waitress appeared and welcomed Dylan then asked if he'd like something to drink. He requested an Arnold Palmer. She nodded and told him to browse the menu and she'd return shortly.

"What's good here?" Dylan asked while perusing the simple menu printed on colored paper attached to a clipboard.

"Everything," was Sheridan's reply. He laughed. "But I must warn you. They change the menu every day. There are only about three items that are consistent. If you fall in love with it, you might never get that particular combination of food again."

Intrigued, Dylan nodded. "Alright, so what do you recommend?" he asked.

"You can *never* go wrong with the flank steak or the chicken mojo, but they stay on the menu, so you can get them anytime. All their fish is amazing, and their specialized sauces and glazes will make you slap yo mama and somebody else's."

Dylan laughed hard. The lady at the table next to them chuckled as well.

"The crab cakes are on the appetizer menu today, so do yourself a favor and start there, unless it will keep you from getting the dessert. Because that's the reason I keep coming back."

Dylan nodded. "I can handle three courses if you've got the time?"

"I do – I cleared my afternoon for you. A gentle nudge from the Holy Spirit told me to," Sheridan winked.

Dylan grinned. He was happy God was making a way for him in this situation. He truly was nervous about it. They decided on their food and ordered. Once the waitress took their orders and menus, Dylan decided to get right down to it. He leaned in since the lady at the next table already proved to be nosy.

"This is something I was instructed to do a while ago. The day I left your office actually, but I admit, I've been hesitant. Not only that, but I'm also kind of clueless. Lately, it's been nagging me, and I decided to start with what I knew. I knew you had some knowledge about it and mentioned you had a friend that does as well, so that's why I'm here."

Sheridan knew exactly who this involved. She also wanted to keep their conversation from the nosy neighbor – not just because she didn't care for nosy people, but you never knew where the Kingdom of Darkness was lurking. She was sure Dylan coming here to meet with her was not a good thing for Team Evil.

"You remember who I told you I met that dreaded night?" Dylan asked.

Sheridan nodded.

"Well, that day I left your office, I had a dream. In it, he told me some things about my purpose, but he also told me that the little one I care for will be able to see him. When I inquired as to why, he said that would be revealed in time and that I needed to teach her not to fear him."

"Wow," was all Sheridan managed as she took a sip of her water.

Thinking of Hope, she wondered why these children were gifted to see what had to be one of God's scariest creations.

"Exactly," Dylan agreed.

The waitress brought over Dylan's crab cakes with jalapeno tartar sauce and lemon-herb slaw before he continued.

"I know she has seen him at least once and it petrified her. We were at the park and she ran to me suddenly and begged to leave. I felt his unmistakable presence then I saw an old woman across the street and knew he was coming for her. Later that night, the incident was on the news. So now, I need to be obedient and teach her not to fear him. I'd also like any insight your friend might be able to give me as to why she's been gifted to see him and if she can see anything else for that matter."

Dylan finally took a bite of his crab cakes and closed his eyes.

"Oh my, God," he said.

Sheridan laughed at his reaction. "Trust me, I know," Sheridan said with a smirk as Dylan quickly ate the remainder of the crab cakes.

"Well, I can tell you this," Sheridan began. "I'm not going to give you second-hand accounts and I know Grey will be willing to talk to you, but he's a bad boy - in a good way," she clarified when Dylan frowned. "You remember the bizarre stories in the news last year concerning a Tallahassee woman being kidnapped, then the mass graves in California and the sex trafficking rings being raided and exposed?"

Dylan nodded. "Of course. You would have had to be living under a rock not to hear about that," he told her as he took a sip of his drink. "What about it?" he inquired.

"The woman who was kidnapped is my friend Grey - the one I told you about."

Dylan choked on his drink. Sheridan had to grab her napkin quickly to prevent herself from spitting out her water after laughing at his reaction.

When she composed herself, she said, "As my girl Grey would say, it's *real* in these spiritual streets. You might want to stop eating for this part," Sheridan warned him.

Dylan coughed and put his fork down as he frowned.

Sheridan took a moment to chuckle then said, "The cop that took down the sex trafficking ring in Miami, is her husband and also a great friend."

"Are you kidding me?" Dylan asked.

Sheridan paused before she answered as their waitress brought over their food. They thanked her, blessed the food and Dylan dug in. The food looked superb.

After taking a bite of her tender and juicy flank steak, Sheridan said, "I can tell you this for sure. Your friend - oh he was definitely at the compound in Miami with them. Grey told me that she was instructed to stay in his shadow for her protection."

Dylan sat back and stared.

"What?" Sheridan asked, as she scooped up some mashed potatoes with gorgonzola butter and sautéed shitake mushrooms. She always got the mushrooms in place of the onion rings if they were on the menu.

"In my dream, I made the comment that I was walking in his shadow and he told me there was nothing to fear. The 23rd Psalm took on a whole other meaning for me."

Sheridan nodded.

"That's funny. Grey said something very similar."

"Except she wasn't dreaming," Dylan pointed out.

"No, she wasn't."

"This is crazy."

"Oh, you don't know the half," Sheridan responded. "I should probably warn you though. Grey is what we call a spiritual nerd. She actually enjoys most of this stuff. Not saying she didn't have the common sense to be scared and cautious, but her faith is like *stupid* at this point! She's been on the frontline of some of the most epic spiritual battles I've ever heard of. I don't know if God will reveal to her why your daughter can see him, but she'll definitely give you some insight that will be priceless in this journey you've found yourself on."

Dylan nodded carefully, not sure how he felt about meeting these people. He'd had some powerful spiritual encounters but kidnapping, drugs, murder, death, and sex trafficking, that was a lot to digest. As disturbing as the conversation was it did not stop him from enjoying his incredible meal of seared tuna steak, cognac pepper sauce, asparagus, and mashed potatoes. He couldn't wait to try the dessert.

Sensing his apprehension, Sheridan placed a calming hand on his forearm.

"I know it's a lot to digest, but it's going to be okay," she assured him. "Ignorance may be bliss, but trust me when it comes to spiritual matters, knowledge is power. And if you've already been warned that this is her gift and something she's going to be dealing with, you as her father, need to prepare her for her gift and equip her with what she needs. If the gift was given to her, it was for a purpose because it is needed. Trust me, our spiritual gifts have literally kept us alive."

Dylan nodded. "Her mother and I want to make sure we're obedient in this. We trust God and we're committed to seeing this through," Dylan said with conviction.

Sheridan smiled then dug through her purse for her phone. She dialed Grey.

"Hey boo," she said when Grey picked up.

"What's up girl?"

"Well, I have a client who has a daughter that is gifted to see your BFF. He's in town for the day. Would you happen to have time to meet with him today?"

There was a pause.

"Wait, not Black Beauty himself?" Grey inquired.

"The one and only," Sheridan confirmed with a chuckle.

"What is up with him and kids?"

Sheridan laughed. "Girl, I had the same thought."

"Well, let me call Neil and see what he's got going on to see if I need to grab a babysitter for Hunter. I'll definitely make it happen, 'cause I already know not to be disobedient." Sheridan chuckled. "Alright, I'll text you the details," she confirmed.

"Okay, see you later girl."

"A'ight, later," Grey said and hung up.

Sheridan looked at Dylan. "It's a go."

He nodded.

Sheridan waved over the waitress.

"By the time we finish our dessert, we should have a plan to meet. In any case, why don't you tell me about this assignment you got?"

Dylan smiled. He would love nothing more than to share how God took his pain and misery and turned it into purpose that transformed lives!

Chapter 22: The Grave

Agent Michelle Fuller
Orlando, Florida

I went back and forth for a day about whether or not to visit my father's gravesite. I knew if I didn't deal with it, it would be a constant distraction, but it was a risk. If this emotional baggage wasn't handled, it would weigh me down and I couldn't afford it. I need to be light on my feet and quick with my thoughts.

I had no intention of dealing with my uncles this early in the game. I needed time to strategize, plan and get rid of my fear of snakes. I shuddered at the thought but knew I was going up against the most formidable adversaries.

I spent six long months with Neil. Sure, his demise was on hold until I dealt with the faulty arm of our weapons trade, but still, his love for his wife kept him out of my seductive grasp. I needed to use what I knew about him to my advantage, but he also possessed the same advantage.

When I'm nervous or anxious I either eat or do my hair. I couldn't afford to be overly chunky right now, so I decided to give myself a new look. It took me about eight hours to install the jet black faux locs.

I accentuated a few of them with the little gold cuffs and admired my handiwork. I added a little fake nose ring. The sapphire stone looked striking on my fair skin. I also added a mole above my lip on the left side. I no longer looked like a swollen mess so that was good.

I slid in the light gray colored contacts added dark lipstick and smoky eye makeup. I fluffed the locs as I stared at myself in the mirror. To the untrained eye, I looked like someone else. Dressed in a classic Adidas tracksuit, I prepared to hop on the road.

Tallahassee was only a four-hour drive from Central Florida. I had gone back and forth with myself enough, it was time to execute. Operation: Settle My Grief was in full effect. I slid on my aviator sunglasses and headed out of the motel.

This was the kind of joint where you could stay for the week and remain under the radar. Sure, I didn't look like I belonged, but I also was surrounded by the people who were too obsessed with their own daily grind to notice me. It was nice, but not luxury. It was clean which is really all that mattered to me. No one would be snooping around here for information unless a crime demanded it. I had no intentions of creating a crime scene in the near future. I hopped in my ride and headed to mourn the father I never knew. If I hadn't been distracted, I would have noticed him noticing me. I would have realized he always noticed me.

†††

Tallahassee, Florida

Four and a half hours later, I circled the serene cemetery looking for anything suspicious that could jeopardize my overall agenda. The goal was to get in and out unnoticed and unscathed. The cemetery was well kept. Flowers adorned headstones throughout the grounds, left by those who kept their loved ones in their thoughts and didn't think it robbery to come and commune with a headstone for special occasions or just because.

It was the middle of the afternoon. The sun was bright, but it managed not to be hot under all the shade provided by the luscious trees. The soundtrack consisted of loud birds discussing whatever the hell birds had to talk about and noisy traffic, horns, rubber on the road with occasional brakes and dissonance of music selections blasting out of open windows. It almost seemed disrespectful so close to a home for the dead. I had done my share of disrespectful things, so I had no room to talk.

I parked some ways down from the place I assumed the groundskeeper was stationed. Once I saw him tumble out of the small building, I realized his drunk behind was the least of my worries. I stared at him in the side mirror. *Was he talking to himself?* I shook my head. Clearly hanging out with the departed had taken its toll.

I didn't know where my father had been buried so I hoped I didn't garner any suspicion by walking around looking lost. Grabbing the white roses off the seat, I quietly exited the vehicle. The family seemed to be pretty solid, so I knew they were the type to have a family plot.

Besides, Tallahassee was their home, so their roots were here. With that thought, I'd start with the big headstones. Turns out the fifth one was my charm. The dark gray granite headstone was large and regal. In bold lettering, it read LAWSON. On one side, beneath their surname was Father, Neville Lawson and the dates of his sunrise and sunset. On the other side, it read Son, Niles Lawson with his alpha and omega beneath it.

There were flowers there, couldn't have been more than a few days old. It was clear this grave was visited regularly. It was immaculately clean. According to the dates, there were no recent birthdays, and we weren't currently within range of a holiday. That meant whoever visited did so just because.

That conclusion made me nervous because any minute now could be a just because. My instincts told me to run, but my heart begged me to stay. I knelt down on the ground and placed the roses on my daddy's side of the headstone. The tears that always seemed to be lurking whenever he was the focal point spilled out and hit the freshly cut blades of grass.

I placed my hand over his name, and all of the emotions that had been swirling inside me for the past several days just came bubbling out. I broke down, right there at my father's gravesite, sobs racking my entire body.

"I'm sorry daddy, I'm so sorry our time was stolen from us. I want to be angry at you, but I can't. Our separation wasn't by your choice. You may not even have known I existed. I wonder, did you know me, daddy? Did you try to fight for me? I never knew I needed you as much as I did until I was hit with the reality of what happened to you. There's a part of my soul that was always missing and now it can never be found even though I know where the missing piece lies. I want you to know that your baby girl is going to avenge your death. Every person that played a part in your demise will be joining you soon and very soon. You're lucky your father has already turned back to dust. I know his sins that cost you your life and if I find out your mother's sins led you to this place too, she's also going to pay. It really is simple. They took you away from me and now I am going to take away everything they love."

I vibrated with anger. It consumed me, but I was also comforted to be near his essence. I laid down and looked up at the sky. The tears continued to fall down my cheeks, but I knew my soul was being cleansed.

A soft breeze began to tickle my face and dry the tears. It was gentle and smelled of summer. I closed my eyes and enjoyed the sensation that money could not buy. When I opened my eyes, the clouds parted, and a beam of light shown through.

The warmth the sun blanketed me with was comforting. The beauty that surrounded me was in stark contrast to the ugliness that lurked in my soul. It occurred to me; I had no control over who I became. They made me and now their creation was coming home to show them exactly what they created me to be. I sat up suddenly.

Looking around, I saw there was an older white lady a few paces down with her hand on a headstone. She did the Catholic sign for Hail Mary. I wanted to tell her Mary couldn't help her, the only person you could depend on to help you, was yourself. With that thought in mind, I got up, brushed off the dirt and grass and removed my sunglasses.

I wiped the tears with my sleeves to discover my smeared makeup. I'm sure I now looked like a well-dressed zombie. That was partially true because, from the moment I found out about my father, something in me had died. Now they would too.

†††

He watched her as she wiped the grass from her clothing. He hoped she would take off her sunglasses, so he could get a better glimpse of her face. He had been the groundskeeper at Slumber Hollow Cemetery for the last 20 years. He knew just about every frequent mourner by name.

The Lawson grave was one that received consistent traffic. It was usually the one he called his Angel that came by almost weekly to visit her son and husband. Sometimes, the older boy would come by. He only saw the youngest one come by once when he first moved back to town. But this beauty here, she was a stranger that didn't belong and didn't fit. He could mind his business, but he wouldn't.

Finally, she took her glasses off. The way she wept over the grave, his first thought was maybe she was a love child that just found out about her father, but she was favoring the son's side of the headstone, not the father's. He thought that odd.

Once he looked at her face, the smeared makeup threw him off, but her skin tone was unmistakable, which gave him his first clue. As she turned to head towards her car, he hid a little more, so she wouldn't spot him.

The resemblance was there, subtle, but noticeable if you knew what you were looking for.

"Sweet Jesus," he mumbled to himself.

He would definitely tell Ms. Angel the next time she came to visit. There was something strange lurking in her family tree.

Chapter 23: Crossing Paths

A few hours later, Grey parked her car into a spot right in front of Sheridan's office building. Quickly gathering her things, she exited the car and walked towards the door, where Sheridan stood waiting.

"Hey, girl," Grey spoke as she walked up giving Sheridan a tight squeeze.

"Hey, hun," Sheridan replied after releasing Grey. "Listen, thanks for meeting him. I know this is completely unexpected."

Grey gave a nonchalant wave and shrugged.

"Girl, it's no problem."

Sheridan gave her friend a grateful smile.

"Come on in. He's in my office."

Grey walked fully inside, her two angelic warriors, Savas and Bojan, entering with her. They greeted Sheridan's ever-present warriors, Tero and Wayland. Sheridan locked the office door behind them because it was after hours, then turned to lead Grey to her office, which was at the end of the long hallway.

As the two friends walked through the lobby, Grey looked over at the empty receptionist desk and sadness washed over her. This wasn't Grey's first time in Sheridan's office since Stacy's tragic passing, but she still expected to see the young woman's smiling face whenever she came in. It hurt deeply to know she never would again. Shaking off the grief, Grey continued following Sheridan to her office, ready to meet her client.

The two women walked inside to find Dylan, patiently waiting on the plush, deep orange sofa. He stood up when they entered. Sheridan's office was designed to reflect a comfortable space. Dylan gave a small smile as the two women walked toward him, and Sheridan began the introductions.

"Grey, this is my client, Dylan Smith."

"Dylan, this is one of my closest friends, Grey."

"It's so nice to meet you," Dylan said as he shook her hand. Grey returned his shake with a firm grip of her own and gave him a bright smile. Still holding her hand, Dylan gazed at Grey in awe.

"Wow, I'm sorry for staring," he started. "But just being able to shake your hand, after all you've been through."

Dylan shook his head, visibly overcome to be standing in the presence of a woman whose very life was a testament of God's divine grace, power and protection. He continued.

"I don't even know you, but I'm grateful to meet you."

Grey, touched by his words, smiled bashfully. It never ceased to amaze her how God used her ordeal to inspire faith in others.

"Aww, thank you," she replied gratefully. "Yes, God has been good to me." Dylan didn't even know the half.

"Why don't we sit?" Sheridan suggested.

Dylan sat on the sofa; Grey took the chair while Sheridan parked it behind her desk.

"So, how old is your daughter?" Grey asked.

"Roni is seven years old," Dylan told her. Grey nodded

"Well, at least she's older than Hope."

"Hope?" Dylan inquired.

"Hope is my goddaughter. She'll be three this year."

"Whoa," Dylan said.

Grey and Sheridan chuckled. Dylan had no idea what he was in for; this therapy session was about to become a crash course in spiritual warfare. Grey gave him a once-over. She couldn't be sure how he would handle what she was about to tell him, but she knew it was best to give him the truth - straight up, no chaser.

"Listen, Dylan, I'm going to cut straight to the chase because I have to get back to my son. His babysitter has homework tonight."

Dylan laughed. She was just the way Sheridan described her.

"My first encounter with the Angel of Death was in New Orleans..."

Grey launched into her tale. When she finished telling Dylan all of her encounters with the angel who'd come to see him on that fateful day, she wasn't surprised to see him staring at her, wide-eyed with his mouth hanging open. Sheridan just laughed, tickled by Dylan's' reaction and Grey's animated trip down memory lane.

"Just breathe," Grey told him.

Dylan shook his head as he put his hand over his mouth. He needed a minute to digest this woman's bizarre story. He wanted to dismiss it, but it was too crazy to make up. Besides, one only needed look to all of the news coverage about the fallout following her kidnapping and rescue as evidence, she was indeed telling the truth.

Grey waited him out. She knew how this sounded, but she was also anxious to hear how he'd met her beloved angel. Dylan shook his head and then stared some more. Grey laughed.

"Why don't you tell me about your encounter?"

Dylan nodded. "Um, wow. That's. That's just crazy."

"Tell me about it," Grey said chuckling.

"How are you so composed as if you're talking about the most mundane thing ever?"

Grey shrugged. "It's just you know, Tuesday," she said with a grin and nonchalant wave of her hand.

They all laughed.

"Well, my encounter isn't nearly as wild as yours, but it was profound in my life."

Grey moved to the edge of her seat. She loved this stuff. Dylan began to recount the events that led up to his decision to take his own life, the argument he had with God and then passing out once Death walked through his closed office door.

"Wow! Your purpose must be extraordinary for God to go to such lengths to stop you from giving his breath back."

Dylan nodded and paused to get his emotions in check. Realizing God's love for him still stirred something deep in his soul.

"Yes, indeed it is, and I am grateful to be walking in it," he responded. "I had a dream after I left Dr. Richard's office, and, in it, the Angel of Death visited me once again. He told me there are many who pull away from their faith when he comes to disrupt their lives. Some refuse to believe because they spend so much of their energy distraught over him just doing his job at the command of the Master. He told me that many miss their assignment. The world around them suffers because they never fulfill their purpose, and it's all because they are stuck in their grief. He told me I was created to bridge the gap between the brokenhearted and YHWH because of what I had been through. He said God would give me the words to minister to those who are grieving."

"Wow," Grey breathed out. "That is absolutely beautiful."

Dylan smiled. "Yeah, I can see that now."

Sheridan wiped a lone tear. She remembered his first visit to her office and the way God used her to get him on this path to purpose. It was so rewarding to see your prayers come full circle.

"So, tell me about your daughter."

Dylan pulled out a picture of Veronica and handed it to Grey. Grey stared down at the little chocolate drop with large afro puffs. Her brow winged up. Dylan laughed.

"Well that was a plot twist," Grey said. "You're from Jacksonville, right?"

"Yeah," Dylan said nodding. "I have some friends there that I think you and your wife should meet."

"That's right, Blake and Jasmine," Sheridan chimed in.

Dylan frowned, knitting his brows together in slight confusion. He looked at Grey.

"You know Blake and Jasmine?" he asked.

"You know them?" she asked, just as confused.

Dylan shook his head.

"Not personally, but I work with their friend Damon. He recommended Sheridan to me because she'd helped his friends with their family."

"Wow! It is such a small world," Grey told them.

"Six degrees of separation is still undefeated," Sheridan added.

Dylan shook his head. *What were the odds?* He told Grey about Veronica's introduction to the Death Angel.

She thought for a few moments then said, "Well the best way to introduce spiritual things to your children is by first introducing them to God. Not just saying their grace or saying their prayers before bed, but actually taking them to church, teaching them about God and encouraging them to have their own relationship, even as little children. Instruct her to pray about things that come up in her life and tell her to see what God has to say about it. You'll be surprised what she comes back with. If she seeks out His voice, He will respond. When they have their own connection to God, it will facilitate a safe place for the spiritual world. Talk about angels with her. If she's naturally inquisitive, she will deduce that there is an opposite to angels but use your discretion in introducing her to the demonic world. Once she gets comfortable, tell her about the Angel of Death. She's already familiar with the subject matter having lost her father, so she has first-hand knowledge of grief and loss."

Dylan nodded. What she was explaining to him made plenty of sense.

"Veronica has been around church all her life. It shouldn't be hard."

"Remember church is different from God," Grey warned. "Church is full of human frailties. Introduce her to God himself and let that be her foundation - not church. Remember to show her that He is love. Don't make Him out to be the big, wrathful God that will send you to Hell, before you know that she completely understands Him as love."

Dylan nodded. Sheridan agreed with her friend. This was practical wisdom Grey was giving him. So many times, people weaponized God. They introduced him to people as a detached supreme being who was all Heaven or Hell. They didn't teach about the Father that was full of love, forgiveness, grace, and mercy.

"Do you have any idea why she can see him?" Dylan asked Grey.

"Honestly, nothing has been revealed to me yet, but I will tell you about his connection to my goddaughter."

Dylan nodded again, grateful for whatever she could provide.

"God released a prophetic word over Hope through our late pastor the day of her dedication. Part of it stated that she was a healer, and that she would carry healing in her hands. Not too long after that, she was attacked by what appeared to be sickle cell. It was touch and go for a minute, she actually coded, but God."

Grey paused for a second to lift her hands in silent praise. Hope's testimony of healing never failed to amaze her. She continued.

"From what I understand, whenever she touches someone to heal them, the Death Angel is there to kill whatever afflicts them for it to never return."

"Wow," Dylan said.

"God used her not just to heal me and my son when I got back from California, but a woman who had been bound by an infirmity for 40 years. It was absolutely astounding to witness. So, with that, I must warn you. If your daughter is gifted in a way that will mess up Satan's plans, she is likely going to be targeted."

Dylan frowned.

"But rest assured, if God put a gift inside of her, He's going to use it. He is invested in her and therefore He will protect her. You and your wife just remain on post and keep her covered. I don't know what the angel's relationship to your daughter is, but he's Hope's guardian. So, when the enemy could no longer get to her, he came for her parents. Be mindful of his manipulative attacks that look like they are random. He never loses sight of his target."

Dylan nodded soberly. This was a lot to take in, but he also knew God had orchestrated this meeting.

"Thank you so much, Grey. I'm so grateful for all that you've shared."

Grey stood up. "It is my sincere pleasure. I know what it's like and being clueless allows for fear. But knowledge is power. I will continue to pray for you and your family. If God reveals anything to me, I'll make sure to reach out."

She extended her hand. Dylan stood with a grateful smile.

"Can I hug you?" he asked.

Grey laughed, then wrapped him in a friendly embrace. He squeezed her back.

"Thank you so much," he said sincerely as he released her. "My wife would have a blast talking to you."

Grey grinned.

"Make sure you bring her next time. We'll do the dinner thing."

Dylan nodded.

Grey turned to Sheridan. "Call me later babes. I need to go relieve Jessica. Neil caught a case."

"Okay, I will."

Grey waved bye then headed out.

When she left, Dylan took his seat on the sofa. He glanced at Sheridan, who watched him with a knowing and amused look.

"I need a minute to digest all of this."

Sheridan just laughed.

"Take your time."

Chapter 24: A Grave Mistake

Angela Lawson pulled up to the Slumber Hollow Cemetery. She normally came to see her husband and son on a regular basis. But lately, it had been a struggle, because once again, she felt betrayed again by the man she'd loved.

How could he not tell her they had a granddaughter? She knew they had yet to prove it, but everything about this situation felt like the truth. From Etienne's letter to the warning of an impending attack on Nigel's daughter, all the jacked-up puzzle pieces seemingly fit together.

She tried to stay away, but she couldn't. She was mad though. She found herself wondering if her son knew about the baby and chose not to tell them. It was frustrating that all these answers were buried with her loved ones. She wanted answers. No, she *needed* answers.

Maybe if she found out more about the past, it could help save her first grandchild's future. She knew her sons. As sweet and lovable as they were, she knew they possessed a fierce protective instinct, and they would do what needed to be done to protect Nigel's child. Both of them loved Nigel's daughter from the moment they found out about her. She did too.

This little girl was so loved, long before she was even conceived. But her first grandchild was her dead son's legacy. How could she stand by and let that be taken away from her? She didn't want to be naïve and assume her granddaughter would run to her with open arms.

Hating to admit it, she had to be realistic. Her granddaughter could be dangerous. She could not want anything to do with them. The thought of that broke Angela's heart.

Sighing, she grabbed the flowers off the passenger seat and pulled her emotions together. Getting out of the of the car, she walked the familiar pathway that led to their family's section. As she approached the large tombstone, she stopped. There were white roses on her son's side of the tombstone.

Instinctively, she looked around the cemetery. There was no one else in the cemetery except for her. She usually came at first light early in the mornings. She loved the morning dew, the breeze, and the scents of the fresh flowers she always had with her. This was odd.

Even if her sons came to visit, they wouldn't bring flowers and certainly not *white* roses. The gesture had feminine energy all over it. Neville's parents were dead and gone. Who would be visiting her son? Something wasn't right. Quickly, she put her flowers down and went to visit her favorite caretaker.

Hurriedly, Angela made it over to the small shed-like structure that was near the mausoleums. She knocked. Moments later, the door creaked open to reveal the most lovable functional drunk she had ever known, Ulysses.

He was a slender man, with wrinkled white skin, covered in grime piled on by a non-consistent relationship with soap and water. He grinned when he saw her, showing off a set of teeth that could use a toothbrush, some mouthwash, and a highly skilled orthodontic specialist.

Always a slight slur to his speech, he managed, "My Angel, you're here. I've been expecting you. I've got lots to tell you."

Angela held her breath as the significant aromas that consistently accompanied Ulysses assaulted her nasal passages. She knew at any moment, her allergies would flare, and her throat would begin to scratch if she didn't stand downwind as soon as possible.

Ulysses was a tragic story, but he was one of God's children and that's why Angela always showed him kindness, love, and respect. She ignored the outside and focused on his big heart.

He called her his Angel because she saved his life one day. When she was visiting her husband and son, she noticed he didn't come out to speak with her. She always came on the days she knew he worked.

When she went to check on him, she found him passed out from one of his drinking binges. He had hit his head and fallen unconscious. Angela notified medical personnel immediately and they were able to resuscitate him.

For the next week while he recovered, she would visit him daily in the hospital. Not only had Ulysses suffered a severe head injury with his fall, but his copious alcohol consumption meant he was also severely dehydrated. Angela would sit and talk with him for hours, help the nurses refresh his bedding and even sneak him plates of food to help brighten his mood. It saddened her to learn she was the only visitor he had, even though she knew both of his parents were alive and well off, in fact, they owned the cemetery where he was the caretaker, along with many others in the city.

All of this flashed in her mind. She blinked.

"What did you say? Why have you been expecting me?"

He stepped out into the light, she stepped back to angle herself downwind.

"Someone was here just days ago, and she was visiting your family's grave."

"She?" Angela inquired.

Ulysses nodded his head as he gave the stubble on his chin a scratch.

"Yes, indeed Ms. Angel. She was tall and awful pretty. Now, I don't know if it was what was real, or you know, my drunken eyesight, but when she turned around to head back to her car, she had tears on her face and her makeup was running too, but she reminded me of you. Her skin was the same color as yours and I noticed how she favored your boy's side of the tombstone and so that's what was in my mind when she turned around. You've shown me pictures, he looks like you. She looks like you. Not in an obvious way, but in a way that's like y'all have so many like features that when you know what you're looking for, you can see it."

Angela gasped. *It couldn't be. She was here? In Tallahassee? At her son's grave?* Angela felt light-headed. She stumbled back a bit. Ulysses caught her by the arm.

"You alright, Ms. Angel?"

The unexpected strong grip of the frail, drunk man alarmed her and brought her back.

"Yes, I'm sorry. Ulysses, I need to go and talk to my sons. Do you have a cell phone?"

"Yes, ma'am, I do."

"I need you to take down my number and call me immediately if she returns."

He nodded and went to get his phone.

When he returned, she said, "Ulysses, I need you to listen and hear me well." He nodded giving her his full attention. "She might be dangerous. Do not engage with her. If she comes to speak to you, act like you don't know the family. Do you understand me?"

He nodded. Angela took his phone and added her number. She handed him back the phone. Ulysses looked at it and noticed she put her name in as Angel. He smiled.

"Yes, ma'am. I understand."

Angela squeezed his hand.

"Thank you for this."

"No problem. You know I always look out for my Angel. I promise to be careful."

"Thank you, Ulysses, but I have to go talk to my sons."

Angela turned to hurry off.

"But wait!" he yelled. Angela turned to face him. "Who is she?"

Angela sighed, "My granddaughter."

Ulysses stared behind her retreating back, dumbfounded.

Chapter 25: Family Discussion

Angela was disturbed, to say the least. She couldn't believe that her granddaughter had been right here in her city just days ago. She wanted more than anything in the world to hug her. To hold a piece of her baby boy in her arms once more.

Her hands shook as she drove through the city. She spoke to the voice-activated Bluetooth system in her car and instructed it to call Neil.

"Hey ma," his smooth baritone voice came over the car speakers. "What's up?"

"I um, just found out something and it's got me a little shaken."

Neil's voice lost all casualness. "What happened? You alright?"

"I'm okay, but I just talked to Ulysses when I went to see your father and brother. He says a woman came to the plot and favored your brother's side. She left a dozen white roses. They are still fresh. I must've missed her by a day or two. You know Ulysses is always under the influence, so his timeline might not be accurate."

"Did he say what she looked like?"

"He didn't give much description, he just told me she was my color and she looked like me if you knew what you were looking for. He said he saw it because she favored my boy's side of the grave."

Neil was quiet for a moment and Angela swore she could hear him thinking through the phone.

"Okay ma, where are you now?"

"I'm just driving around."

"Okay, don't go home right now. She could be watching. Go to the station. I'll be there in fifteen minutes."

"Okay."

"I need to call Nigel."

She ended the call.

†††

Twenty minutes later, the brothers walked into the Tallahassee Police Department. They walked through the busy corridors, while officers and personnel waved at them.

"When you gon join the force Nigel? We could use you!"

Nigel laughed and waved him off. "Y'all don't pay enough."

The officer that asked laughed as they passed him in the hall.

"Hey Lawson, your mom is here looking like a snack. You better get in there before Simmons takes her home."

"Simmons life will end today if he comes anywhere near my mother," Neil said without a smile or breaking stride in his steps.

Nigel chuckled but didn't say anything. Their mother was beautiful, and she didn't look her age. Men, young and old hit on her all the time. He was amused. Neil always took offense.

"You know mama is going find her a man one of these days," Nigel said.

"Shut up, Nigel," The very thought of their mother with a man annoyed him to no end.

Nigel simply chuckled and shook his head at his brother's ambivalence as they made their way into the homicide bullpen. Angela was sitting in Neil's guest chair in his office. An officer was sitting on the corner of his desk, flirting with their mother.

"Man, if you don't back up off my mama, we gon have some problems."

The young officer showed all his teeth. "I was just keeping her company while she waited for you guys."

"We're here so now bounce before I put my hands on you."

The young officer chuckled, reached for Angela's hand, and gave it a gentlemanly kiss. Nigel saw Neil's jaw clench and thought his brother just might lose his cool for real. "It was nice to meet you, Ms. Angela."

"My pleasure," she smiled up at him.

"Negro if you don't bounce, I'm gon hurt you. I'm so not playing."

Nigel chuckled as he took the seat next to his mother.

"Neil, stop being rude. He was just being nice.," Angela chastised.

“He was just leaving so he doesn’t get his behind whipped.” Neil replied at the flirting officer’s retreating back, as he walked out of Neil’s office. Angela scoffed and folded her arms over her chest.

“What are you gon do when I find me a new man?”

Neil paused mid-air as he was about to sit in the chair behind his oak wood desk.

“Say what now?”

Nigel fell out laughing.

“I’m serious. I’m not going to be alone for the rest of my life.”

“Ma, I’m not in the mood.”

“Well, you better find the mood,” she said under her breath.

Nigel leaned in, “Ma, who you been creeping with? I wanna meet him.”

His mother leaned in and winked at him.

Neil slammed his hand on the desk. “Not. In. The. Mood!”

Nigel and Angela laughed.

“We have actual serious issues to discuss.”

“You’re right baby. I’m sorry,” Angela said trying to hide the grin on her face. Nigel sobered his laughing as well and turned serious.

“Okay, Neil told me what Ulysses said. Sounds like she got daddy issues.”

“My concern is how she found out he was her father and what else does she know?” Neil added.

Nigel nodded.

“I don’t care what her issue is, I want to meet my grandchild,” Angela interjected.

Neil sighed and looked at his brother, who put up his palms as if to say, “don’t look at me.”

“Ma, we talked about this. You need to prepare yourself. This is not about to be a family reunion,” Neil told her sincerely.

She sighed. “Figure it out,” she told them with finality. “Now. I am going to go find my daughters-in-law and spend some time with them. Let me know when I’m cleared to go home.”

They nodded, as she gathered her purse and moved to stand. Neil cleared his throat in an attempt to ease some of the tension in the room. Angela looked at him.

“Ma, I’m going to have an officer outside your house for the time being.”

"Okay, baby, do what you need to do."

She stood and walked over to Neil then leaned down to kiss his cheek. Nigel stood up and kissed her cheek.

"Love you ma," they both said.

She smiled. "Love y'all too. Be safe and fix this without taking her life and I mean that."

They didn't say anything as she walked out.

Nigel looked at Neil, "I guess she told us."

Neil sighed.

Chapter 26: Sunday Dinner

The ladies at the kitchen table jumped when Jeremiah and Seth yelled at the TV protesting whatever flag the referee had called on the play.

Mia grabbed her chest. "Is it really that serious y'all?" she asked irritated.

"Yes!" the six men watching the game said collectively.

The usual gang was in attendance with two new faces, Darcy, and Jessica. The women had decided to remove themselves all of the yelling in the living room and commune in the dining room as the children played blissfully undisturbed in their rooms.

"Mia, how do you do it?" Grey asked.

"Do what?" Mia asked.

"Where do you find the time just for you. I have one kid and a husband, and I feel like I have forgotten all about me."

"Well, in my defense, mine are old enough to ignore when I need to," Mia said with a shrug.

The women fell out laughing.

"I wish I could ignore all of them some days," Lindsey admitted. "My God, sometimes I just need a minute to breathe. Me and Jacob have fully bonded now, which I am absolutely grateful for, but now he and Hope gang up on me. Like, can I please have two minutes alone in the bathroom? Why? Why do they want to come into the bathroom with you!"

Darcy chuckled at the young mothers.

"Oh, honey, Daniel is completely ignored. He can cry and stump and fall out when I'm in the bathroom. I don't care, I don't care, I don't care. Give me my peace!" Sheridan said. "Now he just puts his little fingers and toes underneath the door until I come out. I take my precious time."

They all laughed.

"Well Hunter's not walking yet, but he's crawling like a madman. I can't wait for this invasion of my privacy," Grey said sarcastically.

"Well just wait, because it's coming," Mia said. "Isaiah is our weirdest one yet. Whenever Jeremiah goes in the bathroom for number two, he wants to sit on his lap. They are so weird. Better him than me."

"Oh my God!" Grey shrieked.

"Kids are the most invasive, disrespectful, inconvenient little people ever. You just adjust and roll with it," Darcy said. "Eventually they grow out of it. They become teenagers and never want to be around you, so it's a tradeoff. Enjoy the closeness while you can," Darcy said winking at her daughter.

Jessica rolled her eyes playfully and continued to listen to the seasoned women.

"I'm all for the closeness, just not in the bathroom. I mean, Hope basically demanded privacy before she was potty trained. We could always tell when she was pooping because she would go off to a corner by herself and then come back around us. Yeah, you want your privacy but won't give me mine," Lindsey rolled her eyes.

They laughed. "Aren't y'all trying for a new one though?" Sheridan asked.

"Yeah, we are and every other day I ask myself why."

They laughed.

Sheridan rubbed her belly. "Well, I'm trying to get ready for this one and Grey, this is something Seth and I have been working on. As a psychologist, it's my job to be aware of the things that psychologically affect us. We are determined to teach our children good habits and now we're trying to figure out how to teach a three-year old the concept of me time."

"Elaborate please," Genevieve said.

"Okay, when observing my family, my patients and just people in general, I realized that we are so busy, just going and going and going, we never pause when we transition to the next thing. So, for instance. When you wake up in the morning, don't just jump up from sleep to intense mode. Take a minute or fifteen to fully wake up, prep your mind for your day and then get ready. Now the real one is when you get home. The rule in our house is when you get home from work, everybody gets 30 minutes of uninterrupted time to themselves. Yes, we do the hey honey, I'm home, kiss, kiss, hug, hug and then silence! You get 30 minutes to decompress. To get rid of the attitude you have from your coworker or your boss or whatever happened in the news that day. You get time to breathe, take off your shoes, release yourself from the prison of your bra before you are bombarded with house stuff. Seth and I have been doing it for a month and it has worked wonders. When Seth and I talked he told me that me bombarding him with house stuff or kid stuff as soon as he walked through the door aggravated him to no end. He would always say to himself, 'Can I just have a minute.' And I felt the exact same way. As soon as I walk in the house, it's, 'Mommy!' Or Seth is asking, 'Where is this or did I do that?' And I'm thinking I just left these crazy people at work; I need a minute. So, we decided to take thirty."

"Lawd, that could save Jamal's life!" Lindsey said.

They fell out laughing.

"That is good stuff," Mia said. "And my children are old enough to enjoy their thirty minutes too. I know I get on their nerves too because I start fussing as soon as they come home when they ain't did what they are supposed to do."

"That's interesting," Genevieve chimed in. "What if the kid is in trouble? Do you wait before you address it?" she asked.

"Well, I think it's important to know your kid and know yourself. I for one, think it is better to wait because I need to calm down. It even gives you room to consult God or at least say a 'Jesus don't let me kill this child,' prayer before you address it. They also have time to calm down and think about what they did. Think of all the anxiety they have when you approach them, and they know they are in trouble. They just start doing dumb stuff. Lying before you ask a question. Falling out crying when all you did was enter into their personal space, just doing the most. I'm not against spankings, but I do think that we as parents, especially black parents need to understand that not everything can be solved with a belt, not every child is the same and cannot be dealt with the same."

"Yes," Mia interjected. "Because Isaiah is that kid that will do what he wants to do even if he knows it's wrong, own it when you ask him about and take the spanking or punishment. In his mind I guess he figures it's worth it. He drives me crazy! We have got to find another way."

"Exactly," Sheridan said. She continued, "In this day and age with all the police killings, rampant injustices and Lord, what if this crazy man gets in office. The racists are coming out the woodworks. Believe it or not, black people in this country are walking around with

PTSD. Think about it. What happens when a cop pulls you over, or you just see the lights behind you?"

"Immediate panic," Mia said.

"Palms sweating, heart drops. Gripping fear," Grey said, "And my husband is a cop."

Lindsey blinked. She didn't feel any of that and found it profoundly disturbing that these women she knew, loved and respected felt this way just because they saw police lights behind them. Was not having that feeling of fear and panic her white privilege?

"There's instant panic for me too," Darcy said. "Especially when Jessica is in the car with me."

"Just, sheer fear," Genevieve admitted.

"Exactly. We don't even realize how we unconsciously walk around waiting to find out if we or someone we love will be the next trending hashtag. So, all I'm saying this. Don't take away the black mama fear that you have instilled in your children, because they need that. What I'm saying is, try better ways of handling things in your home. Don't necessarily do it the way your mama did because that's what you know. If it was so effective, why do you have the mental and emotional issues that you have? One thing that I am adamant about is self-care. Like PJ used to say, 'How can you poor from an empty vessel?' There is a certain amount of selfishness allowed because you have to take care of you so you can take care of the family God entrusted to you."

"So, what happens after everyone reconvenes from their 30-minute time out," Mia asked.

They laughed.

"Then I go and start preparing dinner. Seth helps out with Daniel and at the dinner table, we talk about all those things. Attitudes are so much better. Whatever drama from the day is left outside the house and we can deal with the issues inside the house with no residue from outside."

They all nodded as they considered what Sheridan was suggesting.

"Any tips for toddlers?" Lindsey asked.

"Well right now, we are teaching Daniel that when he gets home, he gets to have quiet time and after quiet time he gets a reward. It varies from day-to-day."

"Does it work?" Lindsey asked.

"Some days yes, some days no and when it doesn't. We take quiet time shifts. We usually decide with rock, paper, scissors who gets their 30 minutes first."

They fell out laughing.

Chapter 27: Plan B

Kadijah sat on the shoulder of Interstate 10 crying, trembling, and praying as she waited impatiently for her husband to arrive.

"God why is this happening?" she cried out as she continued to rub her protruding belly.

She was five months pregnant, and life had officially gotten insane. This was all too much. She constantly wondered, both in silence and aloud, what exactly it was she carrying inside of her. It had to be incredibly special for all hell to break loose like this. But every time she asked, the only answer that ever came was a *gift.* She didn't understand, and to be honest, her frustration with God was mounting. The spiritual attack was one thing, but not understanding why was testing her patience *and* faith on a completely different level.

Kadijah looked up in her rearview mirror to see her husband's big black SUV pulling up behind her. She swore he was out of the car before it even stopped. Nigel ran to her door and opened it. He helped Kadijah out of the car and quickly moved her to the passenger side, out of the way as cars continued to speed down the highway, oblivious to the trauma she'd just experienced. She was also oblivious to her two angels, Cheveyo and Quan, who had never left her side.

Nigel held his wife tightly as he tried vainly to get his emotions in check. He was fire hot! He kissed her forehead then finally released her, so he could look at her.

"You okay?" he asked.

Kadijah shook her head and held him tighter. She cried hard into his chest. He continued to try to get his temper under control, but it was truly futile. It had been a long time since he'd been this angry about anything, but this wasn't just anything. This was his wife and child - two people about whom he absolutely did not play. Right now, the murderous thoughts running through his head were only second to the gut-wrenching fear that had gripped his heart at Kadijah's frantic phone call. It had yet to completely subside, even now as he held her in his arms.

After a few minutes, Kadijah's tears subsided. He placed his hands on both sides of her face. Her fair skin was flushed red and tear stained.

"Tell me what happened," he demanded.

She sniffed and wiped her nose with the tissue she'd pulled out of her purse.

"I really don't know," she replied on a shaky breath. "I was just driving, and I kept noticing this black car behind me. I was in the right lane so there was nowhere for me to go as it kept getting closer. I just assumed it would go around. The left lane wasn't congested, but instead of getting over, it just kept tailing me. Anytime, I would speed up, the car would too. We went back and forth like that for about two miles. All the while, I'm freaking out because the car won't stop following me."

Nigel listened intently to his wife, trying earnestly to keep his composure for her sake. He wasn't sure he was doing a good job of it though; his whole body practically vibrated with anger. He willed himself to calm down as Kadijah continued.

"I kept trying to get a look at the driver, hoping maybe if I got his attention, he might leave me alone," she explained. "But I couldn't make out anything but a silhouette. The window tint was too dark, like limo black. It was creepy."

"So, how did you end up on the shoulder?"

"I pulled over to avoid getting ran off the road!" Khadijah cried. "At one point, the car got so close I thought it was going to hit my bumper. Then the car zoomed into the left lane but kept swerving into my lane. It was like I was in their blind spot, but I know they knew I was there. I'm blowing the horn and screaming. It was like the car was taunting me. Again, I couldn't see anything, the car was all black and so were the windows. I would slow down and so would the car then finally it just kept coming over in my lane and wouldn't stop. I finally pulled over onto the shoulder, and that's when it took off like a bat out of hell."

Bomani, Nigel's Egyptian warrior, shared a questioning look with his angelic brethren.

"What is Insidious up to now?" he asked.

Quan, the Japanese warrior assigned to Kadijah replied.

"He is only taunting her, not attacking her. The demons with the car only cackled as she became more frightened. They also didn't engage us in warfare."

Lajos, Nigel's Hungarian warrior, added, "Insidious is strategic. It's likely he's trying to send her into premature labor to take his chances with the baby in the NICU. The environment alone poses a challenge to their faith."

"He could also be trying to force Nigel's hand," Cheveyo, Kadijah's Native American warrior, suggested.

"How do you mean?" Bomani inquired.

"They've kept Nigel on his toes, true enough, but nothing significant enough to force his hand to take action."

"You mean to activate whatever plan he has for her protection?" Quan asked.

"Indeed," Cheveyo affirmed. "They learned how the brothers think from Neil. You can bet Insidious has studied all of their mistakes from the battle they just lost."

The other angels nodded in agreement, as Cheveyo continued his assessment of their latest demonic foe.

"He is wise and very strategic. Nothing he does is without a specific cause. So, we need to be a step ahead. Nigel's plan B can't be amateur, and it has to be something the Kingdom of Darkness would never suspect."

Lajos smiled at Bomani who nodded knowingly. Cheveyo, ever vigilant, caught the interaction and gave his angelic brothers a questioning glance.

"I take it you guys have something in mind," he stated.

Lajos nodded as he grinned fiercely. It was now just a matter of putting their plan into motion. Nigel's angelic contingent looked at their charge.

"What kind of car was it?" he asked his wife through clenched teeth.

"Like a Dodge Challenger or Charger maybe," Kadijah answered unsure. She was still visibly shaken. "I didn't get a tag or anything. It sped off too fast. It looked demonic to be honest, like a raging beast."

Nigel nodded as he tried to think. He'd called Neil on his way to his wife and told him this was the last straw. It was time to move her to the safe house, so he could do what needed to be done. Neil had been hesitant because he knew Grey would have to go with her, but he also understood exactly what his brother was going through. That alone had directed his actions and pushed him to finally agree.

Just then, Darryl got out of Nigel's truck and came over. He looked at Kadijah.

"You alright?" he inquired.

"I will be," she said as she sniffled.

"I'm sorry this happened. I'm going to drive your car back for you."

She nodded.

Darryl turned to Nigel and asked, "What's the next move boss?"

"Check her car for any tracking devices when you get it back to the office. Then get to the safe house and wait for my instructions. I'll tell Cynthia to redistribute your work until this is dealt with."

Darryl nodded and went around to the driver's side of Kadijah's car. Nigel opened the passenger door and grabbed her purse. She stared up at her husband.

"Tracking device? Safehouse? What in the world are you talking about, Nigel?"

Nigel walked her over to his truck and helped her into the passenger side.

"Don't ignore me, Nigel."

"I'm not ignoring you baby, but I need to think, and you need to let me. There will be a series of things that are about to happen that will seem strange to you. Just let me do me, I'll explain everything. Just give me a minute, okay." She stared at him reluctantly. "Do you trust me?" he asked.

"You know I do."

"Then act like it," he said as he closed her door then went around to get in the car.

He took a minute to take a few deep breaths as he calmed down. He removed the gun from his hip and sat it in the center console. Kadijah stared at it thinking by now she'd be used to it, but truthfully, she wasn't, and she didn't think she ever would be. She could tell he was thinking because he drummed his thumbs on the steering wheel.

Lajos whispered a name in Nigel's ear. He pulled his phone off his hip then dialed a number. She heard it ring twice before a deep voice picked up.

"Long time no hear from. You good?"

"Nah, actually I'm not. I need you and eleven of your best."

"Trouble?"

"At my front doorstep."

"I understand. Where and when?"

"Tonight. Darryl will get in touch with your travel agent to give details."

"See you soon," she heard the voice say and then the phone went quiet.

Nigel hung up.

"Who was that?" she asked scared and nervous.

Nigel stared at his wife. Her face was full of fear and tear stains. It pissed him off to no end. This had to end.

He said, "I have friends in high places and friends in low places. But if I call them a friend, you can trust them with your life."

His wife stared at him. Somehow, she just knew whoever he just called was from that low place. She wanted to say something, but she said she trusted him, so she was going to have to see this play out.

Chapter 28: What About Your Friends

The next evening, Nigel pulled up to a house deep in the country of Quincy, Florida. The house sat on a large piece of land. The first thing Kadijah noticed about this house she'd never been to was that it was pushed far back from the road and there were no trees anywhere near it.

Pulling up behind them, was Neil, Grey, Hunter, and Beau. When they got closer, Kadijah noticed three black SUVs in the yard along with Darryl's Suburban.

"Where are we?" Kadijah asked.

Nigel looked at his wife then gently kissed her lips. He grabbed her chin and stared deeply into her eyes.

"Trust me, baby, I got you."

She nodded but was officially scared out of her mind.

Nigel hopped out of the car. She saw him pull his shirt down to cover the firearm at the five-thirty position on his back. He came around to the passenger side and opened the door. Helping her out, she grabbed his hand with no intention of letting go.

Beau and Neil got out of the car first and scanned the area. When Grey got out, she noticed the two large black men with even larger guns standing near the entrance. She pulled her firearm out of her purse and put it on her hip, not even trying to conceal it. She scooped up her sleeping baby and kissed his cheek.

Neil was in front of her with Beau bringing up the rear as they walked up to Nigel and Kadijah. With them and unseen to the unauthorized human eyes, were Savas, Bojan, Ern, Koldo, Alvise, Ranj, Cheveyo, Quan, Bomani, and Lajos. All of the angels that guarded these soldiers for Christ nodded at the two powers angels that stood like sentries on the roof. One on the left, the other on the right.

Grey continued to peruse the bodyguards. She didn't know much about street gangs, but something told her she was about to meet some members. There were tattoos, scars and stern faces that were not welcoming.

Grey quipped, "Well this is interesting. I don't know what y'all are up to, but I'm gon roll with it for the moment because I trust that y'all have Kadijah's best interest in mind."

"Please don't start trippin' boo," Nigel pleaded. "Kadijah is already squeezing all the feeling out of my hand. I need one of y'all to keep a level head."

Grey looked over at the men by the door once more, then at her husband.

"I need you to soldier up for me baby," Neil told her.

"Do you know them?" Grey asked her husband.

"I know my brother trusts them, so I trust them."

Grey gave her husband a nod as she caressed Hunter's sleeping back. Looking back at Nigel, she said, "Okay, bro. I got you. I'm down for whatever this is."

The relief that flooded Nigel's face at her willingness told her more than he'd ever admit out loud.

The front door opened. Darryl came out followed by a high-yellow man with long neat locs that cascaded down his back in a tail. He had a scar down the right side of his face. His eyes were amber and hypnotic as he approached them. The stranger smiled when he saw Nigel.

"Long time no see, bro."

Nigel grinned and went to embrace him. He had to do so with one arm because Kadijah didn't let go of his right hand. Neil and Beau chuckled.

"Thanks for coming."

"If you call, you know I'm on the way."

"I appreciate that."

"This is my wife Kadijah and she's carrying my little girl as you can see."

The man extended a hand to Kadijah.

"It's nice to meet you, ma'am."

She shook his hand, shocked by his manners as they completely contrasted his thug exterior.

"I haven't decided yet if it's nice to meet you," she told him honestly.

He laughed. "I get it, but you good ma, you good."

Nigel turned. "This is my brother Neil." Neil stepped up and shook his hand. "Neil, this is Stephan."

"It's so nice to finally meet you, Stephan. Your reputation precedes you."

"As does yours," Stephan replied.

Neil stepped back. "This is my wife Grey and our son, Hunter. This is Beau. I'm not sure how you run things, but he comes along with them. They are a package deal, no exceptions."

Stephan nodded. "I understand."

He reached over and shook Beau's hand. Stephan noticed Grey's Glock 43 on her hip. His brow raised.

Beau said, "She can handle herself if she needs to, but he'd prefer she didn't."

Stephan nodded.

"It's nice to meet you too," Grey told him.

Just then, her eyes flamed, it was only visible to the spiritual beings. Grey blinked and saw two military angels flanking the man in front of her, though she was careful not to react. *Well, that's interesting*, she thought to herself. She knew this little adventure was going to be way more than she ever anticipated.

"Let's step inside, shall we," Darryl suggested.

They all piled into the mundane single-family home. Their neighbors were a mile away on each side, so they weren't too worried about being watched. While they weren't worried about being watched by humans, that didn't mean spiritual eavesdroppers weren't lurking.

†††

Hunter's angels, Alvise and Ranj, followed them inside, the rest of the warriors took up positions around the house. Savas saw a demon across the street lurking in some trees. He grinned fiercely.

"You may as well come out; we can see you."

The demon hopped out of the tree as he stood to his full height of six feet. His beady green eyes glowed.

"Nice move," he told them. "Insidious won't be happy, but he won't stop until he gets that baby. Don't celebrate this victory long. He loves a challenge."

"We look forward to it," Cheveyo said as his eyes flamed the other worldly blue.

The demon nodded then took flight.

Once it was gone, Savas turned to his fellow warriors.

"Bomani, you and Bojan go to alert the Captain they are watching this place. Insidious will not be happy and we need to be ready to combat his next move."

Bomani and Bojan nodded. They took off streaming gold and white lights.

†††

Kadijah's breath hitched as they entered the home to find nine more men strewn about in the living and dining rooms. The house wasn't decorated but had all the basics - sofa, love seat a couple of chairs, a dining room table covered with firearms and a fireplace.

Nigel felt her hand tremble in his. He looked back at her and kissed her cheek.

"I need you to trust me, baby."

Grey's brow winged up at their babysitters. She eyed Neil. "Oh, this just got interesting."

Neil laughed. "I think you're going to be more of a shock to them than they are to you," he told her.

She chuckled. "You might be right."

Hunter began to squirm. She rocked him, but he began to fuss. Neil reached for his son. Once in the comfort of his father's embrace, the little bundle went right back to sleep.

The men of various sizes, shapes, and hues all stood up and moved out of the way for the women to sit. Beau could tell by their colors which West Coast gang they were from but chose to keep that information to himself.

Grey grabbed Kadijah's other hand and pulled her away from Nigel. She was completely at ease once she knew there was angelic protection here. As bizarre as the situation was, and the fact that she couldn't reconcile these men having angels with them was of no consequence. What she did know was they were under the protection of the Almighty and that's all that really mattered. The why's and how's were not her business, but God's.

"Girl, relax. You look like you're constipated," she told her.

Kadijah stared at Grey then finally let out a nervous chuckle. She took a deep breath and sat down at Grey's insistence.

Nigel mouthed, "Thank you," to Grey.

She winked at him. Nigel nodded at Stephan who took the center of the room.

"Ladies and gentleman," he nodded toward Beau. "As he said, I'm Stephan and these are my men." He went around the room and introduced each man. Each one seemed scarier than the last to Kadijah. "I know you all don't know me, but Nigel and I go way back. I promise you ladies and your children are in the best hands until Neil and Nigel do what they need to do to make sure you're safe. No need to worry."

Kadijah just stared as her mind raced. *Was her husband really about to leave her here with these strange men?*

Grey spoke up. "It's nice to meet you fellas. Listen, I don't doubt our safety because I know my husband would never leave me and Hunter anywhere he didn't deem the safest possible place, however, I have to be practical. We are dealing with a woman almost six months pregnant under some stressful conditions. She hates guns and y'all got them sitting around here like what-nots and conversation pieces. I'm here for it, but she isn't. So, can somebody please tell me what are we going to do if she happens to go into labor out here in the middle of nowhere? I can pray the horns off a Billy goat, but I don't know nothin' bout birthing no babies!"

Everybody laughed.

Nigel pointed to a man in the corner. He was lean and looked the most sophisticated of the bunch, but he still had stone cold killer written all over his face along with several tattoos.

"If you go into labor, he's more than capable of handling the situation. There's an area set up for just such an emergency."

Kadijah's eyes got wide as saucers. "Are you freakin' kidding me right now?" she asked incredulously.

"No, I'm not," Nigel said with sincerity. "I wouldn't leave you anywhere without medical assistance at the ready."

Kadijah stood up, "Negro, we need to talk."

She briskly waddled to her husband, grabbed his hand, and led him outside.

When they left everyone fell out laughing.

"Dang she got him locked down like that?" Stephan asked. Neil nodded. "I never thought I'd see the day."

"Me either," Neil replied chuckling.

All the laughing woke Hunter out of his peaceful sleep, and he was not happy about it. Neil rocked his son as he hummed a melody in his ear. After a few moments, Hunter settled back into sleep.

"So..." Grey began. "I figure y'all are from California, forgive me for my naivete, but what gang are you all in? I'm not familiar with the colors?"

The room fell into a less-than-comfortable silence.

"Miss Grey," Beau said. She looked at him as he shook his head discouraging this line of questioning.

"Well, I don't know how long y'all are going to be babysitting us and the conversation has to start somewhere."

She looked around the room once more at the stern, quiet faces and sighed loudly.

"Alright, that's fine. Don't tell me," she said waving her hand in a nonchalant fashion. "But y'all better find some type of conversation otherwise by the time I'm finished, I bet I have all of y'all saved, sanctified and filled with the Holy Ghost. We'll be sitting up here having Bible Study if y'all don't figure out a way to entertain me."

They fell out laughing.

"Y'all laughing, but she's dead serious," Beau told them. "She got me converted," he confessed.

Neil laughed at his crazy wife as he kissed the top of Hunter's head. He knew he didn't have to worry about her. She would be fine. Kadijah was another story. Neil said a silent prayer for his brother. He knew she was outside giving him the business.

†††

Outside, Kadijah was indeed going off.

"Are you crazy? You must be insane. Correct me if I'm wrong, but these are gang members, right? Not only do you want me to stay with 12 strange men in the middle of nowhere, but you also want me to let one of them stick his hands up my hoo-ha and pull your daughter out."

Nigel couldn't help it; he fell out laughing. "Girl, you are crazy."

She stared at him incensed and ready to punch him in his pretty face. Nigel sobered and grabbed his wife's hand.

"I need you to listen to me. You know that I am crazy in love with you, right?"

"But, Nigel..."

"Don't but Nigel me, answer my question." Kadijah sighed heavily and swallowed the swirl of emotions caught in her throat.

"Right."

"You know that I would never put you in harm's way, right?"

She hesitated, but said, "Right."

"Listen, I don't know why all this crazy is happening, but God gave me the assignment to protect you and my child and that's what I'm doing to the best of my abilities. Grey is here for spiritual protection and the rest of them are here for everything else. I'm not playing any games or taking any chances. My methods may seem unorthodox to you, but there is a method to the madness. Rest assured there is *always* more method than madness I promise you. This is strategic. No matter what you think about these men they are loyal to Stephan and Stephan is loyal to me. They are professionals and very capable. I told you, I've got friends in low places too. Sometimes you need a sinner over a saint."

Khadijah frowned. "Why is he loyal to you?"

"That's a story for another day and one I promise to tell you, but not now." Nigel could tell she didn't like that answer, but at the moment, he didn't have time to address it. He reached for his wife's other hand and looked her squarely in her eyes. "I *need* you to trust me. You have Grey with you."

Kadijah rolled her eyes.

"Grey isn't a normal person, Nigel. She'll probably already be BFFs with Stephan by the time we head back in."

Nigel laughed because she was probably right.

"I want you to relax."

"What are you going to do?"

"Whatever needs to be done."

"I don't..."

He covered her mouth with his before she could protest further. The kiss stole all her resistance and fears for the moment. She grabbed his face and let the kiss take her anywhere but here. After a minute, Nigel reluctantly pulled away from his wife. He stared into her face.

"I love you and I love my daughter. I am not going to let anything happen to either of you. If you can't trust anything else around you, trust the promise that God gave us as well as my love for you. I need you to have a little faith in your man. The only reason Phoenix is still alive is because God told me to let him keep breathing. No one here is going to harm you. You know we come from different worlds. I just got on this path you're on. I need to go back to what I know and trust and that's God and my instincts. I'd trust you and my child with everyone in that room before I'd trust you in a church full of saints and a precinct full of cops. Do you understand me?"

She nodded, staring at her husband's handsome face. His eyes were cold steely gray – a telltale sign that he was dead serious.

"I need you to relax."

She took a deep breath. "Okay, Nigel, I am going to trust you and your crazy sister-in-law, but you better figure this out before I go into labor because my baby is not going to be delivered by a man with a kill count and tattoos on his face!" she said with a stomp for emphasis.

Nigel chuckled.

"I'll do my very best. But baby, I promise you, that man is qualified to deliver this baby if he has to," Nigel said as he caressed her belly. Just then their little girl kicked. Nigel said, "See, she's down with it, too."

Kadijah rolled her eyes. "If this little girl comes out acting like you, I'm shipping her back stamped with return to sender on her forehead."

Nigel laughed as he wrapped his arms around his wife and led her back inside.

†††

When they walked back in, all eyes were on them. Kadijah threw her hands up in surrender.

"Y'all bear with me. This is not my cup of tea, but I do trust my husband and my sister-in-law who seems to all of a sudden be right at home."

Grey shrugged. "What can I say, I'm a chameleon. I adapt."

Kadijah shook her head.

"Let's go grab their bags," Darryl suggested to Beau. He nodded, and they headed out.

"Ladies, there are four bedrooms in this house. The master bedroom is for you two, the one across the hall is for Beau and the two in the back are for the guys. There are four bunk beds in each room. I'm assuming you guys will work shifts," Nigel said to Stephan.

"Yes, that's how we roll."

The fridge is stocked, if you need anything Darryl will be the one to deliver any supplies," Nigel shared, as he continued to give them the rundown of the home's accommodations and facilities. He turned to his sister-in-law. "Grey, can you come with me? I need to show you something."

Kadijah eyed her husband. Neil took a seat next to her and gave her Hunter to distract her.

"Take your mind off it and let them do what they need to do. Your only job is to be a safe environment for my niece okay."

Kadijah nodded as she kissed Hunter's sleeping face. She loved her nephew very much. He was the yummiest baby.

In the master bedroom, Nigel was showing Grey all the places weapons were stashed. Some in the headboard, beneath the bed and in the closet.

"Take care of my girls, Grey. Kadijah isn't fragile, but this is just not her scene and I don't see her adjusting to it anytime soon."

"I got you, bro."

"Thanks, boo," Nigel said as he hugged Grey after kissing her cheek.

Neil walked in.

"It would be a shame for me to whip your behind for being all up on my woman before you even got a chance to protect your wife."

Nigel and Grey laughed.

As Nigel headed out, he said, "Thanks, bro. I know I'm asking for a lot."

"Yes, negro you are!"

They laughed as they embraced.

Neil closed the door behind Nigel. Grey put her hand on her hip.

"I know doggone well you didn't come in here to get a quickie."

Neil fell out. "Girl, you need help. No, that's not what I came in here for, but don't tempt a brother. I'm not looking forward to being away from my good thang."

She laughed as she went to him. He wrapped his arms around his wife as his hands slid down to her hips and backside, their standard resting place. She gently kissed his lips.

"You okay with leaving us here?" she asked.

"I am, just pissed I have to leave y'all here. I hate being apart from you, but God has seen us through all the other crazy so why not this one. I know someone has to cover my brother's daughter."

"Good point."

Neil glanced over his wife's face and gripped her chin gently.

"Stay sharp, stay alert and stay prayed up. If stuff gets crazy, call your best friend and tell him to come act a fool."

Grey laughed thinking of the Angel of Death. "I am NOT calling him," she said with finality as she shivered. "Speaking of angels, the fearless leader has two military angels flanking him."

Neil's brow winged up. "Oh, really."

"Yes, really."

"What do you think that's about?"

"I don't know, but I'm sure I was sent here to find out."

Neil nodded. "Nothing is coincidence, and everything is connected," he said repeating Etienne's immortal words.

"Seems like it."

"Well, that actually makes me feel better." Neil's eyes narrowed at his wife.

"What?" she asked innocently. He rolled his eyes at her feigned naivete.

"I know you, Grey," he said. "Just promise you'll try and figure out what his spiritual background is before you start dropping bombs like oh, by the way, angels are walking beside you. I need his focus to not be split, okay."

Grey sighed and rolled her eyes.

"Okay, fine," she relented. "I won't say anything until the Holy Spirit releases me to."

He kissed her. "That's my girl."

She kissed him again as he took it deeper.

“Maybe, we should try for that quickie,” Neil whispered seductively when they broke apart.

She pushed him back. “Boy, stop!”

He flirtatiously bit his bottom lip as he eyed her up and down. She shook her head as she grabbed him by his shirt and yanked him to her. The kiss she placed on his lips told him exactly what she intended to do with him. He had zero objections.

Chapter 29: The Big Guns

The demon stood nervously as he waited for Insidious to respond to the information he'd just provided. Insidious sat in the old, abandoned train station, which he had converted into his headquarters as he oversaw this new war. The Capitol was no longer an option as it was guarded by the Light.

Insidious rubbed his chin. The demon that delivered the news continued to wait anxiously for him to decide what was next. Draven, his right-hand man watched Insidious carefully. He was like no other demon Draven had ever encountered. He sincerely enjoyed watching him work and learning from him.

The demon spoke up, interrupting Insidious' quiet contemplation.

"You should know, your Highness that the light purposely instructed Nigel to summon Stephan in response to your attack on his wife on the interstate."

Insidious' eyes narrowed. "I see."

"I thought you attacked her to purposely get Nigel to do just what he did," Draven stated.

"I did, but I honestly did not expect them to lead him to Stephan."

"Who is Stephan," Draven inquired.

Insidious sighed. "He is one that we groomed from birth to be a soldier for the Kingdom of Darkness. He has the gift of influence and would have been an asset to us."

Insidious sighed again deeply as he lamented the loss of what should have been a valuable weapon in this war.

"He *was* an asset to us until the light blindsided us."

The demon and Draven watched Insidious closely - they were enraptured by the stately way in which he commanded authority. They listened intently as he continued to explain, hanging on to every word.

"Stephan was deep in our side. He knows things, he's seen things, he's a threat plain and simple, but we can't touch him."

"Why not?" the demon asked.

"Once he chose the light he's been under heavy guard. He's got a Job hedge around him."

Draven frowned. "How did he come to choose the light?"

Insidious shook his head. He would never forget when they came to tell him about the fated day they lost Stephan.

He said, "When we knew the light was strategizing to win him for their side, we set him up to die in his sin. He was met in a dark alley by one of his rival gang heads. The opposition got the drop on him, thanks to us, but when he pulled the trigger point blank it didn't go off. From what I heard, there was a flash of light and the opposition dropped dead. Stephan knew then and there he had an encounter with the one true living God. He didn't leave the gang life, but he turned the organization around. Their past reputation still resonates but transformed the entire gang into an organization that takes care of the community. They put an end to senseless killings and put a stop to illegal activities. They turned their cash into legitimate businesses in the community."

Draven shook his head. "So, how did he become loyal to Nigel?"

"The change didn't come without opposition and danger. Stephan hired Nigel's firm to protect his woman, kid, and his mother. Needless to say, he did what he was hired to do. During the gang's transition someone issued a hit on Stephan's family, but Nigel took out the opposition, and he's been indebted to him ever since. I guess Nigel decided now was the time to call in the favor."

Draven shook his head.

The demon said, "But I don't understand. He's a still a gang member. How is the light protecting him?

Insidious stared at the clueless demon.

"Have a seat and let me give you some wisdom." The demon obliged. "Never underestimate God's sovereignty. He loves these feckless humans to no end. He also judges the heart. He's the only one that knows the heart of man. Also, remember He reigns on the just and the unjust. Sometimes His reigning on the unjust is to keep them safe and favored until they choose Him. He gifted Stephan with a spirit of influence. He never intended for it to be used for darkness. We got access to him at a young age, but the light played us. They allowed him to learn our ways, schemes, and systems. Stephan is one of the biggest threats to corruption in his city because of the information he has. They won't touch him, and they let his gang take care of the community without interference because they fear him."

The demon shook his head. He learned more about God from Insidious in one conversation than he ever knew in all the eons he'd been on this earth.

"What are we going to do about Nigel?" Draven asked keeping them focused.

"It's time to bring out the big guns," Insidious told them.

"You mean their niece?"

"Yes, it's time to unleash her like the weapon she is. Tell Lucca to send her to the old woman."

"But what if they are in contact with the old woman?" Draven inquired.

"That's all part of the plan. I want them to be a step ahead of her. Trust me when I say, once they realize who she is their emotions will dictate every move. Strategy will be out the window and it will give me a chance to get to that baby while they are distracted."

Draven and the demon smiled.

Chapter 30: Counterattack

Bomani and Bojan arrived at the old, abandoned church outside of the city limits of Tallahassee. The old insignificant building held none of the majesties of the power that rested inside of it. They acknowledged the powers angels that stood guard on the four corners of the roof.

They nodded and strolled inside to find Captain Valter, Lieutenant Nero and the Angel of Death in a huddle strategizing. Death spotted them and acknowledged their presence. Nero was an Italian warrior with olive skin and dark hair that flowed in waves just past his shoulders. The Captain turned to look. He was Scandinavian, his blonde hair was pulled into a tail at the nape of his neck. He knew their presence meant Insidious was up to something.

The fact that one of Nigel's guardians and one of Greys' guardians are who were sent made it clear, there was an attack coming that no matter what it looked like the underlying plot was to come for Nigel's daughter. They all exchanged a warrior's handshake by grabbing forearms.

When the protocol was done, Captain Valter asked, "What's happened?"

"Insidious is taunting Nigel. Kadijah was attacked yesterday morning on the highway. It forced Nigel to go in contingency mode," Bomani told him.

Valter nodded. He understood. "What did you instruct him to do?" the Captain inquired.

"He already had plans to send her to a safehouse with Grey, for obvious reasons. We instructed him to reach out to Stephan for her natural protection."

The Captain nodded his understanding. The darkness was still upset about that loss. "I see."

"When we got there, there was a demon watching the place," Bojan informed them. "Once he saw Stephan, he warned us he was heading straight to tell Insidious about it. Of course, it was given with threats."

"What are you thinking?" Valter asked his second in command as his face held an intense gaze.

"Captain, surely this will cause Insidious to play his hand with their niece. We've speculated why he's waited to make it known, she's his secret weapon." Valter nodded. "We can't let them be caught off guard. Bomani, guide Nigel to not put this off any longer. Just in case, Insidious is up to more than we suspect, inform him to do it remotely."

"He could use Monet to find her for him. She's more than capable and her special assignment is about to be given to her, she's under a secure hedge and cannot be touched," Death advised.

"Great point," Captain Valter said. "This way we may get an advantage, however, I'm not concerned about Nigel finding out who she is. I'm concerned about Neil."

Bojan nodded. "Savas and I have discussed this. We're ready to guide Grey to keep her husband grounded and to reel him back in."

"But her focus will still be split. She may not be capable of covering Nigel's daughter. Looks like Insidious had a contingency all along to distract Grey," Nero told them.

They all nodded. Death locked eyes with the Captain.

"Send me in."

The Captain shook his head. "It's too soon."

"She's a black female, at 37 weeks her chances of survival are high and complications minimal. Of course, we know that's in the natural. In the supernatural, the Great I AM can do anything, but the human proved statistics will help their faith," Nero added.

Bomani frowned. "You mean forcing her into early labor?"

"It may become necessary," Death informed him.

Only he and the Captain understood what was at stake.

"Yes, Nero, but that's not what I'm concerned about." Again, the Captain and Death exchanged a knowing look. "Bomani, I understand your concerns and yes your charge will be very distressed, however, we can rest assure that Insidious is about to make a move to push her watchman out of place. It ties our hands where Grey is concerned because if the enemy consumes Neil's heart then we lose a valuable soldier as well. Be at ease, Jehovah Jireh has already provided a way around this obstacle. However, it is going to test the faith of Nigel and Kadijah like never before," the Captain said.

“If she goes into early labor, it should force Neil to put his emotions on pause to be there for his brother. Nigel will need him,” Nero informed them.

They all nodded in agreement.

Captain Valter stared at Death, “When the time comes, be ready to make your move. Grey’s gift is activated now, and she will be able to see you. At least her faith won’t be hindered. There’s much that’s about to fall on her shoulders.”

“She can handle it,” Bojan assured them. “We will make sure she does.”

Nero understood there was more to this story than his captain and Death were telling. Nevertheless, he knew there was a reason why and he trusted that Jehovah Jireh would provide whatever was necessary to watch over the promise He’d given Nigel about his daughter no matter what it looked like.

“Inform your fellow warriors,” Valter told Bomani and Bojan. “Insidious isn’t much for physical battles, but we must be prepared for anything.” They nodded. “Godspeed,” the captain said dismissing Bomani and Bojan.

They took off in a glorious splendor. The Captain looked at Nero.

“It is time we told you what Jehovah is up to and why we made this decision.”

Chapter 31: Strategy

Monet cleared her desk to prepare for her next client. The curiosity about the context of this meeting nearly had her on the edge of her seat. If it weren't beneath her to be giddy, she would be but opted to maintain her classiness.

Her skin was the color of caramel and flawless. There was always a regal air around her. Her eyes were brown and cunning. She wore her hair in a sleek bob that framed her face. She was average height with a proportional frame. Time had been kind to her.

Since she'd become a wife and a Christian that tried to die to her flesh on a daily basis, her adventures weren't as colorful as they used to be. Spilling her guts to Charles and giving up all the power she felt she wielded from the secrets she held took a little something from her. She would be a liar if she said there were elements of her past that she didn't miss.

Nigel reaching out to her for a meeting without the involvement of Neil gave her some hope to possibly live vicariously through his shenanigans. She marveled at how similar the brothers were in some regards and then completely different in others.

Sliding a few folders into her locked drawer, she headed out of the office to get a cup a coffee. She and Charles had a late-night last night making love like it was going out of style. He had been gone for nearly a month and she missed her man terribly.

Today, her body was reminding her she was a woman nearly 50 years old and she needed her beauty rest. Grinning with the memories of their love session she headed to the Keurig station in the waiting area outside of her office.

From the adjacent office her assistant, Melissa, was shocked to see her walking by. She was a plus sized woman with mocha brown skin. A short sassy cut framed her cherub face. Melissa came around and stood by her door.

"I could have gotten your coffee for you," she told Monet.

Monet waved her off. "No worries. I needed to stretch my legs anyway. Besides Nigel Sims is my next appointment. I need the brain cells to be sharp."

Melissa smirked. "Girl, when he called his voice dern near melted me into a puddle. If he is half as fine as his voice sounds, I'm gon have to repent for all the thoughts I have."

Monet chuckled as she waited for her coffee to brew. "Well, I'm just going, to be honest. Prepare yourself to repent because those two brothers are eye candy." Melissa fanned herself. "And you know you like them light skinned ones and he is definitely that."

"Oh my," Melissa said.

"And he is very married so look only and don't get caught doing that," Monet said laughing.

Melissa laughed too.

Monet took her black coffee and headed back toward her office.

"You can just let him come on in when he gets here," she told Melissa as she took the first hit of her caffeine fix.

"Will do," Melissa told her as she went back to her desk.

†††

Thirty minutes later, Monet looked up to see Nigel Sims glide into her office. His gait was smooth and confident, but she did notice one thing different about him this time around, there was frustration on his face.

She stood. "Good to see you again, Nigel. What brings you by?" she inquired as she extended a hand.

Nigel took her hand and firmly shook it. "It's good to see you too, Mrs. Wesley. It's a bit of a family matter I was hoping to discuss with you," he told her in his smooth deep voice.

"Well, have a seat and we can discuss it."

He paused then asked, "Do you mind if we close the door?"

Monet raised a brow. She tilted her head and stared at him.

"You know your brother paid me a similar visit. He was much more extravagant with his though. Interesting indeed."

Nigel didn't allow his face to give her any inkling of why he was there.

"Go ahead and close the door," she told him.

He obliged, then took a seat. She gestured for him to go ahead.

"I know we don't personally know each other, but you strike me as a very resourceful woman." Monet gave a noncommittal gesture. He continued. "I need you to understand something up front. My lack of detail has less to do with me trusting you and more to do with me just not wanting to get into all the dirty details - it's personal for me." Monet nodded. "I know you're aware that my brother got deeply involved in some special assignments. Many things were revealed by his involvement in the undercover op including the fact that our dead brother may have had a child."

Monet's brow raised, but she continued to listen without interrupting.

"It's imperative that we find her."

Monet frowned. "How do you know it's a her?"

"That one's going to fall into that lack of details category." She nodded. "Trust me when I say, I'm 99.99% sure it's a woman. She's going to be about Neil's age and my gut is telling me she is just as formidable as my brother and I."

Monet understood he was warning her to be careful and not to underestimate her.

"Well it seems like you have quite a bit of information, why not just find her yourself?" Monet inquired.

"Let's just say I feel it necessary to be strategic in this situation. I've studied some of the steps my brother took dealing with these people. I'm choosing to circumvent his naivete and short-sidedness. I'd rather be pulling the strings than directly involved in this instance. From what I understand about you, you won't have a problem getting this information."

"This too big a job for Lauren Carmichael?" Monet asked inquiring about the woman she caught that they'd hired to snoop on her.

"Um, I'm a married man now and I don't do messy little girls who can't accept rejection."

"Well alrighty then. Do you have information for me?"

Nigel reached into an inner pocket in his suit jacket and pulled out a thumb drive.

"On this, you'll find all the background information I have on my brother and his godparents down in Miami."

"Are they still alive?" Monet interrupted.

"She is his godfather isn't."

"Did they have any children?"

"A couple foster kids. The info is in there too," he told her. She nodded. "I want to be as far removed from this as much as possible until I'm ready to expose myself."

"Why is that?" Monet asked.

"She could know about us as well. She may even be looking for us, just like we're looking for her."

"I see," Monet said. She took the thumb drive. "I'm assuming there's a password on this."

"That assumption would be correct."

"What is it?" she asked.

Nigel smiled as he stood up and rebuttoned his suit jacket.

"That would be the kind of dollars you spent to keep what you want hidden in a black cyber abyss."

Monet leaned back in her chair and gave him a look of admiration.

"Wow, you're a clever one, aren't you?"

Nigel simply winked at her then said, "I'll wait to hear from you."

He let himself out.

Monet chuckled as she inserted the thumb drive in her laptop. When it prompted her for a password, she typed in: zeroesandcommas. When the file opened, all she could do was laugh.

As she flipped through the information, she realized this was no laughing matter. She wondered why these brothers were so desperate to find their long-lost niece. She didn't get the vibe from Nigel they were looking to have a good old-fashioned family reunion.

It wasn't her business though. She'd just let the information tell her what she wanted to know. After an hour, Monet was familiar with the file. She shook her head as she picked up the phone to call her best friend Cassia.

Chapter 32: Ghosts of Sins Past

It was a moment of truth that Sheridan honestly wasn't in the mood for. She didn't think she ever would be, but it was necessary to the forward movement of the twin sisters that had endured so much pain, trauma, and abuse.

Sheridan sat in her office with Simone, Tiara and their father, Percy. Fifteen minutes had passed with nothing but silence. Sheridan honestly didn't even know where to start. Simone had confided in her the abuse she'd endured while in her father's care and Sheridan had been completely undone.

The horror made her sick to her stomach. It was time for Percy to know and understand the part he played. His arrogance and selfishness blamed everyone and everything. While the complete blame wasn't all on him, his role was significant and transformative.

Sheridan observed them. Tiara was the most comfortable. She didn't know this man. He was just the sperm donor in her mind. There was zero connection to him. Now that she knew what had been done to her sister, she had no need to connect with him, but she did agree with Sheridan that this meeting was necessary.

Charles had commuted her sentence and pardoned her. Every day she worked on becoming a whole person and striving for the best version of herself.

Simone sat enraged. She watched as her father kept checking his watch like he had something better to do. He really was clueless, and it bothered her. How could he claim to love her so and never know she lived a nightmare in his home many nights?

Percy sighed loudly, "Can we get on with this?"

Before Sheridan could speak, Simone stood up. She got in her father's face. He flinched at the sudden intrusion of his personal space, obviously taken aback by his daughter's show of aggression.

"Yeah, let's get on with this. You nasty, selfish, no good excuse for a human being. You are a waste of skin. You claimed to be somebody's minister. You claimed to have rescued me from the hell my mother left me in. Do you know what you did?"

Percy stared wide-eyed. He had no idea what she was talking about.

"I was the best father to you. I kept a roof over your head. I made sure you had three meals a day and I protected you."

Sheridan thought Simone was going to hit him at that last confession. Instead, she reared back and cackled like a mad woman. Sheridan squirmed in her seat. Tiara dropped her head and shook it.

Percy was deathly afraid. The last time he saw his daughter, she was demon possessed, called him out and viciously attacked him. Simone snapped back into focus. She got close to his face and whispered angrily.

"Protected me! That is the most laughable thing you have ever said. When your wife was away you had your little nasty boyfriend come and keep her side of the bed warm. You didn't think I knew he was creeping in and out. But I knew. I knew because he crept in my room every single time he was there and raped me while you slept in the room down the hall tangled in the sheets of your fornication and adultery. You failed me as a father!"

Percy gasped as tears formed in his eyes. "You're lying! There's no way!" he shouted.

Sheridan and Tiara both sprang up and grabbed Simone as she lunged for him. She managed to scratch his cheek before they pulled her away. Simone was breathing so hard her chest rose and fell conspicuously.

"She isn't lying Percy. This is your daughter's truth. You need to accept it. She needs you to own this so she can move forward in her healing," Sheridan said as gently as she could.

He stared as tears ran down his face.

"It can't be true. He would never..."

Simone screamed so loud that Emma Lee ran into the office. When she opened the door, Sheridan put up her hand.

"It's okay mama. Just family airing their dirty laundry."

Emma Lee scowled at Percy. She couldn't stand him. Sheridan saw her mother's resistance.

"Ma, I'm okay. I'll handle it. Emma Lee searched her daughter's face for the truth. When she was satisfied with what she saw, she nodded and closed the door.

Sheridan and Tiara continued to keep their grip on Simone. They watched as Percy's brow furrowed like he just realized something. Sheridan sighed with relief. It would help Simone greatly if he could own his part. Percy stood up.

"Were you behind his death? Did you take my lover from me?"

All three women stared in sheer disbelief. Sheridan was about to let go of Simone and slap the mess out of him herself. Her angels glorified and sent calm to her.

"You're a cold selfish bastard," Tiara said. "I hope you rot in hell for all eternity."

She let go of her sister, grabbed her purse, and headed out.

"Doc, I'll see you for my next session, but I'm done with this."

Tiara quietly exited the room as she shook her head.

Sheridan couldn't blame her. She wanted to leave too. Simone continued to breathe hard. As Sheridan gripped her arm, she could feel the heat coming from her. Her rage was palpable.

Simone viciously snapped, "I didn't pull the trigger, but I dern sure requested it."

Percy jumped up enraged like he was going to come at his daughter. Sheridan pushed Simone back and stood between them.

"Have you lost your mind? You will meet your maker today if you lay a hand on this woman!" Sheridan threatened.

Percy yelled and screamed as his pain erupted. Sheridan and Simone just stared at him with no emotion whatsoever. Completely unbothered.

"Sir, you need help. You need to seek a professional and it can't be me," Sheridan told him.

"This isn't over," he threatened his daughter.

"Actually, it is. Goodbye, *daddy!*"

Percy cut his eyes at Sheridan and stormed out of the office. Simone broke. Sheridan went to her and held her as the sobs overtook her. Some time had passed before Sheridan was able to calm her down.

"If you want to be delivered from this, truly delivered from all of this, I will help you, but you have to want it."

Simone nodded.

Sheridan asked, "What happened to your father's boyfriend?"

Simone shrugged. "I don't know. This demon came to me one night and asked me if I wanted him to stop hurting me."

Sheridan gasped. "You knew it was a demon?"

Simone nodded. "By that time, Janet had already appeared and remember I was dedicated to the darkness at the age of five. I was definitely tapped in."

"How did you respond?" Sheridan asked afraid of the answer.

"I nodded. He said all you have to do is speak it. So, I did. I spoke his death. A week later my dad lost it during a news segment that detailed his murder from a carjacking."

Sheridan nodded. "That's when you realized you had power."

Simone nodded. "What was I to do? I had been so helpless all my life. People constantly abused and misused me. I was a child! I saw what power I had, and I embraced it. I swore no one would ever hurt me again. That was my voluntary segue into the darkness. The power is what lured me. Little did I know it wouldn't be worth the cost. Those stains on my soul are permanent."

"They don't have to be," Sheridan reassured her. "The Blood of the Lamb is more powerful than any darkness you embraced."

"I want to believe that, but it's hard."

"It's a process. But you will. How do you feel about going to church?"

Simone frowned. "Uh..."

Sheridan laughed. "Okay, baby steps..."

Chapter 33: Caught Off Guard

Two weeks later, Neil and Nigel were summoned to Monet's office. To say they were shocked by such a quick turnaround was an understatement. Though Nigel had inquired, she refused to give him any information over the phone and she insisted that both the brothers be together when she gave them the details.

As they pulled up to the parking lot, Nigel looked at his brother. His usually confident face told a different story today - he was anxious.

"I got a bad feeling about this, bro."

"Yeah, me too," Neil agreed as he got out on the passenger side.

"First of all, how did me, you and dad look into this, find nothing and Monet has the information for two weeks and strikes gold?"

Neil shrugged. "I honestly don't know. But one thing I had to learn when I was navigating the spiritual battlefield God had me on. Some things are blocked spiritually and when certain pieces are moved into position then other things can be revealed. Maybe the information we needed to find her wasn't available until now."

"That's a good way to look at it," Nigel agreed, as they fell in step with each other through the parking lot. He knew this was vital information they desperately needed to know, but he also could sense this would be an emotional bomb he wasn't sure their family could handle. He sighed.

"What are we going to do about mama?"

Neil just shrugged. "I honestly don't know."

They briefly made eye contact as Neil opened the door to The Rahab Center for Redemption. The center was the second of its kind. Monet had opened a facility to house women and children who were trying to recover from life's trauma. It was a safe haven to all that needed it.

Nigel strolled up to the receptionist's desk. Before he could state their business, the petite woman stood and told him, Monet was expecting them, and they should go right up. Neil raised a brow but remained silent.

They took the elevator up to the fifth floor where Monet's office suite sat at the end of the long corridor. Melissa, her receptionist, greeted them.

"Hi, gentlemen. Monet is expecting you. Just go right in," she told them as she held open Monet's door.

As the brother's walked past her their opposing colognes tickled her senses. One was sexy, the other was woodsy. Both made her mind go somewhere she'd have to repent for later. Monet was definitely right about them. One scoop of chocolate and one scoop of vanilla she thought as she closed the heavy cherry oak wood door behind them. She shuddered once at the thought of being caught up in that swirl then headed back to her office.

Monet stood up and came around to greet both brothers with a firm handshake.

"Have a seat, please," she offered directing them to her visitor's chairs.

Monet strolled to her seat. Today she was rocking a red pantsuit that managed to make her look regal, classy, and formidable. Taking her seat, Monet began.

"I know you both probably have a lot of questions as you should. However, once the investigation was complete, I realized this was bigger and deeper than any of us anticipated."

The brothers looked at each other then back at Monet.

"Who is it?" Nigel asked impatiently.

In lieu of an answer, Monet slid them each an identical black folder. Almost as if they were twins, they reached for the folders. Neil opened his first. The picture staring back up at him made his heart drop down to his toes.

"What the hell is this, Monet?" he demanded.

"The truth," she said.

Nigel frowned and opened his folder. The uncharacteristic expletive that fell off his lips didn't shock anyone in the room.

Neil was seething. "This cannot be the truth!"

"It is," Monet said. "Like I said, when I realized who it was, I knew."

Neil tossed the folder back on her desk. "I'm out," he said and stormed out.

Nigel didn't even attempt to stop his brother from leaving. It wasn't that he didn't care. It was simply that he could barely wrap his brain around what they'd just learned. He was still staring at the picture confused, hurt, and severely pissed off.

"Should we go get him?" Monet inquired.

"Nah, he's gon need a minute," Nigel answered simply. His brain was racing a million miles as he finally tore his eyes away from the picture to look at Monet.

"I just got one question. How did you find her, and we never could?"

"You were right. It was your instincts that made me consider the strategy. She was looking for you too. The people Cassia put on Mrs. Matthews saw her go and visit the old lady. Apparently, she's got daddy issues," Monet told him.

Nigel closed his eyes and took a calming breath.

"Thank you. I am in your debt."

Monet nodded. "I may call in that favor one day."

"You've earned it with this."

Nigel scooped up both folders and stood. He needed to go find his brother, and they needed to think up a new strategy - and quick.

"What are you going to do?" she inquired.

"I'm not sure, but I wish I would have put a bullet in that traitorous heifa's head a long time ago."

With that, he was gone. Monet stared at her copy of the file. With the truth now on her side, she stared at Agent Michelle Fuller's face. She could see the resemblance to her father and therefore a resemblance to their mother.

She shook her head and quietly whispered. "Lord, have mercy."

Chapter 34: Coming to Terms

Nigel got off the elevators in the lobby area and began looking for his brother. He was pissed too, but he knew Neil felt a totally different sense of betrayal about this revelation. He and Fuller had been close. They were partners. He had mad love for her until she revealed her true identity as part of the organization who kidnapped his wife and killed their brother. Neil had actually shot her.

As Nigel strolled through the lobby not knowing how to feel he noticed all the women and children who were roaming around the center. He realized some of them were skittish around him. He understood it. He wanted to smile at them to let them know he wasn't a threat, but he just didn't have it in him at the moment.

After searching the lobby for Neil to no avail, he headed out to his truck. When he opened the door, the sun was bright and blinding. He put up the black folders to block it, but quickly realized his brother was not outside. Then it hit him, he knew exactly where Neil was. He surmised that learning the devastating truth of their niece's identity was what made him miss the obvious.

Nigel headed back into the building and went to the men's restroom. He wasn't shocked to see his big brother coming out of the bathroom stall with the back of his hand over his mouth. They locked eyes. Gray eyes stared back at gray eyes. Anger stared back at anger.

Neil didn't say anything but went to the sink where he rinsed out his mouth. The thought of his niece kissing him and trying to seduce him made him sick to his stomach. After he washed and dried his face, he stared at Nigel.

"I know, bro. I know," Nigel told him. "But you didn't. You didn't."

Neil shook his head. "This is some sick mess man."

"I agree, but I need you to get it together," Nigel told him. "We need to read this file."

"I don't want to read the file man."

Nigel just stared at him for a moment then sighed. "Look, I get it. I really do," he said in a sympathetic tone. "But we don't have time for this."

Neil looked at his younger brother and then did something he hadn't in a long while - he cussed. Nigel took a step back and gave him some space. It had been a minute since he'd heard his brother use foul language.

"A'ight, bro," Nigel said.

"I need a minute to process this, okay?" Neil told him angrily.

"And I need to know everything right now," Nigel countered.

Neil sighed heavily.

"I get it," he said after a few moments. "Do you. I'll meet you in the car in a few minutes."

Nigel nodded and left the restroom.

When he left, Neil stared at his face in the mirror. He was seething with pure anger. There were many things about this whole insane journey that pissed him off. Aside from the attempted rape on his wife, this was next in line. The way they felt about family was being challenged and he didn't care for this feeling.

Then there was the guilt. If they would have found her sooner, could she have been a different person? Could they have given their mother a piece of her dead child back? Could they have saved her?

Neil knew enough about Fuller to know the question of could she change to know they would be wasting their efforts. He also realized she hadn't been bred by the gang but recruited. She was too old to have been bred by them. That was some relief because it meant his brother hadn't been a part of the gang.

Still, he hated the feeling gnawing in his gut - *what if their brother wasn't who they thought he was?* That thought he couldn't handle, so he dismissed it.

Neil looked up at the ceiling towards the heavens and whispered a quiet prayer.

He said, "Lord, I need you. I don't trust myself or my motives in this situation."

He sighed again, then headed out. His angels, Ern and Koldo, had never left his side.

†††

In the truck, Nigel was sitting in the driver's seat completely engrossed in the file. Neil opened the door and got in. He put his head back and closed his eyes as the air conditioner blew in his face.

"You good, bro?" Nigel asked without looking up from the file.

"I will be," Neil said dryly.

"Listen, I know you in your feelings about this a lot different than I am, but I need to let you know what's in this file."

Neil sighed for what felt like the fiftieth time in the past five minutes.

"Alright. What's in it?" Neil asked without opening his eyes.

He steeled himself, mentally preparing for the worst.

"First of all, we need Monet on our team, permanently. Boss lady is thorough. Second, your wife was right. She was a twin, the first one didn't make it."

Neil's eyes popped open as he stared at his brother. Nigel looked up and nodded.

"Yeah, the curse didn't bypass Niles. I know you came to the same conclusion that I did, maybe Niles wasn't who we thought he was, but to me, this says that if he was otherwise he would have been spared from the curse."

"Maybe, but remember Black Pearl wasn't an Untouchable, Lucca just used her because of her power. He just got caught up," Neil said.

He'd seen more betrayals than his brother had. It was strategically intelligent to assume the worse, govern yourself accordingly and be surprised when it was the best instead of the reverse. Nigel didn't push, he knew his brother was in a dark place. The darkest place he'd ever seen him in was the day they interrogated Fuller. Neil actually scared *him*, and he was the loose cannon, which was disturbing, to say the least.

"Whoever was watching him, sent old girl to seduce him and she was a member of a local gang, one of the Untouchable founders was using. The intention was always to raise their child up in the gang."

"So, she voluntarily agreed to lose her firstborn? How did she know she would have twins?"

"She couldn't have. Maybe she had planned a long con with him, but once she discovered she was carrying twins, it didn't matter."

Neil shook his head frustrated. "What else?"

"Apparently, she went to see Mrs. Matthews asking about her father and how he died. Did he have any family and what not?"

"How did Monet get that?" Neil asked impressed.

"Your girl had listening devices planted in the nursing home. There are transcripts."

Neil's mouth dropped open. He reached for the transcript and perused it. He just shook his head. He didn't know why he let Monet continue to shock him. There was a reason she was one of the most notorious and respected madams to ever play the game. After all, the intelligence gathering of a madam went all the way back to the Bible days.

"What else?" Neil asked. "Anything on her travel pattern?"

"Yeah, looks like she was in Atlanta before she went down to Miami. Then there's nothing."

"If Mrs. Matthews told her about the family, she could be heading this way via car. There would be no tracing her flight info."

"What's in the transcripts about it?" Neil asked.

"There's nothing that says she got the information, but we can't be for sure. She could have taken the old lady for a walk or something where Monet wasn't listening, you know."

Neil nodded as Nigel continued, "Well, if she knows it's us, she knows she can't just half step so she's going to need time to prepare, strategize." Neil nodded again as his brother continued to theorize. "I can't see her having a personal vendetta against my daughter. No scenario I run in my head gives her cause to personally have it out for my firstborn."

"Well, you just said it. Your first born gets to live, her twin died. Fuller doesn't need much to go on," Neil pointed out.

"Dang, I guess I missed that one."

"Also, she's a soldier. She doesn't need a reason to follow orders and you can bet someone from the Untouchables is still around and they are pulling her strings dangling revenge in her face. Remember, ego and pride are her downfalls and she's pissed at me and you. She knows how we feel about what we love. She could just come after your daughter as a means to be the most effective way to hurt and cripple you."

Nigel thought over the knowledge his brother dropped. The fact that Neil came to these conclusions and he didn't made him realize finding out who their niece was had affected him just as deeply, it just manifested differently.

"You're right, bro. But just so someone says this... Is there any way possible she wants a family, her real family? Alonzo turned because of Marcus. He gave up his freedom and power all for his son."

"Michelle is different Nigel and I'm personally not even going to let myself entertain that thought. When someone shows you who they are, believe them. She ran a double bluff on me without batting an eye. With the exception of her giving up her fear to me, that was her only mistake. She's good, man, she's good."

Nigel nodded.

"I tell you what though, now that I know who she is, I have no problem shooting first and letting God sort out the details."

Nigel stared at his brother. His eyes were steel gray.

"Neil..."

"Just drive bro, I'm not trying to hear nothing you have to say. I'm over it."

Nigel shook his head, put the car in reverse and drove off.

Chapter 35: Safe Place

Neil could not explain all the emotions and turmoil that were going on inside of him. He truly did not understand why his family had to endure such drama over and over and over again. It was like a perpetual cycle of emotional bombs that was designed to cripple their sanity. Even if he did have complete understanding, he still didn't think it would make sense to him.

Nigel dropped him off at the precinct. He didn't even bother going back inside to deal with stuff he knew he needed to. His sole desire right now was to get to his wife, wrap himself around her and receive the comfort only she could give. He had text Beau after his initial shock and told him to bring Grey and Hunter back home. He would personally bring them back the next morning. He didn't care, he needed his wife.

He was struggling the most with handling the dark side Fuller managed to bring out of him. He vividly remembered the day they interrogated her. He meant every threat he told her. It was very scary to admit, but it was the truth and he needed to deal with it.

Grey was his tether. She could always reel him in when he went too far, but he didn't know if she could reach him from this dark place. Then there was guilt. In his mind, when this moment of truth happened, he assumed he would have been using all his efforts to keep Nigel in check. Now, they both would be loose cannons. In this instance, he would fail his baby brother. He couldn't protect him like this. He just wasn't strong enough to shield Nigel from himself as well as handle his own emotions about it.

Logically, he knew it wasn't worth it, but emotionally and territorially, he wasn't trying to hear that. She didn't take Eva from him, but she took Eva's sister from her. She helped them hold his wife hostage, and she'd plotted for months to seduce him just so she could kill him.

Even if she was capable of change, he didn't want her in his life. This was a family reunion that just wasn't going to happen. It didn't matter how he sliced it, she had to go. He could not make his peace with her being in their lives. He just didn't see it happening. He drove home in silence, his head throbbing mercilessly.

Twenty minutes later, he pulled up to his home. He used the remote to open the two-car garage and pulled his pickup truck inside. He let the garage down before he hopped out of the truck. His footsteps were slow and heavy. This new revelation was weighing him down mind, body, and spirit. Something had to give.

When he came into the house, he entered through the hallway behind the kitchen. As he came around the corner, he saw Grey entering from the other side. She had the baby monitor in her hand. He figured she heard the garage door open.

"Baby, what is it? What's wrong?" she asked as soon as she laid eyes on him.

Neil didn't respond as he approached his wife. He reached for her and pulled her into him. Taking her mouth, he kissed her desperately.

When he released her, she said, "Okay, what's up babe?"

"I need you." She stared at him. His eyes were a dark gray. Something was very wrong.

"Neil..."

"No, I don't wanna talk. I just need to be with you right now."

She frowned. He reached down and grabbed her hand leading her to their room.

Grey was sincerely confused. She'd seen many of his mood swings, but this was a new one. It had to be serious if he pulled her away from Kadijah. She held his hand and let him pull her to their bedroom.

When they entered it, he closed the door and pressed her up against it. He kissed her again completely catching her off guard.

When he released her, he asked, "Is Hunter asleep?"

"Yeah, he fell asleep on the drive." He nodded as he attempted to kiss her again. "Wait, baby... Hold up," she said trying to figure out what was going on.

He put his forehead and nose on hers. It was a common intimate gesture, they shared. It made her relax a little bit though she was still worried about him. This wasn't like him.

"Baby tell me what's up," Grey pleaded.

"I'm in a dark place and I need you. I don't want to talk about it right now," he told her frustrated. Grey frowned. Neil stared into her eyes and pleaded, "Just be my wife right now. I need you to make love to me."

She watched his eyes and saw the unshed tears magnifying the cold gray. She nodded then kissed him on the forehead. When she did, the tears slipped down his cheeks. It was rare he freely let his emotions show without her having to pry them out of him. Whatever this was, it had deeply hurt or angered him. She would do her very best to take the pain away.

Grey kissed his tears away as he held her tightly. She led him to their bed. There were no more words as she slowly undressed him leaving a trail of kisses. Neil blanked everything from his mind except for his wife and this moment. Her touch was like a soothing balm. It never failed to comfort him when he needed it the most. She undressed and joined him on the bed.

Slowly she showered him with love, affection, and adoration. She whispered in his ear how much she loved him and believed in him. She continued to use her words to speak life to him and over him. The tears continued to fall down his cheeks.

She grabbed his face, "Look at me, Neil." He opened his eyes. They were a vivid green as he stared into her big brown ones. "I'll always love you, baby. All of you. Your dark, your light, your good, your bad and your ugly. I will never stop loving you. I need you to know that." He nodded as she spoke. "Tell me you know that."

He hugged her and squeezed her tight as he whispered in her ear. "I know baby. Thank you for loving all of me."

Grey kissed him passionately as she continued to give him what he asked for. His release was just what he needed to relieve the tension and the headache that had plagued him since the revelation.

Grey continued to place soft kisses on his face, neck and chest. He ran his hands through her hair enjoying the warmth of her body on his. Wrapping her in his arms, he decided he wasn't ready to let her go yet. They lay there in silence as Neil continued to hold his wife tight.

She desperately wanted to know what was wrong but knew she needed to let him confess it to her on his own terms. Neil shifted to lay behind his wife. He buried his face in the back of her neck as he pulled her to him.

"I know you want to know what's bothering me, Grey. I can feel the tension in your body," he quietly spoke. "Just give me some space. You already know I wouldn't keep anything this serious from you. I just... need a minute, okay."

She nodded as she squeezed his hand. He sighed with relief and closed his eyes. It wasn't five minutes before she felt his breathing change. She knew he had fallen asleep. Sleep, however, wasn't going to find her, so she began to silently pray for whatever was going on. She wasn't in the mood for the enemy today and she wasn't about to let anything come into her marriage - that just simply was not an option.

An hour later, Grey finally dozed off only to be woken by Hunter's cries. She jerked awake and sat up. When she sat up, Neil grabbed her wrist.

"I'll get him, baby," he told her.

She stared at him and raised a brow wondering how long he had been awake. Neil climbed out of bed and slipped his jeans back on. A few minutes later, he came back in kissing their son's chubby cheeks.

"How's daddy lil man?"

Hunter garbled nonsense in reply. Grey smiled. She loved to see her husband with their son. It stirred something deep in her soul to see how much he loved his seed. She grabbed his shirt off the floor and slipped it on.

Neil and Hunter sat on the bed as he continued to play with his son. Grey kissed her baby boy. Hunter continued to giggle as his parents made a fuss over him.

"Uh oh, somebody needs a diaper change," Neil said.

"So that's why he woke up hollering. I'll go grab a diaper and wipes."

Grey left as Neil held his son close to his chest and kissed the top of his head. When Grey walked back in, she heard him say, "I love you, Hunter. As long as there is breath in my body, I will protect you from anyone or anything that seeks to bring you harm. No matter who they are. Your daddy loves you so much."

Again, there were silent tears running down his face. Grey was beyond alarmed now.

"Okay, Neil, I can't. Like I just can't. You have got to tell me what is going on?"

Neil looked up at her startled, a rarity. He hadn't noticed her return.

"You heard that, huh?"

"Yeah, I did. Now start talking," she said with her hands on her hips.

He nodded knowing she was all out of patience with him as he lay Hunter down and started removing his dirty diaper. Grey handed him the new diaper and wipes.

Neil let out a deep sigh, then said, "Nigel and I met with Monet today."

Grey frowned. "Why?" she asked

He continued changing his son's diaper as Hunter giggled. "She had some information for us. Apparently, Nigel enlisted her to find our niece because he had a feeling that she might be looking for us and he wanted to have the strategic advantage." Grey's brow continued to furrow deeper. "Monet never ceases to amaze me, but she found our niece."

Grey shrieked and startled their son. Neil closed the fastener on the new diaper then scooped the baby up as Grey stared at him dumbfounded. He walked out of the room to dispose of the soiled diaper in the genie as he calmed Hunter back down.

When he walked back in, Grey was still staring at him in shock.

"Who is she, Neil?"

He sighed as he rocked his son. "It's Fuller. Our niece is Agent Michelle Fuller."

There was a sound that came out of Grey's mouth, but neither of them could decipher it. She shook her head in disbelief.

"How in the..." she stopped not even sure of the question she wanted to ask. Neil took a seat on their bed as he continued to hold his son close. Hunter was sucking on his fingers oblivious to the drama that was unfolding around him.

Grey climbed on the bed and just stared.

"You were right," Neil told her.

"About what?" she asked half afraid.

"Apparently, she was a twin, she's the second born. The first one didn't survive."

Grey gasped as she clutched her chest. "Wait! Just wait a minute! I need to process this."

She jumped down off the bed and began to pace. She was heated. She had no love for this woman and now she had to accept her as family. Grey continued to pace and think. Neil just let her because he knew when the shock wore off, she would get back to him. It took a few minutes, but after a while, everything began to register. Grey stopped her pacing and looked at her husband.

"Okay, I get it now. You're no longer worried about Nigel taking her out, you want to."

Neil simply stared at her. His silence provided all the answer she needed. Grey moved to sit next to him.

"Oh, baby... I get it, I really do, but you can't."

"Grey, once she figures out who we are to her, she is going to come after everything I love. That's you and my son. I already told you if anyone ever comes for my seed, there is no trying to convince me of anything, and you already know I will nut up about you in a heartbeat. It's really simple, find the threat and eliminate it before she even gets a chance to come for mine. I cannot tell you how many ways I've plotted to take her out and make sure there's never a trace she ever existed."

Grey frowned. He was dead serious. This was too much. This was his family, but he was right. Fuller wanted revenge. She escaped from federal custody to ensure she'd get it. This was a woman on a mission. Not just any woman, but a highly trained, highly skilled vindictive woman.

"But baby, your mother..."

"I know," he said. "I'm torn because I could never admit it to anyone but you and Nigel. And you two shouldn't have to carry that burden. I would be taking her only link to her dead son, but I know this woman. My mother will never be able to see her clearly. All she is going to see is Niles. Fuller isn't going to stop until she gets what she wants. I believe she's a threat to Nigel's daughter but only because of the blood she carries. She's a threat to my child because of her need to cause me harm. She needs to finish what she started. Her ego and her pride won't let her settle for anything less."

Grey nodded. She finally got it. Their brother's daughter wasn't coming for Nigel's daughter, she was a way for the enemy to regain access to their bloodline. She knew they couldn't touch Hunter, but Neil wasn't trying to hear that right now.

At that moment, Savas, touched her shoulder, "See Grey," he instructed.

Her eyes flamed as revelation hit her. She turned to her husband and grabbed his face to ensure she had his full attention. "Baby, you gotta listen to me," Grey implored. "We had it wrong the whole time. Remember Simone told me it was not a coincidence." Neil frowned. "This isn't just about the babies. It's about you and Nigel."

"What do you mean?"

"Don't you see? If you or Nigel take out your niece, it's murder. Now that you know who she is, the enemy is betting on the fact that you will simply take her out rather than risk her coming after your family and causing any harm. The enemy doesn't need to take you out, he's dangling the perfect coup de grace in your face to make you take yourself out. Your gift, they've been after it for decades. They can't touch you, but you can. It will destroy your family. Your mother will not be able to reconcile with that. Think about it, baby. Just think. I know how you feel right now, but I know your heart. Inside and out and you won't be able to live with this. You won't. Your anger is clouding your judgment right now. If you and Nigel are the reason why they lost the war for this state, why not find a way to take you both out so you'll never be a problem again."

Neil stared at his wife. He understood, but he really didn't care.

"She's a threat to everything I love, I can't say that I can just stand back and do nothing. I can't just let her come for you and my son," he said.

"But we are okay, she can't touch us, don't you get that."

"I can't take that risk, Grey. I can't."

She sighed.

"We've seen God come through in so many ways. Don't you trust Him?"

"You're right," he started callously. "And you know what else I've seen? I've seen demon-possessed men come for you. I've seen a man try to force himself on you. I've also seen my daughter die. I've seen my pregnant wife get kidnapped. I've seen what I thought was my best friend get killed right in front of me. Even though it wasn't her, her life has to be spent in hiding. I've studied the crime scene photos from my brother's brutal murder for years," he recounted angrily.

Tears ran down Grey's face. Hunter's gentle coo directly contrasted the ugliness currently surrounding them.

"Baby, I get it. I really do. I can't say that I wouldn't want to take her out if the opportunity presented itself," she paused and looked him squarely in the eyes as she spoke. "But this isn't who you are. It's not."

She studied his hardened face and noticed his eyes were back to gray. "I don't have any more cheeks to turn, I'm sorry," he responded resolutely.

Tears swam in Grey's eyes. "This isn't who you are, Neil."

"Maybe it is," he said as he held his son close.

His angels Ern and Koldo, looked at each other.

"Insidious is formidable indeed," Ern said.

Koldo, his Basque warrior, nodded, "He found a way to manipulate them and never step out of the boundaries Father set."

Savas and Bojan sent strength to Grey. She would need to fight for her husband like never before.

Chapter 36: Battle of the Sexes

Two weeks of being babysat and Kadijah was over it. They had just cleared the house of the chicken smell. She could add poultry to the growing list of things that made her nauseous. She felt bad, that she was torturing these strangers with her dramatic mood swings, emotions, and nausea.

She didn't understand how Grey just rolled with it. Then she remembered Grey was kidnapped. This incarceration had to be more pleasant than that, which explained why their current situation didn't even phase her. She wanted to go home. She wanted to talk to her husband. All she got was a few texts throughout the day. She didn't understand how Grey was able to leave for a day and she wasn't. She was beyond irritated.

What were they doing? Had they found their niece yet? She hated to admit it, but she wondered if he used Lauren Carmichael to locate his niece. After all, she was, "the best." She shook the idea from her mind because that anxiety upped the risk of having her baby delivered by this bootleg doctor.

Grey noticed Kadijah's anxiety. The bouncing leg was a giveaway. Grey sighed.

"Girl, I'm not gon tell you no more to relax. It's going to take as long as it's going to take."

"I'm trying, Grey," Kadijah rolled her eyes. "This just isn't my scene and I'm so uncomfortable."

Grey remembered the discomfort of her pregnancy so it's not like she couldn't sympathize. It's just that she was adaptable, and it was frustrating to deal with someone who wasn't. Thankfully, she'd had an idea.

"I had Darryl bring me something this morning."

"What's that," Kadijah asked curiously.

Grey pulled a pack of playing cards out of her back pocket. She shook the box.

"You interested in a game of spades? I hear they got some hard-core players."

Kadijah raised a brow. "You know I love you sis, but I can't be your partner."

"I'm not asking you to. I would never cheat on Nigel with his wife."

"I feel the same about Neil. Now that we're agreed, who's playing."

Kadijah managed to get herself up with some effort. She took the cards from Grey and wobbled over to the table. Grey grinned. Once Grey sat down to play, Hunter let out a wail in protest to something.

Grey shook her head. "Beau, you want to take my place?" she asked in annoyance. The big man chuckled at her reaction and walked over to the table.

"Sure, I'm down."

Grey went to the master bedroom. "What you in here fussing bout, sir?" she asked playfully when she entered. There was Hunter, attempting to pull himself up in his crib, wailing and reaching for his mother.

Grey picked him up. She cradled him close to her chest and kissed his forehead.

"You hungry?"

Grey took a seat on the bed, then began to breastfeed her son. As she fed her son, she could hear the trash talking and laughing. Grateful that perhaps this would take Kadijah's mind off the obvious, at least for a little while. She pulled out her phone and sent Neil a text:

She's getting a little stir crazy. Work smart but work fast.

Grey returned to the fray after Hunter had been fed and changed. She was enjoying seeing Kadijah have fun and relax. Watching the spade table for a few minutes, she was about to get comfortable until she tuned in to the debate in the living room. She turned to listen in.

"Man, these females don't want a grown man. And they definitely don't want an alpha-male in their space. They too busy trying to be a man to get a man."

Grey raised a brow as she placed kisses on her son's face. One of the young men saw her standing up. He quickly offered his seat to her. She smiled. For these to be hardcore "thugs," they were so polite. Grey took a seat then crossed her legs.

"All I'm saying is a brother is still looking for his queen because I keep running into Miss Independent who is more concerned with proving she's my equal than my woman. How do I get an attitude because I hold the door for you? I mean dang. Can a brother be a gentleman?"

Grey frowned.

One of them added, "Tell her to be your equal when it's time to kill them bugs!"

The guys fell out laughing. Some of them high fived. Grey chuckled. She decided to stay out of it.

"Nah, but for real man, I'm frustrated. I love her, but she trippin'. That's why when Stephan hit me up for this trip, I was like, bet. I need a break. Do you know before she blew up, I was about to propose!"

"What?" one of his guys asked, shocked. "See sometimes God has a way of saving you when you just determined to be stupid. I told you not to marry that girl. She don't want a husband, she wants a child. I'm telling you. God just spared you from a lifelong headache."

"Oh my," Grey said.

"I'm just saying," the dissenter shrugged looking at Grey.

"No disrespect," the brokenhearted told Grey.

"None taken," Grey said as she bounced Hunter on her lap.

"Do you have an opinion on it?" another asked.

"That's not enough information for me to make a blanket statement about the sista, so I'll pass," Grey replied. "However, I am a woman who appreciates a chivalrous man. Not all women do. It's a preference thing. Sometimes it's not worth the fight."

"You know how old ladies look at you when you let your woman open her own door and your big manly behind standing there very capable."

Grey chuckled. "I get it, I really do. But you're not in a relationship with the old lady, or your mama for that matter. That's not really a battle that's worth the war. If you have real fundamental differences then I agree with your boy, take a minute to reassess before pledging her forever," Grey told him.

"Okay, I gotta ask," another said. "You stay with a gun on your hip, you're very take charge as we've all seen. It's hard to believe you just fall in line when your husband says so."

Grey shot him a look. "Fall in line though? Mkay, I see we are going to have to work on your descriptive words. Ain't nobody falling in line. It's called respect for the man I married," she quipped. The young man who'd made the comment at least had the good sense to look sheepish. Grey shook her head slightly and trudged on.

"I get what you're saying, but don't get it twisted now. My husband is the King of his castle. It's true, I am an alpha-female, but he's an alpha-male. I don't subscribe to the notion that there can only be one alpha and the other has to be a beta, at least not if they are different genders. Because I strongly believe you can't have two big cats in a house be it alpha/alpha or alpha/beta. Two queens cannot operate in one castle, period. No mama's boys accepted!"

"Amen," Kadijah interjected to show gender solidarity.

"No offense, Grey, but I've only been around you for a few weeks and most men couldn't handle you," one of the men said honestly.

"Well, the one I said I do to, doesn't *handle* me. He loves me and it's just that simple. Why do y'all act like a strong woman is some terrorist unleashed on the male species that needs to be *handled* or *tamed*?"

"Strong women want masculine men when it's convenient for them and it's like they get their rocks off trying to emasculate a brother. They want a grown man in the bedroom and a little boy in the other rooms of the house," another chimed in.

"Well, see you're not dealing with a grown woman, but a little girl playing dress up."

"That part," Kadijah said as she slammed a trump card.

"Care to elaborate?" he asked.

"Sure," Grey said as she passed Hunter over to Mason, the bootleg doctor as Kadijah had not-so-affectionately named him. Her son had migrated to him for some reason. She was cool with it because kids were the best judges of character. "Take me for example, clearly an alpha female, however, there's something I understand about being with an alpha male. An alpha female in a relationship with an alpha male understands that the control she yields is because he gives it to her."

"You mean, he allows her to have it," one of the guys interjected.

Grey shot him a lethal look.

"Ouch," another one said.

"*No,* I mean he *gives* it to her. The word allows implies, she's under some type of rationing system, which a relationship should never be. I said what I said. If he's truly an alpha male he's always in control of the situation. However, you can be in control without being controlling. Neil and Nigel are clearly both alphas, but you never see them bump heads when they are in the same space? Why? Because they are wise enough to know that just because they have dominating personalities doesn't mean that they dominate in all things. They each are strong in certain areas. They always give priority to whoever is best suited to handle the situation. Their father taught them that. For that same reason, the alpha male gives control to the alpha female because he recognizes things she's better suited at handling than him. It's not about ego for him. An alpha that is controlled by his ego is a beta playing dress up! And because she is also an alpha, he can trust her to handle things in his absence or incapacity at a similar level in which he would even if it's in a different way than he would. If she understands this, it should boost her ego instead of creating a grab for power. They work together. Teamwork and keeping God first is the key."

She paused to gather her thoughts.

"For instance, think about a flame from a lighter. There's the blue flame and the orange flame. Which one is hotter?"

"The blue one," one of the men said.

"Which one burns?" she quizzed.

"They both burn," he continued to answer.

"Exactly. But why," she asked rhetorically. "Because they are the same flame one is just closer to the source of oxygen. The blue flame is the foundation for the orange flame; therefore the orange flame gets her power from the blue flame. But they are still the same flame. You aren't trying to get burned by the orange flame, but you definitely don't want to get touched by the blue one. That's the way I see two alphas that work together in a marriage. My baby doesn't have an ego, so he lets me shine because he knows when I shine, he shines too because I carry his name. And I have zero problems with him doing his thing. Hell, it turns me on."

Everyone fell out laughing.

"So no, as an alpha female I do not feel threatened by an alpha male and he definitely doesn't feel threated by me."

"What's up with feeling threatened in your relationship anyway?" Kadijah interjected. "I mean you made the choice to be in a relationship with that person. How jacked up are your insecurities that you would feel your significant other, your intimate partner would be a threat. That is insane. I don't care if you're alpha, beta, delta, or omega, for that matter. If you are not mature enough to be a partner to and with your significant other, you don't need to be in anybody's relationship and you dern sho ain't got no business being anybody's spouse!" With that, she slammed down another trump card.

"And mic drop," Grey said laughing.

The men were stunned at Kadijah's bold statement. Grey could tell by their faces they didn't expect anything like that to come from her.

"I told y'all, don't sleep on my girl. Just 'cause she not violent like the rest of us, don't mean she is anybody's pushover."

They all nodded expressing a new admiration for the women they'd been sent to protect.

Chapter 37: Fast Friends

Stephan watched Grey from afar as she managed to keep Kadijah calm, yet again. He was thoroughly fascinated by this woman who talked about God every chance she got but felt right at home with his bunch of misfits.

Beau walked up to Stephan. "She is intriguing, isn't she?"

Stephan caught the subtle accusation in Beau's voice and smiled.

"Chill big man, it's not even like that. My heart beats for one woman."

"That's good because Neil would kill you about *that* one."

"Oh, that's fa sho. I peeped that day one. No worries, we're very professional."

Beau nodded. "Mr. Sims wouldn't have hired you if you weren't. I think he's worse than Neil."

Stephan laughed. "Nigel is one scary negro. Trust me, I know. Neil seems to trust you emphatically with what's most precious to him."

Beau nodded. "I'm a professional too. Besides, I love Miss Grey and I would never let anything happen to her or my lil homie, Hunter. We've been through a lot together. She's special and she has a way of taking God's most wayward creations and loving them in spite of."

Stephan rubbed his chin as he continued to observe Grey distracting Kadijah with Hunter.

"Yeah, she does have a way about her. I really wonder what makes her tick."

As if Grey could sense her name in their conversation, she looked up at them. They looked like they were up to no good to her. She walked over to them on the wrap around porch.

"What are you two up to?" she asked, hands on her hips.

They laughed.

"Nothing, Miss Grey. I'm gonna head in and hang out with Hunter for a bit."

Grey raised a brow. She watched as Beau went back inside the house then turned her attention back to Stephan.

"Can I ask you something?" he began.

"Sure," she said as she leaned against the railing. "What's up?"

"What have you observed about your *babysitters*?" he asked with a smirk.

She laughed. "Oh, you heard that."

"I hear everything," he said confidently.

"I'll remember that," she told him. "Well, I've observed that you guys are well organized. You work as one unit. Each man completely trusts you. They may not completely trust each other, but they trust that you trust everyone. If that makes sense."

He nodded and glanced up at his boys that were in eyesight. "Perfect sense."

"They are scared of me and nervous as hell around Kadijah."

Stephan laughed.

"I will neither confirm nor deny that."

Grey grinned. "No need, I know I'm right. I can be very off-putting, but I assure you, I'm harmless."

"Harmless?" Stephan repeated with a chuckle. "I don't think so. You may not be a direct threat to them, but harmless you are not."

Grey smirked and shrugged.

"What else?" he asked.

"Whatever Nigel did for you it was serious. Because your mind is here with us, but your heart is with whoever holds it. And your face lights up when you talk to her, and the rest of the time no one even sees your teeth."

He stared at her then laughed.

She shrugged and answered the unspoken question in his eyes.

"The way you watch me with my son tells me you miss the loves of your life, something awful. The way you handle Kadijah shows me you have a great respect for the role a woman plays in bringing forth life."

He sighed. "They are my heartbeats."

"Son or daughter?" Grey asked.

"Daughter. Man, she's got me wrapped around her finger."

Grey grinned. "I just bet. Tell me about the lady who's got your heart."

He smiled wide showing all his teeth. It made Grey's heart smile. She missed her heartbeat something awful.

"Chantal is the realist chick I know. She been riding with me since middle school. The epitome of a ride or die."

"Wow, that's a long time."

"People say that all the time, but it doesn't feel like it. We've spent 20 birthdays together and I can't wait to spend another 50 with her."

Grey smiled. "Any more kids?"

"We can't have any more of our own, but maybe we'll adopt."

"Oh, I'm sorry to hear that."

"Don't be. God has been good to a knucklehead like me. I'm grateful."

"Amen," Grey said.

She wanted to broach the subject of God but didn't feel the release in her spirit.

Instead, she asked, "What did Nigel do for you to make you take this assignment with zero hesitation?"

Stephan whistled and rubbed the back of his neck.

"That's the kind of thing you don't really talk about," he said cautiously. "But what I will say is, he's the reason I can still hold my wife and baby girl in my arms."

Grey nodded. She wouldn't be asking anymore about that. Stephan asked a question of his own.

"How did you become so observant? I thought you worked in like accounting or something."

She laughed. "Let's just say I'm married to a real one."

Stephan laughed. "Clearly."

Grey laughed too. "I was observant before him. I'm one of those people who is always observing, but I don't know that I'm doing it until something is different and I immediately notice something is off. Being around Neil made me more conscious of it. Being around Nigel made me learn how to draw conclusions."

He nodded. "So, none of this rubbed off on your sister-in-law, huh?"

Grey laughed. "My sister-in-*love* is cut from a different cloth. Her strengths lie in other areas. Don't be fooled by her girly ways. She'll grow a pair when she needs to."

Stephan laughed. "Okay."

"She's really nervous right now. And she's a die-hard pacifist so all you violent negroes make my dawg nerves bad."

He laughed. "Then how in the world did she manage to be *your* friend and marry Nigel of all people?"

Grey laughed. "Well, Nigel is a charming little something, I tell you. She tried to resist him, but in the end, destiny was too much for her to argue with. And as for me, I wasn't always like this. I mean, I always exercised my second amendment rights living in a stand your ground state you know, but I wasn't always at this level. I'll have to claim guilt by association on my new outlook on life."

"What happened?" he asked sincerely curious.

"You must not watch your local news, sir."

"I try not to..." his voice trailed off.

Pushing off the railing, he stood to his full height as he turned to stare at her. His eyes grew wide. She knew realization had just hit him.

"You're the woman from Florida who was kidnapped." Grey raised a hand and grinned sheepishly.

"Guilty," she said.

"Wow," he said staring at her still. "And Hunter... you were pregnant with him during all this?"

"I was," she nodded.

"I see you thorough, huh?"

Grey hollered in laughter. "I wouldn't say all that."

"Well, what would you call it?"

"Blessed and extremely favored and doing the work of the Lord."

Suddenly, there was a sound like someone stepped on a tree branch. They both turned. Stephan's hand flew to the butt of the pistol he kept on his hip. Grey had her gun out and in front of her. It was pointed at the ground at a 45-degree angle, but her finger was not on the trigger.

Realizing it was just a branch falling off a tree across the street, they both relaxed. Grey holstered her weapon. Stephan looked at her and raised a brow. He knew she was trained because she didn't immediately point the gun at anyone or anything and she didn't put her finger on the trigger, which meant she had control and she wasn't panicking. Her speed had to be part training, part natural ability. She was a paradox indeed.

"Weren't you just about to preach?" he asked.

"Let me tell you something. My baby boy is in that house. I take zero chances with his life and safety. God loaned that gift to us to keep safe. I take my job very seriously. You want to see me act a monkey fool? Threaten my child."

Stephan threw his hands up in surrender. "A'ight thug mama. I got you."

Grey rolled her eyes and went back into the house as Stephan laughed and shook his head. She was alright with him. He really wished she and Chantal could meet.

Chapter 38: Family Ties

Agent Michelle Fuller
Supai, Arizona

When my feet hit the desert sand after the helicopter dropped me off, I got pissed just on principle alone. It was too hot for this foolishness, but a girl had to do what a girl had to do. I pulled the brim of my hat down lower and slipped on my sunglasses.

I had to look up this remote place and familiarize myself with it. This city was found deep within an inner gorge of the Grand Canyon. It was arguably the most remote place in the United States, a population of less than 600.

It was so basic even the U.S. Census Bureau had been known to miss it. It was one of only two places in the U.S. where the mail was carried out by mule train. The pilot rambled and told me the village had a small café, lodge, post office, school, church, clinic, police station and a general store.

When we flew overhead, I saw the beautiful falls the pilot called the Havasu Falls. It was home to the Havasupai Indians. As annoyed as I was, the history lesson was valuable because knowledge was always power.

Dressed in a tank top, cargo shorts and Timberland boots, I grabbed my duffle off the ground and swung it over my shoulder. I knew because this hole in the Grand Canyon had a very tiny population, everyone would know I didn't belong.

I refused the donkey to ride into town and told the local, I would trek it. He looked at me strangely, but I had zero cares to give. The desert heat was merciless, but I was fueled by something much stronger - revenge.

It was time me and my dear sis had a nice chat. I risked getting to one of my storage units in Central Florida and got some cash and weapons. Found a local hacker and got him to get me into the FBI. I screwed him and slit his throat. It wasn't personal, I simply couldn't afford to leave a trail of witnesses.

Hacking into the FBI I discovered what damage had been done as the organization came crumbling down. Needless to say, I was very disturbed about the vials of blood that were listed in the reports. I was bothered and flattered that after they contacted Neil about my escape, he told them to move the vials and keep them under heavy lock and key because I could possibly try to retrieve them.

I found that to be extremely interesting. It gave credence to the gibberish Lucca was talking about. Though I loathed the man, I couldn't wait to stop him from breathing, but Neil was a solid cop. He believed in facts and evidence. If he believed there was something to the vials, then I had to readjust my thinking.

Lucca said I lacked imagination. I couldn't be caught out here in these streets unprepared because I was shortsighted. Maybe I shoulda kept the hacker alive and paid him to be my personal do boy.

He was a smart one. He managed to detect a hack on my files that originated from here. That was odd because who would be looking for me, here. After further digging, I almost fell out of my chair when I discovered Neil's partner Eva was alive and well.

I don't know how she managed that one, but she'd be interrogated soon enough. The ping on her IP address got me fairly close. I would have to find a place to set up surveillance and wait for my opportunity to make sure this little family reunion went exactly the way I wanted it to.

†††

Early the next morning, I watched from the house across the street as Eva saw her children and husband off. She stood on the porch with a smile as she waved goodbye. Taking a sip of her coffee, she sat in one of two rocking chairs on the porch.

I heard the old lady I had tied up gag.

"Listen, lady. I got business here. When I'm done, they'll come and find you. If I hear one more peep out of you, you die. It's really simple. Do you understand me?"

She nodded as she looked at me with tears in her eyes. The duct tape I had over her mouth was covered in her tears. I ignored her and continued to watch Eva.

I dug through my duffle, pulled out my Beretta and put it in my waistband. I put my hat and sunglasses back on then grabbed the remote detonator off the table and headed across the street.

The nosy old lady told me that Eva's husband was usually gone for about two hours every morning. After he dropped the kids off at school, he went for a run and then a swim in the Havasu Falls. He did this on a daily. Apparently, these falls were about 15 miles away.

Routine was so comforting to the average Joe, but to a woman like me, it was space and opportunity. I slipped out of the front door and headed across the street. It didn't take her long to focus on me. Her skin was bronze denoting our Hispanic heritage. Her five-foot-three frame was petite and compact, which I already knew was misleading. I would not underestimate her. I knew she was deadly. Her brunette hair was long and wavy, she wore it pulled back into a ponytail.

She immediately went rigid deciding either she didn't know me and *thought* I was a threat, or she recognized me and *knew* I was a threat. I saw her hand moving toward a table.

I spoke clearly, "Uh-uh." I held up the detonator in my hand. She stared. "Touch that gun and you die."

She pulled her hand back.

"Who are you?" She asked.

I removed my hat and glasses. She gasped and spilled her coffee all over her. She cursed as the hot liquid splashed on her exposed thighs. All she was wearing was a fluffy purple robe covered in butterflies. I was impressed by the foul language she used to consult me about what I was doing here.

I walked onto the porch and put my glasses back on but chose to leave the hat off. After all, it was hot as Satan's butt crack out here in the middle of nowhere.

"How do I know that's really rigged to something?" she asked as she stared at me with anger practically leaping off of her.

"Would I bluff?" I asked smugly.

I pushed a button on the detonator, and she heard the beep come from behind her. She stood up and looked at the side of her house. It was clear she would be cooperative now. She glanced across the street.

"Did you hurt her?" she asked referring to the old woman.

"She'll live," I told her.

"I'm going to assume if you wanted to kill me, I'd already be dead. So, get to your point and get the hell away from me."

"You're a smart woman, but then we do share the same DNA, so I shouldn't expect any less."

She stared at me. "You know," she stated more than asked.

I nodded. "Now, my question to you is how are you still alive? I killed you."

Anger turned her Hispanic face a tint of red.

"I don't die that easily."

I whipped my Beretta out and pointed it in her face. "Enough with the rhetoric. My time is precious and limited. I'm here for a purpose and I don't appreciate you wasting my time."

She spit at me. That was ballsy. It landed near my boot. I looked at her and had to take a deep breath because I almost ended her life right then and there for the disrespect.

"Answer me," I said.

"You murdered my sister in cold blood, you coward."

It was my turn to be stunned. I quickly recovered.

"You had an identical twin?"

"Had being the operative word."

That took me for a loop. "Are there any more of us?" I asked.

"Not to my knowledge," she said.

"How did you find out about me?"

"Our sister had a file on you. I didn't find it until after you killed her."

"Why were you tracking me?"

I could tell my question disconcerted her.

"My sister's blood."

I winged up my brow. "An eye for an eye, aye sis?"

She nodded. I could see it in her eyes. She wanted to kill me with her bare hands. I couldn't blame her, but that would interfere with my current plans, so she'd just have to get in line.

"Why are you here?" she asked me.

"I recently discovered I had a whole family I knew nothing about. I was informed of my father's murder and the fact that I was hand selected to take out my uncle. I was also informed about a curse, though I'm not sure how much I believe that."

She listened intently.

"I won't give you information on Neil or Nigel. You'll have to kill me first."

"I don't need you to give me information on them. I will deal with my uncles on my terms, but I'm here because I need you to deliver a message."

"To who?"

"To Neil."

"What's the message?"

"Tell him Lucca sought me out to spill the family tea. I'm not happy about being used and lied to and for that, the organization has to pay. Therefore, give him my word that I will not willingly help them touch Nigel's daughter. I want no parts of it."

She frowned at me not knowing how to take my words.

"However, him, his wife and brother are all fair game. Tell him to prepare for me because I'm coming for all three of them with a rabid vengeance he's never seen before. They need to get their affairs in order to be sure their little ones are taken care of."

She frowned. "But they are your family. Your flesh and blood. Why?"

I cut her off. "Neil and I have a score to settle. It will cause him more pain if I take his wife out and I gotta deal with Nigel because he will never let me keep breathing if I take his brother from him."

"But why not try to mend your relationship with your uncles?"

"That's sweet and I know you're trying to manipulate me. Trust me, Neil wants my blood as much as I want his."

"That may not be true. You don't know him. He forgave me for betraying him."

I chuckled. "This isn't Madea's Family Reunion sweetheart. Now, I must be on my way. I have no beef with you so if you stay out of this, you and your family won't catch my wrath by default. Consider it the least I can do out of respect for our sisterhood. I'm pretty busy handling all the people I have to kill right now, and I sincerely don't have time to deal with you. If you come for me because you can't let go of the past, you'll understand why they call me Black Widow. It would be wise for you to let bygones be bygones."

She stared but didn't comment.

"Thank you for your undivided attention. Now, if you attempt to move from this spot before two hours pass, I'll detonate. Not only will it blow up your house, but your dear neighbor has one rigged to her place as well. It is well within your disarming capabilities now that I know who trained you."

She smirked knowing her full cover was blown.

"In two hours, handle your business. But call your bestie and give him the heads up now," I said nodding to her cell phone sitting next to her pistol.

I knew I threw her for a loop with that one, but it benefited me to let Neil know I wasn't coming for his niece. It gave me time to ensure they would have to regroup. I stood up and tucked my gun back in my waistband.

"This was fun. Let's not do it again," I told her then bounded off the porch steps.

I disappeared into the house across the street. When I came out, I had my duffle back on my shoulder and brandished the detonator, so she could see it.

"Clock starts now," I yelled.

I hopped off the steps, hopped in the neighbor's vehicle and headed out of this pile of rocks.

Chapter 39: Forewarned is Forearmed

When Fuller was out of sight, Eva scooped up her phone as her hands shook. She quickly set a timer for two hours and then dialed Neil. He didn't answer. She cursed and dialed him again. No answer. She wanted to throw the phone but knew her mobility was limited. Taking a deep breath, she calmed down. She waited ten minutes then dialed Neil again, this time she Face Timed him.

He picked up, "Listen, Eva, I can't...," he paused his dismissal as her face came in to focus. She could tell he had been walking and had stopped.

Eva swallowed hard. "Neil, Fuller just left my house?"

He frowned. "Say what?"

"She found me, and she's coming for you and Nigel. She plans on killing Grey too." She saw the anger leap onto his face, but she knew she had to tell him everything. "There's more Neil," Eva continued. "Lucca told her everything about who you are to her and her father. They came to her to help them get Nigel's daughter. She's pissed at them for taking her father and knowingly using her to seduce her uncle."

Neil's eyes widened. "They knew?"

Eva nodded her head in confirmation. "Yes, and I could tell she was disgusted by it. She told me to tell you that you have her word that she will not willingly be a part of any harm to Nigel's daughter."

"Why willingly? That's odd."

Eva shrugged. "That's what she said."

Neil's jaw clenched as realization hit him. "She knows about the blood and knows there's a possibility they could get it and use it."

"Maybe," Eva added. "I get the feeling she's not into the spooky side of this. I think it's safe to say she's not on good terms with the organization and wants to cripple them by refusing to help them, but that doesn't change her original agenda."

"Killing me and my wife," Neil said. "And Nigel."

Eva nodded at him through the phone. He sighed.

"Okay, I need you to send me everything you can right now."

"I can't. I can't move for another...," she paused to check the time, "...Another hour and forty minutes. She's got my house and the neighbor's house rigged with explosives."

Neil let out a slew of colorful expletives. Eva frowned. It wasn't like him to get down like that anymore. But then again, this wasn't your average daily circumstance.

"What are you going to do Neil?"

He stared into the camera. She could see his eyes were now a steel gray.

"I'm going to bury my brother's daughter."

With that, the line went dead.

Chapter 40: Mommy Dearest

Agent Michelle Fuller
Lakeland, Florida

It took some time, but I found her. I was becoming obsessed with my past and needed to find all the answers I could, so I could take out my uncles, take out the rest of the organization and live my life the way I wanted to.

Never again would I be loyal to anyone or anything. Family. Ha! That was a joke! I watched my mom as she served one of the customers in the mom and pop diner.

I was in Lakeland, Florida and she was hiding, but I was here to give her the shock of a lifetime. I wasn't seated in her section as I continued to just sip my coffee and watch her. She caught my eye a couple of times and I could tell I was familiar to her, but she never came over and said anything to me.

Many things caught my eye in this place. The restaurant's whack homely décor I assumed was to make one feel at home. What a crock! What home? I never had one. As a matter of fact, death to all TV programming that sold me the pipe dream of what happiness was supposed to look like. Hollywood was the real dream snatcher. It sold you fairytales that didn't exist in real life, but yet you spend all your coins and all your emotions trying to attain something that was a myth to begin with. Whatever evil genius came up with that is one well off sadistic bastard.

I don't know, maybe I was too bitter and pessimistic. Some people may have gotten the pipe dream. Like the family sitting arguing over whose turn it was to pick tonight's movie. If I were sentimental, they would have been adorable, but I'm not so alas, they annoyed me instead.

The drunk guy behind me was drinking coffee like the cure to his pain was in the bottom of his next cup. Funk, caffeine, and whatever alcoholic poison he chose made for the most disrespectful odor.

Whenever his waitress walked by her movement made his funk assault me. I wanted to turn around and choke him for being offensive to my nose, but the look on my mom's face would definitely be much more satisfying. So, I exercised restraint. Not something I'm generally good at.

Besides, I'd have to stand in a decontamination chamber for an hour just to get his stench out of my clothes. I never realized how messed up in the head and heart I truly was. All these conflicting and contrasting emotions. This mess right here was for the birds.

I ignored any positive emotions I felt finally laying my eyes on her and channeled all the negative energy I had. I had stuff to do and she was an obstacle in my way.

I specifically came in close to the end of her shift. I saw her take care of her last customer and head to the back of the kitchen as she removed her apron. I threw some bills on the table and slipped out of the front door.

I pulled my hoodie on over my head as I headed to the back of the building where the staff exited. Leaning up against the wall where I would be hidden when she opened the door, I waited patiently.

Well, maybe not patiently. I had one foot against the brick wall, and it tapped though I tried hard to stop it from doing so. Minutes later, the door swung open. I had to put my hand up to keep it from slamming into my face.

As it slowly closed, I saw it was her that exited. I waited a few seconds to see if anyone else came out. Thankfully, we were all alone. I took a few steps, careful not to make any noise. She was looking down and digging in her purse.

Once she had her keys in her hand, I knocked her in the back of the head with the butt of my pistol. She made a muffled sound as I caught her before she hit the car door. I shoved her into the back seat after I grabbed the keys, hopped in, and took off.

I drove to a tiny storage unit I had acquired earlier that day. I pulled up to the door, put in my code and lifted up the gate. Dragging her in, I tied her to the chair with the rope I had placed in there earlier. She was still knocked out. I closed the gate.

I grabbed the spray bottle and sprayed her face. She screamed back into consciousness but quickly silenced herself when she saw my gun pointed at her face. Her eyes were wide as saucers and I saw just how much my sisters looked like her.

"Who are you?"

"Hi, mom! Remember me, I'm one of your twins!" I answered sarcastically.

It took her a minute to remember me. Guess she realized I wasn't Eva and her dead look alike.

"Oh my God, is it really you, Nyla."

"Who the hell is Nyla?"

She blinked and stared. "I'm sorry sweetie. What did they name you?"

"Who is they?" I asked.

"The organization, who else?"

"Where's your mark?" I asked.

"On my ankle," she said. "You don't need the gun. I won't hurt you. Rest assured, I can, but I won't."

I smirked. "Cocky for a woman tied up with a bruise on the back of her head."

"I am an Untouchable. Never forget that. You caught me slipping. Now please untie me so we can talk."

"Let's not and say we did," I told her.

I went and got another chair and sat in her face. I placed my Glock on my thigh, so she would know not to try me.

"While I know we are flesh and blood you should know I have zero problems blowing your brains out and leaving your corpse here to rot okay mommy dearest."

"I would expect nothing less from one of their assassins," she replied simply, returning my cold tone with a flippant air of her own.

"Why did you let them take me away from you?"

"It wasn't my choice. You were bred specifically to be an assassin."

"Why?"

"Because of who your father was. You were trained to be able to take out your real bloodline. They knew the light was up to something, so they decided to breed their own seed in the same bloodline as a weapon to take out the family should it ever be required."

I frowned but managed to quickly fix my face.

"What happened to my father?"

There was this look that came over my mother's face. It was sadness and maybe some regret, but there was definitely pain. She really did love him. A tear slipped down her face.

Before I knew it, I was wiping it for her. She smiled. I scowled and chastised myself for being weak.

"I was tasked to seduce your father because when they found him in Miami, they knew it was an opportunity to get to the bloodline. They also knew about the curse Lucca manipulated Black Pearl into casting on the bloodline, so they recruited me because I was a twin, and it was a good possibility that I would have a twin. Mind you this was before the organization became the organization. The head guy kept tabs on the gangs in Florida. He had been hatching the plan to create the Untouchables for years before executing it. That's where we came in. We were part of a local gang in Florida."

"I was made an Untouchable, not born one?" I asked for clarity.

"Exactly. Neville was a twin also, but the second one died at birth. They knew Pearl would not break the curse, so I was tasked with getting pregnant by him and just in case I didn't get twins on the first round, I had to convince him this was long-term, so I could get pregnant again if we lost the firstborn. So, I was in it for the long haul, which is why I fell in love with him. The minute they found out I was having twins; he was on borrowed time. I wanted out. I wanted to leave the gang and be with your father. I told him everything. He told me his dad could protect us. The night we were supposed to leave, they murdered him."

Her face almost broke my heart. She sat there, and she wept. I gave her the time she needed because honestly, I was emotional too. Once she composed herself, she went on.

"I went to his funeral but left when his dad spotted me. The only reason I was still alive is because I was carrying you and your brother. I was afraid and didn't want to end up dead. To ensure my loyalty they took you from me after your brother didn't make it out of the hospital. They told me they would kill you if I was ever disloyal to the organization again. So, to keep you safe, I stayed and became who they wanted me to be. I gave birth to your sisters and they were allowed to stay with me, but they had a special assignment too. They came after we found out your grandparents had another baby boy.

That was strategic on the organization's part. From birth, Eva was groomed to become a cop. Her moves mirrored their sons though neither of them ever knew it. Do you know your sisters? Have you met them? How are they?"

"One of them is dead," I said flatly.

She jerked like that actually caused her pain.

"What happened?"

"I killed her for betraying the organization for Neil."

She gasped. "You killed Eva?"

"No, I killed the other one who was pretending to be Eva." She just stared. "Like you said, they created me to do the things that I do."

"How's Eva?"

"Why do you care?"

"Because she's my child?"

"So am I?"

"I know how you're doing. You are holding me at gunpoint. I think it's safe to say there isn't going to be any family dinners."

"I have fifteen bullets in this gun. You could eat all 15 right now."

"Do what you want. I'm tired. If you're going to kill me, kill me. If you're going to continue to interrogate me, let's get it over with so I can go home to my cat."

"Why are you working that pathetic job?"

"I gotta eat. When the organization crumbled, I broke ties and started my own life. They took the love of my life away from me. They snatched my only surviving child right out of my hands and held you hostage from me and they wouldn't let me have contact with my twins once they were put in the field. Then they let one of my daughters kill her sister on their behalf. The organization and everybody in it can burn in hell for all I care."

There it was. I saw it. Her rage. It was powerful. I contemplated whether I should recruit her. I could use someone to have my back out here in these streets. Who better than my own flesh and blood? She had as much disdain for the organization as I did. But I don't know. We were all ruthless. I didn't doubt the information she told me was true, but she could turn around and slit my throat. I knew I was capable of doing so to her, so I couldn't trust her.

"Why Nyla?" I asked.

"You were named after your father. He loved you so much Nyla. He wanted you and he wanted us to be a family." She looked away, the sadness returning to her eyes as she spoke.

"But they took that away from me. Your father was a good man. He just carried the wrong bloodline. I'm sorry sweetie. I'm so sorry."

I choked back the tears that threatened to escape any minute now.

"What's your name?" she asked.

I stared at her contemplating whether or not to give her the truth. She was beautiful even through the tears, red eyes, and flushed cheeks. Hispanic, brown eyes, dark lush hair. She looked very much like an older version of Eva. I realized I didn't look like her, but her heritage did run through my veins. I know my father was fair skinned. Looking at her and remembering what the pictures of him showed me, I understood the tone of my skin. I used to wish I was dark. Like midnight. Oh, how I loved beautiful black skin, but one too many slave masters had tiptoed in the slave shack and ruined the melanin content Mother Africa had bestowed upon the generations before me. For some reason that angered me. Now, I knew I carried Hispanic blood in me too. I was a blank canvas with all these colors that were spilled, mixed together and voila, there I was. I blinked and gathered my thoughts on the present.

"Michelle. My name is Michelle Fuller."

"It's nice to meet you, Michelle. I can tell by the rage that's just below the surface you feel a certain way about the way you were raised. Your father was taken from you and I chose to give you up to save your life. I know how lonely it was being trained as an assassin and raised as an orphan, but you are so special, Michelle. Never forget that. I know you don't believe me, but I love you. I've always loved you."

"Prove it," I told her. "Help me take down what's left of the organization starting with Lucca Prescott."

My mother grinned fiercely.

"It would be my sincere pleasure."

Chapter 41: Sampson Steele

Orlando, Florida

He swept the floor of the hotel lobby with care and pride. The tranquility the quiet afforded him gave him peace, which was something he craved. The life he led prior to this was consumed with war. The task of cleaning a hotel likely seemed menial to many, but to him, it was peace in the midst of any storm.

Most people lived lives that allowed them to be oblivious to all the evil in the world. He wasn't one of those people. He'd had a front-row seat. He craved the simple. The uncomplicated. The basic. He could have vacuumed the floor and others on staff questioned why he didn't, but again, the electric cleaning device robbed him of the quiet.

Now that the spacious lobby had been swept, it was time to mop. His favorite thing to do in the wee hours of the morning. Sleep didn't find him often, but when it didn't, he chose to be productive. No need in being wasteful of time or complaining about what he couldn't control. If he wasn't cleaning, he was working out.

Doctor's had prescribed every kind of pill to help him with his insomnia, but none of it worked. Man-made pills were no match for the demons in a man's mind. His memories would always be with him. With the exception of a lobotomy, they were seared into his brain and there to stay.

His decisions would forever be a weight on his heart. His actions would weigh down his soul. He was what he was and now he was trying to be something different.

As he prepared to mop the floor, *she* invaded his thoughts. From the moment he saw her climb out of her car dressed in all black, she'd captured his attention. She was sexy. She was sensual. She was dangerous.

Every time he saw her, she was a different person, but she couldn't fool him. He was fixated on her and every time he mopped the large lobby, he thought of her.

There was something significant about washing away all the dirt and grime that others so carelessly left behind and making something look new. He often felt there were layers of emotional dirt and grime that people carelessly left behind that covered her soul. Which he thought accounted for her rough exterior.

He wondered if his love could wipe it clean and reveal the hidden shine that he could see the moment she turned that fateful day and gave him a glimpse of her pretty face. He had dissected her looks and thought he had a pretty good idea of which parts of her were real and which were masks.

He understood why people wore masks on a primitive level, but he craved her natural look. Yes, she was stunning with makeup on, but without it, he could see who she could've been had she not taken the path that led her to be so cold, calculating, and dangerous.

He recognized himself in her. He imagined if he ever decided to say something to her that she would continue to play her game of charades. He chuckled, thinking how fun it would be to play the cat and mouse game with a worthy opponent, who didn't even know she had already been bested because her soul mate was her opposition. He could see right into her soul because it mirrored his.

The thought jarred him. He didn't even know this woman and yet he felt like she was his soul mate. He didn't believe in much, he had been raised not to, but life had handed him some undeniable encounters that he had to give respect where respect was due.

What he felt for her was real. She needed him. He knew that on a divine level. He simply knew it. She'd left earlier that day, and he knew the reason he couldn't sleep tonight is because she hadn't made it back safely yet. He worried about her. The peace he'd managed to find in his current life dissipated every time she was gone and didn't return until he knew she was safely tucked away in her hotel room.

He admired his handiwork as the white tiled lobby floor gleamed. He smiled thinking of her face glowing the way the floor did as a result of his love. Seconds later, he shook off the daydream. That woman was absolutely dangerous. It would be undeniably suicidal to get involved.

She possessed the traits of nature's most savage beasts. She entered a room without warning like a tornado. She consumed everything in the space she was in like a hurricane with no regard for the damage left behind. There was a part of her that held the calm he knew.

The eye of her storm was her heart and he knew if he could get to it, he would possess it, but the vicious wind and rain that surrounded it wasn't going to let him anywhere near it. He had a feeling that the love she could give would crush him like a tsunami, but the fault line that had to release that wave was a big one. He didn't know if he had the energy to be the one to trigger it.

He sighed and put up the cleaning supplies in the janitor's closet located just off the lobby. He took one last look at his work, then exited through the main doors of the hotel. He waved bye to the nighttime clerk and headed to his room.

The lights on the car entering the parking lot momentarily blinded him. When he regained his focus, he realized it was her. Her room was near the lobby area. He watched as she parked.

Grabbing the black book bag, she always carried, she closed the door and looked around like she always did but didn't see him because he remained in the shadows. She *never* saw him, but he always saw her. He wondered what made her so paranoid, but his instincts knew he needed to stay as far away from her as possible. She entered her room.

The uneasiness he felt all day finally released. He shook his head and headed to his own room. He stripped, taking off his boots and custodial jumper leaving on his boxers and t-shirt. He sat down on his bed and wondered, what if? The question was loaded and the only way to answer it was to expose his heart to her.

Since he'd given up his past life he stayed on the path of least resistance. She was nowhere near that path. Opening up to her meant opening the door to the past he'd shut and locked down never to return to again. He pulled off the t-shirt he wore and pulled off his socks. He lay down and stared at the ceiling.

Ninety-nine percent of his mind said walk away. However, that one percent that connected her to the night his life changed forever, he couldn't dismiss. His mind said no, but his heart screamed yes! It was those conflicting thoughts that chased him into a restless sleep.

†††

They lurked outside his hotel room. Insidious was seething.

"I told you, he is smitten with her," Draven informed his malicious leader.

Insidious rubbed his chin as he pondered. He locked eyes with Sampson's guardian angel that stood guarding the door with his weapon drawn and his eyes aflame. He needn't worry. Insidious was not here to attack, simply gather information.

"I see."

"How do we intervene?"

"First, I need to know who he is. Get me information on him as soon as possible. Reach out to the Strongman in this region and find out why he has angelic protection. You know nothing Father does is coincidental. This was divinely orchestrated I'm sure, but I don't know why."

"I'll get right on it," Draven said.

"She's very vulnerable, we need to make sure she isn't subject to falling for him," Insidious warned. "As we know, love is a powerful force to try and contend with."

"What can we do? We don't have permission to attack him and he's guarded."

"Always remember, don't focus on what you can't do. Focus on what you *can* do. Have you forgotten our leader is the prince of the power of the air? Use it!" Insidious demanded. "Gather up your little imps and minions. He may be under protection, but she is not. She belongs to the darkness. Make sure they continuously whisper to her spirit that she is unlovable, unredeemable, and unworthy. Plant every type of doubt in her mind and for goodness sakes don't ever let her forget about her mission for revenge."

Draven smiled as he nodded. He flashed a petty smile at the angel that watched them closely. It was a good plan, once again Insidious found a way to wreak havoc and not violate the sovereign will of God.

Chapter 42: The Admirer

Agent Michelle Fuller
Orlando, Florida

The next day there was still a heaviness in my heart, but it no longer kept me from breathing. To prove it, I inhaled and let out a deep breath. I grabbed the bag with the Zaxby's grilled cobb salad minus the fried onions plus the Mediterranean dressing off the passenger seat along with my black Louis Vuitton bookbag and headed to my room.

I got to the door, but before I could unlock it, I realized I didn't want to be alone. Talk about a strange feeling. My solitude was the air I breathed. You see, this is why they say ignorance is bliss. I was a perfectly fine sociopath until that demon Lucca dropped a bomb on me. I sighed then turned to head to the lobby.

Earlier, when I'd checked in, I had seen a small dining area where they served a continental breakfast. I hoisted my bag on my shoulder and decided to walk on over. I figured the risk was pretty low seeing as how I looked very different from the way I did when I first arrived.

It was about a three-minute walk, but when I entered the modest lobby, I was grateful that there wasn't anyone seated at the tables. The staff at the front desk was more than enough human contact to make the ether around me feel less lonely.

Before I walked in, a couple holding hands beat me through the door. They were heading to check in. I gave them the once over and then headed to the table furthest away. I took the seat with my back facing the corner, so I could watch everything.

Never leave your back facing the door, especially when you're solo and no one was there to watch it. I put my bag in the chair next to me and opened my salad. My stomach wasn't growling, it was cussing. I hadn't really eaten anything since Beelzebub spilled the tea on my family tree. Today was the first time I'd even had an appetite, which further let me know going to Tallahassee, though risky, was the right thing to do, even confronting my mother.

I drizzled the dressing over the salad and dug in. I chewed so fast I bit my doggone tongue. The expletives I let out were both more colorful and louder than I intended.

"Careful Miss Lady, the salad ain't gon get up and run off the table."

I was about to cuss out whoever decided to insert themselves into my private affairs, but when I looked up, I had to pause. He was beautiful.

Chocolate.

Masculine.

Full lips.

Soft eyes.

Thick lashes.

Bowed legs.

Straight white teeth.

Dimples.

I dug in my bag for the bottle of Voss water, I always kept with me and took a sip. The water must have cleared the haze of lust because I realized he was wearing a custodial uniform.

I grimaced.

"Don't you have a floor to mop or something," I said, my tone dripping with disrespect.

He smiled, and I swear there was a twinkle that appeared when those thick lips parted into a full smile. He sauntered over to my table and took a seat. Oh, he was bold, but stupid nonetheless. In the five seconds we stared each other down, I contemplated 10 different ways to take his arrogant behind out.

"Now, Miss Lady," he said. "I know your mama raised you better than that. Didn't someone tell you to never judge a book by its cover?"

My body was betraying me and telling me we wanted to entertain him, but my mind was telling me this wasn't the time or the place to make friends.

I barely recognized the tamed and sexy tone of my own voice when I finally responded to his question.

"My mama didn't raise me."

"Oh, is that why you have identity issues?"

I glowered. "Excuse you?"

He gestured to my hair and eyes.

"New hair, new eyes and I don't believe that mole was there before."

Sweat pooled at the base of my spine. Before he knew what was happening, I had a knife to his throat. I viciously asked, who the hell he was. He frowned and put his hands up.

"Uh, I'm the owner of this place. The name's Sampson. Chill out, Miss Lady. I didn't mean any harm."

"Why are you stalking me?" I demanded.

"Not stalking. Noticing. You intrigue me."

"Well, I'm not flattered."

"I didn't ask you to be." He looked at the hand that still held the knife, then back at my face.

"You mind removing the knife from my throat before someone takes notice. Clearly, you're trying to stay low key."

He was right. I frowned and looked around. The couple that checked in was no longer there and the woman at the counter was glued to some drama on TV and hadn't noticed our little exchange.

Reluctantly, I put the knife back where I'd had it, in my pocket.

He stared.

I stared.

"I hate to think of such a beautiful woman with so many issues."

"I've got more issues than Jet Magazine. Walk away and I'll be out of your hotel within the hour."

"Don't rush out on my account."

"I've overstayed my welcome. Trust me." I looked him over once again. "By the way, if you're the owner, why are you walking around looking like the help?"

"Cleaning relaxes me."

"If you say so."

He reached for my hand. Something powerful shot through me at his touch. I looked at him like his name was Radio.

"You're going to want to *not* touch me."

He put his hands up in surrender. "My apologies, I sincerely didn't mean to make you uncomfortable. I truly apologize that was not my intention. It's just you've fascinated me for whatever reason since you arrived."

The frown on my face must've alerted him that I wasn't liking the direction of this conversation.

"I make it my business to know who's in my motel. But like I said, you caught my attention. Again, I meant no harm. You have my word that whoever you are and whoever you're running from, I'm an ally, not a threat."

He stood up. I watched him move with an innate sensuality that made me bite my bottom lip. I could tell by the cocky grin that I was caught.

"I *am* flattered," he said, then grinned and walked away.

Yum, going and coming it's all good, I shamelessly stared at him walking away. When he was out of sight, I had to process what just happened. I put a knife to his throat, in public, in broad daylight and he politely asked me to remove it, so I don't bring attention to myself. Yeah, that's not normal. He was different, but I wasn't in the mood.

Once again, my appetite was lost. I threw away the salad and grabbed my bag. I hated myself for doing it, but when I got to the door I turned back to see if he was there. Those eyes stared holes into mine.

My feet defied me and refused to move. His bowed legs headed my way closing the gap between us. He stopped just out of arm's length and made a show about doing so. Guess he'd learned his lesson about my quick reflexes. So stupid he was not.

He smiled and said, "Just in case you go in your pocket again or pull your gun." I rolled my eyes irritated he could see my concealed weapon though I wanted to chuckle. "Have breakfast with me tomorrow."

"No," I replied simply.

He grinned. "I'll be here at *our* table at 8 AM. If you want to share a meal with me, show up. If not, don't. I'm a very simple guy when it comes to dating. I don't beg. I don't plead. And I don't persist where there is resistance."

With that, he turned his back and walked away. As an extra blow to my ego, he did not look back. I smirked and headed out the door.

Chapter 43: Decisions

Agent Michelle Fuller

Sleep eluded me the way white supremacy eluded justice. REM and I would not be sharing an intimate embrace tonight. There was this feeling in the pit of my stomach that I didn't recognize, and it scared the bejesus out of me.

I wanted this man, desperately. And get this, I didn't want to kill him afterward. I wanted him to hold me. I wanted him to comfort me. I wanted him to make love to me. Now that was new and completely unexpected.

This man had the potential to distract me in ways I didn't even know existed yet, but I knew he was capable. For that reason alone, he had to die.

Chapter 44: Emotional Roller Coaster

Agent Michelle Fuller

To say that I was shocked that it was 7:55 in the morning and I was sitting at *our* table waiting for Sampson to arrive is beyond an understatement. This was the kind of bull that fairy tales were concocted from. Not only that, I had taken out the faux locs and I wore my hair in its natural state, silky black curls along with the girliest maxi dress I could find in Walmart last night when I finally gave up on going to sleep. I wore no makeup save for some mascara and lip gloss. Who was I?

My.

Self.

What was it about this man that made me remove all the masks I wore? If that wasn't bad enough, I still hadn't decided on whether or not to kill him. One thing I did know was that I'd have to kill him before I let him touch me because if I didn't, there was no way I could find the strength to take him out after. I didn't believe much in divinity, but the way this one encounter had me spinning out of control, it may just have been divine intervention.

If that's the case, God was trying to use him to intervene and stop me from exacting revenge on my dear uncles. That thought only pissed me off more. Once again, they were being protected and who was looking out for me... no one! Nobody ever did. I was born to simply be used and abused. Somehow Sampson felt different. I don't think he wanted to use me or abuse me, but was I mature enough to accept that? I honestly didn't know.

I checked my watch, it was 7:59 AM. If he stood me up, I might burn this whole hotel to the ground. Sheesh. I'm tripping, hard! Mid-eye-roll the door opened and caught my attention. I had to do a double take.

Gone was the ugly custodial jumper. He was wearing dark denim distressed jeans that managed to still look masculine and a black t-shirt that pressed up against him in a way that made my hands jealous. It had one white word on it: dope. He wore black Timberland boots. Listen, a man that wears Tims in the summertime is begging to be dragged back to my bed and devoured. I literally squirmed in my seat as he approached *our* table.

"Lawd have mercy," I whispered as he sat down across from me.

His smile was genuine, and those dimples sent a panic through the ether of my soul.

"I must say, I'm surprised to see you here."

"Not as surprised as I am to be here," I retorted. "Trust me on that."

"So, why did you come?"

"Sleep deprivation makes you do strange things."

He chuckled. "You're funny for a stone-cold killer."

My eyes bugged out of my head. I was speechless. There was no judgment in his tone, but he was so matter of fact I felt completely vulnerable and exposed since he looked me dead in my eyes without flinching daring me to deny my truth. His fearless boldness was unnerving. This man disarmed me constantly. I was definitely going to have to send him to find out if God was real or not.

Before I could respond he said, "We recognize our own kind."

I sat back in my seat and stared. I stole a glance at the other patrons going about their business of eating their complimentary breakfast ignoring us. Finally, the cotton in my mouth dissipated and allowed me to speak.

"Do tell."

"I used to be a Navy Seal. I had quite a few, let's call them, special assignments. Like I said, we recognize our own kind. Though, I'm pretty sure Uncle Sam never foot the bills for your kills. Free-lance, I'm guessing."

"It's complicated," is how I responded. Hell, if it worked to explain a Facebook relationship status, surely it could explain the ratchet and tragic story of my life.

"How complicated?"

"More than you could handle."

He leaned in closer and the sexy woodsy scent he wore attacked my nostrils and made every nerve I had stand on end.

I.

Exhaled.

"Try me," he said cockily.

“I’d rather just scratch this itch that’s between us and go our separate ways,” I said seductively.

He chuckled. “Oh, you think I’m easy, huh? Don’t let the name fool you. I’m not out here in these streets like that. Nah, Miss Lady, you’ve got to earn *this*.”

I stared at him baffled. “Are you gay?”

“That’s an immature assumption.”

My temper spiked quick! “Come for me negro.” He looked at me bemused. “You don’t know me like that, I suggest you watch your mouth.”

“My, you have a temper.”

“It’s a good asset to have in my profession.”

“I don’t trust easily, so I’m extremely selective about who I lay with and who I sleep next to.”

“Who said anything about sleeping?” I smirked.

His eyebrow shot up in amusement. He leaned in even closer and whispered in my ear, “What I have planned for you will *require* you to go to sleep to recover. I’m a grown man, you better recognize. Let that be the last time you disrespect my manhood.” He sat back in his seat and looked me squarely in the eye.

“Do we have an understanding?”

I don’t know who in the heck this negro was, but he was getting on my third nerve. The man continued to render me speechless. All I could do was manage to nod my understanding. I had to suppress a shudder from the tingle his velvet whisper left behind. Thankfully, he changed the subject. Murder was easier to discuss than love any day.

“So, tell me something, this current path you find yourself on. Are you in danger?”

“Yes,” I found myself confessing.

“You could always just walk away.”

“I can’t. I have some personal scores to settle.”

“Oh, so there’s revenge too, huh?”

“It’s what gets me up in the morning.”

He frowned, and I felt like he was disappointed in me. That stung. I had to get out of here. This man was tearing me down every second I spent in his presence.

"If revenge is a means for you to stay above ground, I get it, but if the issues are completely separate, I'm going to advise you to let it go."

"How dare you?" I questioned beginning to get mad and loud.

"Hey, chill out with all that," he said looking around. Our conversation had been hushed up to that point. Once he was satisfied, we were no longer of interest to others, he continued, "If you honestly thought I was a threat to you, you would have already *attempted* to take me out. I'm as real as they come, Miss Lady. From the moment I saw you, something in me wanted to protect you at all costs. I can't explain it."

"I don't need protection. I can protect myself," I snapped.

"I'm sure you can, from any external enemy. I'm here to protect you from yourself. That's the one person you've never been able to conquer."

His words slammed into my chest so hard I had to gasp. Tears welled up in my eyes, but I refused to let them fall. He stood up and reached for my hand. I hesitated but gave it to him. He pulled me out of my seat.

I grabbed my bag. With my hand in his, I followed him through the busy lobby. He led me to an office behind the check-in area. He opened the door then closed it behind me.

I stared at him completely baffled. He pulled me into his chest and squeezed me so tight yet so gentle, I broke. I cried and cried and cried and cried some more.

Vivian Green said it best. I was on an emotional roller coaster. My body shook with all the feelings that coursed through me. At some point, I even let out a wail. He was steady and continued to hold me upright. There were a few times I thought I'd fall because my knees betrayed me and buckled, but he never let go.

I don't know how much time had passed but I finally pulled myself together. I stared into the kindest eyes I had ever known.

"I'm sorry," I said shyly when I managed to get my emotions under control. "I got snot all over your shirt."

He laughed. "I do have a washing machine."

He released me to go get me some tissue off his mahogany oak desk and the emptiness that ensued from being out of his embrace was overwhelming. He wiped the tears gently from my face and handed me more tissue to clean my nose.

I turned my back and handled my business, hoping that I didn't have any random fluids or pieces of tissue lint on my face when I turned back around.

I faced him. He stared down at me. I'm guessing he was an inch shy of six feet. He placed his hands on the sides of my face and stared at me. There were no words, but I felt it. This connection. He knew what I was capable of and it didn't scare him. Apparently, he was capable of it too.

Finally, he spoke, "I know you have a lot of demons, but I can love you past all of them if you let me."

"Why do you want to?"

"You don't know my story, but I have seen many evil things in many evil places. When I look at you, I don't see evil. I see a woman that is in desperate need of unconditional love. I was given a second chance. I think you deserve one too."

I swallowed hard. "You don't even know my name."

"I want your real name and I know that's not what you had them put in the system. When you tell me that, then I'll stop calling you Miss Lady."

"You can call me Black Widow."

He smirked. "That's cute, but I'm not interested in your assassin name. What's your *name*?"

I looked into his eyes and sighed.

"My name is Michelle. Michelle Fuller."

He smiled. "No, it's not."

"That's the name I was given," I confessed.

"Then what would you like to me to call you?"

I stared at him and then it came to me. The name my father had given me.

"Nyla. Call me Nyla."

He smiled. My heart smiled and I'm pretty sure it had never done that before. He gently pressed his lips against mine and pulled me into him.

Innocent was how it started. Like we were introducing ourselves through the kiss. Then he nibbled my bottom lip and I lost it. I went limp in his arms. My knees betrayed me again, and they buckled.

Intensity came next. His tongue danced with mine in a rhythm I had never known before. His lips were soft. His mouth was warm, and I could taste the traces of Listerine he must've used before coming to see me. I knew he could taste the cherry Starburst I had eaten trying to remedy the dry mouth my nervousness caused in anticipation of seeing him again.

Passion followed. The sounds we made as we continued to declare our desire for one another was like a sweet melody that could only be created by us. The smacking. The moaning. The breathing. How can a kiss be torturous and so fulfilling at the same time?

I wrapped my arms around his neck to steady myself and returned the passion that stirred deep in my soul. I don't know how much time passed, but when he pulled away and stared into my eyes, something deep within me had shifted.

Breathlessly, I said, "I want you."

He grinned. "The feeling is definitely mutual, but like I said, I'm not that easy."

I frowned.

"There's nothing virtuous about me so you don't have to do the chivalric dog and pony show with moi," I replied.

"Just because you don't know your worth, doesn't mean I'm blind to it or my own." I frowned at him. "I'm not gay, and I'm not necessarily the guy who wants to wait until marriage, but we still don't know each other, and our pasts aren't exactly squeaky clean. Caution is the word of the day. I have a feeling that being with you in that way, there's no turning back. And I don't know that I can handle a sample of you without getting the whole package. You're damaged, and damaged people are unpredictable. I don't mean that in a negative way, but the truth is the truth."

I stared at him. How he read me so well, I would never understand. "I'm not really sure what to do with you," was all I managed to say.

He smiled then said, "Now that you've let some of the burdens off your chest, go and really think about what you want. If you want revenge, then you can't have me. That's a never-ending rabbit hole that I'd rather not be a part of. I would rather spend my days loving you than killing for you. I'm done with that life. Now, if it's about your safety, we can tie up any loose ends and go live a normal life anywhere in the world. It's up to you. You let me know what you want me to do."

I pulled away from him. The look of panic on his face both warmed my heart and frightened me more than any Stephen King novel ever could. It did my ego good to know his attachment to me was as bad as mine was to him.

"Like you said, we don't even know each other. It hasn't even been a full 24 hours that I was aware you existed. I don't even know your last name. How dare you ask me to give up my revenge for uncertainty."

He glowered and stepped closer to me. It was the first time I'd seen a dark emotion on his face. Oh yes, he was indeed a killer. I'm not sure how I ever missed it. Yet somehow instinctively, I knew he'd never hurt me. So, I didn't even flinch.

"Don't get it twisted. There is nothing uncertain about this. You know it and I know it. Listen to your better angels for once and choose the path of least bloodshed."

"I can't," I said defiantly. "I have to finish this."

"You don't."

"I do."

He reached out and grabbed me.

"Nyla, can you honestly look me in the eyes and convince me that you believe the trade-off is worth it?"

Again, tears swam in my eyes. I couldn't answer his question and that made me want to panic. I chose to be a coward instead of a grown woman. I snatched away from him.

"Girls like me don't get happy endings," I said solemnly. I'm sorry Sampson. Goodbye."

With that, I grabbed my bag and fled the scene. I didn't dare look back because I knew the sorrow in his eyes would have broken me beyond repair.

Chapter 45: Pillow Talk

Agent Michelle Fuller

Laying in Sampson's arms provided me with something I had never before experienced in my life - *peace*. How was that possible? Couldn't get too excited though. Yes, he was in my bed, but not the way I wanted him to be.

About two hours after I fled the scene, my heart ached in a way I can't explain. I swallowed every bit of pride I had and set my ego to the side, which is something I had never done in my life. I went back to his office and knocked on the closed door. To my surprise and dismay, he opened it. We stared at each other for a long while.

Finally, I built up the courage to speak. "I still have yet to make a decision and I honestly don't know what I'll choose, but what I do know is that I need you to hold me. Just once. I feel like I can't go the rest of my life never knowing what it feels like to be wrapped in your arms with the rhythm of your heartbeat soothing me."

There was this pained expression on his face. He nodded and told me he would be at my room at eight. I don't know what was up with him and the 8 o'clock hour, but at 7:59 PM he knocked. I answered.

This time he was wearing a white t-shirt and some silver basketball shorts with socks and athletic slides. His legs were thick and hairy. He made my mouth water. I had to suppress my desires because I knew he was dead serious about not going there with me. Truthfully, I couldn't even blame him.

He came in, closed, and locked the door, then reached for my hand. I donned a night-shirt and some boxers. I know I looked a hot mess. Seems like he opened the floodgates of my tears. I had been crying on and off all day with no Lifetime movie to blame for my reckless emotions.

He asked, "How do you want to do this?"

"I want to be the little spoon."

He nodded and climbed in behind me. He pulled me into his body. I listened to his steady breathing. I felt his heartbeat against my back. I held the hand that held me and then I closed my eyes. I don't know how much time passed, but when I woke up, I was grateful.

We ended up ordering a pizza. Once that was devoured, we fell back into a groove that felt both natural and familiar. He lay on his back and I lay on his chest mesmerized by his pheromones. How could the scent of his skin soothe me? As he held me, he played in my hair and massaged my scalp. It's like he was trying to melt away everything ugly inside me.

I hated that he didn't kiss me. I wanted to kiss him but didn't want to risk losing this embrace by pushing too far too fast. So, we just chilled. We took silly pictures. The conversation flowed effortlessly. He made me laugh. He made me think. He made me happy. Being in his space, made me content.

If I was truly honest with myself, it made me uncomfortable. I wasn't used to happy. It was foreign, and I didn't know how to embrace it. It was like the vegetable that you knew was good for you and it really didn't taste bad, but it looked weird and so you were hesitant to say, yeah, I like that.

When I got uncomfortable with real life, I reverted to the life that was normal for me.

"You know my moniker. What was yours?" I asked as he ran his finger over the red hourglass tattoo at the base of my spine.

"I really try to leave that part of my life in the past."

"Please?" I begged. I wanted to know the part of him that was most like me.

He sighed. "I'll tell you the name, but only if you promise not to ask any follow-up questions."

I rolled my eyes, but said, "Okay, I promise."

He looked me in my eyes and laughed.

"You're lying."

I grinned. "No, I promise. Tell me, please."

"My name was Savage."

I stared at him for a moment without blinking. That one word told me everything I needed to know.

"You good?" he asked when I remained quiet.

"Yeah."

"No questions."

I shook my head. "Nope, none."

"Don't go digging into my background Nyla. My name possesses the type of flags that will get a knock on your door or a bullet in your head if you poke too close to my secrets okay."

"Okay."

"I'm serious. Respect my choice to leave the past behind me."

"Okay," I said exasperatedly. "I got it. Don't go snooping."

He kissed me on my forehead which only made me want to kiss him. I decided to cut to the chase.

"Why are you here in my bed holding me and getting attached to me when we both know there is a very real possibility that I am going to break your heart?"

"I wish I knew," he said as he continued to absentmindedly play in my hair.

I felt that on a spiritual level, so I didn't press him anymore.

I asked, "Do you believe in God?"

"Why do you ask?"

"Because if He is real, you seem like somebody He may have sent to distract me."

He laughed hard.

"I don't know about all that. I'm not exactly the poster child for churchgoers."

"But do you believe?" I asked again.

"Absolutely."

"Why? Were you raised in church?"

"No, actually I was raised by atheists."

"Okay, this ought to be interesting." He chuckled and began to share.

"My parents were very much intellectual atheists, so I never got any kind of religious anything from them except that it was a lie."

"What's an intellectual atheist? I thought atheism was the whole deal," I interrupted.

"Well, there are intellectual atheists who truly believe in rational thought that a supreme being isn't a reality. They just see science and nothing more. Whereas an emotional atheist is one who believed and some tragic event, likely some type of death of a loved one, caused them not to believe. Really, their feelings are just hurt, and they are throwing an emotional tantrum. Something that doesn't exist can't be the source of your pain if it's not real."

"Hhhmmm, makes sense."

"Me, I was just indifferent. It didn't matter to me one way or the other. One night in Afghanistan during a raid, my whole squad was wiped out. I had been shot as well. I propped myself up against a dingy wall and waited to die or be captured. I found some religion that day because I prayed that if God was real, do not let me be captured behind enemy lines. I didn't mind dying but being captured wasn't an option. I knew way too much information. I saw this light, it was bright and white, and I thought it was the proverbial tunnel that people always refer to when death is near, but I also saw a wing. It was a huge white wing. After that everything went black. When I woke up, I was in a hospital and they told me it was a miracle I was still alive."

"Whoa," I said as goosebumps saturated my flesh.

"I spent a week in the hospital and on that last night I was in my room and I felt a presence in there with me. I opened my eyes ready to kill and I saw this huge being with wings, turning and walking away. I asked, 'Is this real?' He turned and said, 'It's not yet your time,' and then he vanished.

"What did he look like?" I asked caught up in the story now.

"I don't know that white light blurred his face. I just saw the wings and heard the voice. I had no choice but to believe then."

We were silent for a long while.

"Did you ever see the angel again?" I asked.

He chuckled. "It's funny you asked that. I saw just the wing and only for a second standing by your room the day you checked in."

I frowned. "Are you serious?"

"Yeah. I saw you pull into the parking space and get out. I have to admit, you looked so sexy in all that black. I stared so hard I almost started drooling." I laughed. "When you went into the room and shut the door is when I saw that wing. I blinked, and it was gone."

"That's really crazy. I doubt very seriously an angel would be protecting me," I said dismissively.

"Maybe not," he responded. "I don't know how it works, but maybe it was my guardian angel's way of letting me know to look out for you beyond the immediate attraction I had for you. I mean my life was spared for some reason, right?"

"Interesting theory, but I doubt it. No one ever looks out for me. I look out for myself."

He shifted our bodies and turned to face me. He kissed my nose.

"This may be our only night together and I have to accept that, but I really want to know. What's going on with you? Why is this revenge so important?"

I tried to pull away, but he gently pulled me closer to him.

"Stop running Nyla. I'm not going to hurt you. And your secrets, whatever they may be are safe with me. You know you can trust me. You never know, I might be able to help you."

I sighed because I did trust him, and I had no idea why. I wanted to spill my guts to him the minute his hand touched mine while we sat at *our* table.

"How often do you watch the news?" I inquired.

"Often."

"Ever heard of the Untouchables?" He frowned even as he nodded. "I'm one of them."

He blinked and just stared.

I laid it out. I told him about my double cross of Neil. Meeting with my mom and the tea she spilled, the part I played in Grey's kidnapping, Neil shooting me, and my being arrested and escape from federal custody. I also told him about the spawn of Satan and all that nonsense he told me about my family tree. I even told him, what I'd done to my sister in order for her to deliver a message to Neil about the terms of my plan. To his credit, he didn't jump up and bolt for the door.

"So, the feds are looking for you?" he asked when I finished my spiel.

"I'm sure I'm at the very top of their list. So, you see, there is no future for us. I'm a wanted woman. When I deal with my uncles, and I deal with Lucca, I'm going to disappear, but I'm going to be looking over my shoulder for the rest of my life."

"I hear everything you're saying, I truly do, but I don't see the point of your revenge at the expense of your happiness. Your uncles aren't going to come for you unless you come for them and you already said you have no interest in harming your niece. One phone call to Neil can shut it all down and you know that. And Lucca and the organization, aren't as big a threat as they used to be. He's bluffing. The U.S. Government has torn them apart. We can be together somewhere that has no extradition to the U.S. and be done with all of it. You're trying to prove a pointless point Nyla. You're not protecting yourself and you're not righting any wrong that you didn't earn. I'm sorry but that's the truth. Karma always collects her due."

I was heated.

"You don't get to dictate to me how to handle the affairs of my life! You don't know what it feels like to be me! To have everything decided for you and taken from you! To be manipulated and used. I didn't ask you for your approval. This decision belongs to me, Sampson."

"You're not being rational," he defended his position.

"And you're not being realistic," I yelled back. "This isn't some freakin' fairy tale. It is real life. We're not going to fall in love, get married, have 2.5 kids and live happily ever after."

"I've waited a long time to cross paths with someone I wanted to share time and space with. I don't need a house and kids or even a happily ever after. What I need is you and time. Time to spend with you. Loving you. Being loved by you. Making love to you. Being free with you. Not being told what to do or following anybody's orders no matter how jacked up they are. You're that woman for me and I know I'm that man for you. Don't take this opportunity for peace away from us both."

I turned away from him as the tears burned my eyes.

"I can't be what you're asking me to be, Sampson. I can't."

"Please, let it go. For me. For us."

I felt defensive. "I thought you didn't beg," I said nastily.

He scowled, but said, "I don't, and I did... for *you*."

"I'm not who you think I am. Trust me, I'm doing us both a favor."

"What you're doing is being a coward," he said dismissively.

I plopped down on the bed, done with the conversation. I expected him to get up and leave, but he didn't. The silence was thick and painful. He was angry with me. I felt the strong emotion coming from his skin. He was asking too much. I broke the silence.

"Why can't we be together after I handle my business?"

"I told you, I don't want any part of that life anymore. I'm done. With the exception of protecting what I love, which isn't much. I'm done with that. And who's to say you'll even make it back from handling your business?"

My temper spiked at that.

"First of all, you're really trying my patience. I'm not some amateur in the game. I can handle myself."

"And it's that kind of arrogance that can get you killed. What part of my whole squad got taken out are you not listening to? I was part of a very elite team. I don't care who trained you and how you were trained, I will give you a run for your money, trust me on that. But there is always someone out there better than you. Or one mistake, one moment of distraction and you could be taken out."

I rolled my eyes.

"I appreciate the care, but you can save it. I don't need it. I know what I'm doing."

"The risk you're taking isn't even necessary. You're picking a fight based on your pride and your ego and nothing more. If you can't see how asinine that is, then I can't help you. I worked too hard to get my peace and sanity back Nyla, and I'm not going back. Not even for you."

There it was.

Our stalemate.

Our crossroad.

Our impasse.

I sighed and so did he.

I cried and so did he.

Sometime later, he reached for me and held me tighter than I had ever been held before. I found peace in the steadiness of his heartbeat and sleep finally enveloped me.

When morning arrived, the sun came through the window bright and disrespectful. I threw my hand over my face and rolled over. Something was missing. I opened my eyes. The space next to me was empty and cold. I called out for him. No answer.

I heard his words in my head, "I don't beg. I don't plead. And I don't persist where there is resistance."

He was gone. An ache I had never known pierced my heart.

I wept just like they say Jesus did.

Chapter 46: Loose Ends

Agent Michelle Fuller

Once I got myself together, I wasted no time getting the hell out of dodge. I almost didn't check out, but I needed to be careful of the trail I left behind. Neil and Nigel were smart, and they could possibly be on my scent after I left their brother's grave. All loose ends needed to be tied up.

I threw on my favorite pair of bleached severely distressed jeans and a t-shirt with a black fist pump. I pulled my unruly curls up into a messy bun on top of my head, slid in my gray contacts and added my infamous mole.

I needed to find a tanning salon soon. I needed to darken my skin as soon as possible. I threw everything in my duffle and then grabbed my bookbag and headed to the lobby wishing upon any star that I would not run into Sampson while secretly hoping he would come and rescue me from myself.

My heart was heavy, I felt so sluggish, but my decision was made. It is what it is. I slid on my giant sunglasses and dumped my bags in the car then headed over to the lobby to check out.

There was a line which pissed me off to no end. I had to wait for these whiny people and all their complaints. Everything and anything irritated me. There was a kid wailing about something. Whoever was speaking on the TV had the most annoying voice ever and the little kid standing in front of me was staring at me instead of paying attention to whatever electronic device his parent had given him.

Little brat.

I wanted to smack him or flip him off. Neither of which was appropriate, I'm aware. After 15 minutes, it was my turn. My attitude was on a hundred thousand trillion.

"I need to check out."

"What's the name?"

"Rochelle Johnson." He looked up at me puzzled. "What the hell are you staring at? Just check me out!" I demanded.

"Um, Mr. Steele wanted me to give you this note. He said you would be checking out some time today."

I frowned.

"Who the hell is Mr. Steele?" I asked.

"Um, the owner," he said his white face turning bright red.

He had that look that you get from all white men when they think the "angry black woman" was about to snatch them. In this case, though, I likely was. I snatched off my sunglasses.

"Arrogant bastard," I said under my breath. "Give me the note," I demanded.

Poor thing, his hand shook as he slid me the note. I took it and stepped out of the line. His handwriting was in all capital block lettering like an architect. It read:

NYLA,

I KNOW I WAS WRONG FOR NOT SAYING GOODBYE, BUT I KNOW YOU CAN UNDERSTAND WHY I DIDN'T. YOUR REFUSAL TO GIVE US A CHANCE, DOESN'T STOP THIS NEED I HAVE TO WANT TO KEEP YOU SAFE. I KNOW I CAN'T GET YOU TO STAY SO I WON'T ASK, BUT PLEASE, COME BACK IN THREE DAYS. MEET ME AT OUR TABLE AT 8 PM. THERE'S SOMETHING I NEED TO GIVE YOU. I NEED YOU TO TRUST ME. STAY SAFE.

LOVE,
SAM

I was floored. Shocked and angry. Why didn't he give me the letter himself? We both knew my curiosity wouldn't let me ignore his request. I fought back the tears and went back to finish checking out.

"Do you have something I can write on?" I asked, politely this time.

Nervously the young guy slid a piece of paper and pen my way.

I scribbled: *Nothing but death can keep me from it.*

I knew he'd recognize the line from what turned out to be both of our favorite black movie of all time - *The Color Purple*.

I slid the note back to the guy and handed him cash.

"The bill has been taken care of," he informed me.

I nodded and left to put some distance between me and the best thing that had ever happened to me.

Chapter 47: Pissed Off

Agent Michelle Fuller

My heart was broken.

I needed something to remedy this pain that was determined to take me out. I needed somewhere to focus my anger. Tears ran down my face as I drove down the highway heading nowhere fast. I needed to slow down because I couldn't risk being pulled over.

That's when it hit me. I dug my cell phone out of my bookbag and called my mother.

"I expected to hear from you sooner."

"I've been busy, but I finally figured out how to take out the pretty boy."

"How?" she asked.

"I'm going to tell him I have information on my niece and to meet me at your diner. I'm going to stand him up. You're going to tell him who you really are. Tell him to meet you for drinks after your shift. I'm going to give you something to spike his drink. It will be time lapsed and give you plenty of time to leave him with plenty of witnesses to say you all did not leave together. I'll bring enough money for you to relocate when I drop off the package. You've got three days to get your life in order. Understood?"

"See you in three days."

I hung up already starting to feel just a little bit better.

Chapter 48: Ma!

Darcy was in the kitchen preparing a fancy brunch for her and Jessica. There was something going on with her child and her spidey senses were tingling. It was time to have a real talk with Jessica about life, boys, sex, and relationships. She knew most parents dreaded this moment, but not Darcy.

She wished her mother had given her a heads up. She wished her mother had explained things to her and not just say don't do it or damned her to hell for sex. The church had such a long way to go in that area.

Sex was natural, and everyone craved it at some point. It needed to be properly addressed and parents needed to prepare themselves for the inevitable. Some children would remain virgins, but many would not. She hoped and prayed that Jessica would save herself, but in the event, she didn't, she wouldn't send her baby girl out in the world clueless to figure it out on her own, especially not with other teenagers and the internet as her source of information.

While Darcy was comfortable now that she had prayed, she didn't think Jessica would be. However, she was just going to have to get over it because her spirit was warning her, it was time.

Jessica came downstairs rubbing her eyes in her favorite nightshirt.

"Good morning, ma. What's all this?"

"Good morning, baby. I just thought you and I would have some brunch this morning and have a little girl chat."

Jessica eyed her mother suspiciously as she reached into the refrigerator to pull out a bottle of water.

After she took a sip, she asked, "Girl talk?"

Darcy ignored the inquisition and said, "Why don't you set up the table I have on the back porch with the plates, flatware, and glasses. I'm almost done."

Jessica shook her head but was obedient. She knew her mom was being fancy because they weren't eating out of the plastic and the glasses were champagne flutes. Jessica set the table and poured the orange juice into the two flutes as her mom began to bring out the food she prepared.

Darcy had made Belgian waffles with pecans, a bowl of fresh mixed fruit, a plate of assorted cheese, scrambled eggs with cheese, bacon, and chicken wingettes, all flats, the way her baby loved them.

Jessica's mouth watered as the aromas from all the food assaulted her senses. She knew she likely didn't want to have this conversation with her mom, whatever it was, but the woman had definitely played her hand well. She was not about to miss out on this meal.

Darcy took her seat and reached for Jessica's hand. She blessed the food. They begin to fix their plates. The eight angelic beings that surrounded them begin to spread out and cover the large backyard.

Darcy decided to go straight for the jugular.

"So, I haven't seen Marcus in a while, what's going on with you two?"

Jessica shifted in her seat and paused midbite.

"Um, I've just been busy, you know."

"Do you expect me to believe that? You two were inseparable."

"Ma, I really don't want to talk about Marcus right now, if you don't mind."

"Okay, we can talk about something else." Jessica sighed with relief, but it was short-lived. "Are you still a virgin?"

Jessica choked on her waffle. Darcy sat back and let her compose herself.

"Ma!"

"Jessica!" Darcy replied in kind.

"Why would you ask me that?"

"Why wouldn't I ask you that?"

Jessica rolled her eyes. "Yes, ma, I'm still a virgin."

"A virgin-virgin or just a technical virgin. Have you done other things?"

Jessica had a coughing fit. Darcy wanted to laugh so bad, but she had to keep a straight face at least for this part.

"Girl drink some water."

Jessica finally took a few sips of her water, then calmed down.

"Ma!"

"Girl, if you don't stop calling my name like it's 911. We are having this conversation, so make your peace with it."

Jessica put her head down beyond embarrassed.

"No, ma, I'm a real virgin, I haven't done anything. I had one kiss."

That got a raised brow from Darcy.

"With Marcus?" she asked.

Jessica nodded. She was afraid to look at her mother.

"Are you mad?"

"No, baby, you're 14 years old. It was inevitable. I adore Marcus and I know he comes from a good home, so I can at least be grateful for that."

Still, with her head down, she said, "I'm sorry I didn't tell you."

Darcy reached across the table and lifted her daughter's chin.

"Hold your head up baby, okay."

Jessica looked at her mother piercing her heart with her husband's gray eyes.

"Okay, mama."

"Besides, if you're grown enough to be swapping spit, you should be grown enough to own it."

Jessica's eyes bugged out of her head. Darcy fell out laughing. Jessica did too and the tension in the atmosphere dissipated.

When they calmed, Darcy spoke, "Okay, this is how this is going to go. I'm going to lay out the rules in my house and where I stand on this issue and then you can ask me any question you want to about sex, babies, relationships, whatever. For this brunch, I'm not your mother, I'm your friend, but *only* for this brunch," she warned.

Jessica laughed.

"You think you can handle that?" Darcy asked.

"Yes, ma'am."

"Okay, I would love it if you remained a virgin until your wedding night. I don't know if I can adequately explain to you what that does in a marriage. But it saddens me that your husband won't likely be a virgin because society just doesn't raise them that way. That is a phenomenon not very common these days."

That statement made Jessica wonder what all Marcus had done with Candace. The jealousy that spiked, caught her off guard. Darcy saw her daughter shift uncomfortably and intuitively assumed correctly. She hoped Marcus wasn't out there having sex, but he wasn't her responsibility, Jessica was.

"In my house," Darcy continued, "I'm not here for it. Respect my home, you understand?" Jessica nodded. "You can officially date at 16, group dates while you're 15, but that comes with stipulations, such as who the group is and whether or not I've met his parents. Understand?"

Jessica nodded.

"Babies are real. Being a parent is real. Babies cost money. Being a parent makes everything take a backseat. If you got dreams and goals, they become delayed. I will always support you no matter what, but I will not take on the responsibilities you create for yourself. Do I make myself clear?"

Jessica nodded.

Darcy stared.

"Yes, ma'am."

"Sex is more than just a natural thing that leads to procreation. It's also spiritual Jessica. It is the connecting of two souls in the most intimate way. It doesn't matter if the two parties involved have feelings. God's law trumps natures. I truly hope, wish and pray you wait, but I know that I can only be responsible for one vagina and that's mine."

Jessica choked on her cheese.

Darcy laughed. "Maybe feeding you during this conversation was not my brightest idea."

Jessica laughed. "I'm sorry, ma, I just wasn't ready."

"Would you like me to use one of your street terms for it?"

Jessica threw up her hands. "No! Please don't. We can stick with scientific terms."

Darcy smirked. "I thought so." She continued. "After four daughters, you learn the hard way that you only get one and that's the only one you have any say over."

"Were my sisters virgins when they got married?"

"Again, that's not my place, but I have given them a heads up that if you come to them to be open and honest with you about the things they learned when discovering their sexuality."

Jessica nodded. She didn't mind that, she loved her sisters and had a great relationship with each of them.

"Thanks, ma."

Darcy winked at her baby girl. "God has such a beautiful destiny in store for you, of this I am confident. Mistakes don't change your destiny; they just derail or delay it. Don't take the scenic route to your destiny baby. Do your very best to keep mistakes to the bare minimum. The way you do that is by watching the pitfalls of others, not to judge them, but to gain perspective. Let wisdom be your life-long teacher."

Jessica nodded.

"If you decide to have sex, I want you to come to me and tell me, immediately. Yes, I will be very disappointed, maybe even hurt, but I'll get over it. I want you to protect yourself and I will be putting you on birth control. I don't want you to think of that as a free pass to just go out and put miles on your body baby girl, it's precautionary. It's no different than wearing your seatbelt when you get in the car. You don't plan to get in an accident, but just in case you do, the seatbelt is there to do what it can to keep you safe. You will be paying for your own birth control though. If you're grown enough to be doing it, you're grown enough to carry the weight that comes with it. I also would want you to carry your own condoms and use them every single time. Do not depend on a man to supply them and do not listen to the nonsense that it doesn't feel the same. If he's not your husband, that isn't his privilege, period."

Jessica nodded completely shocked at what her mom was telling her. She'd discussed this topic with her friends and none of them reported a conversation like this with their mom.

"Ma why are you being so cool about this?"

"Because I wish I knew half of what I'm telling you when I discovered my sexuality. I would have and could have made better choices. Just know that opening yourself up to sex opens up a whole new world of dangers. Babies, though challenging, are the good part. There are several diseases, some that won't ever go away. You're going to discover your bodies pH balance and what can throw it off. It can open you up to infections that are very uncomfortable. When you join your body with someone else's, they invade your natural balance and throw it off. Sometimes, infections result from that."

Jessica made a face that said, "gross."

"Exactly," Darcy laughed. "Now, that's my spiel, so go ahead and ask away."

Jessica was hesitant.

"It's okay, baby, I'm your girlfriend with experience, remember. Don't be shy. Everything you're feeling is normal and nothing to be embarrassed about."

Jessica nodded and took a deep breath. It took a few moments, but asked, "How does sex feel?"

"Girl, it's good!"

Jessica fell out laughing. "Oh my God, ma!"

"Well, it is. The Bible says that everything good, God created. And we know He created sex."

"How you gon bring the Bible in this, ma?"

"Uh, because it was created by God. In the Bible when they say so-and-so *knew* their wife, they talking about getting busy girl. The hundreds of thousands of the children of Israel didn't get dropped off by the stork."

Jessica shook her head as she giggled. Her mother was slap crazy.

"Now, let me be honest. You know your father wasn't my first because of the rape, but there were two others before I met your father."

Jessica's eyes widened.

Darcy laughed. "Girl, I wasn't always the first lady." Jessica laughed. "Besides, even though, I was raped my first time, the sexual appetite was awakened."

Something occurred to Jessica. "Is that what King Solomon meant when he said, 'Don't awaken love before her time?"

"That's exactly what it meant. The more you dabble in sexual activities, the more your appetite increases. It's like a rabbit hole. Make sure you're ready before you open that door. At 15 I just don't think you are. You're a very intelligent young lady, but some stuff you're just not mature enough for and age doesn't determine that. When I said sex was good, I meant that, however, it didn't become good until I was in love and the man that I shared my body with cared about my pleasure as well as his. I didn't have an orgasm until I was married to your father. So, all the other times amounted to a waste of my time and unnecessary miles on my body. I can guarantee you a 16-year old boy doesn't know what the hell he is doing. He has one thing on his mind. Getting the same thing from you he discovered in the shower by himself."

This time Jessica fell out of her chair laughing at her mother. Darcy laughed. She was so grateful she and her baby girl could have this candid conversation. When Jessica sat back down and composed herself, she was wiping tears from her eyes.

"Mama, you are crazy."

"No baby, I'm real."

"Speaking of masturbation. Is it wrong?"

Darcy sighed this was such a sketchy subject. "You won't find it specifically mentioned in the Bible. Have you ever done it?"

Jessica put her head down.

"Look at me, baby. It's okay."

"Once."

"And how did you feel afterward?"

"Convicted."

"Then there's your answer. That can be a very gray area for some people, but the reason you felt convicted is because you have a relationship with God, and you spend time with Him. While it is a natural thing that even little kids discover on their own, it doesn't make it okay. When you are trying to justify behavior that isn't necessarily named as sinful, you should ask yourself, does it edify God? Our bodies are the temple of the holy spirit and denying your flesh is part of your walk with God, masturbation is pleasing your flesh, period. We are called to die to our flesh, which means denying it. Now, it's likely you will do it again because you have whetted your sexual appetite, but I warn you, it can become an addictive behavior. Anything that has more control over you than you have over it is a stronghold. You pray and ask God to help you with that, okay."

Jessica nodded.

"Mama, I think I love Marcus."

"I know you do, baby." Jessica looked up at her mother shocked. "It's so apparent when watching you two. So why did you cut him off?"

"He actually cut me off when I told him I didn't want to be his girl."

"Why didn't you want to be with him?" Darcy asked shocked at her daughter's confession.

"Well, when he kissed me, it caught me off guard and I started feeling things in my body. Kinda similar to what I felt the one time I did masturbate." Darcy nodded. "And I got scared. I don't think I'm ready to handle being that close to a boy yet. I want to save myself, but that seems like it will be really hard ma."

"Oh, it won't be easy, but if that's your desire, God can keep you. But you have to let Him keep and use that way of escape that He gives you. But baby avoiding men for that reason is going to have you emotionally stunted. While you might be physically ready, you won't be emotionally ready. Marcus is a different story I know because y'all are best friends. Technically, you guys have been dating, just without the physical part. I wouldn't stand in the way of your friendship but would lay out rules, you two would need to abide by until you're 16. However, if you're not ready, that's okay. Understand, relationships require your heart to be invested. That's a whole other monster."

"Tell me about it. Candace saw us kiss and she's been acting a monkey fool ever since. Marcus says they aren't together, and I believe him, but I know something happened between them."

"And how do you feel about that?"

"It drives me crazy thinking he's been with her," Jessica said with disgust.

"Ooooh wee! Someone is jealous."

Jessica put her head down as Darcy laughed.

"It is natural to feel some type of way about the person you care about being involved with someone else but let me make this clear. Jealousy is a nasty emotion and one you do not want to entertain. It's okay to be territorial and at times a little possessive, but you can't have what someone doesn't freely give you. The only person you can control in a relationship is you. You cannot change a man. You cannot stop other women from wanting your man. It's his job to let them know he isn't available. Only he can set the boundaries for other women. If he cares about you and respects you, he will. If he doesn't, get out, run the other way, and do not look back. Your self-respect is just that, *self*-respect. If you don't respect yourself, no one else will."

Jessica nodded. She stood up and hugged her mother.

"You are the best mother ever."

Darcy laughed. "I love you baby girl."

"Love you too ma, thank you. Can I come to you if I have questions later?"

"Of course."

"Will I be talking to my mother or my girlfriend?"

"Girl, I don't know. The holy spirit gave me a special dispensation for this conversation. I did a lot of praying." Jessica laughed. "I will always be here to listen to you and if I feel like I'm going to be irrational because I'm your mother, I promise to step back, pray and then come back and talk to you. How's that?"

"That's a deal," Jessica said smiling.

Darcy realized she was raising a beautiful, well-shaped daughter in the age of social media. The 21st century was its own beast to contend with. She couldn't take her mother's style of parenting from the 20th century and think it was going to serve her well.

She needed to talk to the Creator of all things. He created her daughter, and it didn't matter what times were like, He knew how she was shaped and formed, therefore He would know how to parent her.

"Come on, let's go get dressed and drive to the outlets for some retail therapy," Darcy told her daughter.

"Really?" Jessica squealed.

"Really."

Jessica jumped up.

"After we clean up this mess."

"Deal," Jessica said as she began to clear the table."

Darcy smiled. She whispered, "Thank you, Lord, please keep my baby girl safely behind your hedge of protection."

Chapter 49: Heart of Steele

Agent Michelle Fuller
Orlando, Florida

Three days later, I arrived by 7:55 PM and parked myself at *our* table. The lobby was fairly empty save for the clerk that checked me out. He still looked afraid of me. I chuckled.

If Sam stood me up tonight, I would indeed burn down this hotel and everything in it. Missing him was a constant throbbing pain in my soul. He was my every waking thought and he haunted my dreams. I couldn't escape the hold he had on me though I desperately wanted to.

The door opened and there he was. I looked down at my phone not surprised to see it was 7:59 PM when he strolled in. He was dressed in gray sweatpants and a black shirt with matching sneakers. He was trying to send me into cardiac arrest. The man oozed sexiness from his pores.

We'd talked about what gray sweatpants did to a woman, so I know he wore them on purpose. Jerk. He sat down, and his sexy cologne assaulted me yet again. I hated him. No, I loved him, but still, I hated him.

"You look amazing," he said.

The smile that graced my face betrayed the image I wanted to display. I was dressed in all black because he loved me in it. I wore a pair of faux leather leggings and a black top that exposed one shoulder. My freshly purchased tan had my fair skin looking sun-kissed and copper like a brand-new shiny penny. My hair, now auburn was straightened and worn in a sleek ponytail.

"Thank you. The gray sweats, really?"

He grinned cockily. "Hey, I had to try."

I laughed, and the tension melted.

"What's up with you and the 8 o'clock hour?"

He smiled. "Maybe one day I'll tell you, but not today."

I rolled my eyes. "What am I doing here, *Sam*?"

He slid the manila envelope he brought in with him on the table.

"What is this?" I asked.

"Open it."

I rolled my eyes, sat back, and picked up the envelope. When I opened it, I stared down at some documents. I pulled out a passport, a driver's license, and a social security card. There was also a note and a single key. I stared at him frowning. I opened up the passport and there I was, Nyla *Steele*. The picture was one he took of me that night. My new driver's license and social security card read the same name. The note had an address on it. Tears welled in my eyes.

"What is this, Sam?"

"I know I can't stop you, but if you need to get away, I want you to have the means to."

"You gave me your last name?"

"I figured if things were different you would have chosen to take it."

"If things were different, I would choose everything about you," I confessed.

Tears welled up in his eyes but didn't fall. He cleared his throat and sat up straighter.

"And this key?" I inquired shifting the subject.

"That's my place. My spot to disappear. Now it's yours. Just get there, call that number and I'll meet you there."

A tear ran down my cheek.

"If you want the feds off your back, it's a good chance I can make that happen?"

"How?"

"Let's just say I've been saving my get out of jail free card, just in case I needed it."

"I can't take that from you."

"It's not taking if I willingly give it."

"Why are you doing this?"

"You know exactly why I'm doing this."

"Thank you." He nodded and stood up. "Where are you going?" I asked.

"I told you. I don't want just a sample; I want the whole package. I'm not willing to settle for anything less."

With that, he leaned down and kissed my cheek.

"Be safe love."

He turned and left me sitting there crying and staring at his retreating back. I sat there for about five minutes feeling sorry for myself then I got mad.

I slid the contents back into the envelope and stuffed it in my backpack. I slung it over my shoulder as I began to wipe the tears from my face with the back of my hand. I strutted to the counter with purpose and got Simon's attention.

He looked petrified. I could care less.

"Which one is his room?"

"Um, ma'am... I can't."

I whipped my .22 out and placed it on the counter. "I am not going to hurt him, but I will hurt you if you don't tell me which one his room is."

"It's room 2... 2... 219," he said looking like he'd just peed on himself.

I wiped my face again.

"Thanks, Simon. Don't worry, I won't let him fire you," I told him as I dashed out.

The cleaning lady in the lobby stared at me like I was crazy. I flipped her off and headed to room 219.

I knocked.

No answer.

I knocked again.

I knew he was in there; I could feel him. This time I banged on the door. Finally, he opened it.

"Nyla..."

I covered his lips with mine and kicked the door closed. He pulled away and stared at me.

"I can't," he said breathlessly.

I let my eyes pierce his. "What if I walk out that door and you never see me again," I asked desperately.

Tears welled in his eyes, but they fell down my cheeks. He snatched me up. I wrapped my legs around his waist as we tumbled onto the bed.

Hours later, we finally gave it a rest. I resisted the Sandman that was trying to take me under. I wanted to hold on to this moment as long as I could. While he slept, I pondered my life and all my choices. Never in my existence had I been connected to another human being in such a way. Yet deep inside, I knew it wasn't enough. It just wasn't.

I wasn't built for this. I wanted to be, but I wasn't. What if I stayed? I would always be restless. Knowing they got the best of me would always haunt me. I couldn't let it go, I just couldn't.

What was wrong with me?

I began to cry, like really and truly cry. Sobs rocked my body. Sam stirred. He just pulled me into him.

"Shhh."

I held on for dear life and cried until I was exhausted. When I had no more tears left to shed, he pulled my face to his. He stared into my eyes and I knew he could see deep down into my black soul.

"You're still going, aren't you?" he asked.

I nodded. The pained look on his face broke my heart.

"I won't ask you to understand but I am who I am, and you are who you are. We have to accept that about each other. You don't understand the wars that rage on the inside of me. My demons are loud, and they'll never let me be happy."

He nodded. "Nyla, I promise you my love can roar louder than any demon you're facing. But you have to let me."

"I'm familiar with my demons. I don't know love. It's safer to stick to the devil you know."

He stared at me like my words bruised him beyond repair. He leaned in and placed the sweetest kiss on my lips.

"I'm going to hold you as long as you allow me to."

I nodded and lay my head on his chest. I closed my eyes exhausted from our mind-blowing escapades and scraped raw from my emotions. We both knew when the sun came up, I would be gone, for good this time.

Chapter 50: Father, I Have Sinned

When Sampson woke up the next morning, Hurricane Nyla was gone leaving nothing but the pieces of his broken heart in the wake of her unsolicited devastation. Now he had to find a way to put the pieces of his life back together, though he felt like he may never be whole again. He gave her a piece of him the night before. He knew it was a mistake to go there, but what's done was done. The woman had a way about her that forced a man with principles to throw caution to the wind. Now came the consequences, regret, and pain.

Dragging himself to the shower, he stared at his reflection in the mirror. He closed his eyes. He could see her, feel her, smell her. He sighed then turned on the shower letting the steam fill the room.

Climbing in he decided this was the one and only time he would let himself break over a situation he knew was dangerous before he even spoke to her. He cried as the powerful jets of spraying water mixed with his sorrow. She was gone.

As bad as it hurt, he knew if given the chance he'd have done it all over again. It was just something about her that pulled at him. He couldn't explain it. She was a part of him even before he knew her name. For his sanity, he needed to let her go, but for his heart to keep beating, he needed to keep hope alive that she'd change her mind and come back to him. He'd known her for a week and she'd completely changed the trajectory of his life.

After he showered, he headed into his office. An hour passed before he gave up getting any work done. He needed to talk to someone. He headed out.

"Hey Simon, I'm gone for the day. Hold it down. Call my cell if you need me."

"Uh, okay. No problem," Simon replied confused.

Simon didn't know what was up with his boss, but he knew it had everything to do with that crazy lady he was smitten with. Simon had known Sampson for years. Though not privy to all his secrets he knew a few. He knew enough to know they were two peas in a dangerous pod. He wasn't so sure they were good for each other and he was glad she was long gone.

Sampson strolled into the sanctuary of the All Souls Catholic Church that sat across the street from his hotel. When he needed to clear his head and the gym didn't work, he'd come here from time to time to just sit in the sanctuary.

He didn't pray, he didn't light a candle, he never owned rosary beads, he simply enjoyed the stillness when there was no service. There was something so amazing about a sanctuary open for any and everyone to come in when they needed solace. He'd always thought of the church as a shelter for the weary.

Father Jonathan usually left him be, though sometimes if no one was in his confessional, he'd come and sit with him. A few times they chatted about his past, God, angels, Heaven and Hell. Father Jonathan had become his friend without him even realizing it.

Since his departure from the military, outside of his hotel staff, he had no one. Both of his parents were gone. He had a sister, but they barely kept in touch with each other. He kept tabs on her and sent her money once a month to make sure she was never in need.

He hadn't been able to form successful relationships after his time in the navy. He knew war. He knew warfare. He knew combat. But once he was discharged, he wanted no parts of anybody's war.

There had always been a longing in him to belong to someone and have someone belong to him. He saw the ugliness of the world and in his opinion the only thing that could counteract that kind of evil was love. As jacked up as his other human relationships were, he knew when he met *her*, all the love he had yet to give would be ready, willing, and able. Never in a million years did he plan to give his heart away to someone who was too afraid to hold it and petrified to let him hold hers.

The church was beautiful with its ornate décor and stained-glass windows. The large wooden pews gleamed with fresh polish. The large crucifixion that sat behind the altar always seemed ominous to him.

A few people had come in to light a candle and pray as they held their rosaries at the front of the church. He knew there was someone in the confessional, because of the hushed whispers that filled the quietness around him. He'd never been to confession. He didn't buy into the concept that he needed a mediator to talk to God.

He figured if he could have a divine encounter in the trenches of Afghanistan with no middleman, one wasn't needed. He thought about that angel nearly every day, but he realized sitting there he never talked to God after that night. True, he had tried to become a better person, but with the exception of seeing the angel wing when Nyla breezed into his life, that was it.

Why was that? How could he have such a miraculous encounter with God and not seek more beyond that moment? He looked up when he heard faint footsteps approaching him.

"My friend! It's good to see you," Father Jonathan said in his cheerful voice.

Sampson smiled and looked up at the older man. Father Jonathan was about 5-feet-5-inches. His priestly robes covered a robust belly. He had a receding hairline, and his white skin sported many wrinkles, but his eyes were kind and his spirit gentle.

"Father Jonathan, it's good to see you too."

The older man frowned. "Oh, my son, what burdens your spirit today?"

"How can you tell?"

"Son, a blind man could tell something was wrong with you. Tell me what's going on."

"Father, I'm in love, but she doesn't love me back."

"Oh, well I'm sorry to hear." The priest pondered for a few moments as he observed the sad demeanor of his friend. He asked, "Are you sure she doesn't love you or is it she doesn't really know *how* to love you?"

Sampson chuckled. "You've always been insightful, Father. That's exactly what it is, but she doesn't want to *learn* how to love me either."

"Scripture says *Love is patient, love is kind. It does not envy, it does not boast, it is not proud. It does not dishonor others, it is not self-seeking, it is not easily angered, it keeps no record of wrongs. Love does not delight in evil but rejoices with the truth. It always protects, always trusts, always hopes, always perseveres. Love never fails."*

Sampson nodded taking in the words the priest recited from memory.

"I know a man like you wouldn't just give his heart to any woman. You, my friend don't trust very easily. So, she must be special. I told you a long time ago, God was trying to get your attention. I think He finally has it. Why don't you just sit here for a little while, just be still and listen."

Sampson stared up at Father Jonathan confused. The priest chuckled as he patted Sampson's shoulder.

"You don't honestly believe that He brought you back from death without reason, do you?" the priest asked mischievously.

Sampson didn't answer, but he remembered what the paperwork said. His time of death was 8 PM. Miraculously, he was brought back two minutes later. It took him a week to recover, but every time a clock struck 8:00 he was reminded, he walked this earth because God wanted him to.

Father Jonathan left Sampson to ponder his words. Nyla came into his life like a hurricane so maybe it was an act of God, but why? If she was the reason he was still breathing, how come she was gone? The guardian angel that was assigned to him stood valiantly behind him as Sam took the priest's advice and sat still to see if God had something to say.

Chapter 51: The Voice of the Lord

Hours had passed, and Sam still sat right there in the pew. Every now and then Father Jonathan would come out to see if he was still waiting. For his part, Sampson had never been instructed to sit still and listen for the voice of God.

As he sat, he realized he desperately wanted to hear it and he made up in his mind he would sit there until he did. With all the drama Nyla had going on he knew only something truly divine could guide him out of this mess he'd gotten himself into.

As messy as the situation was, he somehow felt he was right where he was supposed to be. Perhaps that's why he was willing to sit and wait to hear something. He needed to know for sure if this was what he believed it was and not just his loneliness leading him down the path of destruction.

His guardian angel stood valiantly over him. He had watched over him daily since that fateful night in the Afghanistan raid. The angel had been assigned to Sampson to watch out for him in the midst of corruption and guide his steps until he crossed paths with destiny. Now, his job was to order his steps to the path that led him to his Lord and Savior, Jesus Christ.

Patience and discipline were something that was second nature to Sampson as a sniper. Sitting there being still wasn't difficult. Believing that some supreme being was going to speak to him was the difficult part.

"Be still my child. My hand will reveal itself soon. When it does, move with haste. You'll know what to do," a still small voice said.

Sam's eyes got huge as the tears involuntarily spilled down his face. He felt this enormous presence all around him. He wiped his face and looked around completely baffled.

His guardian angel chuckled. The audible voice of the Lord God Almighty was a force to be reckoned with. Just then Father Jonathan walked into the sanctuary. He could tell by the look on his face that God had just given his dear friend an encounter he would never forget.

The priest prayed faithfully for Sampson's salvation. He understood this moment just got him one step closer.

"Father, I heard him."

"I knew you would. Now, go, son. Your steps are being ordered. Never forget that."

Sam nodded as peace settled in his heart. He left the sanctuary with a new focus. To be ready to move with haste when the hand of God revealed itself.

Chapter 52: Confrontation

Neil and Nigel entered the lobby of the G & M Hotel.

"You really think she's here?" Nigel inquired.

"This is where the trail led. Let's find out," Neil pointed and headed towards the counter. They stood in line.

In his office, Sampson watched the two men that just walked into his establishment. His instincts told him somebody was going to come looking for Nyla sooner or later. They had only missed her by a day. He was grateful for that.

He assumed, these were her uncles, especially since the lighter skinned, slimmer one had similar features of hers. They seemed to be complete opposites. The taller one wore jeans, boots, and a t-shirt. He wore a gold badge around his neck.

The other was dressed fashionably in navy blue suit and tie. The suit and tie did not fool him. He recognized the outline of his gun and knew he was a southpaw.

Sampson was still dressed in his custodial uniform but decided to confront them. He exited from his office and made his way into the lobby.

The brothers were next in line. He stood off to the side and waited to see how they would approach. When they got to the counter, Neil flashed his badge.

"Good evening, my name is Detective Neil Lawson. My brother and I are searching for our niece. We got a tip that she may have stayed at your establishment. Do you mind taking a look at a photo?"

The clerk said, "No, not at all."

Neil pulled out a picture of Michelle Fuller. It wasn't an official photo, but one from their days undercover.

"Oh, that's Roche..."

Before he could finish, he was interrupted.

"Excuse me, Simon, I'll take it from here," Sampson interjected.

Nigel turned around to see who was being rude.

"Yes, sir," Simon said and motioned for the next customer to approach the desk.

Neil and Nigel sized up the custodian. They exchanged a look.

"From the way, ol boy fell in line, I would say you're more important than your uniform would suggest," Neil said.

Sampson nodded. "I'm more likely to find out what's going on in my establishment as the help versus the owner any day," he told them.

Neil nodded and extended a hand. "Detective Lawson."

Sampson shook the hand offered. "Sampson Steele, owner."

They both admired the firm grip each other displayed. Nigel followed up with his own strong handshake.

"Nigel Sims."

"You're looking for your niece, is it?" Sampson inquired.

"Yes, your boy was just about to tell us..."

He got cut off. "Why don't we take this to my office?"

The brothers exchanged another look then nodded. They followed Sampson behind the counter to a cove of offices that were hidden by the wall.

"Aye, where's your bathroom?" Nigel inquired as Sampson reached his office.

"It's around the corner to your left."

He nodded and headed off. Neil knew his brother was going to contact his right-hand man Darryl to look up information on the owner now that they had his name. He followed Sampson into his office and took the seat he offered. Sampson headed behind his desk and took a seat.

"Can I get you something to drink?" he asked.

"No, I'm good," Neil declined.

"Should we wait for your brother?"

"Yes, let's."

Sampson nodded.

Neil asked, "What branch of the military did you serve in?" Sampson's brow winged up. "It's the way you carry yourself."

Sampson nodded. "Navy."

"Seal?"

"Indeed."

"Thank you for your service."

"Thank you for yours," Sampson nodded.

Neil nodded his thanks.

Nigel came in and shut the door. "What are we being thankful for?"

"Sampson served in the military," Neil informed him.

"Oh no doubt, probably a Navy Seal," Nigel said confidently.

"You have a good eye," Sampson said trying to hide his shock.

"Yeah, I do, but we recognize our own kind. Besides, Seals have a very distinct air about them."

Sampson had to catch himself, that statement was exactly what he'd said to Nyla.

"Something wrong?" Nigel inquired.

"Nah, it's just you don't give off a military vibe."

"Oh nah, homie, I'm nobody's soldier. But I am highly trained at taking lives that need to be taken, you feel me."

Sampson sat back in his seat and folded his arms in front of his chest.

"It's nice to know we're going to skip the BS and level with each other."

"I like you, I really do," Nigel told him. "I hope you are an ally instead of an obstacle. Where's my niece?"

Neil decided to sit this one out and observe. He could appreciate a worthy opponent, but there was more to this. Something was nagging at him. He had to give it to Fuller, she had definitely thrown them a curve ball with this guy.

"Why are you looking for her?"

"We don't want her to miss out on this family reunion."

Sampson smirked. "You're funny. Listen, I'm not going to insult your intelligence by trying to convince you she wasn't here. She's long gone, and I don't know where she is. Even if I did, I wouldn't tell you."

Nigel's brow winged up.

Neil leaned in. "I recognize a man in love when I see one. Your protective instinct is understandable, but I caution you. She's more treacherous than you can imagine. It's best if you stay out of family affairs."

Sam scowled showing the first sign of a temper. "I know exactly who she is, and I know who you two are and why you want to find her. For the record, I begged her to leave all this behind and come have a life with me, but she's driven and unfortunately, I haven't been able to stop it."

"Then you can understand what I will have to do should the situation call for it," Nigel told him with a straight face.

There was fire on Sampson's face, but he managed to keep his cool. "I'm going to ask you this one time. Find a way to deal with this that doesn't take her life."

"The choice has always been hers," Neil informed him. "And she continues to make the wrong choice."

"I understand what's at stake here, I really do, but you don't understand what's on the other side of an unfavorable outcome for her."

"What's that?" Nigel asked his own temper spiking.

"If when this is over, she's not breathing, she won't be the only one," he told them as smooth and calm as ever. "I do not want to be your enemy, but I have no problem doing what needs to be done to avenge what I love. All I'm asking is that we find a better solution."

Neil and Nigel exchanged a look.

"It's obvious you truly do love our niece. That much is clear, but if unconditional love wasn't enough to talk some sense into her, what likelihood do we have? Your girl is a loose cannon that has already taken plenty from me. For me it's about one thing, protecting what I love. So, you do what you have to do sir. For the record, I truly wish she would choose you, but if she doesn't, then like my brother always says, it is what it is." Neil stood up and headed out the door. He was done with the conversation.

Nigel remained seated, but said, "This is really jacked up. I truly am sorry we couldn't help each other. I'm always here for black love. You seem like one that would fit right in with the fam, to be honest."

Sampson nodded in agreement, "Yeah, in any other situation, we'd likely be good friends. You know, she wants no part of bringing harm to your child," Sampson told him.

"I know and for that I'm grateful." Nigel stood up as well. "If she agrees to let bygones be bygones, I can move on. It will take some convincing, but I can make sure my brother moves on as well, though I don't think she'll be invited to the cookout."

"That's fair," Sampson said. "If I can convince her otherwise, I'll let you know."

"You do that," Nigel said and pulled out his card.

He dropped it on Sampson's desk and left to find this brother. Sampson sat back in his chair and sighed. His heart ached. All he wanted was to hold her in his arms and all she wanted was revenge.

He had come so far from the life he used to lead, and he sincerely didn't want to go back. He already knew the depth of what he felt for her would activate the *savage* in him if harm came to her. He didn't doubt for one second that her uncles were formidable warriors, but so was he.

Chapter 53: Impasse

The brothers rode in silence for a long while stuck in their own heads trying to process what just went down.

Finally, Neil broke the silence, "Where are you headed?" he asked.

"To my wife. I miss her and I'm tired of being away from her and my baby girl."

Neil nodded. He missed Grey and Hunter as well. It had been weeks of following leads and strategizing on their part. He was more than okay with reuniting with the woman he loved.

"Thoughts?" Neil inquired.

"He would kill for her without a second thought," Nigel said matter-of-factly. "We may have to neutralize him as well."

Neil nodded. "I assume you already sent his info to Darryl to get the scoop."

"You know it, waiting on it to come through."

"He's formidable," Neil said.

"I agree, but you know what's jacked up. I want her to let this whole thing go and be with him. I want that for her. If we've learned anything in all this, it's that love can transform the darkest of souls. She needs this. If she chooses him, mama wins, though she might not get to be in her life, but she wins, and our loved ones are safe. What happened to her that she's so broken, she can't see it?"

"I don't know, but whatever it is, it's deep."

"Daddy issues? Mama said she went to see Niles grave. I mean why risk all of that to drop off some roses to a man you didn't even know."

"That's a good assumption."

"If she stays on the course of revenge, she'll be even more ruthless than before because of what it's costing her."

"Yeah, I considered that too," Neil admitted.

Nigel sighed. "Why is our family plagued like this. I mean seriously, we're missing something. There's something bigger at stake here. It has to be. This is insane. I'm sincerely torn about this man."

"I'm not," Neil said flatly.

Nigel looked at his brother and frowned. "You serious, bro?"

Neil looked at him with such a no-nonsense glare he understood not to ask the question again.

"Well dang."

"I've hit my quota of betrayals this lifetime. I'm good. I'm not here for the foolishness. It's hard for me to believe that she's capable of change. I will never trust that woman, period. There will be no family reunions and chilling like all is well."

Nigel wasn't quite sure how to reach his brother. It was usually him that needed to be talked down off the ledge. It never occurred to him that their roles would be reversed.

The way Neil handled him when he was out of control wouldn't work on his brother. They were built completely different. He would have to talk to Grey. She was the only person on the planet capable of reaching him. That worried him though because Grey had her own issues with their niece.

Nigel sighed. Neil continued to silently steam. He wanted this over and done with. He wasn't heartless. He was okay with her being locked up, but he already knew she wouldn't make the civil approach easy. The lengths she went to escape prison made it abundantly clear she had zero intentions of returning to a cage.

Silence enveloped them again as they each returned to their own mental battles. Thirty minutes passed before either spoke a word.

Nigel said, "I know you've considered this, but I'm going to say it out loud."

Neil sighed, "Yeah, maybe God is trying to intervene and give her a way out with this Sam guy. But if she doesn't take it, that's not on us. That's what free will is all about."

Nigel sighed frustrated. This felt so unfair. He sincerely believed his niece when she said she wanted no parts of bringing harm to his daughter. He also understood that she could be used against her without her consent, but that didn't bother him as much as maybe it should have.

He didn't know if his faith in God had gone to another level or if he saw something in her that Neil wasn't capable of seeing. Blood was thicker than water. She was made an Untouchable but born a Lawson. That had to count for something.

She had a stake in the perpetuation of their bloodline whether any of them acknowledged it or not. Why would she risk going to see

Eva just to send a message that essentially was a warning sent to protect his baby girl?

He didn't know when his heart began to change for her, but love was finding a way through the darkness that had begun to settle in his heart. He stole a glance at his brother. His face remained stoic. He wouldn't press the issue anymore. He'd just get them home safely to the women they loved.

Chapter 54: Home

When Nigel pulled Neil's truck up to the safe house they hadn't said a word to each other since he brought up divine intervention. They weren't mad at each other, they just stood on different sides of an issue. Well, not completely different sides. He hadn't fully converted to Team Michelle, but he was willing to consider the possibility.

He still couldn't wrap his mind around it, but there was something about the love he saw for her on Sampson's face. He recognized the fierceness of his protective nature because it was like looking in a mirror. Weren't they essentially all connected in this tug-of-war to protect the women they loved?

Speaking of the woman he loved, there she was. Kadijah was standing on the porch beneath the porch light. He jumped out of the truck and headed for his wife. Neil climbed out of the truck as well. They both nodded at the four men standing watch.

"If I wasn't a beach ball, I'd run and jump in your arms," Kadijah told him as he neared the porch.

Nigel grinned and picked up his pace. He grabbed her and picked her up then laid a kiss on her that made her head spin.

"Uh, can y'all stop blocking the doorway with all that please?" Neil politely asked.

They laughed as Nigel shifted them out of the way, but their lips never parted.

Inside the house, Grey was coming towards the front door carrying a fussy Hunter, Beau not far behind them. Neil smiled when he saw his wife and son. He couldn't wait to be in his favorite spot. He needed the peace it brought him more than he ever had before.

Neil reached for his son. Grey handed him over and was not shocked at all that he stopped crying once Neil put him on his chest.

"He missed you," Grey told him.

Neil kissed the top of Hunter's curly head and reached for his wife. She wrapped her arms around him and squeezed him tight. He kissed the top of her head. Grey looked up.

"You okay?"

"Not really," he told her honestly.

"Okay. It's gonna be okay."

Neil leaned down and kissed his wife. Grey grabbed his face and took the kiss deeper. She missed her man. Nigel and Kadijah came in.

"Uh, now who's in the way."

He was ignored as Neil continued to kiss his wife.

"Um, that's my queue to leave," Beau said. "I'm going back to bed."

Nigel and Kadijah laughed as they headed into the kitchen to sit at the dining room table. Stephan came in from the kitchen.

"Welcome back man. You good?"

"Yeah, I'm good."

"Alright, I'll give y'all some privacy. Holla at me in the morning."

Nigel nodded. He looked over to see his brother had yet to let Grey breathe.

"Um, negro. Come up for air!"

Neil continued to indulge in the kiss for a few more moments. When he finally pulled away, he kept an arm wrapped around Grey.

"Stay out of grown folks' business!"

They laughed. Grey headed over to Nigel. He stood up to give her a hug as Kadijah stood to hug Neil.

Nigel whispered in Grey's ear.

"I can't reach him, sis. It's on you."

Grey squeezed him to let him know she'd heard him. When he pulled away, he locked eyes with her for a split second before releasing her.

Neil kissed Kadijah's cheek. "How you feeling, sis?"

"Uncomfortable as hell."

They all laughed.

"So, are we going to be debriefed or what?" Grey asked.

"Let tomorrow worry about itself," Neil said before Nigel could answer. "Babe, go grab anything you need for the night."

"We're leaving?" Grey asked confused. "Yeah. We'll be back first thing in the morning."

She nodded without protest, then went to the room to gather her and Hunter's things.

"You good, bro?" Nigel asked.

"Yeah, I'm good," Neil said as he kissed his son again.

Nigel stood up and handed his brother his truck keys. Neil took them. Grey came out of the room with Hunter's car seat and portable bed and an overnight bag.

"Good night y'all," Neil said as he placed Hunter in his car seat and grabbed the bed.

"Night," Kadijah said.

When they left, Nigel closed and locked the door.

"What was that about?" Kadijah asked. "Are y'all okay?"

"Yeah, we're good. I'm pretty sure that's about being alone with his wife after a few weeks."

Kadijah laughed.

"Speaking of...," she stood and reached for his hand.

He grinned and gladly took it.

Chapter 55: A Stolen Moment

Neil checked his family into a nondescript motel about ten miles up the road. He went straight to take a hot shower and wash the day away.

Grey got Hunter settled in his portable bassinet. He was fed, dry and prayerfully in for the night. She missed her husband dearly. Sharing a bed with a grumpy pregnant woman was not the business. She was grateful for this little reprieve.

She was propped up in the middle of the bed when Neil came out of the bathroom with a towel wrapped around his waist. He leaned down to kiss his baby boy then turned out the light.

Grey muted the TV as he climbed into the bed and lay his head on her bosom. Grey ran her fingers through the waves of his Caesar haircut. He closed his eyes and enjoyed being close to her again. Her scent, her heartbeat, and the feel of her silky skin beneath his calloused hands all soothed him like only she could.

"You gonna tell me what went down?"

He nodded. "Not right now though."

"Okay," she said as she leaned down and kissed his forehead.

"I missed you," she said.

"I missed you too, baby. You have no idea."

"Show me," she said. He looked up at his wife. She had a sly smile on her pretty face. "Don't act like you didn't bring me to this cheap motel to take advantage of me."

He grinned and leaned up to kiss her.

When they were done, Neil slept peacefully on her bosom. She began to cover him in prayer. She wasn't sure what all went down while he was away from her, but she knew this battle was far from over.

When she was done, she peeked over at their son then finally dropped into sleep. Their angels had never left their side.

Chapter 56: Divine Strategy

Nigel paced back and forth on the back porch of the safehouse as he continued to pray. He loved being all alone in the wee hours of the morning talking to God. Five AM was the time he tried to approach God's throne with consistency. His angels were right by his side.

"Lord, these puzzle pieces are flying at me left and right. I know they all fit together, but I just don't see how. You have to show me what's going on. I know only you could change my heart towards our niece. I know that's all You and none of me, so tell me why. Tell me how to fight this battle."

He continued to pray and pace. Finally, he took a seat on the rocking chair and just sat still. He closed his eyes and rocked as he let his mind settle. Bomani, his Egyptian warrior, glorified and placed a hand on his shoulder.

Nigel remembered that Etienne told them they could find strategies for war in the Bible. He nodded. "Thanks Father. Now, please, order my steps."

Nigel went into the house being careful to keep quiet. There were two guards on duty, but everyone else in the house was asleep. He went to the Keurig and popped in a k-cup of his favorite coffee blend, then grabbed his phone and his Bible. After he'd poured the coffee adding no sugar or cream, he headed back to the back porch.

Nigel took a sip of his coffee then picked up his phone. He loved technology and utilized it every chance he got. He Googled "famous battles in the Bible."

As he scrolled, he found a site the listed remarkable battles in the Bible. As he searched through the list, one of them gave him a vibe. Nigel picked up his Bible and turned to 2 Kings 6:8-20. He read the passage carefully. He stopped at verse 20 like the site suggested, but something nudged him to go further. He read the next three verses before the topic change.

21 When the king of Israel saw them, he asked Elisha, "Shall I kill them, my father? Shall I kill them?" 22 "Do not kill them," he answered. "Would you kill those you have captured with your own sword or bow? Set food and water before them so that they may eat and drink and then go back to their master." 23 So he prepared a great feast for them, and after they had finished eating and drinking, he sent them away, and they returned to their master. So, the bands from Aram stopped raiding Israel's territory.

That part was crystal clear. He knew exactly what God was telling him. He pulled out his phone to take out some notes, so he could reflect on what he just read. He knew within these verses God have given him a strategy for his family. He would use whatever revelation he got from this passage to construct his prayers going forward.

He typed:

2 Kings 6:8-22

✔ God can reveal the plans of your enemy so you know where to set your watchman

✔ The enemy will regroup and plot against the seer, but DO NOT fear. The same God has an angelic alliance ready to wage war on your behalf

✔ Pray for God to BLIND your enemies from being able to see you and lead them to YOUR fortified place. You have the advantage on your territory

✔ Do not repay in kind but show them love/kindness and send them on their merry way. This enemy is no longer a threat.

Nigel mused over what he wrote. He felt his discernment kicking in. He prayed.

"Father let every step the enemy takes be exposed. Show me where to set the watchman. Blind our enemies to everything we do. Blind them to our children. Blind them to our weaknesses. Blind them to our strategies. Show me how to bring our niece home where she can be protected from the plot the enemy has against our bloodline. Father show her she is safe with us and nowhere else. Give us the heart to show her love, kindness, and forgiveness. Remove her as a threat and make her an ally. Make this family whole again and restore what the enemy tried to steal all those years ago. In Jesus name I pray, amen."

Nigel felt himself relax. It's true he didn't know what lay ahead, but he knew that God was in the details and that was enough for him to finally have peace. He knew he'd need to talk to Grey and the sooner, the better.

Chapter 57: The Debrief

A couple hours later, Nigel kissed the back of his wife's neck.

"Wake up sleepy head," he murmured.

Kadijah whined, "Babe, you just let me go to sleep a few hours ago."

He chuckled. "You complaining?"

She giggled. "No, but my brain needs sleep to function."

"Well, it's not going to get any right now."

He repositioned himself and kissed her. The kiss managed to clear away the cobwebs.

When he released her, she said, "You keep this up and you're gonna make this baby come early."

He laughed and began to kiss her neck as she surrendered to the moment and embraced the man she loved. She loved that he took his time and was never in a rush when they shared these intimate moments. What the man could do with his hands consistently blew her mind.

For his part, Nigel took care to prove to his wife just how much he'd missed her in these last few weeks. He knew he didn't ever want to be apart from her like that again. He wanted this situation over and done with, so he could get on with the business of living his life with the woman he loved.

When they were finished, he was smug, and she was sated.

"Come on, let's go take a shower because Neil and Grey will be here soon."

"I can't feel my legs, Nigel. You take your own shower and I'll take mine. I do not trust you."

He laughed. "I would never..."

She cut him off. "No, sir. I am too fat and feeble to be fooled up with you in the shower. Now go! I can at least catch a fifteen-minute nap."

Nigel laughed hard as he kissed his wife then headed for the shower.

†††

An hour later, Neil and Grey along with Hunter walked through the front door to find the house still quiet. At the table sat Beau, Nigel, Stephan, and Kadijah. Neil closed and locked the door behind him.

Kadijah stood up to reach for Hunter.

"I missed my baby," she said as she put kisses on his chubby cheeks.

Nigel stood up and greeted his brother with a hand clasp and one-armed hug.

"You good now?" Nigel asked.

"I'm lighter on my feet," Neil replied with a shrug.

Nigel laughed. "Me too. Real light."

They laughed.

Neil and Grey took a seat. Nigel exchanged a look with Grey, she gave a slight shake of her head to let him know she hadn't been able to help Neil deal with whatever he was going through.

"So, what did y'all find out?" Stephan asked.

"It's complicated," Nigel said.

"How so?" Grey asked frowning.

He understood Neil hadn't told her anything by her question. He guessed he could understand that. His brother was more concerned with being with his wife than bringing the ugliness into their long-awaited reunion.

"Agent Michelle Fuller is a mess of conflictions. She's got daddy issues and we believe she might know the truth about the part the organization played in Niles' death. She went to visit his grave and brought roses."

"What?" Grey asked shocked.

"Yeah," Neil said.

"She also is in love with a very dangerous man, but she's choosing to pursue her revenge rather than settle down with him," Nigel informed them.

"Wait, what?" Kadijah commented in shock.

"How dangerous is this guy?" Stephan asked.

"Darryl just shot me the information this morning. He was honorably discharged from the Navy. He was a Seal with many of his missions marked classified. We have no idea, but we can guess. Any more digging and I'm sure somebody would've come looking for whoever was snooping."

"Oh! One of them kind, huh. How in the world, did she end up with him?" Grey asked.

"He owns the hotel she was staying in," Neil added.

"Is he a threat to y'all?" Beau asked.

"He doesn't want to be, but he will be if harm comes to her. He made that very clear," Nigel informed them.

"This is too much," Kadijah said rubbing her belly with both hands.

"The only thing you need to be worried about sis is having this baby," Neil told her. "We'll deal with the rest."

"I think there's bad blood between her and what's left of the organization since she wants no part of harming my daughter," Nigel interjected. "She made that clear to Eva and Sam."

"But the organization can use her if they want to," Grey added.

"True, but I believe she would do everything in her power to prevent that."

Grey studied him. "Bro, you seem to have a change of heart about her."

"I do."

"Why?" Kadijah and Grey asked in unison.

"The look on Sampson's face told me everything I needed to know. There's a chance that we can end this with our family still intact, *all* of our family," he said while eyeing his brother.

"And your stance on this?" Grey asked her husband.

"There will be no family reunions. I don't care."

Grey nodded but chose not to indulge the dissent.

Nigel chose not to say anything to his brother either but instead addressed the rest of the group.

"Listen, the way we took down Alonzo and the organization was with love and forgiveness. Sampson has the love to offer her. We need to offer her the forgiveness and trust God to do the rest."

"That's a good theory bro, but on the other side of that is death for the people I love. I'm not risking it. I don't trust her. You heard what Sampson said. She chose to pursue revenge rather than to live a life with him. Her decision has been made and we need to govern ourselves accordingly."

Beau frowned. He'd never seen Neil quite like this.

"Well I know your mother would be very happy if this ended favorably for everyone," Kadijah added. "She constantly worries over it."

"My mother needs to embrace reality. I know this woman. Do y'all get that? I *know* her. Do I believe God can do anything? I absolutely do, but she also has to *let* Him. She isn't going to stop until she gets what she wants. I for one am not going to sit back and let her have it. She knows she's family and she still chooses to exact revenge for some mess she started in the first place. So, no, I'm good on the whole kumbaya. I'll pass."

Neil got up and left the table to head outside to the front porch. Nigel and Grey exchanged a look.

"Oooweee he is hot with her," Kadijah said.

"I'll deal with Neil later," Grey said with a sigh. "What else can you tell us?"

"I've been thinking. Eva is aware of their mother and so is Fuller. Maybe we can track the mother. She has to be working with somebody and I'm guessing her mother is the only one she would trust enough to let in on her plan."

"Good point," Beau agreed.

"I'll call Eva and see what she knows," Nigel said.

"And what about me and my team?" Stephan asked.

"For the time being, y'all head back. If I need you, I'll let you know. I'm going to put Darryl on Kadijah and I know Beau will likely stick around for Grey." Beau nodded his agreement. "She's going to come to us that we can be sure of. My mission is going to be to find a way to reason with her. I know she'll stay in some kind of contact with Sampson. My thought is to set up a meeting with me, her, Neil, Sam and my mom to see if we can reason this out."

"Do you trust her not to try anything?" Kadijah asked.

"Yeah, I don't think Neil would be okay with your mom being exposed like that?" Grey added.

"Listen, y'all taught me all about spiritual warfare and I was slow to believe. Now that I'm fully invested, y'all gotta act like y'all know better. Do you think I came up with this plan on my own? Trust me. Love and forgiveness can tear down this breach, but we gotta be strategic and we gotta be smart. Do I trust her? No. But I do trust

Sam. There's something about him. If he gives his word, it's ironclad. Remember he has a vested interest in a truce being drawn as well. He loves her fiercely. Trust me on that."

They nodded.

"I don't think her ending up at that hotel owned by the one man that could see her like no one else ever could was happenstance. It was absolutely divine intervention. God is up to something. Everybody at this table knows I take zero issue with doing whatever needs to be done to protect mine. I just don't think that's what God wants this time around. I think there's something about her. She's our flesh and blood and has managed to still be standing even though her dad and most of her siblings aren't. You think its coincidence that the two who were connected to Neil are still breathing? Even when it looked like Eva was gone, she wasn't. He *shielded* them, and I truly believe that whether he's aware of it or not. I think it will be to our family's detriment to take her out before we know why that is. I also think Neil's resistance to this is further evidence that this is bigger than what it is. Y'all know, I'm usually the hothead and he's the rational one. Just think about it."

Stunned faces surrounded him.

"Ah, the grasshopper has become the teacher," he said.

They all fell out laughing. Nigel would always be a clown, no matter how serious the situation.

"What are we going to do about Neil?" Kadijah asked.

"Neil is mine to deal with. I got this, y'all. No worries," Grey told them.

Their angels had never left their side. They stood around listening and proud that Nigel had begun to use his gift of discernment to see the bigger picture. He and Grey together could do much damage to the Kingdom of Darkness. She had to get her focus off Neil's emotions and back on the spiritual side of things.

There was a reason Insidious used Fuller to come for them. He knew what he was doing, but they were confident that the Great I AM knew exactly what He was doing too.

"We need to pray," Stephan said shocking everyone but Grey and Nigel.

He stood and extended his hands. Everyone grabbed hands, with the exception of the one hand Kadijah had wrapped around her nephew. Stephan led them in a powerful prayer asking God for protection, wisdom, and patience. He also prayed for Neil's calloused heart.

They said, "Amen," in unison when he finished.

The angelic beings grinned fiercely. They had just surrendered to the will of God leaving their personal agendas behind.

"Hey Grey, I need to holla at you for a second," Nigel said. She nodded. "Follow me."

Chapter 58: The Dynamic Duo

"What's up boo?" Grey asked when she and Nigel were on the back porch.

"Are you familiar with the battle in 2 Kings chapter 6?"

Grey's forehead creased as she thought. "Is that the one where Elisha tells his servant there are more with us than there are with them?"

"That's the one," he confirmed.

"I love that scripture. What about it?"

"Etienne told Neil and I to get our war strategies from the Bible. This is the one God led me to. I took notes based on what I felt the Holy Spirit was revealing to me. I need you to take a look at them."

"Okay," she said, not sure what he was getting at.

Nigel pulled up his notes on his phone and handed it to Grey. She read through them. Her memory of the battle was vaguely jogged, but the second point in his notes stood out.

"You're showing this to me because the enemy came for the seer?" He nodded. "Yes, but you're the one God is revealing the plot of the enemy to, not me," Grey told him.

"That's true, but I still wanted you to be aware. You cover me, and I'll cover you. Kadijah may not be focused on anything other than the baby right now. Neil isn't ready to hear this yet. Especially those last three verses in that passage about not killing them and instead preparing a feast for them."

"You're right. My baby is definitely not dealing with this well. I'll be on my spiritual toes so to speak. I got you, boo. No worries."

"Grey." She eyed him carefully, he rarely called her by name. "I felt a specific need to tell you about this. He may not be revealing the warfare to you, but there's something you're able to see that I'm not. So be ready."

She nodded.

"Okay. I'll be ready."

Their angels nodded. They knew these two gifts working together could do a whole lot of damage. With each of their spouses emotionally distracted, they would need to cover each other for the parts of the battle only they were able and available to see.

Chapter 59: A Gentle Touch

Neil stood on the porch with his hands in his pockets staring out into the open road as the dewiness of the morning settled him. He knew he was extremely emotional about this situation, but he couldn't help it. He was seriously agitated with everyone around him telling him how to feel and what he should be doing.

He didn't know what was in the Kool-Aid everybody was sipping, but he was good on that. There was also another conflict he was in the middle of that he didn't want to acknowledge. He wasn't talking to God, but God was most definitely speaking to him. He wasn't trying to hear it though.

He heard the door open, but there was no need to turn because he already knew it was his wife. Coming up behind him, Grey slid her hands around him possessively squeezing him. She lay her cheek against his back.

"You know, you look awfully sexy standing up here in these sweatpants staring off into the distance."

Neil smirked.

"Is that why you came out here? To flirt with me and feel me up."

"No, but when I saw you standing there, exuding sexiness the way you do, I had to put my agenda on pause."

He chuckled. She felt the rumble of his laughter through his back.

"You smell good, too," she said squeezing a little tighter. "I'm ready to get you home and take full advantage of you."

"Oh, is that so?"

He felt her nod against his back. Reaching for one of her hands, he pulled it to his lips and kissed it.

"Thank you for making me smile," he said.

"I try to do what I can do when I can do it."

He laughed as he turned around and wrapped her in his arms. He stared down at her towering over her five-foot-five frame. Her big brown eyes stared up at him. He kissed her nose.

"I love you."

"I love you," she said.

"I need some space on this thing with Fuller. I gotta work through it on my own."

"You didn't tell me she was here in town at your brother's grave."

"I know, I'm sorry. Please don't take it personal. Nigel and I were just working through it the best way we saw fit."

She nodded then asked, "What can I do?"

"What you always do, cover me in prayer."

"Promise me when you're ready to talk about it, I'll be the keeper of your secrets."

He smiled at her. "Always."

She stood on her tip toes to kiss him. He took the kiss a little deeper.

"Oh yeah, it's time to get you home, girl." She laughed. "Go get my child so we can go work on another one."

"Um, you still owe me a push gift for the first one homie," she said with a smirk.

He laughed as she headed into the house. He slapped her backside for good measure as he watched her walk away. Her walk still mesmerized him.

Chapter 60: Bundles of Joy

Sheridan was tired, but happy as she stared down at her baby girl. Seth was the last of the triplets to have his new bundle of joy enter the world. They were all only weeks apart.

Emma Lee fussed over her daughter as Seth took his baby girl from his wife. He was so in love. Rebecca Nicole Richards decided she would come two weeks early and she would come in the middle of the night. He grinned as he rubbed her tiny hand with one of his fingers.

He leaned down and kissed his wife's forehead. "You were a true soldier," he told her. "I'm so proud of you."

"You owe her a push gift," they heard a voice say.

They turned to see Grey coming in carrying their son Daniel.

Seth laughed.

"Daddy!" Daniel screamed.

"Hey lil man," Seth said as he leaned down to embrace his son.

"Is that my stister?" Daniel asked wide eyed.

"It is," Seth told him.

Father and son sat down to get to know the new addition to the family.

Sleepily, Sheridan said, "Thanks for getting him and for bringing him up here to see the baby," she said to Grey.

"Oh, it's no problem. If you need us to help the first few weeks just let us know."

"I definitely will," she said.

"How you feeling?"

"Girl, like I got hit by a Mack Truck."

Grey laughed. "Sounds about right."

"Alright now, mama needs her rest," Emma Lee began to fuss.

Grey leaned over and kissed her friend's cheek.

"I'll see you later. Oh, and I have bags of stuff for her. I went to buy one outfit and it was all downhill from there."

Sheridan shook her head. "Grey, do not start spoiling this child already."

Grey shrugged and waved bye.

"You get some rest baby. We'll take care of baby girl."

"Okay, ma," Sheridan said as she closed her eyes for some much-needed rest.

Third Trimester (Nov., Dec., Jan.)

Chapter 61: Lying in Wait

Agent Michelle Fuller had organized a plan to deal with those who had wronged her. Truthfully, her ire was toward Neil. Hurting him beyond repair before she took his life was simply necessary. She couldn't let the offenses given to her by him pass without retaliation.

Sampson had complicated everything and caused her to be slightly off her game. After she dropped off money and the poison to take out Lucca to her mother, she decided to set her sights on Nigel. One, it would emotionally cripple Neil. Two, it would neutralize one of Neil's advantages over her and three, it would thrill her to no end.

Deciding to breeze into town, take Nigel out and then leave to regroup for Neil and Grey was what she'd come up with. She'd been in position all day. She sat in a parked car with darkly tinted windows across the street from Nigel's security company.

All day she watched and noted employees, clients, patterns, and anomalies. This isolation gave her time to think and reflect on everything she'd gone through in the last month.

Since she'd left Sam's bed, she'd been a nomad, sleeping in various motels or whatever car she currently drove with the exception of the first week she'd spent in one hotel to rid herself of her snake phobia. She'd gone to a local pet store and purchase three snakes.

Forcing herself to live with the despicable creatures until she could pick one up and successfully hold it for five minutes. It was the most traumatic experience of her life, but she was determined to make sure she had every advantage in this war with her uncles.

Her mother had alerted her that Lucca had been dealt with once and for all. Though her heart was still broken over leaving Sam behind, things were looking up for her in her journey for revenge, so she focused on her good fortune and kept Sam where he belonged. In her rearview mirror.

Someone walked out of Nigel's building pulling her thoughts back to the present. She wanted to make a splash to announce her arrival with a bang. Her plan was to plant a bomb under Nigel's truck that she could detonate remotely.

She knew he closed at six. The day before, she'd given a couple hundred dollars to the homeless man that lurked in the area who told her that Nigel left between eight and nine every night. She was confident it was enough to buy his information and his silence.

For some reason, she wasn't interested in useless killing anymore. It baffled her, but she didn't have time to psychoanalyze herself. She needed to handle her business and figure out a way to still be with Sam when all was said and done. It was now 7:30 PM and she hadn't felt comfortable vacating her spot to plant the bomb.

She assessed there were several cameras all around the building. She knew he was on high alert. Unbeknownst to her, five demons guarded Fuller ready, willing, and desperate to battle any angel that got in their way.

†††

Across the street at Nigel's security firm, not only were there natural protectors, but there were spiritual ones as well. Angelic sentries had been sent by Captain Valter to guard the building while they awaited Fuller's arrival. She thought she had been undetected, but she'd been heavily surveilled by forces beyond her wildest imagination.

While Bomani and Lajos had never left Nigel's side. The minute Fuller hit their region; she was under watch. They knew the Almighty would protect their charge. They simply awaited instructions.

A messenger angel arrived on the scene. The demons watched in aggravated impatience as the message was delivered. They knew if a message was sent it could be sent from Captain Valter or directly from the Throne Room of Heaven.

The messenger angel's emerald robes shimmered as his wings retracted to stand near the large warrior angel guarding the front of the building. Both angels threw up their wings to cover their faces and hide their hushed conversation.

"Greetings brother," the warrior angel said.

"Greetings. I bring you a message from on high."

"What is it?"

"Father says, stand down. Blind Nigel and his people from seeing anything she tries to do."

Without hesitation or question, the warrior said, "I will alert his guardians. Go to the old, abandoned church on the outskirts of town and alert Captain Valter."

The messenger angel nodded and took off in a majestic emerald light, his expansive pearl wings glimmering as he flew away. The military angel looked at his fellow comrades.

"There is a message from on high. Jehovah is about to intervene. We don't know how, but we will trust His directive."

He flew away and went to alert Nigel's personal guardians of the message.

†††

Inside the office, Nigel was winding down his day. Every hour on the hour, his rotating shift of security reported what they saw. So far nothing of any substance had panned out.

He didn't care for being high strung all the time. He constantly prayed for this to be resolved. His work usually got him pumped. The challenges, even though dangerous were fuel for him, but not this one. This one weighed on his heart.

He kept thinking about his mother and how this would ultimately affect her in the long run. She'd already suffered so much loss. He had completely washed his hands of trying to convince Neil of anything. It was insane.

He had never seen his brother so rigid about a situation. Even Grey hadn't been able to get him to budge. All he could do was pray for his brother to see that there was a better way and pray that Fuller loved Sam enough to take the better way.

He knew his mother would want a relationship with her, in the best-case scenario. Neil wouldn't be able to get on board with that. As far as he was concerned her two options were a final black dress or an orange jumpsuit, there was no in between for him.

Just then the military angel entered in a stream of white light. Bomani and Lajos drew their weapons. One stood behind Nigel, the other in front. They were expecting their fellow angel was alerting them to an impending attack.

"Stand down, brothers. We have just received a message from the throne room."

Bomani and Lajos looked at each other then sheathed their gold flame coated weapons. They understood that if a message came from on high and not their captain, they were about to witness divine intervention.

"What's the message?" Lajos, a Hungarian warrior asked.

"The directive is to stand down and blind Nigel and his people to anything she tries to do."

Again, Nigel's two guardians exchanged a look then nodded.

"We will take care of it," Bomani, the Egyptian angel said.

With that, the other warring angel took flight to head back to his post. Lajos threw up a shield around Nigel. They were confident that the other angels on duty would take care of the other employees.

They were confident without hesitation they could trust the Ancient of Days. They couldn't wait to see what He was up to.

†††

Across the street, the five demons realized the angels weren't going to strike. They all put up their weapons but continued to stand guarding the building. They did not look ready to engage in warfare.

Demons were aware that sometimes God allowed things to happen and when they saw their opportunity to try for mayhem and destruction, they went for it, usually not quite thinking it all the way through.

The leader nudged Fuller. "Go now."

Inside the car, Fuller felt like this was the time. She had been watching and was shocked to see two of the security guards go inside and the others retreat to the back. She had judged, she could make it across the street, plant the bomb and get back in her spot within five minutes if she ran at full speed. She could detonate it as she pulled out and disappeared.

The cover of dusk was her friend, dressed from head to toe in all black, she got out of the car, the small but deadly device in the pocket of her cargo pants. She gently closed the door behind her and moved to the edge of the parking lot. Traffic had a steady pace, but she managed to get across the street without incident.

The five demons were surrounding her. Two of them watched the angels with their weapons drawn. They knew they were watching them but didn't move to intervene. They would take full advantage. The other three were whispering to Fuller reminding her of why she wanted this revenge. Constantly reaffirming that she was the victim and she needed to right these wrongs against her.

When she stepped on the property a powerful wave of nausea rose up in her. The cramp that hit her stomach took her down to her knees. The demons stopped trying to figure out what was going on.

Fuller's eyes got wide as saucers. She didn't know what was happening to her body. She put her hand over her mouth and gagged. Sweat began to bead up profusely on her forehead. She managed to get to the bushes that lined the building before she was violently ill.

She was shaking like a leaf on a tree as tears rolled down her cheeks. When the vomiting stopped, she stood up but swooned from the dizziness that the nausea caused. Something deep within her fueled her fury.

Determined to complete her self-appointed mission she looked around to see if her illness had brought any attention. She half expected to be surrounded by men and women with guns but was shocked to see the parking lot was still empty. Not wanting to miss this golden opportunity, she pressed her way.

The angels watched in anticipation as the demons encouraged her to continue on her mission. She pulled the device out of her pocket and continued to head towards Nigel's truck, though she walked along the bushes behind the parking spaces and not in front trying to avoid the cameras as long as possible.

She crossed between two sedans that were two spaces down from his truck. She wanted to put the device in the front of the vehicle to ensure maximum damage to the driver.

Just when she crossed in front of the second sedan, the wave of nausea struck her again. This time she went to her knees on the asphalt and dropped the device. She vomited all over the concrete and the bomb.

She shook like there was a personal earthquake erupting inside of her. Her hands began to sweat. There was a stomach cramp that made it hard for her to stand. When she reached to pick up the device a cramp struck her again, she yanked her hand back and clutched her stomach letting out a muffled groan.

She heard people talking and looked up. A group of pedestrians was walking along the sidewalk in front of the building.

"Ma'am are you okay?" one asked.

"Can we help you?" Another inquired.

She waved them off and ran as fast as she could pass them. She dipped and dodged the cars on the busy street nearly getting hit. She was in so much pain she thought she was going to black out.

Finally, she made it to the car, jumped in, started it and pulled out like a bat out of hell narrowly missing a car as she spun out into traffic. The demons were right there with her irate over what had just taken place.

The strangers walking down the street were in complete bafflement at what they had witnessed. They never saw her face.

"Should we knock on the door and tell whoever is in that building that they have a mess to clean up?" one asked.

One of the angels quickly flew over to them and impressed upon them to keep it moving.

Another said, "Nah, let's stay out of it and get out of here. That was weird."

They all nodded in agreement and kept walking.

The angel knew the device had not been armed, but it was still dangerous. Besides, he was confident Nigel would find it and eventually put the pieces together and follow the ordered steps Jehovah Jireh had just laid out.

†††

Twenty minutes later, Nigel and Darryl exited the building. They were talking about other cases the firm was working on, though they still remained watchful of their surroundings. As they crossed the parking lot, one of the angels flapped his wings in their direction.

"You smell that?" Nigel asked.

"Smell what?" Darryl asked.

"Smells like..." Nigel sniffed. "Ugh, vomit," Nigel said covering his nose and mouth.

Darryl looked out into the parking lot and saw the mess near his car.

"Yo, somebody puked in the parking lot, in front of my car."

They both stared at each other knowing they had the same thought. How was someone in the parking lot ill and no one saw it? They both pulled their guns and walked slowly towards the bodily fluids as they scanned the parking lot. It could have been a distraction.

Darryl got on the radio and told the other security guards to come to the front of the building. When they got to it, Nigel looked down.

"What is that in the middle of it?"

Darryl leaned in careful not to get any on his shoe.

"Looks like some sort of electronic device."

Nigel looked around. This was strange indeed. His discernment was on fire. Bomani and Lajos were right by his side.

"We need to bag that and get it to the lab as well as a sample of the vomit. Where there's bodily fluid, there's DNA. I got a feeling I had an unplanned family reunion."

"Boss, how did..."

Nigel cut Darryl off. He had this peace he could not explain even though everything in him told him that was an explosive device.

"No worries. God was looking out; of that I am confident."

His team moved in and retrieved the device along with a sample of the bodily fluids. Before Nigel left, he let his forensic team swab his cheek and then he headed home.

For some reason, he felt like he shouldn't tell his brother about this just yet. It was difficult not to include him, but he truly believed God was up to something and he knew he needed to obey.

Chapter 62: Shock

Fuller sat in a ball on the shower floor of the pay by the hour motel in tears where she had been for the last fifteen minutes. The crying would not stop. How could this be happening to her? And to top it all off, she wasn't able to retrieve the device and was keenly aware that she'd left her DNA at the scene of the abruptly interrupted crime.

Professionally she was pissed at herself. Personally, she was overwhelmed and confused about her conflicting emotions. As she sped through the city trying to figure out what was going on something occurred to her.

She had always been in tip-top shape. Very rarely did she get sick and she was careful about the food she put into her body. She hadn't even eaten anything that day for her to have food poisoning. That wasn't it. It was something else.

Then it hit her, it had been about a month since she'd been with Sam and in all her plotting, planning and scheming she hadn't realized that her cycle was late. Her cycle was like clockwork. The same day every month no matter what.

She'd appreciated Mother Nature for that because her promiscuity could leave a girl wondering. Nothing was foolproof though she had been on birth control since she was a teenager, that was until she'd gotten arrested. Sam was the first and only man she had ever slept with unprotected. This was insane.

Her hands were shaking as she pulled into the parking lot of the CVS down from the seedy motel she resided in for the moment. Keeping her head down, she ran into the store and bought five pregnancy tests, the most expensive ones. She kept her head down though she could tell the clerk was silently judging her. Making sure to avoid all cameras as much as possible, she jumped back in her car and headed to the motel.

Once inside she drank every bottle of water there was in the room and waited for her bladder to protest what she forced into it. She peed in a cup and then dipped all five tests in according to their directions.

She waited.

She paced and bit her nails as she watched in abject horror as each one revealed the same thing.

Pregnant.

Pregnant.

Pregnant.

Pregnant.

And yep, PREGNANT.

She stared in disbelief.

She cussed.

She screamed.

She cried.

She ranted.

All of her shenanigans came to a screeching halt when the nausea rose up again and she was violently ill.

In the shower, the water was now turning cold. Her eyes were swollen, and her footing wasn't steady, but she managed to climb out of the tub. She headed straight for the bed.

There was no drying off or application of her precious coconut oil. She flopped onto the bed and pulled the cover over her distantly aware that she'd probably catch a disease from the tub and the sheets.

She didn't care.

Life had just handed her the biggest plot twist that she never saw coming and she had no idea how to move forward from this cruel twist of fate.

The five demons that surrounded her were in sheer disbelief of what they had just witnessed.

The leader said, "We have to tell Insidious."

"I'm not telling him."

"Neither am I!" another protested.

"You're the leader. You deliver this news."

The leader shook his head.

"The light is going above and beyond to snatch her from us. We need to be prepared for anything. I say we take her out. Better dead than a soldier for them."

They snickered and salivated at the thought of snatching this soul into the pits of hell.

"I'll talk to Insidious."

Chapter 63: Prayer Warrior

Nigel lay awake in bed. He could not sleep thinking about how close he could've been to death knowing the only reason he didn't see it until he did was because his flesh would have definitely intervened to interrupt whatever God was doing.

He had zero patience to wait for the results of the DNA test, but his discernment already told him what he knew it would reveal. It was his niece. He also knew deep down in his soul her unexpected sickness was because she was carrying a child.

What really prevented him from sleeping was the Holy Spirit telling him not to tell his brother about this. Every time he reached for the phone, he heard a resounding, "No!" It went against every loyal instinct he had but being disobedient was not an option. He wasn't a stranger to spiritual warfare, but he'd never been the point man. This was a crazy weight to bear and he honestly didn't like it.

However, that didn't change the importance of what he had been tasked to do. Something was stirring in the atmosphere. If their niece was pregnant, he knew it had to belong to Sampson and that was okay with him. He also knew that life came from God, and Satan could never, so this was God's will. Who was he to judge how God worked out His sovereign will?

His angels glorified sending strong conviction for him to pray. They felt the attack coming for his niece. Once the enemy discovered this unexpected move by Jehovah, they would pounce.

Nigel sat up.

Kadijah stirred. "Baby..." she said groggily.

"Go back to sleep love. I'm good."

Kadijah nodded and rolled back over.

Nigel climbed out of bed and went into the living room after closing the door behind him. He began to pace as he tried to think strategically. There wasn't a baby in their bloodline that the enemy didn't come for. True enough the curse was broken, but that didn't mean that the enemy couldn't attack another way. Nigel began to pray.

"I call on Jehovah Nissi to put a hedge of protection around our niece and her unborn child. Lord, I know you sent this baby. I don't know why, but I know it's for a reason. I plead the Blood of

Jesus over Sam's seed. Send your angels to protect her even though she's lost. Your Word says you reign on the just and the unjust Father. She's lost. Don't hold that against her. Don't hold that against this baby. This child has Lawson blood running through its veins. I call on Jehovah Sabaoth to fight on her behalf. Lord fight for her until she can fight for herself. I serve the enemy notice this day. You will not have my niece. You will not have her child. You will not take away her chance at redemption. Now Father restore what the enemy has taken."

Nigel continued to pace in silence for a few minutes.

He started again, "Father, I cover my brother right now. Lord, free him from the burdens that haunt his heart. Show him who you are in this situation. Don't let him rely on his own understanding, but on Your sovereignty. We need You like never before. You didn't bring us this far to leave us. Do not let Neil become victim to his emotions. Be his strength where he's weak. Lord, You find a way to reach him like only You can. You know his heart. You know what's going on in a way Grey and I could never know. Bring this family together. We need to stand united against the plans of the enemy for our family. Unify us in heart, mind, and spirit. Equip us to tear down the plans of the enemy and make this family whole, in Jesus name I pray..."

Nigel continued to pray as his angels continued to burden his heart. There was an attack coming for his niece. She needed a watchman on the wall. He was it.

Chapter 64: Bad News

The demon arrived at the abandoned train station. Before he went in, he paced outside trying to prepare himself to deliver the devastating news of what the light had done. When he returned, he was supposed to be delivering the news that Nigel was out of the equation, delivering a clear pathway to his daughter.

This message was so far from that, he didn't know if that was even an option anymore. He flew inside to find Insidious and Draven in deep conversation.

"The stakes are getting high, we must consider back up plans for our back up plans," Insidious told him.

"Insidious, I have some important news from the front lines," the demon interrupted.

Draven turned around with a snarl on his face. "How dare you..."

Insidious interrupted the dress down by touching his arm.

"No, this is important because he's afraid to tell me. What happened?" Insidious demanded.

"The light..." the demon said nervously.

"What about the light?" Insidious questioned fiercely.

The demon hesitated. Draven pulled his sword and took a few steps in his direction.

"Speak now or be silenced forever."

The demon swallowed nervously. "The light intervened on our attempt to take out Nigel."

"That's normal and was expected. We had permission to attack," Insidious said annoyed.

"What happened?"

"Yes, it is normal, but not *how* they intervened."

Insidious felt a sick churning in his belly. His eyes narrowed as he spoke through clenched teeth. "What happened?"

"Fuller is pregnant."

Insidious and Draven stared blankly.

"She got sick at the scene, dropped the device and left her DNA. Nigel's discernment is going to lead him straight to her."

Insidious fell back into his chair, completely thrown off by the news.

"Let me think," he demanded.

It took a while as they watched in silence as he pondered with his clawed fingers rubbing his scaly chin.

Finally, he spoke, "As much as I despise the light, I have to admire a well-played chess move. I never saw this coming. I guess that's why He's sovereign and I'm not," Insidious said with slight admiration in his voice.

"What's so genius about it?" Draven asked tired of Insidious' dramatic approach to everything.

"It's genius because the light made a move we could never make. Only Father can give life. Which means that even though the child was conceived in sin, it was His will to bring it forth. So many of His precious Christians miss that simple fact. They demonize the mothers and most times the babies born out of wedlock, but one can never know the mind of God and why He decided to send the children He sends. Even if you believe it's just nature running its course, Father created nature and how it works so it's still His sovereign will. In this case, I know He sent this baby to change Fuller's heart. We'll have to wait and see if it works. She still has free will. I have no doubt her getting sick at his establishment was so that Nigel could discern she was pregnant, which would in turn possibly stay his hand of execution against her. After all, this child would be his dead brother's grandchild and his mother's first great-grandchild. First, it starts with compassion and then love rears its ugly head. We can't stand against that."

"You're right, which is why we feel that we should take her out. Better dead than converted," the demon said.

Insidious frowned but decided simply because he was annoyed to let them try.

"Great idea. Go take her out."

The demon nodded.

"I'm going with you," Draven said.

"No, you're not," Insidious told him. "I need you here. I have another assignment for you."

Draven frowned but nodded.

The demon assigned to Fuller took off with glee.

When he was gone Draven turned to face Insidious, "What do you have for me to do?"

"I just saved your life."

"What are you babbling about?"

"You will watch your tone and your words when you address me," Insidious said with a deadly hiss.

He whipped his darted tail around and yoked Draven. Draven dropped his sword and stared in shock as his throat was squeezed with a vice-like grip.

"Like I said, I just saved your life. When will you learn? You think the light went through all that trouble to allow her to conceive to let me take her out just because I feel like it. She may not be protected, but that child is. It has Lawson blood running through it and the curse is broken. Which is another slap in my face. I should have seen this coming. I should have expected it. That baby can not only change Nigel and Neil's heart towards her, but it can change her black heart. Rest assured that child is protected and the moment they try to harm its mother, the light is going to respond. All I did was set foot on a protected warrior's property and the light responded. Trust me on this. God is omnipresent, unlike our master. He doesn't have to go through his angelic alliance to get a strategy in place. Just His voice will summon angels by her side."

Draven stared wide-eyed. He really didn't care for Insidious because he handled things so differently, but it was moments like this where his brilliance showed up that he had to give respect where respect was due.

Humbled, Draven nodded.

Insidious released him. "Now, we need a new plan. Our best bet is to ensure Neil's heart never accepts her."

Chapter 65: Not Today Satan

The demon flew through the city ecstatic about unleashing the spirit of death on Fuller. One more added to the pit of hell was always a point of happiness for him. When he arrived back at the hotel, the other demons were impatiently waiting for him to get back.

"What did he say?" one asked immediately once he arrived on the scene.

"He babbled about nonsense, but his final decree was for us to take her out."

They grinned and looked over at Fuller asleep beneath the covers.

"How should we do it?" one asked.

"Get someone to tamper with her brakes. I love vehicular deaths."

"Perhaps send someone to rape her then kill her. Let's violate the womb holding this child."

They grinned and salivated at the prospects as they continued to ponder scenarios on the most devastating way to take her out. Once they finally had a heinous plan, they were about to go into action when they felt a powerful presence descend upon the room.

They stared in absolute horror as the 16-foot Angel of Death dropped down into the motel room. His massive 18-foot black satin wings that were tipped in crimson were spread expansively. He cast his Shadow over the bed to cover a sleeping Fuller. She was completely oblivious to the war that raged all around her.

"Retreat!" their leader yelled.

"Not so fast," Death said as the golden cuffs on his wrists glowed and released chains that yoked each of them by the neck and lifted them into the air. They gasped as they were strangled clawing at the golden cuffs around their throats.

The first chain began to retract drawing a scared demon closer to Death's face. Death's obsidian black diamond face never flinched or gave any expression. Staring into his diamond eyes that flashed the colors of the rainbow put a panic deep within the demon as it tried to beg for mercy that would never be granted.

"It was your idea to have her raped and violate her womb, was it not?"

The demon wouldn't answer. Death smiled, a disturbing rarity that told of impending doom. The demon stared in terror knowing his fate was sealed.

Death released the chain and snatched him with his large hands. Tossing the demon behind him, the demon screamed as he plummeted into Death's shadow. The other demons heard him burning and screaming and then it was silent. They shook in fear and tortured anticipation of what awaited them.

The next one was dragged to face Death. "A car accident, was it?"

Silence.

This time Death didn't smile, he snarled as his scythe appeared in his outstretched hand. He twirled it horizontally like a baton and without warning took the head of the demon and watched him turn to black ash. Death blew his breath and bright multi-colored fire consumed the ashes.

The other demons trembled and continued to try to escape the clutches of the golden cuffs around their necks. It was frivolous, to say the least. The next demon tried to negotiate.

"I'm sorry. I won't touch her, I swear. If you let me go, I will exit this region and never return."

Death was genuinely amused, another rarity and chuckled.

"That's new. "You're right, you won't be returning."

The demon's beady yellow eyes bulged as the golden cuff got tighter and tighter. The cuff began to heat up with a glowing fire. The demon shrieked as he was incinerated.

The other demons stared helplessly awaiting their fate. The fourth one remained silent as he stared into Death's eyes.

"Anything to say?" Death inquired. The demon shook his head. "I'll make this quick then."

Before the demon knew what happened, his neck was separated from his body by the scythe of Death. The fifth trembled profusely.

Death said, "Calm yourself. You won't be sent back to the pit this day. Go tell Insidious that I am the one who guards this child. He's lived a long and bothersome existence. This is his only warning.

If he comes for this child again, I will end his existence. This is not a suggestion, but a command. Do I make myself clear?"

The demon nodded as he stared into the unique eyes and trembled. The golden cuff released, and the demon fell to the ground.

"Make haste," Death said as the demon scurried away.

Death turned to stare down at Fuller sleeping peacefully beneath his Shadow. He removed his shadow, she squirmed but didn't wake. He placed his large black diamond hand over her head and whispered to her spirit.

"Go see your sister, she will help you take your next steps."

Death removed a golden key from beneath his wing and placed it around her neck. He gave her the gift the Great I AM had instructed him to. She was always meant to have it, but because of the path Jehovah knew she would take, he would not allow it to be revealed until the appointed time.

Then Death cast a small piece of his Shadow around it to hide it from all spiritual eyes, the light and the dark. Only he knew it existed. The Ancient of Days kept many of his secret strategies trapped within him. No demon was powerful enough to breach his fortified diamond skin, therefore, the enemy couldn't ever launch an attack until God himself decided to reveal it. He dutifully obeyed the voice of the Lord.

Death placed his hand over Fuller's belly and told the child, "Be still. Your mother needs her strength to make this next journey."

With that, the Angel of Death and his Shadow took flight leaving his brilliant midnight blue aura trailing behind him.

Chapter 66: Run Tell That

Insidious stared dumbfounded at the frightened demon as he recounted the horrific encounter with the Angel of Death.

"There is no defense against him. We were all just at his mercy. The way he took each one out was different. I've never seen any one angel war like that."

"Enough!" Insidious yelled frustrated. "How come I never heard about the Angel of Death joining the war?"

"Everyone is afraid to even speak his name," Draven told him.

"What is the deal with him and children?"

"My sources tell me he became so indignant after he found out about the attack on Hope that he volunteered to defend her. Then he was set as her guardian."

Insidious considered. "But he doesn't guard Neil's boy?"

"He doesn't need to," Draven said. "He's his own shield."

"Right. Who else is Death fond of?" Insidious inquired.

"Grey," Draven said while rolling his evil eyes.

"Interesting indeed," Insidious said while rubbing his chin. "Spread the word. For the time being Fuller's child is absolutely off limits. We can't afford to have our numbers dwindle because of our arrogance. He doesn't seem to need his fellow angels assistance or the prayers of the saints to handle his business."

Draven nodded.

"I'll get the word out."

Insidious sat back and pondered. *What was up with Death and these babies?* He needed to know this, so he could figure out a way around this arduous obstacle.

Chapter 67: Sister Love

Agent Michelle Fuller
Supai, Arizona

Desperation caused you to do dumb things. There was so much more going on that I understood I needed to take a step back and figure it out. I felt like Death was chasing me and it was only a few steps behind lurking in the shadows.

None of this made sense. Killing used to be easy. Now there were all these complications. I could have taken Nigel out and then that vicious nausea felt more like an invisible attack than a pregnancy symptom. I don't know much about being pregnant, but I'm sure my "morning" sickness is *not* normal.

I was starting to believe Satan's minion when he said I lacked faith and imagination. There was something in the ether. I don't know if it was good, evil or both, but I was keenly aware that we humans were not alone in this world. There was no other logical explanation for what was happening to me.

I was so desperate, but I couldn't go back to Sam. I still hadn't decided what to do about the baby, but I couldn't keep hurting him. I couldn't go back to him if I wasn't going to stay. I couldn't tell him about this baby if I wasn't going to keep it. I couldn't keep being flaky. He deserved better than that.

There was this inexplicable pull I had to go and see my sister. I know I was taking my life in my hands, but where else could I go? I trusted my mother only in the context of us possessing the same agenda. Once that alignment diminished so would our bond. Eva was different though. Sure, I'd once tried to kill her, and threatened to blow her up, but we had more in common than anyone else in this game.

Both of us were Neil's partners and betrayed him. He forgave her. I needed to figure out how to get him to forgive me. If I had any chance of surviving long enough to even make a decision to keep this baby, Neil had to be on my side. Innately I knew he was the key to this whole thing.

Right now, there was no way in hell. I knew it deep down in my soul. Neil was the single most threat to my existence. I know

Satan's patsy warned me about my niece being capable of rendering me useless, but that was something on a spiritual level I had yet to comprehend. Neil was a real life, flesh, and blood threat to my ability to keep breathing.

This time I opted to take the donkey ride into town. I didn't have the energy to walk the long trek. I had to stop three times to vomit up the little bit of food I managed to keep down in the last two days. It seemed this baby gave me a good behavior reprieve, but the minute I hit Arizona, all bets were off. I was miserable.

I know I looked like a zombie. I wore a casual pink sweat suit, which was regrettable in this desert heat. So, on top of losing fluids from nausea, I was also profusely sweating. I told the guide to stop a block from Eva's place. I would walk the rest of the way.

He continuously tried to make sure I was okay, but I just waved him off. He kept offering me water, but I knew that would make me vomit as well. I was scared out of my mind, but options were down to the bare minimum. I reached for something I never had before - faith. Well, faith, my guns, and knives. I grabbed the weapons I stashed behind the old lady's place the last time I was here.

Slowly, I approached the door across the street and knocked. Waiting for someone to answer felt like an eternity. A Hispanic man opened the door. I made sure my hands were visibly down by my side.

He frowned at me. "Can I help you?" He asked.

"Is Eva here?"

"Who's asking?"

"Michelle."

"Hold on a second," he told me and closed the door in my face.

A minute later the door snatched open. I was staring down the barrel of a gun.

Raising my hands in surrender, I told her, "This is my white flag."

"Give me one good reason not to drop you where you stand."

"I'm your sister."

"That didn't stop you from taking out *my* twin."

I was about to attempt another reason, but the nausea rose up with a vengeance. I ran off her porch and was viciously ill... again. I gagged until this little human stopped torturing me. When I looked up at her tears ran down my face.

"I'm pregnant and I'm scared."

She stared in utter shock. I waited breathlessly to see how this would go. A minute later, Eva put her pistol in the small of her back and motioned for me to come in the house. I cried in sheer relief.

She looped her arm in mine when I made it up the stairs and closed the door behind us. Oh yes, something divine was indeed looking out for me. Maybe not me, but definitely this baby. But why?

Chapter 68: Family Reunion

Supai, Arizona

Fuller, Eva, and Juan sat at their intimate dining room table staring at each other in silence for a long while.

Juan said, "I'm going to leave and let you ladies deal with your familial drama. I'll pick up the girls and take them out for a while to give you all the time you need. I want all this drama to end and if it takes a leap of faith to befriend the enemy, I'm willing. Our girls need a normal life. We owe that to them."

He stood up and kissed his wife's cheek, then headed out.

"Why come here?" Eva asked when Juan had exited.

"Would you believe me if I told you that something outside of me pushed me to come to you."

Eva stared at Fuller for a long while.

"I would believe that."

"Why?"

"Because that voice is the reason, I'm alive today."

Fuller nodded. "Care to share?"

"In time."

"How did you end up pregnant? I know you were trained better than that."

"A sperm. An egg. You know the usual suspects," she responded flippantly.

"I. Will. Shoot. You!"

Fuller sighed, "You're right I was trained to know better."

Michelle told her sister about all that she had been through since she left her on the porch with a bomb. She told her about meeting their mother and stumbling into Sam and her choice to pursue revenge instead of him.

To say Eva was blown away was an understatement. It looked like God had a way of getting the attention of His most wayward creations. She had no doubt the divine was guiding Fuller's steps even if she had yet to acknowledge it.

"One thing Lucca said that stuck with me is that I lacked faith and imagination and it would be my downfall. So here I am, taking my first ever leap of faith. That's how I ended up on your doorstep."

"Have you ever heard of the term, spiritual warfare?"

"Sounds vaguely familiar."

"Well, you're about to get a crash course in it."

"Okay," Fuller said apprehensively.

"Lucca is the devil incarnate and even though I still haven't decided if I truly trust you, I trust nature has stepped in and put a pause on all your sadistic ways by doing the one thing that is guaranteed to have you taking a step back and reevaluating your life."

Fuller put her hands on her flat stomach. "A baby."

Eva nodded. "Let me make you this smoothie that helped calm my nausea. It was brutal with my second baby. Juan's grandmother used to make it for me."

Fuller nodded. "Mind if I watch you make it?"

Eva smirked but nodded. "I'm not going to poison you, girl."

"Professional paranoia."

"Be my guest."

Eva gestured for her to follow her into the kitchen. She eyed Fuller for a full minute.

"What?" she asked confused.

Eva picked up the block of knives on the counter and put them in the refrigerator.

Fuller fell out laughing. "Now who's paranoid?"

"Let's just put everything in the fridge and be done with it. So, we can have an open honest conversation and still be living to tell about it."

Fuller rolled her eyes. "Okay fine."

Eva pulled the gun out of the small of her back and placed it in the fruit crisper once she'd cleaned it out. Fuller pulled the small .22 she kept in her ankle and handed it over. Eva pulled the four-inch blade she habitually kept hooked on the back of her bra.

Fuller nodded her approval. "I'll have to try that one."

Fuller pulled out the 9 mm that was on her waist and handed it over. Eva pulled out her clutch piece. A small bodyguard .380 that was in her ankle holster. All were placed in the refrigerator.

"Should we pat each other down or do we trust that we're clean?" Eva asked.

Fuller stared for a full minute sizing her sister up. "We should pat each other down," Fuller decided.

They both found one more pistol and one more knife. They laughed as Eva began to make the smoothie that saved her sanity during her second pregnancy. It was a blend of yogurt, fresh ginger, peaches, bananas, pear nectar and fresh lemon. When that was done, they sat on the sofa in the cozy living room.

"I was Neil's partner for nearly 20 years before they activated me. In that time, I'd fell in love and had three babies. Neil was like a brother to me. He took a bullet for me and that changed the game. The organization lied. Neil was the antithesis of everything they taught us to believe. He truly loved me and would always have my back no matter what. So, when I had to choose. I chose my babies and my friend but knew they wouldn't let me just leave. Our sister, my twin, faked her death when we were 16, she was over it early in the game. This was her place. Though she got out of the organization she continued to gather as much information as she could. Once I started having kids, she started working on my exit plan. So, I enlisted her help when they activated me. We tracked and found Neil and planted the information about the shipment, so I could get him out of the game. I never knew you were one of us. The night before the weapons shipment, my sister took me down. I woke up days later trying to put everything together and found out she was dead. I was sick thinking Neil did it, but in my heart, I knew he wouldn't have, even with my betrayal, he would never do that to me. I went back and found more information my sister had that revealed you. Needless to say, you were at the top of my kill list. Before I could figure out how to do that, you showed up at my house... uninvited."

"I'm sorry about that," Fuller told her.

"No, you're not, but thanks for trying to be a decent human being." Fuller chuckled. "No matter how hard I tried, there was this conviction that kept telling me to let it go. I know I've changed in the last year, but I honestly didn't know that I had truly changed until I told Juan one night that I was letting it go. I would not seek revenge on you. I would let God handle you."

Fuller frowned. "You believe in God?"

"I do. And I know He's the one who sent you to my front door in your time of need. I know because had He not worked on me prior to it, I would have ended your life the moment you showed up. Shortly after I told Juan I was letting it go. Nigel came to see me.

He believes that this is bigger than all of us and that you and I being attached to Neil and being the only ones to survive all the craziness in our family was for a bigger purpose. I could believe that about myself, but not about you. That is until you showed up here with child. God works in mysterious ways."

"Why would God care anything about me?"

"He created you. But to be honest, there is truly a vested interest He has in your father's bloodline."

"Why?" Fuller asked curiously.

"Remember when I brought up spiritual warfare?" Fuller nodded. "Welp, here's your crash course."

Eva began to tell Fuller everything she knew that had transpired in the organization and in her family. Neil had debriefed her on everything on his end and she'd told him everything that transpired on her end. It took a couple of hours, but Fuller sat there with her mouth wide open.

"And you believe this? All of it?"

"Believe it? I lived through most of it. Let me tell you what happened to me in those eight months I was in hiding..."

Chapter 69: A Weary Soul

Flashback - Eva's Story

She woke disoriented and with a throbbing headache that made her squint as she stared up into the iridescent light. She blinked slowly trying to take inventory of the condition she was in. Her instincts told her not to move because she didn't know if she vulnerable to an attack.

Closing her eyes, she minutely moved each limb and each finger. Her ears were tuned in to any noise, but she was surrounded by silence. It was almost deafening. Her brain was hazy, and her memory alluded her. Laying there completely still, she tried to figure out where she was and what happened to her.

Like a flash of light, it hit her. She sat up and immediately regretted it as she grabbed her viciously aching head.

"Ugggghhhh," she cussed in agony.

She recognized the space she was in. This was the spot she and her twin were holed up in while they tried to get Neil out of the organization. She took a deep breath and stood up shouldering the pain, so she could figure out what the heck was going on. She wondered how long she had been unconscious.

Searching for her cell phone, she continued to hold the back of her head. Someone clocked her pretty good. Her cell phone was sitting on the table in the small kitchenette. Grabbing it, she saw the battery was down to one percent. Just before the phone died, she saw the date and time. It was three o'clock in the afternoon two days from the last day she remembered.

"What in the world is going on?" she asked out loud half afraid a strange voice would answer.

She squinted as something next to the counter caught her eye. It was a note. She hurried over. There was an unmarked bottle of prescription pills next to a small envelope that read: *jumeaux* - it was the masculine word for twin in French. It was a code they used. She opened the pills and recognized the 800 milligrams of ibuprofen. She dry swallowed two of them and ripped open the note.

Twin,

I'm sorry for hitting you. I left you plenty of 800s. The headache will subside in a couple days, but I had to. I know if I had told you my plan you would talk me out of it. Our plan is good, but risky. You've got three little girls who need you around to raise them, so they don't end up like us. I'm going to take your place. Hopefully, I'll be back before you find this. If not, it went bad. If it goes bad, lay low and then as soon as you can, get back to your family. I love you. It's been amazing spending time with you these last couple months, albeit plotting illegal activities, but you know how we do. :-)

Love you,
Me

Eva's heart sank into the pit of her stomach. She knew before she knew. They had been separated for many years, but the connection of twins couldn't be broken by time or distance. She scrambled to find the charger for her phone.

Once that was taken care of, she pulled out her laptop and began frantically searching the internet. Tears ran down her eyes as she read the news report of the raid gone wrong and the cop from Tallahassee whose body had been identified as hers.

The tears wouldn't stop. She began to gag as she thought about Neil being in a place where he could take her life. How? Why? That wasn't the plan. She viciously scrubbed away the tears and then hacked into the police files searching for the report.

When she found it, she read it, but it didn't give her any concrete information on what happened. Her heart was shattered in a thousand pieces. Her sister was dead and possibly at the hand of her best friend. The weight of the double life she lived came crashing down on her mind, body, and soul.

Eva curled into a ball and wept. An hour passed before she could move. She had to get out of there because she didn't know who knew what, who was looking for her or how close they were. She missed her husband and her children terribly, but she knew she couldn't see them until all this mess was settled.

As long as the organization was functional, she had to stay away from the people she loved the most. Knowing she needed to get out of Florida as soon as possible, she packed her bags and left.

Two Months Later

Mobile, Alabama

Eva sat at the back table in the run-down diner picking over her food. She had been staying at the hole in the wall motel across the street for the past two weeks. The diner had become her second home. She ate there every day. The food was decent enough.

She loved the fact that she continued to be a nobody. At least she thought she was. The plump woman who waited tables in the establishment moseyed her way over to Eva's table.

"Are you alright, dear?" she asked.

"I'm good."

"You don't look good. Do you need help? A place to stay?"

"I'm fine."

The woman sat down across the table and placed her hand on Eva's. "No baby, you're not fine. You've lost weight in the two weeks since you've been coming here. Listen, let me take you over to my church. I know they can help you get on your feet."

"I said, I was fine," Eva snapped.

"Okay love. I'll leave you be. Just know, I'm praying for you."

Eva dropped money on the table and hurried out of the restaurant.

Five Months Later

Santa Monica, California

Eva sat on the wooden bench at the end of the pier. It was early, and the sun had only begun to peak out for the day. The salty sea air whipped her hair around as she stared toward the vast Pacific Ocean contemplating.

Over the past few months everywhere she turned someone was invading her space and noticing her. No matter who she encountered they continued to try to get her to a church. It was the oddest thing. She couldn't seem to stay anywhere more than two weeks.

The pain of being away from her husband and children along with the pain of believing Neil had taken her life and knowing her sister died in her place was beginning to be too much to bear. Her mind was strong, and she could go on if she wanted to, but she didn't feel like she deserved to.

She had been deceitful all her life and had caused irreparable damage to the lives of so many. Why should she go on living with all the hurt and pain she had caused? She felt like if she took her life, somehow the scales in the universe would balance out. A tear slipped down her cheek.

There was a couple in the corner of the pier hugged up having an intimate moment that she noticed. Her soul ached to be held by Juan one more time. Her heart broke at the thought of never seeing her children again. And her spirit was crushed knowing that she'd betrayed the best friend she'd ever have.

It was time to balance the scales. She scooted to the edge of the seat. She would have to make the jump quick otherwise the couple could pull her back, but no one was coming after her this deep in the Pacific Ocean.

What Eva could not see were the demons all around her. They had tormented her for months now once she'd spiraled down into a state of depression. They constantly whispered things to remind her of all the wrong she'd ever done and to make sure she bore the full brunt of guilt for everything that had happened. They also put fear in her that at any moment, someone from the organization could take her life or the lives of the ones she loved if she ever returned.

Eva scooted a little closer to the edge of the bench. Suddenly an old Asian man walked up to her.

"May I sit?" he asked politely.

Eva wiped her face. "Sure, I was just leaving."

He took the seat and grabbed her hand. She stared at the withered hand on hers and then looked into his face. He had the most beautiful eyes she'd ever seen. They were gray. No green. No hazel. She didn't know what color they were, but they sparkled.

Suddenly a feeling of warmth flooded her body as she found herself sitting back down.

"Whatever you think you know, you don't," he told her.

"I'm sorry. What are you talking about?"

"The weights on your heart, my dear."

"I don't know what you're talking about," she said nervously. This was freaky.

"You do indeed." He turned to face her. She was mesmerized by his kind eyes. "You feel that tug on your heart, don't you?" She nodded. "Why do you resist?"

"I don't deserve forgiveness."

"No one does, but that's why it's called grace."

"Too much has happened. I can't go back."

"Love is a powerful force. It has a way of shining through the darkest of places."

"Why does God want me?"

"He created you for something great, but if you end your life, you'll never fulfill your destiny."

"What is my destiny?"

"You must turn and face your fear and then follow the steps as He orders them."

"I don't know if I can do that."

"Of course, you can."

"Are you what they call a prophet?"

He smiled and stood up but didn't answer. "Choose Him, He's already chosen you."

Eva dropped her head as she felt this overwhelming sense of belonging. When she looked up, the man was gone. She stood up and looked behind her. He was nowhere to be found.

"Where did he go?" she asked out loud.

The couple in the corner of the pier looked up at her strangely.

"Where did who go?" the man asked.

"The old man?"

"Ma'am, are you okay? Do you need help?" the woman asked.

She waved them off frustrated as she tried to understand what just happened.

The demons began to protest as they felt the hope within her springing forth. In the spirit realm, a flash of light hit the pier. Two warring angels appeared on the scene. They drew their fierce ancient weapons preventing the demons from pouncing.

"She's ours!" one of the four demons yelled as he drew his weapon.

"I beg to differ," the fierce warrior threatened as the majestic blue flame coated his weapon and ignited in his eyes.

The demon charged. The angel engaged. Weapon met weapon as they clashed. The other demons joined the fray as did the other angel. She had no idea that she was important enough to God for angels and demons to be fighting over her very soul.

Eva realized she'd had an encounter with an angel, though it went against everything rational in her mind. She knew what she saw. She knew what she heard. She knew what she felt.

"Jesus, this is real."

That majestic and powerful name being uttered from her lips in faith pierced every demon's ear and stunned them all. The two warring angels took full advantage delivering final blows to the four demons as black ash rained down and they were no more.

All of a sudden, Eva felt a little lighter. The haze that had plagued her mind was gone.

"Ma'am, do you need help?" the woman asked her again.

Eva smiled. "No, thanks, I'm fine."

She stood up and headed to her car. It was time to go home. Whatever she had to face; she was willing to face it. She didn't know she would be escorted all the way home by two fierce angelic warriors.

Chapter 70: Love Covers A Multitude of Sin

Hours passed as Eva and Fuller exchanged information. They had a mutual respect for each other's journey but was far from trusting one another. They looked up when the door opened, and Eva's three daughters filed in. They were stair steps in age. The youngest eight, the middle girl was 10 and the oldest was 12.

"Hi, mommy!"

"Hey, ma!"

"Mommy!" the youngest one squealed.

Eva greeted each of her daughters with hugs and kisses while Juan carefully eyed Fuller.

"Who's this?" Maria, the middle daughter asked.

"This is Michelle. She's someone from my old life. We were just catching up."

The girls waved at her. Fuller smiled and waved. The three girls were beautiful replicas of Juan and Eva's combined genetics. She found herself wondering if she was carrying a boy or a girl. Her hand unconsciously went to her belly.

"Mama, I'm hungry," Erica, the baby girl said and headed to the fridge.

"Don't open the refrigerator," Eva and Fuller yelled at the same time making all the girls jump.

Juan and the girls turned to stare at them. Eva sent Juan a look. He caught the hint and knew not to even ask.

"You know what girls... let's go pick up a pizza," Juan suggested.

The girls stared at their mom and then their dad.

"That's a great idea. Get one with extra cheese and pepperoni," Eva said trying to normalize this awkward moment.

"Will you be staying for dinner?" Juan asked Fuller.

"No, I won't," she said politely.

He nodded. Eva saw the relief on his face. The girls and Juan headed out. Eva and Fuller looked at each other then fell out laughing.

"It's probably time I get out of here," Fuller said.

"What are you going to do about the baby?" Eva asked sincerely.

"I don't know, but I promise you I won't do anything without first letting Sam know."

"Thank you. That's all I can ask," Eva said.

"You've been amazing to me today. Thank you."

"You've helped fill in some gaps for me too. So, thank you," Eva told her.

Fuller fidgeted for a moment.

"What is it?" Eva questioned.

"Do you think Neil will ever forgive me? I know it's crazy, but I really want a relationship with my grandmother. I'm not really sure why maybe it's because I look like her. My thoughts surrounding this baby is I never had a mother, so I don't know how to be a mother. I feel like she's the mother I need in my life. I know it's crazy, but I do. Suddenly I'm wanting things I never even thought of all because of this baby. I know I can't have that until I fix what I broke with Neil."

"I honestly don't know. I believe he's capable of it, but actually doing it, I'm not sure. In Neil's mind, you tried to harm Grey. That's a capital offense in his heart, you know. She's something very special to him. I've been through all his major relationships, but Grey was different. She made him different. It's like he was functioning, but not really living until he met her. I tried to right my wrong. You didn't. If there's a way you can think of to show him that you're different. If there's a right you can wrong, that may work."

"Can you talk to him for me?"

"I can't let Neil know just yet where you and I stand. That's not wise. I'm barely on solid ground with him. But if I get the chance to talk to Nigel, I'll tell him and see what he can do."

Fuller nodded. "I understand that."

Eva reached for her hand and squeezed it. The gesture made Fuller break down and cry. Eva shocked herself by leaning over and pulling her sister into her arms.

Fuller clung to her sister for dear life. She hadn't felt that kind of love since Sam held her and she knew her sister genuinely cared. It scared her and pleased her at the same time.

Eva stroked her sister's hair as she tried to calm her down. Even though she hadn't thrown up since she drank the smoothie, she knew she was already weak. She wanted to calm her down for the sake of the baby.

Ten minutes later, Fuller pulled herself together. Eva gave her some tissues to clean her face.

After Fuller blew her nose, she said, "Would you believe I never used to cry?"

Eva laughed. "Totally. You're making up for lost times."

"I think that it's Sam."

"What do you mean?"

"After that first kiss, something in me shifted. Like I felt it. It's like he turned on the emotional switch I had been disconnected from all my life."

"Sounds like true love," Eva said smiling.

"I don't know about that. But then there's this baby. How can this one thing change my life so drastically? Even after Sam, I was affected, but not like *this*."

"The bond of a mother to a child is like nothing you will ever experience in your life."

Fuller nodded. "I should go."

"Don't forget your guns in the fridge."

They stared at each other and bust out laughing. Fuller retrieved her guns and knives. Eva walked her to the door.

"I don't know if I'll see you again, but thank you," Fuller said then shocked herself by reaching out and hugging her sister.

Eva welcomed the embrace and squeezed her sister. "Survive sis," Eva whispered.

"I'll do my best," Fuller replied then pulled away.

They shared an unspoken glance and then she was gone. Eva closed the door and leaned against it.

"God, I don't know what you're up to, but I trust you."

†††

Later that evening when everyone was settled and tucked away in their beds, Eva slept peacefully. Her heart and soul weren't weighted down anymore. She was emotionally free.

He appeared like the Shadow he was towering over the sleeping couple in all his black beauty. The golden key dangled from his massive hand as he watched them sleep peacefully. The Angel of

Death placed the golden key around Eva's neck then cast a piece of his shadow over it to keep it hidden as well.

He knew the Great I AM would allow her gift to be revealed when it was necessary. Her act of compassion and love activated something she never even knew was on the inside of her, but the all-knowing, all-powerful God of the universe knew because He decided before the foundations of the world that it would be so.

Chapter 71: Lord, Have Mercy

Agent Michelle Fuller

I was in the darkest place I had ever known. The ether of my soul was polluted and convoluted. My heart was so heavy. My mind was tormented. It's funny, this is the most confused place I had ever been in, but yet I knew exactly what I needed to do.

I was caught between two opinions. I was double-minded. I was lukewarm. So why didn't I just do it? Because I wasn't worthy. Because I was afraid. Because I knew how to be bad, I did it well. I did not know how to be good and I would definitely be a disappointment.

I sat on the floor in the dark because I couldn't stand to look at myself. How had my life gotten this bad? The faces of every person I savagely murdered in the name of my inbred idealism haunted me. Countless eyes - blue, brown, hazel, gray - they haunted me. In the darkness they stared.

I heard all the voices that begged for mercy when they stood on the business end of my weapon of choice. They asked me for mercy, and I gave none. Now, here I am in need of mercy. I was such a hypocrite. Now that I had love in my life, now that I was carrying a seed, suddenly life meant something. But wasn't that what a parent did? Fight for the life of their child.

My dad would have fought for me had he been allowed to live. My mom didn't fight for me and I didn't want that for the child I carried. I wasn't going to be her. As the tears cascaded in rivers down my face, I made my decision. Not for me, not for Sam, but for this baby that I already loved so completely.

Lucca's words reverberated, I was no match for both good and evil to be coming at me with everything they had. I got on my knees and bowed my head. Surrounded by darkness, nothing in the room was moving, nothing stirred. The silence was deafening. I tried to open my mouth, but I could not.

†††

Fuller may have thought she was all alone, but she was not. In the darkness, Insidious was there. He instructed his demons not to touch the baby, but he said nothing about touching her. She belonged to them. She served Satan and she was not a child of the light. He knew this was why God had given her womb the breath of life. The Creator of all things knew it would make her consider switching sides. Not if he could help it. He continued to whisper and torment her.

"You will never deserve mercy."

"You are not worthy."

"He can never love you."

"You're a murderer. A stone-cold killer."

"Jesus can never love you."

"You say you love this child, but you don't. You can't. You're not capable of it."

"If this child lives, it will pay for your sins. You're better off getting rid of it and saving yourself the pain."

"Sam isn't going to risk his freedom for you."

"It's all an illusion. It's all temporary. You know who you are. You know who you were created to be."

"God is not real. How could a merciful God allow you to end up in this life? You know the truth, don't fall for the lie."

As he continued to torment and torture, Fuller grabbed her head wishing the viciousness would stop. She let out a scream of frustration. Insidious only increased the attack.

At her wit's end, she screamed, "Father, have mercy!"

Insidious stared wide-eyed in disbelief. This chief sinner had called out for help. He felt the faith leap off of her. She believed. Mercy showed up!

Chapter 72: Choose Ye This Day

Insidious braced himself as he felt the presence of unmistakable light all around him. They revealed themselves. Surrounding this weeping sinner stood Captain Valter, Lieutenant Nero, *and* Gabriel. He was undone.

"Brother, you would come to defend the likes of her?" Insidious asked Gabriel.

Gabriel responded by pulling out his qama dagger from the golden sheath at his waist. In all his emerald brilliance his frame was 18-feet in height. His two sets of brilliant pearl colored wings were expanded and stretched 22-feet. His shimmering skin was the color of alabaster. His golden mane flowed freely to his shoulders.

His emerald accented cuffs began to glow with righteous indignation. Insidious nodded. He wasn't one for battle. He knew how to fight, and he fought well, but he preferred to run the show, not be the show. He snapped his fingers.

Ten malicious demons descended into the room that he'd had waiting just in case the light tried something like this. Their green, red and yellow eyes glowed with evil as they all held their weapons at the ready.

The Captain and Lieutenant pulled their weapons as well. Their eyes flamed a brilliant magnificent blue, while that same flame danced across their weapons.

"You won't have her without a fight," Valter warned.

"My sentiments exactly," Insidious hissed.

His demons charged. Weapon met weapon as the battle began.

†††

Fuller was in awe that her cry out to God, stopped the merciless taunting in her mind. She had no idea that spiritual warfare on behalf of her soul waged all around her. She wanted to call for spiritual help, but she was paralyzed with fear.

What did that look like? What did that feel like? What did that mean? Something in her belly began to flutter. She immediately grabbed her stomach and thought of her child. It wasn't about her anymore. She would face this moment head on if there was even the slightest chance, her child would be okay.

Insidious could feel her heart changing. He was fit to be tied. He screamed out and sank his claws into Fuller's head. Fuller screamed out as this sudden massive headache took her breath away.

Gabriel turned at her cry. He knocked back another demon and threw his dagger at Insidious. Insidious snatched his hand back and retreated, the dagger missing him by millimeters.

The fury in Gabriel's eyes put a strong fear in Insidious' heart. He had to decide how much trouble this one soul was worth. He looked around as his demons fought valiantly, though it yielded little to no effect. These angels were not trying to let this soul go. He never understood God's love for these feckless humans, especially ones as depraved as this one.

Gabriel warned, "Back off and live to fight another day. Touch her again and it's me and you."

Insidious fumed. He wanted her so bad, but there was always another way.

He yelled, "Retreat!"

The seven demons left gladly obliged. The three angels encircled Fuller as they watched the demons leave.

Insidious warned, "This isn't over."

They ignored him and waited for him to leave. Fuller was still down on the floor full of fear at making the confession she knew she needed to. Lieutenant Nero touched her as his body glorified bathing the room in a brilliant white light. His touch silenced all that was in her.

She fell to the floor and said, "Jesus, I'm sorry. Forgive me."

She collapsed on the floor and waited for hell to come and snatch her away. Instead of minions from the seventh circle of hell coming to drag her away, what she felt was a warmth that spread across her chest.

The weights she had always carried in her mind, heart, soul, and spirit began to feel lighter. Her mind began to have a singular focus. She felt mercy. Mercy said she was forgiven. Mercy said she loved. Mercy said she was good enough.

Fuller could not stop the heart wrenching sobs as the one true living God began to forgive her of her sins and cleanse her of all unrighteousness. The angels stood in awe as they watched the love of God descend upon this wretched soul in desperate need of divine mercy, grace, forgiveness, and love.

They looked up when they felt the presence of another warrior. The Angel of Death stepped into the room. His infamous shadow with him. He remained silent but watched until the transformation was complete.

When Fuller sat up, she wiped her eyes. Death reached down and removed his shadow that hid the golden key around her neck. The other angels gasped! Death in all his beauty exited without saying a word.

Chapter 73: A Hesitant Heart

Monet sat in her breakfast nook with a cup of coffee, still in her expensive yellow satin pajamas. She took a sip of the steaming black Cuban coffee and stared out into the brightness of the early morning. She loved the bay window in their kitchen.

Charles and Corbin were out of the house, so she was all alone to deal with the dream she'd had. The dream was so strange that after she finished it, she found herself in Charles' office praying and asking God for clarification. He responded and she declined.

God was indeed tripping. Now she felt bad, but there was no way this assignment was for her. She took another sip as she watched her neighbor pass by on her morning run. Her thoughts drifted back to her dream.

In the dream she was running. Every time she would come to a dead end, she saw these flashes of parts of buildings. They would flash quickly. They all looked ancient and they were all doorways. No, not doorways, but gateways. She would keep running until the next dead end with the same results.

Finally, she stood in the middle of the maze and screamed, "Let me out of here."

She heard, "The only way out is through my will."

Monet awoke with a start. Charles had stirred and reached for her pulling her in close. Her heart was pounding.

He asked groggily, "You okay?"

"I'm fine," she lied. "Just a crazy dream."

Sleep engulfed him and that was it. Monet lay in her husband's arms wide awake until Charles and Corbin left the house. In the office she prayed.

"Lord, what is your will?" she prayed.

When she heard nothing after a while, she decided to pick up a Bible. She took the Bible and sat on the couch and begin flipping through it.

Out of nowhere, she heard, "Stop!"

Monet frowned. "Okay, God I know you're the supreme being and all, but that was scary. Can you not do that again? Thanks."

The angels that had recently been assigned to her chuckled. When she looked down, the Bible was turned to 1 Chronicles chapter 9. She began scanning before she read and was shocked to see "The gatekeepers" in verse 17. That's what she'd seen in her dream, lots of gates. She ignored all the names because she didn't know who those people were and skipped down to verse 22 that talked about 212 people being chosen to be gatekeepers.

As if God himself was pointing it out to her, the verse jumped out. *"The gatekeepers had been assigned to their positions of trust by David and Samuel the seer."* The next verse that stood out read, *"The gatekeepers were on the four sides: east, west, north and south."*
The next verses that stood out read, *"But the four principal gatekeepers, who were Levites, were entrusted with the responsibility for the rooms and treasuries in the house of God. They would spend the night stationed around the house of God, because they had to guard it; and they had charge of the key for opening it each morning."*

Monet shook her head. What in the world was God trying to tell her? Surely, she had not be chosen as anybody's gatekeeper. As Monet sipped her coffee she continued to reflect on her morning with God.

She didn't feel worthy to have such a trusted position. She wasn't even sure what it entailed, nor she did she know which gate she was supposed to keep.

Frustrated she said, "God, you've got the wrong girl, I'm sorry. I can't do this."

Monet headed to the sink, poured out her coffee and headed to get dressed and go to work.

Chapter 74: Face-to-Face

Another late night at the 24-hour gym Neil tried to burn off his frustration. It remained a moot point as it always had. He just couldn't get on the same page with his mom and brother. Yes, it would make everything nice and tidy, but it was far from nice or tidy. It was reality.

He just didn't see this playing out in any way that made them one big happy family. He couldn't bring himself to trust her. The deceit was too deep and if he was honest, still raw. Forgiving is one thing, forgetting and befriending was something completely different altogether.

The gym was practically empty, save for another young woman and a few staff members. Sweat poured from him like a faucet as he got off the elliptical machine. He headed to the showers to get out of the wet clothes and head home. He was tired of carrying this. Something had to be done one way or another.

Neil showered and changed into a black Nike sweat suit. He closed and secured the locker he kept at the gym when something felt off to him. He pulled his firearm from his hip and turned to see what was going on.

Stunned, he stared. "You must have a death wish Michelle. What the hell are you doing here?"

Fuller stood dressed in black yoga pants and a black sweatshirt with a hood over her head and her hands raised in surrender.

"Hear me out, Neil."

"What the hell are you doing here?" he asked again.

"I need to talk to you."

"About what?"

"Can you put the gun down?"

"I don't think so."

"Neil. I'm trying here."

"And I care because..."

"I want this to be over and done with. I'm walking away."

"I don't believe you."

Fuller sighed. "Neil, this isn't a setup. This isn't me trying to manipulate you. Look at me. Look at where I am. Why would I risk my life and my freedom?"

Neil kept the gun trained on her. "I don't know what you're up to, but I will never trust anything that comes out of your mouth. My family will never be safe with you around."

She sighed and dropped her head. She only had herself to blame for this. When she looked up at him, he was shocked to see tears in her eyes. He frowned.

"Neil. This isn't a trick or a trap. This is me throwing myself at your mercy."

"Why now? What happened?"

She hesitated. He pulled the hammer back on his pistol to change it to single action.

"Okay, okay," she said lifting her hands higher in surrender. "I'm pregnant." Neil frowned. "I don't want any part of this life. I don't want revenge anymore. I just want to be with the man I love and our child, that's it. I can't relax and believe that's possible if I'm always looking over my shoulder for you. I know you're the real threat to my life and not Nigel. I would never partake in hurting his child. Never."

"I didn't start this war, you did."

"So, let me end it."

"Problem is, I can't trust you to believe it's really over. You could be lying."

"I could have taken you out just now, but I didn't, think about that."

He looked at her like she was stupid.

"You can't be serious right now. I know you too well for that," he said through clenched teeth. She sighed. "Yeah, you want revenge, but your pride and ego require me to suffer first to know I was bested by you. You wouldn't come for me until you hurt me beyond repair, by coming for Grey and then you would make sure I knew it before you took me out. Let's not forget you'd drag it out as long as possible. You're too savage for a merciful kill. Let's not pretend that you're someone you're not. Do not insult my intelligence like I missed something."

She grimaced in frustration. He knew her too well. Well the old her. She couldn't deny he was right.

She asked, "What happened to that man I was undercover with? What happened to that man that fell in love with Kane's kids?

The one that took each of those girls at that facility as personal burdens? The one that rescued the young girl from that strip club?"

"You happened to me. Eva happened to me and my dad happened to me. It doesn't matter how long you've known someone or how good of a person they seem to be, humans are capable of epic levels of deceit, betrayal, and selfishness. My family will never pay the price for my naivete. You need to leave. Show up anywhere near me again and Sam is going to need a black suit. Do I make myself clear?"

"I'm sorry I hurt you."

"Apology not accepted."

She nodded. "I'll leave." She turned.

"Wait." Stunned she looked back at him. "Does Sam know about the baby?"

She shook her head not even the least bit shocked he knew about Sampson.

"Why not?"

"It's complicated."

"Uncomplicate it. He has a right to know and he needs to be a part of any decision you make."

In his mind, Neil understood if Sam knew about the baby, he'd fight like hell to make sure it was not aborted.

"Why do you care?"

"It's my brother's grandson. That baby is my blood."

"So, am I," she said incredulously.

"Not anymore," he said with finality keeping his gun trained on her.

She nodded and turned to leave. He let her go because he sincerely wanted her to tell Sam about the baby. From one father to another, he owed him that. Once he was satisfied, she was gone, he headed out, though he kept his pistol by his side, just in case it was all a setup.

Chapter 75: Say What?

Once Neil was in his truck, he circled the parking lot to see if Fuller was anywhere lurking. Satisfied no one was going to follow him, he called Nigel.

"Bro, it's like 3:00 in the morning. What's up?" he said groggily.

"Fuller just confronted me at the gym."

There was a short pause. This time Nigel's voice left all trace of sleepiness and was fully alert.

"Tell me everything now," Nigel demanded.

"She came to confess she wanted to let this all go and just walk away."

"Why now?"

"She says she's pregnant with Sam's baby and wants to live a life with him and not worry about looking over her shoulder for me."

Nigel sighed.

Neil frowned. "What the hell am I missing, Nigel?"

"I knew she was pregnant," he confessed.

"What? And you didn't tell me. What the hell Nigel?"

"Calm down, bro?"

"Don't tell me to calm down. I'm all out of patience Nigel."

"Bro just meet me at our spot. I'm on my way. We need to talk."

Neil hung up without responding. He was thoroughly pissed the hell off. Deception was everywhere.

He dialed Beau.

"What's up boss man?" Beau asked after the first ring.

"Be on alert. Fuller is in town. I don't know if she's stupid enough to try anything, but I have to go meet Nigel. I will be a little longer."

"No worries, Neil. Your fam is safe with me."

"Thank you, man."

Neil sighed as he hung up the phone and made a U-turn to head to his mother's house.

Chapter 76: Family Affairs

Nigel got out of bed.

"Where are you going baby?"

"We are going. I don't have time to call Darryl and I don't want to leave you here alone. Fuller is in the city."

"Wait, what?"

"Babe just get up and throw on something, please," he said with irritation in his voice.

Kadijah turned on the bedside lamp and stared at her husband trying to figure out this new mood of his. Clearly, he was upset.

"What's wrong Nigel?"

"Neil thinks I betrayed him. We need to talk, and I need to clear the air."

She frowned. "He found out your niece is pregnant?"

"Yeah."

Kadijah sighed. She knew it bothered Nigel something serious to keep that information from his brother, but he had to be obedient to what God was telling him to do. She felt bad for him.

Neil was already in a dark place and this did not help. His brother was supposed to be his closest ally. She couldn't imagine how he felt knowing Nigel intentionally kept something this game changing from him.

No more protesting on her part. She climbed out of bed and threw on some sweats and some sneakers. She didn't even have to ask where they were going. They would be meeting up in their tree house. She would be in her mother-in-loves big comfy recliner with her favorite blanket and knocked out. She would let her husband know that she loved him and his brother but once she was asleep this time not to wake her up. He could grab a spot on his mom's couch or come back home, but once she was in that recliner, he better not bother her.

Nigel quickly dressed. He put on some black sweats and a black t-shirt, then stepped into his wheat Timberland boots that were by the bed. Kadijah watched as he put his gun on his hip and tightened the drawstring. She licked her lips then chastised herself and reminded herself, now was not the time.

Nigel went into the bathroom. She heard the water running and him brushing his teeth. She followed suit, then followed him out the door.

†††

In another part of town, Grey was awakened by her cell phone ringing. Absentmindedly she reached toward the noise and fumbled until she grabbed it. With one eye open she saw Neil was calling.

"What's wrong baby?" she asked when she answered.

"I'm headed to meet Nigel at our spot. I just didn't know how long I was going to be gone and I didn't want you to worry."

"You sound pissed. What happened?"

"Nigel's been keeping stuff from me!" he snapped.

"What did he not tell you?"

"Well I'm sure plenty, but the most important thing is that Fuller is pregnant with Sam's baby."

Grey sat straight up. "Say what now?"

"Yeah. That part."

"Wait, go back. What happened?"

"Fuller confronted me at the gym."

"She did what!" Grey practically screamed into the phone.

"Grey, chill out before you wake the baby."

"Negro, you better make this make sense before I start acting a plum fool. Who the hell does she think she is? I will..."

Neil cut her off. "She came to me to apologize and ask me to let this go. She tried to convince me that she was done with it and just wanted to go be happy with Sam and this baby."

"And you don't believe her."

"Hell no!"

"Why not?"

"Why would I?"

"Neil, a baby changes things."

"You have to have a heart for it to change. Fuller has an empty black hole where hers is supposed to be."

Grey sighed. "Baby, I am not a fan of your niece you know that. But I need you to throttle back on your anger for a minute and just think. It's some bizarre stuff happening, and you know Nigel has a good reason for not telling you."

"I am so tired of everybody telling me what to do with *my* anger," he snapped then let out an expletive.

"Whoa, calm down before you piss me off. I'm just trying to reason with you."

"And I'm just trying to keep my family safe. Her job was to kill me. She willfully deceived me, the Bureau and was sent in to take out players in her *own* organization. This is a woman that cannot be trusted. Period. Why is that so hard to understand?"

"Nobody asked you to trust her Neil. We are asking you to trust God."

"Okay, I tell you what. When He speaks to *me* and tells *me* something different then I'll listen. Until then, I'm locked and loaded, ready, willing, and able. I do not want to discuss this anymore!" he snapped.

Grey sighed. "I'm just going to say bye, because if you hang up on me, we are going to have some problems."

"Bye," Neil said then hung up.

Grey fell back on the bed.

"You heard him God, only You can get him to see this from any other perspective. I trust that You got this handled because the way my attitude is set up right now, I am not going to be helpful. Fix it Jesus."

Her angels, Savas and Bojan exchanged a look. Savas reached down and touched her sending her peace, so she could get some sleep.

Chapter 77: Hashing It Out

When Nigel exited out the backdoor to their mom's house, he saw his brother's feet dangling from their childhood treehouse as the light from inside shown bright.

Nigel sighed, "Lord, I don't want anything to come between me and my brother. Please work this out. We need you, in Jesus name I pray. Amen."

Nigel had a ball of nervous energy as he approached the tree house. He climbed up as Neil moved his long legs out of the way.

"Hey bro," he said as he took a seat on the other side while his long legs dangled as well.

"Start talking Nigel," Neil said with his arms folded across his chest.

"I wanted to tell you, but God told me not to," Nigel said bracing for a reaction.

Neil was about to snap when it registered what his brother had just said.

"What do you mean?"

"I mean, the night she came to my office to try to take me out, when I realized what was going on, I felt the strongest conviction not to tell you. As soon as it went down, I reached for my phone, but I heard, 'no' so clearly. I had to back off and trust Him. I've been praying nonstop asking God what He wanted me to do."

"What happened at your office Nigel?" Neil demanded.

He told his brother about what they found outside when they were leaving and what they ended up seeing on the security cameras. The anger that was set on Neil's face looked permanent. He also told him how they all seemed to be blinded to what she was outside doing. No one on the inside saw it on camera and none of the security outside was in place when she arrived. He didn't believe that was happenstance.

"I didn't know for sure she was pregnant, when I saw the video, because anything could have made her sick, but it just came to me. The DNA test though did match mine as a family member, so I knew it was her."

"And this bomb?" Neil asked frowning.

"Remote trigger, but she apparently never activated it. I guess when the pedestrians came along, she knew she had to get out of there. Because if I had caught her out there like that, it woulda been lights out."

Neil nodded trying to process all of this. It took him a few minutes before he said anything. He was pissed. He had snapped at his wife and upset her. He didn't want to do the same with his brother. In all this craziness they were his allies.

Nigel gave his brother the space he needed to calm down. Silence enveloped them as the sounds of the fall night was filled with the mating calls of the cicadas. The air was breezy with the scent of summer transitioning into fall.

Neil took a deep breath. "Why do you think God told you not to tell me?"

Nigel looked at Neil like he was slow. "Um, bro, you haven't exactly been emotionally stable in this situation." Neil wanted to defend himself but nodded. "I mean, in the beginning, I was on the same page, but too much bizarre stuff was happening, and I had to take a step back. Then I started praying and it's like my discernment just went into overdrive and I could see what wasn't obvious."

Neil nodded. "Okay, what did you see?"

"You really ready to hear this, bro?"

Neil frowned. "No, but I guess I need to. Because her coming between you and I is not an option. We deal with this tonight."

Nigel nodded. "For me it started with Sam. I mean I know he was a valid threat, but I just didn't get that vibe from him. You know how I can just feel people. I immediately liked him and felt some type of way about being at odds with him. I also know how much true love truly changed me. Fuller is more like me than she is like you so that's the angle I took it from. I knew that Sam truly loved her just from that one encounter. Like y'all taught me it's not about flesh and blood, but it's spiritual. Mom's reaction never sat right with me. Once Fuller made it clear that she wasn't a willing participant in anything to do with my baby girl, it put me in a different mind frame. I know you haven't assessed any of this because that's just not where your head is but think about it."

Neil listened intently.

"Both Fuller and Eva were connected to you. Your partners. They are the only two left alive from their mother. Their mother is too, but I'm not sure if she's on the up and up. I know both of them were living foul, but maybe they are still alive because of you."

Neil frowned. Nigel gave it a second. "You mean the shield thing?" Neil asked.

Nigel nodded. "After everything that went down, Eva ended up giving her life to Christ."

"Bruh if you looking for Michelle to be converted, you might as well believe in fairy tales," Neil said.

"I'm not so sure bro. Hear me out. At the end of the day Fuller is Niles' daughter and she didn't get pregnant until *after* the curse was broken."

Nigel saw it click for Neil in his facial expression.

"I got a feeling that this baby she's carrying is spiritually protected which is why God basically told me to step off. I mean He's dealing with Fuller. We haven't even had to touch her. Every encounter we've had she's either running or apologizing. There's more to this bro and you need to deal with whatever is going on in your heart because I'm telling you, she is part of this family's spiritual legacy."

"Don't you think I would if I could," Neil said frustrated. "I can't!" he snapped.

"Why is that bro? Think about it. You don't think you being the one they betrayed while simultaneously being the reason they are still alive is coincidence, do you? It's strategic. All I'm saying is bro, don't let the enemy win."

"Even if I choose not to take her out. I can't trust her. I don't see myself welcoming her with open arms," Neil said honestly. "She's wanted by the Feds. She killed Federal agents bro. Her fate is sealed."

"Some stuff God is going to have to work out however He sees fit. I'm not trying to have my great niece or nephew born in prison though."

Neil sighed. "If she stays away from me and mine, I won't pursue her."

"I can work with that. Just promise me you won't take her out. I know you don't believe she's for real, but I do. She's on our side, whether she realizes it or not."

Neil sighed. "I guess I need to spend some time with God," he said.

"Couldn't hurt," Nigel said laughing.

Neil chuckled. Nigel reached for his hand. Neil clasped it as they embraced.

"Let me get home to my wife. She's pissed at me," Neil said.

Nigel laughed. "Well, I'm on my mama's couch because Kadijah told me if I woke her up again, she was going to cause me great harm."

Neil laughed. "She's in mama's recliner, isn't she?"

"Knocked slap out."

They laughed as they climbed out of the tree.

"You better take some ibuprofen now for those back problems you gon have tomorrow," Neil teased.

Nigel gave his brother the finger as he waved bye exiting through the yard, while he went into the house through the back door. The weight had been lifted from his heart. He knew that they'd finally gotten through the hard exterior and now it was up to God to do the rest. He was grateful.

Chapter 78: I'm Sorry

It was nearly 6 AM when Neil finally made it home. He took the scenic route, needing to think and clear his head. This was crazy. Why did God insist on giving him the hardest emotional circumstances to deal with? What was it about their family?

He pulled into the garage and turned off his truck. He sighed because he knew his wife was pissed at him. He unfairly took out his frustrations on her. He went in the house to find Beau sitting in the kitchen sipping a cup of coffee.

"You good boss man?" Beau asked.

"I will be. Thanks for looking out for them while I got this stuff sorted out."

"No problem. Need me to stay?"

"No, I'm good. Take off when you finish your coffee."

"Heads up, Miss Grey is *hot* with you."

Neil chuckled. "I know. I've been working on my apology speech."

"Good luck," Beau told him as he raised his coffee mug in salute.

Neil shook his head and headed for the stairs. First, he went to Hunter's room. The chocolate bundle was wide awake and busy chewing on his toes. Neil laughed and scooped him up. He kissed his baby boy and took a seat in the rocking chair.

"What's up lil man?"

Hunter squealed and grabbed his daddy's face with his slob covered hands. Neil laughed. This little boy brought him so much joy. Who was he to say that the child his niece carried couldn't transform her? Hunter had certainly changed him and Grey.

He also realized how much he missed his son. Since this ordeal he had been away from home more than he wanted to be.

"I'm sorry daddy's been gone so much lately. I promise to be around more often."

He kissed the top of Hunter's head as he inhaled his sweet baby scent. Neil pulled his son into his chest and began to rock as he closed his eyes. He was beyond tired.

A while later, Grey walked in to find her husband and her son knocked out. She was pissed at Neil, but the scene before her melted her heart. She wasn't surprised when Neil jerked slightly and opened his eyes. He could always sense another presence around him.

"Good morning," she whispered.

He looked around a little confused. "Good morning baby. How long have I been sleep?"

"I don't know. I'm not sure *when* you got home."

He ran a hand over his face to clear the cobwebs. "I'm sorry. I came in to kiss Hunter, but found him up and then, I don't even know."

"It's cool," she said.

"No, it's not. I owe you an apology." She leaned against the doorway. "I'm sorry for snapping at you. Thank you for being incredibly patient with me these last few months. I talked to Nigel and I'm working through my issues. I know I haven't been the easiest person to deal with."

"My mama said, if you can't say anything nice, don't say nothing at all." He grinned. "Apology accepted," she told him. "You need to get some rest," she said as she walked over to take Hunter.

He barely stirred as she took him from Neil and placed him in his crib. Neil rubbed his bearded chin as he watched his wife in her thigh length red satin gown lean over the crib to put the baby down. How she stirred him so easily he never could understand.

Grey rubbed Hunter's belly to soothe him when his eyes fluttered. Moments later his eyes closed again. Grey turned around to find her husband coming toward her. She recognized the look on his face. She rolled her eyes. He grinned and reached for her.

Possessively he pulled her into him as his hands roamed the satin barrier between them and kissed her deeply.

"Why don't you put me to sleep?" he suggested against her neck.

"You so nasty," Grey said giggling as she wrapped her arms around his neck.

"Let me *really* apologize to you," he whispered seductively as he nibbled her ear lobe.

In response, she kissed him back letting him know all was about to be forgiven.

Chapter 79: If You Send Me, I'll Go

A word had been ringing in her spirit for over a week now. She had yet to share it with anybody and figured God must be trying to tell her something. The word itself was intimidating so instead of taking the time to research it, she hesitated.

Finally, she could no longer ignore it. They sat at the dinner table. Genevieve listened as David told her about his day.

He asked, "What's wrong cutie? You seem distracted."

"Nothing, it's just I think God is trying to tell me something. I'm not sure what it is and really, I'm not sure I want to know."

David chuckled. "Which means, it's important. What are you hearing?"

"It's just one word - gatekeeper."

David put down his fork. "Oh my!"

"Well that doesn't make me feel better."

He laughed. "It wasn't meant to."

"What do you know about gatekeepers?" she asked him.

David sat back and thought. "I know that when Nehemiah finished the wall, the first thing he did was install gatekeepers. Back then cities had to be fortified before they would begin to conduct business. A gatekeeper had to not only be trustworthy, but alert. I mean think about it. If the gatekeeper couldn't be trusted, he'd make one heck of an inside man for enemy. Back then their walls were their security. If the people assigned to watch the entrance couldn't be trusted, they could let the enemy walk right in. A breach in the security."

Genevieve absorbed all that her husband and pastor was revealing to her.

"Do you think He's telling me I'm a gatekeeper?"

"Perhaps," David said not completely sure.

"A gatekeeper of what though?"

"This city."

"Oh!" she said. "That actually makes sense. But in this city, where are the gates?" she asked sincerely.

David thought about it and put a finger up signaling for her to hold on. He left the table and returned a minute later with his Bible.

"I've seen something somewhere that may apply here," he told her as he flipped through his lovingly worn Bible. "It can't mean the exact same thing it was back then, but maybe there's a clue to help you get an idea of what God is trying to tell you," he said as he continued to flip. "Do me a favor," he said. "Google gatekeepers in the Bible and tell me what the results are?"

Genevieve put down her fork and grabbed her phone and began the search.

She said, "Ezra 2:32, Nehemiah 7:1, 1 Chronicles 9:22..."

"That's it," David said snapping his fingers. He quickly flipped and scanned. "Yep, here it is. In 1 Chronicles, it says the gatekeepers were on the four sides - east, west, north and south."

Genevieve nodded.

"I wonder which gate I'm supposed to cover and why."

"Keep seeking Him baby. He will reveal all. You just make sure you're obedient when He does."

She nodded.

"You're right baby. Wherever He sends me, I will go."

He nodded. "That's my girl."

She grinned as they prepared to enjoy the rest of their dinner.

Chapter 80: The Unexpected Gift

Kadijah lay on the examining table with her arm behind her head as she stared at the monitor waiting to see her baby girl. Nigel leaned down and kissed her forehead as the doctor put the clear gel on her protruding belly.

Kadijah grinned.

"What?" he asked.

"It tickles."

"Oh."

He leaned down and kissed her lips unable to resist her beautiful face. The way she glowed as she carried his seed never ceased to gently squeeze his heart. He couldn't believe he was three weeks away from being a father, completely in love with the woman that carried his baby and happier than he could ever imagine.

"What was that for?" Kadijah asked smiling.

"Because I love you. Thank you for bringing my baby girl into the world. I know it hasn't been easy."

Kadijah snorted when she laughed. He laughed too.

"That's an understatement. Good luck getting another one out of me. As a matter of fact, I am going to need a push gift for this one."

Nigel and the doctor laughed at her.

Insidious was present as he was for all of Kadijah's doctor's appointments. He lurked as closely as their angelic protection would allow. Cheveyo, Quan, Bomani and Lajos continued to guard their charges and keep Insidious at bay. Suddenly, they felt the unmistakable presence of Death. They all turned to see him strolling down the hallway with ease.

"What is he doing here?" Insidious asked.

No one responded as Death made his way into Kadijah's exam room. Insidious was fit to be tied as he watched as Death placed his massive black diamond hands on Kadijah's belly.

"What are you doing?" he screamed.

No one responded. Insidious watched as the doctor continued his examination.

The doctor put the device on her belly. "Let's get a look at this little lady and see how she's doing. Have you guys picked out a name yet?"

"Not yet," Kadijah said as she felt the wand moving across her abdomen. Kadijah frowned. "Where's the heartbeat?"

The doctor frowned; he was wondering the same thing. "Hold on, let me check something," the doctor said.

Nigel frowned. "Doc is there a problem?"

"I'm checking..."

He could see the fetus on the monitor, but he was not seeing or hearing the heartbeat. Standing up, he put his stethoscope on Kadijah's belly as he listened intently, with the same result. The flat look on his face told them all they needed to know.

Kadijah screamed.

Insidious stared incredulously at the angelic beings, he grinned fiercely.

"Well that was unexpected. Can't say I saw that coming, but who am I to argue with the sovereign will of Father. I'm disappointed, but I can't say I'm not thrilled we won't have to deal with her as a child of the light."

He strolled off with confidence.

Their angels looked at each other. They turned to see Death still holding Kadijah's belly. Suddenly, he began to shimmer, he was no longer made of black diamonds, but clear diamonds. He shimmered to the point he could no longer be seen. Even his Shadow disappeared.

†††

Grey and Neil arrived at Nigel and Kadijah's apartment as soon as Neil came home. Grey had been praying nonstop since she'd heard the news. She didn't believe it. She couldn't believe it. This little girl was a promised child. *How can she be...* Grey couldn't even bring herself to think the word, let alone say it out loud. She thought about getting Hope to pray for Kadijah's baby, but for some reason, she wasn't feeling that in her spirit. Her faith wouldn't let her stop fighting for her niece.

When they got out of the car Grey said, "Neil, this isn't true. It's not true."

Neil just shrugged. "Baby, I don't know what to say. This is crazy."

"God promised them this child. All the warfare we endured to discover Black Pearl's curse and to break it. This isn't true. It can't be."

Neil wanted to believe what his wife was saying, but there was no heartbeat. He went around to the car and held his wife.

"It's going to be okay, baby."

Their four angelic beings surrounded them as they continued to send Grey strength to stand as a watchman on the wall. The look of devastation on Nigel's face when he opened the door broke Grey's heart.

She grabbed him and said, "Nigel, I need you to fight for your baby girl. Do not give up."

He had no response.

Grey went inside to find Kadijah sitting on the sofa in tears.

Neil asked his brother, "So, what... How do you..."

"The doc told us they would induce the pregnancy and she will deliver a stillborn. They gave us the option to go home and prepare ourselves instead of doing it right then. Kadijah was so hysterical, I decided we needed to come home and try to regroup before they went forward with it."

Neil had negative thoughts, but he wouldn't utter them. Nigel was caught between his faith and his heart, a precarious place to be. Kadijah had lost all hope and faith, while Grey was pacing and praying trying to figure out what was going on.

Grey got down on her knees and placed her hands on Kadijah's belly as she began to travail in tongues. She continued to pray when her eyes suddenly flamed. Grey felt the unmistakable presence of Death all around her. She became angry as she opened her eyes.

There he was in all his black beauty standing behind Kadijah with his hands wrapped around her belly. Grey's eyes filled with tears of rage.

He shook his head and said, "Don't let what you see determine what you know to be the truth. All warfare is based on deception.

This is a test of their faith, not yours." Death put a finger to his lips signaling for Grey not to tell what she'd seen.

Grey stared blankly as a fire hit her belly. She continued to travail in tongues as Kadijah squeezed her hand.

When Grey finished, she said, "We need to get you to the hospital."

"I can't," Kadijah said.

"You can, and you will." Grey went to Nigel. "You have got to trust the God we serve and the instruction He gave you. Your first-born child will be a little girl and all the ones after her will be boys. God is not a man that He should lie. I know it looks dire, but this is the time for faith and not fear. Bro, when you dropped us off at the safehouse you asked me to trust you and I did because that was your lane. You had me there for spiritual protection. This is my lane, let me drive. Trust me when I tell you, we need to get her to the hospital now. You said there were things I would be able to see that you could not. Please, trust me."

Neil grabbed his wife's hand and squeezed it. He couldn't speak, his voice was thick with emotions, but he needed her to know he had her back.

The tears Nigel had been holding back spilled down on to his cheeks. His eyes were a vivid green as Grey's words gave him a glimmer of hope.

"Okay, sis. Okay."

†††

When they arrived at the hospital Grey felt evil all around her. Insidious had demons on post. He wanted to see for himself the baby delivered stillborn. Grey's gift was in full effect. The presence of Death had never left her, so she knew he was there, but he'd also given her instruction. She wouldn't let his presence unnerve her. She knew his shadow was a place of peace and refuge, so she held on to the that.

When they got out of Nigel's truck, Kadijah grabbed her stomach and began to scream out in pain. Nigel panicked, while Neil rushed in to get the paramedics. EMTs arrived and quickly put Kadijah on a gurney as they wheeled her through the emergency room.

Nigel didn't even realize he was praying as the tears silently ran down his face.

Neil understood his job was to cover his wife as she covered his niece. They followed the gurney as far as they were allowed to when Kadijah and Nigel disappeared behind the double doors. Grey watched in abject horror as the Angel of Death appeared before her. She watched as he went from black diamonds to clear diamonds. He literally looked like a silhouette of water. He winked at her.

She gasped and clutched her chest. Neil caught her when her knees got weak.

"What is it, baby?"

Grey grabbed her husband as she tried to process what she was seeing. She shook her head and refused to say what she saw.

"Just keep praying baby, keep praying."

An hour later, they were allowed to see Kadijah. Her blood pressure was up, and the doctors decided to induce labor because now her health was in jeopardy. There was still no heartbeat. All Nigel could do was hold his wife. He had no words and had cut off his emotions. He was functioning on autopilot and trying to treat it like it was a mission.

He felt like if he detached himself, he could handle it. The minute he let himself feel the inevitable, he didn't know if he'd be able to close the floodgate. They had given Kadijah a sedative to sleep. Everyone remained quiet as Grey continued to pray.

†††

In the hallway, Insidious stood with a grin on his face. "I know the light is up to something. It can't be this easy," he said to Cheveyo and Quan, Kadijah's warriors.

Their faces remained stoic.

"Why did Death strike her? Where is he? He has to be here to take her spirit." Their faces remained stoic. "Answer me!" He demanded.

"What difference does it make?" Cheveyo asked. "Isn't this what you wanted, for her to be touched by the hand of Death?"

"The Spirit of Death, not the Angel," Insidious said snarling. He didn't trust that angel so until he saw proof he would remain as close as they allowed him.

†††

Grey watched as Death, still crystal clear kept his hands around Kadijah's belly as the doctor's continued to check the ultrasound. There was still no heartbeat. Her mouth was agape as she finally understood what he was doing. On instinct, she reached out and grabbed her husband. She understood she needed his gift in this very moment. There was information she would possess that could make her a target.

Puzzled, Neil stared at his wife, her grip on his arm was so tight. He decided to just fall back and let her do her thing. Grey watched as the blue shield surrounded the room. She knew he both concealed her presence as well as protected her. She definitely needed to be hidden for whatever was about to be revealed to her.

Savas and Bojan grinned. They loved to see her operate in her gifts.

In her mind, Grey spoke, "It's been an attack from you all along, not the Darkness, but the Light," Grey said.

"Not an attack," Death corrected her. "A strategy. If the enemy thinks she's mine, there's no need to try and attack her anymore. It gives us the window of opportunity for an attack free arrival. Black baby girls have the highest survival rate at this stage, so this was the best window of opportunity."

Grey nodded. "But why? Wasn't she protected by the promise from God regardless?"

"She is," Death told her, "But her brother isn't."

"Oh my God, oh my God!" Grey finally understood what was happening. "All warfare is based on deception. He's a second born so he's..."

Death nodded. "His shield couldn't be activated until after he was born because he needed to remain hidden."

Bojan, her Serbian warrior, touched her temple and began to give her understanding. Grey grinned fiercely as she remembered that the strategy God had given Nigel to blind their enemies to their strategies. She was in complete awe of the God they served. Jehovah Sabaoth was truly amazing.

†††

An hour later, Kadijah had been rushed to have an emergency c-section. This day kept getting worse, but Nigel remained by his wife's side determined to be her rock. The fact that Grey just wouldn't give up kept him hoping against hope even in the eleventh hour and fifty-ninth minute. Kadijah's blood pressure continued to rise so the doctors and nurses moved with controlled chaos as they got her open.

"What the..."

Nigel heard followed by some choice expletives. The next sound he heard was music to his ears. He heard a baby's cry. His knees buckled as he looked over to see a wriggling baby screaming at the top of her lungs.

He heard the nurse scream, "Doctor, there's another one."

"What?" the doctor said as he looked down to see another baby. He passed the first one on to the nurse as they pulled the second one out. His voice wasn't as loud as his sister's, but he whimpered.

Nigel stumbled back into the nearest wall. "There's two?"

The doctor turned to grin at Nigel.

"Looks like your wife had a stowaway. This little guy hid behind his sister for your wife's entire pregnancy."

Nigel blinked. "What?"

"Someone get this man a chair before he passes out," a nurse said grinning.

Death in all his black beauty strolled out of the room. His task was complete. Her brother would conceal and protect their existence until they were ready to let the truth be known. As a mouthpiece for God, she was the sword and her brother the shield. Together they were a mighty force to combat the plans of the Kingdom of Darkness. The sword and the shield.

Chapter 81: A Sovereign God

Nigel and Kadijah were in absolute awe as they held their children. Not only did God deliver on His promise, for their baby girl, but He sent them an *unexpected gift* of a son. Grey was a mess of tears. Neil managed to quickly wipe away the few that slipped his guard. This was simply amazing.

Kadijah held her son close to her bosom. Nigel held his daughter falling deeper in love by the second.

"Grey. How did you know?" Kadijah asked.

Neil nodded for her to tell them. She told him what she'd seen when they went in for the c-section. When Nigel ran out to confirm the twins, he was flabbergasted.

"Well, when I got to you guys' apartment, I felt the presence of the Angel of Death. When my spiritual sight was opened, and I saw him, I was heated. He told me that it was a test of your faith and not mine and reminded me that all warfare is based on deception."

Kadijah and Nigel both stared with their mouths agape.

"When we got to the hospital, he was holding your belly when the doctor was checking for a heartbeat, mimicking death to back the enemy off and allow for the delivery because while she was protected by God's promise, her brother wasn't."

"Whoa."

"Are you serious?"

Grey nodded. Neil continued to shake his head. Nigel's brain began to catch up with his emotions.

"Wait, so he's the second born. Is he a shield?" he inquired.

Grey nodded. "She hid him in the natural and now he'll hide her in the spirit. A dynamic duo indeed."

Kadijah shook her head. She could not believe it, this was crazy. She went from trying to prepare her mind to delivering an almost full-term stillborn to going home with two babies. This was insane, but she was so grateful.

Just then, there was a knock on the door. Neil went to open it. It was their mother with the biggest grin on her face and a bouquet of balloons.

She came in, "Oh I can't wait to meet my baby girl." She stared. "Who's the other baby?"

Nigel grinned. "Ma, we got a surprise. Apparently, we had a stowaway."

Angela shrieked. Neil and Grey laughed. "You mean, I get two new grandbabies."

Kadijah nodded. "You want to meet them?"

"Uh, yeah!"

They all laughed. Nigel walked over to his mother.

"This is your granddaughter, Gideon Nicole Sims."

"You named her Gideon? Oh, I love it. What does it mean?"

"Gideon means, one who destroys, and Nicole means the people's victory."

"Oh wow, what a powerful name you have little one."

Angela smiled and savored her first moments with her granddaughter. There was a slight ache, and a silent prayer sent up that she'd be able to hold her first granddaughter in her arms as well.

"You want to meet your new grandson?"

Angela smiled as she wiped away a tear. Neil took his niece from his mother. He was already in love with her. Nigel handed his mother their son.

"Meet Griffon Neville Sims."

Angela looked up and smiled. "You gave him your father's name?"

"It was Kadijah's idea," he confessed.

Angela blew her a kiss. "Thank you," she mouthed as her emotions overtook her. "What does his name mean?" she asked.

"His name means fierce fighting chief."

"Wow," she said as she looked down at the precious bundle of joy.

"Hey, why the G's?" Neil asked.

Nigel and Kadijah shared a look. "We wanted to pay homage to their watchman. The one who never stopped fighting for them."

Neil smiled. Grey gasped.

"Oh my gosh. I'm so honored. How sweet. I will always fight for these tiny warriors."

Neil leaned over and kissed his wife's forehead. He was so proud of her.

"Can I hold Griffon?" Grey asked. She'd said a silent prayer over Gideon when she held her and now she did the same with her brother.

Angela gave him up, but only because she could grab his sister, which she quickly did. Neil laughed. He stood up and nodded for Nigel to follow him. They headed out of the room.

Angela got up. "How are you feeling love?"

"I'm tired ma. I'm going to need so much help."

Grey and Angela laughed.

"You will have it," Angela said. "Is your dad on his way?"

"He'll be here tomorrow. Technically, we had another three weeks."

"Right. Can I get you anything?"

"Um, one of my babies."

They laughed. Angela handed over Gideon then looked at Grey. She laughed and gave up Griffon. Their angels were glorified rejoicing for the miracle and protection of the birth of these children with powerful destinies. It was always their honor to witness the sovereignty of God triumph over the evil plans of the enemy.

†††

Outside the room, Neil looked at his brother.

"How do you feel?"

"Tremendously blessed and scared as hell."

Neil fell out laughing. "Y'all won't be alone in this."

"I know, but still. Not only are there two of them, but they are here a month early."

"Hey, you're a strategist, you'll get it figured out."

"Speaking of strategy. What about Fuller?"

"Not today. You leave her to me. You just enjoy being a new dad."

"Neil, try not to kill her."

Neil laughed. "No promises."

Nigel shook his head as they headed back in.

†††

The demons lurked outside the hospital room but couldn't hear anything. Neil's shield was in full effect. They wanted to know what was going on in that hospital room.

Insidious had them posted outside the operating room, but they were blinded to everything that happened. The only thing they could report back was that they didn't look like a family who had just experienced the death of a baby.

The demon left in charge said, "Let's go tell Insidious that the light pulled a fast one."

"But what?" another asked.

He shrugged. "I wish I knew."

The angels grinned fiercely as the demons walked away empty handed. They couldn't wait to see Insidious' reaction to the truth.

Chapter 82: Dropping Bombs

Nigel sat at his desk staring at the wall. There was a feeling of dread churning in his belly. The waiting was torture. He was sitting on a bomb that needed to be dropped as soon as possible.

It could be life or death if he didn't get the information where it needed it to be. He had left word with Eva and Sam two days ago that he needed Fuller to call him. No one seemed to know where she was. He was hoping and praying that she got in touch with either her sister or her lover before it was too late.

As the time kept ticking, he wondered if he should have just told Eva and Sam what was going on. That way, she could get the information faster, though it was still no guarantee. No, he needed to be the one to tell her because he also needed to talk some sense into her.

"God, let her call me soon," he prayed aloud.

He realized he was sincerely concerned about her safety. Their dynamic was so strange now. His babies had been safely born, but he still felt like there was a threat.

When his people discovered what they did, the angst got stronger. He hoped Neil had let go of the idea of taking their niece out but because no one knew what she was up to and she wasn't with Sam, her situation remained precarious.

His phone rang. It was a blocked number. His heart dropped as he picked up.

"Hello."

"I heard you've been looking for me."

"Can you hang up and video call me?"

"What do you take me for an amateur?"

"Not at all. I'm not snooping on you. I just need to see your face and I need you to see mine. I have something important to tell you."

"So just spit it out."

"You asked Neil to trust you and he didn't. How did that make you feel?" Silence. "I'm asking you to trust me. I know Sam has told you I'm your advocate. We gotta start somewhere Chelle."

It was the use of an affectionate nickname that softened her.

"Hang up," she said.

He did. The phone rang a few moments later.

"What's this about?" she demanded.

He could see that she was seated inside of a car. He guessed by the background that she was pulled to the side of a road on an interstate. The blur of cars passing by told him that much.

"It's about your mother."

She frowned. "What about my mother?"

"She betrayed you."

Her fair skinned turned red. "What do you mean?"

"Lucca is still alive and their working together."

"What the..." He nodded. "There's no way. How do you even know this?"

"When we were trying to figure this out, it was my idea to follow your mother because she was connected to you and Eva. I got her information from Eva and put one of my guys on her. Eva told me you had her take out Lucca so when he was spotted, I knew it was a double cross. You need to be careful Chelle. If she betrayed you, there's a follow-up plan. She's coming for you."

He saw the anger on her face and that she was fighting back tears.

"I have to go," she said angrily.

"No! Do not hang up this phone Michelle and I mean it." She paused at the authority in his voice. "Now, we are no longer a threat to you, but she's a real one and Lucca is Satan himself. You have so much more to lose. Do not go after them!"

"I'm not just going to sit back and let that witch get away with this."

"Calm down!" he demanded. "Now I need you to listen. Lucca already has an arrest warrant out. Let me handle this and do this by the book. I have the staff and resources."

"Why the hell did you tell me if you were going to stand in my way?"

"I told you, so you would be careful and not walk into a trap. If you hear from her, I'm begging you not to go."

"I can't promise you that."

"Think of your baby Chelle."

Tears welled up in her eyes, but they didn't fall.

"I won't be safe as long as she's out there. Lucca warned me. He said, 'If you continue to refuse to do your part for our side in this war, you'll find yourself all alone fighting both good and evil and sweetheart as skilled as you are, you're no match for both sides to be coming at you with everything they've got.'"

He shook his head. Lucca spoke that right into existence. She should have known then a double cross was coming.

"Let me handle it."

"Why would you do that?"

"You're my family. It's my job to keep you safe."

"Does Sam know?"

"I didn't tell him the details."

"I have to go."

"Wait. Come to Tallahassee. My mom really wants to meet you."

"This is not some happily ever after group hug. I am wanted by the FBI. You just want to keep a leash on me. Listen, I'm not that girl. I can handle myself. Thank you for looking out. I really do appreciate it. I'm out."

"Mich..." the call ended. "Crap!" he said and slammed down the phone.

He thought about it for a minute, then picked up the phone and called Sam.

"Sampson Steele," he said picking up after the third ring.

"Nigel Sims."

"Did you get in touch with her?"

"Yeah and gave her some rough news. I'm afraid she's going to do something stupid and not let me handle it."

"What's the news?"

Nigel told him what he found out.

"That's unfortunate. I'm guessing your decision to tell her was to ensure she doesn't walk into a trap."

"It was, but I don't know if she'll be able to resist going after them. I have a plan to get Lucca arrested. I'm working on her mom."

"Can you send me what you have on them?"

"Yeah, what's your email?"

Sam gave it to him. Nigel scribbled it on a Post It note.

"I'll shoot it over as soon as we disconnect."

"Okay. Nigel, you have my word, I'll keep her safe."
"Thank you."
Nigel hung up slightly relieved. He needed to deal with Lucca once and for all.

Chapter 83: A Hard Pill to Swallow

Neil had just finished typing up his last report. It was getting late, he was tired, but there was this weight on his heart. It had been there for a while, but today it was truly a heavy load to bear. He knew he needed to go home, but he also just needed a minute to get himself together.

His two angelic guardians never left his side, but there was also six demonic spirits lurking and tormenting his spirit. The angels could do nothing about them because Neil had invited them in with his disobedience and double mindedness.

Neil got up and shut his office door. He lay across the worn brown couch that sat in the corner. His long legs dangled off the edge of the loveseat. He knew God was trying to deal with him, but he was resistant because in all honesty he really wasn't trying to hear what God was saying.

It was crazy how he knew as much as he did about God and had seen more than most people on this earth ever would, but still wasn't trying to line up with God's will. He felt very much overwhelmed and underappreciated. He was mentally, emotionally, and spiritually exhausted by this ongoing family drama that just never seemed to end.

He couldn't pray. He hadn't been able to for a while now. He threw an arm over his face to block out the light in his office. Then he reached for the words of David - one of his precious psalms. The one that rested in his spirit was Psalm 13.

In his heart he prayed. *"How long, O Lord? Will You forget me forever? How long will You hide Your face from me? How long shall I take counsel in my soul, Having sorrow in my heart all the day? How long will my enemy be exalted over me? Consider and answer me, O Lord my God; Enlighten my eyes, or I will sleep the sleep of death, and my enemy will say, "I have overcome him," And my adversaries will rejoice when I am shaken. But I have trusted in Your lovingkindness; My heart shall rejoice in Your salvation. I will sing to the Lord, Because He has dealt bountifully with me."*

The last part convicted him, but still he resisted. His angels Ern and Koldo had never left his side.

"He's praying again," Ern said.

"Indeed. Now is the time. We must reach him now, while his heart is available," Koldo said.

"But how?" Ern inquired. "He isn't listening to anyone around him."

"Maybe he needs to hear from those who aren't around him," Koldo suggested. "We could appear to him as them."

Ern grinned and touched Neil's temple. Neil's eyes began to feel heavy. He fought it because he needed to get home, but after a few minutes, he dropped into sleep.

The vision came quick. He was in Nigel's office staring down at Fuller who was tied to the chair, just like she had been when he realized she'd betrayed him and participated in the kidnapping of his wife. Only this time she was very pregnant. The wound from where he shot her continued to bleed out.

"Help me, Neil. Don't let me die here like this."

He frowned. "No."

"How can you turn your back on me? I'm family," she said with tears running down her face.

"I can't believe you have the audacity to ask me for mercy when you have never in your life afforded it to anyone else. You reap what you sow. That's not on me, that's on you."

"What about the baby?"

He turned his head. He couldn't think about the baby. Children had always been his weak spot. When he did, he jumped as he realized his father and Etienne were sitting on Nigel's desk staring at him.

His father was the spitting image of him, except his full beard and mustache was white. Etienne's pecan brown skin was contrasted by the stark white small afro. They both stared at him with disapproving looks.

"Now, I know you know better than that boy," Etienne said his usual orneriness in full effect. "That girl needs help!"

"Not from me she doesn't," Neil said angrily.

"Son."

He shivered at the sound of his father's voice. He hadn't heard that sound in over four years. Tears welled in his eyes.

"Dad."

"She's our flesh and blood."

"She's evil," Neil countered.

"Well that baby is innocent," Etienne inserted into the convo.

Neville reached over and patted Etienne's shoulder. "I got this old friend."

Neville stood up and walked toward his son. To Neil it was like looking forward in time through a mirror. His father's eyes were a vivid green and he knew his was a dangerous gray.

"Is she evil or is she a victim of evil?" Neil didn't answer. "Son, I know I'm not who you thought I was, but redemption is possible, but only love can facilitate it."

"You're asking for too much."

"Was it too much when Jesus died on the cross for your wretched soul?" Etienne asked.

Neville turned. "Let me do this, please."

Etienne waved him off and folded his arms across his chest.

"Son, I know this isn't easy, but you have to see beyond this moment. You have to see beyond your anger."

"This isn't my mess to clean up. The burden should not belong to me."

"You're right and I'm sorry, but if I were still here, what do you think I would do?" Tears welled in Neil's eyes, but he refused to let them fall. "I love you son and I trust you to do what I taught you to do. Don't break your mother's heart."

Etienne walked up. "I told you even though your cross was a lot to bear that you would never buckle under the weight of it. But it seems that you are. Could it be because you are trusting in your own strength instead of the God that trusted you to carry the cross? Could it be that you are ashamed and hiding your burdens from your wife, the one who Jehovah called to stand beside you? It's time to release those secrets. They have allowed the enemy access to torment you. Son this battle doesn't belong to you, it belongs to the Lord. Give it back!"

Neil awoke with a gasp. He stared up at the ceiling as the weight of the vision rested on his mind. Conviction began to settle on his heart. Everything in him wanted to fight it. Ern and Koldo felt the struggle in his spirit.

"He needs to go home to his wife now. She can war for him," Koldo said.

"Her hands will be tied until he surrenders," Ern warned.

Neil continued to sit on the couch and think about the vision he'd had. Something had to give. He was tired and couldn't go on like this. He made the decision to go home to his wife and tell her about his private struggles. Neil grabbed his keys and shut down his office.

The leader of the demonic contingent warned, "We won't let him go that easily."

"Neither will we," Koldo said as they glorified and expanded their wings to surround Neil.

Chapter 84: Secrets of the Heart

Grey sat comfortably on the couch wearing one of Neil's t-shirts as pajamas reading a book with Barrington curled on top of her feet. Something felt off to her. She checked her watch. It was nearly midnight.

"Daddy, should be home, right Barry?"

The cat stared at her blankly then licked one of his paws before closing his eyes again. She rolled her eyes at the cat.

"You get on my nerves, you lazy bum," she told him.

He ignored her. She heard the garage door open and shut. Barrington's eyes popped open as he stood up on his haunches. Grey frowned and then she felt it too. Something in the atmosphere wasn't right.

Her angels Savas and Bojan looked at each other. They felt the attack coming. They each pulled their ancient weapons as they glorified. Their eyes sparked a blue flame as the same blue flame coated their weapons.

Savas stood in front of Grey. They knew Hunter's two naval angels were glorified as well.

"It's time for the showdown," Bojan said.

Savas nodded. "He's warring in his spirit," Savas confirmed.

"She's going to have to go to war for him. It has to break now," Bojan said. "The attack must be coming for their niece."

Grey felt a stirring in her spirit. A minute later, Neil appeared in the living room. With him, were his two warring angels, Ern and Koldo. Koldo locked eyes with one of Grey's warriors.

"It's time."

They nodded. They felt the demonic resistance coming. Ern and Koldo glorified as well, their bright white light beaming in the spirit realm as their eyes flamed blue and their weapons were coated with the same blue flame.

"Hey baby," she said.

"Hey," he said smiling at his wife.

"You hungry?" she asked.

"Not really."

"How was work?"

"It was work."

She put her book down and stared at him. "What's up babe? You got a weird vibe."

He came into the living room and sat next to her on their light blue sofa. She turned to face him. He leaned over and gently kissed her lips.

He said, "I promised that when I was ready, you'd get my secrets."

"Okay."

He kicked off his work boots, removed his firearm and badge then got comfortable on the couch. He reached for Grey. She lay on his chest as he wrapped her in his arms.

"This is really hard for me to admit."

"Okay."

It took a few minutes before he spoke again. Grey began interceding for him in her heart. She felt a struggle in the atmosphere.

Outside they descended on their home. Neil's doublemindedness had come to a point of no return. The spirits that tormented Neil's mind and heart were Burden, Defiance, Disobedience, Rebellion, Resentment and Shame. He welcomed them with his lack of decision to trust God.

The six demons came ready with weapons drawn and evil eyes all aglow. As Grey continued to intercede, Neil squeezed her harder.

Finally, he said, "I knew."

Grey frowned. "You knew what?"

"What I was to Fuller."

"What do you mean?"

"I knew I was her shield or rather her child's shield."

She sat up and stared at him. His eyes were a vivid gray as they penetrated hers.

"How?"

"That night she confronted me at the gym. I couldn't shoot her. I wanted to, but I couldn't and that was before I knew she was pregnant. Then when she told me about the baby it's like I just knew. Some part of me always knew there was a deeper connection to her."

"So why..."

He cut her off. "Because I was over it. I was tired of being me. Sometimes it feels like it's too much. It feels like my feelings don't matter. That I'm just supposed to get over stuff and let people walk all over me. Take advantage of me. Be everything to everybody when stuff is constantly being taken away from me. And then I feel guilty for feeling the way I do because it comes off as selfish and immature."

Grey listened with an open heart and an open mind. She could absolutely relate to him. Her life wasn't exactly a bed of roses. Though she was grateful his cross wasn't hers to bear.

"Sometimes my cross feels too heavy."

She could tell he was fighting his emotions and maybe even some inner demons. She felt so much resistance in the atmosphere.

"You gotta tell me everything baby or I can't help. You can be honest. This is a safe space."

He continued to fight it. She sat up on his lap and stared down at him.

Grabbing both his hands, she said, "Free yourself. Whatever this is, free yourself."

He sighed.

"To be honest Grey, I'm just not feeling whatever God is doing and it pisses me off that I have to be a part of it. You know I see the worst in people often, so I know life is cruel, but I have whole heartedly served Him and did everything He asked of me, but it doesn't seem to be enough. There's always more to give, more expected of me. I put my life on the line. My brother was savagely murdered. You were kidnapped. Those girls. My dad died. He should be here. We need him. Why didn't God heal him? This is his mess, not mine, but I'm expected to clean it up. It's like his death unleashed spiritual land mines that we just keep stepping on. Then my partners keep betraying me. Eva was like a sister and Fuller, I risked not coming home to you to keep her safe. And I'm just expected to roll over and take it. How? This is insane and on top of all of that, my family is constantly at risk. How do I know I won't lose you or Hunter and just have to accept it as His sovereign will? So, when the threat is within my capabilities to neutralize, then that's it. I'm choosing my family because I can't trust Him to keep you safe. I don't know the mind and heart and God, and He could just up and decide to snatch you away from me. Look at Aliaksana! What she went through. Look at Maksim! He traded his life for yours. I'm extremely grateful for his sacrifice, but this stuff weighs on me baby."

Grey choked up at the mention of the name of the man that gave his life for hers. It still weighed on her heart as well. Then on top of that, he had to deal with seeing murder every day on his job.

"We never know what His decision is going to be, but we have to live with it. And with this Fuller nonsense, you gotta be kidding me. When I realized what I was to her it pissed me off to no end. I don't want to be that for her. I don't want to turn any other cheeks. Why train me to be who I am and then tell me not to be who I am? My natural instinct is to take her out. Plain and simple. I'm over it!"

Tears ran down Greys' face. His emotions were palpable. It was like they were tangible, and they were strangling them both. He was royally pissed at God.

"Neil, let's say you protected me and Hunter and took Fuller out, knowing that is not what God wanted you to do. Then what?"

"I was willing to face whatever consequences I had to, to keep you safe." Grey shook her head. "Grey, I'm ashamed of who I've become. I know I know better, but I sincerely cannot help the way I feel. I've tried, but I can't find the place in my heart to accept this woman in my life and wipe her slate clean. I can't. It's different for my mom and Nigel. I mean, all that hell we went through was to ensure Nigel's daughter would be okay. That opportunity wasn't afforded to me. It's not about what's fair. I've seen too much on my job to be that kind of shallow, life isn't fair, but it's about being too much. Grey, it's too much!"

Grey nodded.

"The fact that you're ashamed means you want to change, you just don't know how." He nodded but didn't speak. "Neil, this isn't about your faith in God, this is about your trust in God. You don't trust Him, not completely. I get it, I really do, but we have to remember that it's never about us. Think about when God confronted Job. Who are we to think we know better than God's sovereignty? We may not understand it, or even like it, we just need to respect it. We don't say it's too much when God's sovereignty causes us to be blessed, prosperous and favored. I know, baby. I know it's easier said than done, but it's necessary. Her life is on the line. Her eternity is on the line. If she dies at your hand, she's going to bust hell wide open. I know you're angry with her, but does that give you the right to accelerate her appointment with eternity? If I left this world today, at least you know where I'm going. With those others, in God's sovereignty he knew they weren't going to change, but if He's telling you to back off, there's a reason. There's hope for her."

"Baby, I hear you, I really do, but I'm telling you, there's something very ugly forming in my heart and I need you to fight for me because I can't fight for myself when I'm the problem. It's starting to really scare me."

His plea ignited something in her. In the spirit, Grey's eyes flamed. She tried to pray.

"Father in the name of Jesus..."

The words would not flow.

"Oh...

The words felt stuck in her throat. She tried again.

"I come against..."

Again, the words were cut off.

In that moment, the six demons descended upon their house. Barrington ran back to the baby's room the minute he sensed something evil. Their four angels sprang into action. Weapon met weapon as they began to clash.

Savas took on two of them with his two broad swords. Bojan kicked one back as another was on his back. Ern swung his morning star to knock back another demon. Koldo took flight with his pike aimed for a heart.

Grey pulled Neil into her bosom and she cried out, "Jesus!"

She began to travail in tongues. As she uttered the cryptic language that the demons could not comprehend the angels glowed even brighter. Her prayers were giving them uninterrupted power.

They continued to war with the demons that had been plaguing Neil. They understood they had to be strategic in the way they took them out. Each one had a specific hold on Neil.

Savas took Shame out first, by bringing his two swords together in an "X" separating his head from his body. Black ash rained down.

Neil felt a weight lift. Grey continued to travail.

Defiance struck Bojan in the side as he plunged his long sword into Burden raining down black ash. Bojan cried out in pain. It was short lived because Greys' prayers immediately began to heal.

Righteous indignation rose up in Ern. He swung his morning star over his head then brought the spiked ball down on Defiance sending the demon back to the pit as his black ash rained down. Disobedience, Rebellion and Resentment were bigger and stronger. They were not going down without a fight.

Grey continued to fight. Now she was calling on the name of Jesus. She couldn't get out any other words. The name was a piercing sound in the ears of the demonic forces. Because Grey had called on that matchless name, in the heavenly realm, the Son of God that was seated at the right hand of the Father began interceding for Neil as the battle raged on.

The angels felt fierce power course through their beings as they felt the prayers of the Lamb of God strengthen them. They fought valiantly.

Savas took on Disobedience. Bojan took on Resentment while Ern and Koldo both took on the nasty demon Rebellion. Rebellion was a force to be reckoned with because rebellion could lead to witchcraft and they would be having none of that.

"He needs to surrender," Koldo said as they continued to war with Rebellion.

"Go," Ern told him. "I'll hold him off."

Koldo took flight and went to Neil's side. Neil held on to his wife as she continued to hold him and cover him.

"Surrender Neil. It's time to surrender," Koldo whispered to him as he placed his glorified hand on Neil's shoulder.

In his spirit, Neil heard the words. There was still resistance in him. Koldo repeated himself.

Finally, Neil said, "I surrender. Father, I surrender my will for yours."

The weights dropped.

Stunned Disobedience and Resentment froze in place as Savas and Bojan took them out. Koldo flew back to help his partner.
Grey heard Neil's confession. She cried out in praise and worship.

All four angels flew up and attacked Rebellion at the same time. Koldo struck out with his pike piercing the demon's abdomen. Ern brought his morning star down on the demon's head as Savas and Bojan sliced with their swords. Then he was nothing more than a black mist.

As the weights fell off Neil, he squeezed his wife. She felt his warm tears on her shoulder. Finally, her words were free. Fire from on high fell down into their living room surrounding them. Grey felt an enormous presence all around them.

She began to interpret the tongues that had just flowed through her, *"God says, if you can forgive her and love her through this, she will finally understand the depth of my love for her and lay her burdens down, so she can surrender to my will for her life."*

There was complete silence as they absorbed what God had just spoke. Their angels returned to be by their sides. In respect of the power of the presence of the Lord, they fell to one knee and bowed their heads.

In Hunter's room, his two guardians fell to one knee and bowed their heads as well. Grey shook with the power that ran through her. Neil continued to hold on to his wife as the words of the matchless King pierced his heart, his spirit, and his soul.

It was a long while before either of them spoke. When Neil finally let his wife go, he stared into her tear stained big brown eyes. She stared into his eyes that were now a dark green. She had never seen them quite like that.

"You get it now?" she asked. He nodded. "We're going to trust God together through this. We are going to show love no matter what and we are going to trust that we will come out on the other side safe, whole and *together*."

He nodded and pulled his wife into his chest. He squeezed her so tight. This rib of his always knew how to hold him down. For that he would be forever grateful. She never judged his insecurities but covered them in prayer.

Barrington trotted back into the living room now that he was satisfied the baby was no longer in danger. He looked at Neil and Grey like they were crazy and then trotted off to the back of the house to find a room without people in it, so he could sleep in peace.

"Thank you," Neil said as he continued to hug his wife.

"Thank you for trusting me with it."

"You're the keeper of my secrets, who else would I tell?"

"Nigel?"

"Nah, and don't think I don't know y'all been plotting on me either."

She smiled. "But I would never give up the contents of your heart baby."

"I know," he said kissing her on the forehead.

"So now what?" she asked.

"Now the enemy has a real problem. Once I let her in my heart, she's mine to protect."

Grey smiled. "I'm proud of you." She kissed him. "Come on, let's check on Hunter and then go to bed."

Grey stood up and pulled him off the couch. She loved how he towered over her. Reaching up, she wiped the tears off his face. He grabbed both her hands then leaned down and put his forehead and nose on hers. She smiled at the familiar gesture.

"Thank you for having my back."

"I will always watch your six, baby. You have gone above and beyond to prove your love for me. It's my pleasure to do the same. You have gone to war for me countless times in the natural. It's only fitting I do the same for you in the spirit."

Neil sighed with relief. His heart had never felt as full as it did now.

"Do you think I have it in me?" he asked.

"Of course, you do. You love with such fierceness, so that's why you have to be careful who you let into your heart. You're more than capable and that's where the conflict came from. Your heart and your mind couldn't reconcile. But double mindedness has been defeated and cleared the way for God to do something great. Like you said, Satan better watch out. Her uncles are united and they coming for him because y'all will not let him have your brother's daughter!"

"Amen." Grey smiled. "I need to call Nigel."

"Right now?" Grey said frowning. She looked at the clock. It was after 1:00 in the morning.

"Yes, right now."

Neil dug his phone out of his pocket and dialed his brother. As the phone rang, he grabbed his wife's hand and led them up the stairs.

"Bro, you good," Nigel said when he answered with a hint of sleep in his voice.

"Better than good, bro. Let's go get Niles' baby girl."

There was a brief pause. "You serious?"

"Yep."

"What happened?"

"We serve a mighty God. See you tomorrow."
Neil hung up on his stunned brother.

Chapter 85: Moment of Truth

Agent Michelle Fuller
Undisclosed Location

I paced back and forth like a maniac. I was biting my nails and fighting nausea as I waited for Sam to arrive. His voice was both happy and trepidatious as I told him that I was at his safe house and needed him to meet me there ASAP. He said it would take him a few hours.

I was going crazy. How did I let this happen? This was insane. How could I, the infamous Black Widow, be pregnant? The word pregnant might as well have been a foreign language because I had no understanding of what I should be doing or how I should be doing it. I was completely lost and totally confused.

The nausea was driving me insane. I hurried to the restroom and was ill yet again. At this rate, I was going to be skin and bones. It had only been two months since I found out I was pregnant, and I was already over it. Just be done already, I thought. I realized I was making myself sicker with all the worry and pacing so I decided to just lay down and go to sleep.

Sampson had me tucked away in his cabin deep in the woods. This place was as remote as they come. It was very rustic and threw me off for a second when I first came in. I didn't really picture him for this type, but nonetheless, it was him.

I was grateful there were no stuffed animal heads looming over me. That was so tacky. I realize coming from me, it's probably tasteless, but still, I never understood the need to have a partial corpse as decoration.

I plopped down on the sofa after rummaging through his pantry trying to find something to settle my stomach. There was no ginger ale in sight. I needed to pass out before I drove myself crazy. I propped my feet up on one of the throw pillows then lay back and closed my eyes. Mercifully, I fell asleep.

†††

Something woke me. I don't know if it was his presence being this close to me or my body simply being done with its nap, but when I opened my eyes, the door opened. My heart and my mind settled.

He stared at me. "Nyla, are you okay?"

I sat up on the sofa and stared at him. "I'm not sure."

He frowned as he closed the door and walked in. "What do you mean you're not sure?"

"Sam, I'm pregnant."

Time stood still as he stared at me in horror and disbelief.

"You're what?" he asked for clarification.

"That night we were together. We didn't even consider protection. I hadn't been on birth control because I was locked up for months. And now I'm pregnant." He just stood there completely baffled. "Sam, I need you to say something. I need you to tell me it's going to be okay."

He rushed over to me and held me. I squeezed him back and cried. I missed him so much. I was terrified. I didn't know anything about being anybody's mother.

He grabbed my face. "Please tell me you're going to keep this baby," he asked with utter fear on his face.

"Of course, I'm going to keep the baby. Why else would I tell you?"

"So, what does this mean?"

"I get it now. I really and truly get it. This love thing. Once I found out I was carrying our baby it's like a light bulb came on and I could see all the errors of my ways. I have to put a stop to this. I have to end this feud with my uncles, but I'm afraid. Lucca is going to go after my niece. Apparently, they had twins. He's going to try and take those babies out. I know he is."

"Okay, calm down, baby. Calm down."

"I have to stop him."

"No, you don't."

"Yes, I do. I'm not asking for your permission. It has to be me. You just don't understand."

"You're carrying my baby Nyla. I'm not about to condone you going off on some dangerous mission no matter how noble the cause. Nigel is more than capable of keeping his children safe from Lucca."

"No, I have to do this. It's the only way I can make it clear to my family that I'm not a threat. It's the only way I can settle the score between me and Neil. If not, my child could be in danger from him."

"You really think your uncle would try and take out your child?"

"No, but he would definitely take me out and I can't risk my baby's life for my mess. You need to trust me on this. I need to do this. I have done many wrongs and it's time I started righting them."

He sighed and stared at me. He kissed me. My heart thudded in my chest. I never thought I'd feel his soft lips on mine again. I loved everything about this man. We kissed for what seemed like an eternity.

Finally, he released me. "I need to think Nyla. You need to let me think."

"Okay, but I need to tell you who my family really is."

"What do you mean who they really are?"

"You said you believe in angels, right?" He nodded confused. "Well, you're going to want to hear this."

After I laid out everything Eva told me, Sam stared at me with his mouth agape.

"This is bigger than my revenge or Neil's inability to trust me. I owe it to my father to right the wrongs forced upon our family legacy. I owe it to this baby because I don't know who it might become. But what I do know is that because Neil and Grey broke that curse, this baby will live. Everybody has done their part for this family. It's time I do mine. Lucca needs to be handled by me. I opened the door to Pandora's box. It's time I shut it once and for all."

Chapter 86: The Prayer of Agreement

The next morning, Grey and Neil arrived at Nigel's apartment.

"Good morning," he said opening the door. "Negro you even look like you got saved again," Nigel said referring to the peace that rested on his brother's face.

"Here you go, first in thing in the morning," Neil said chuckling.

Grey grinned. "I told you. I would handle him."

"I know that's right, boo," Nigel said while hugging Grey.

"I see y'all got jokes. Where's my sister because y'all about to get on my last nerve."

Grey and Nigel laughed. "She's in the nursery with the twins."

Nigel let them in. Along with them came their six angelic warriors. Nigel took his nephew from his brother and kissed his chubby cheek.

"What's up, lil man?" Hunter gurgled something incoherent then smiled up at his uncle. Nigel laughed.

When they walked into the living room, there was nowhere to sit.

"Excuse the mess y'all."

"Um, we moving?" Neil asked.

"Yeah, man, there isn't any space in this two-bedroom with two babies. They got more crap than us and they haven't been here but two months. God pulled a fast one on us and we were so not prepared. I got Cynthia working round the clock trying to find us a place. She's a beast and negotiates like me. She spends my money better than I do."

Grey chuckled as she cleared some boxes off the sofa for them to sit.

"Grey is that you?" They heard Kadijah yell.

"It's me."

"Help!"

Grey laughed. "Well, let me go lend a hand to the new mommy."

Neil took a seat on the couch where Grey cleared space.

"Man, what the heck happened to you last night?"

Neil just shook his head. When he looked up, he said, "I was very much in danger of becoming someone I didn't want to be. I went home and had a heart-to-heart with my baby, and you know Grey. She went to war for your boy and God did that."

Nigel said, "That's my dawg," in Chris Tucker fashion from the movie *Friday*. "That girl know she dangerous with a prayer on her lips."

Neil laughed at his silly brother. "I was in a dark place, bro. She brought me back to the light. I'm sorry."

"Forgiven and I understand. Man, I've been praying like crazy for this family."

Hunter grabbed at the gold chain with a cross that his uncle wore around his neck.

"Well, it worked. Thanks for standing in the gap when I couldn't." Nigel nodded. "So, what's the plan?" Neil asked.

"Well, apparently Sam thinks he has a way to clear her with the Feds."

Neil frowned. "You can't be serious."

"I am. I don't know the details and if it's that kind of pull, we don't want to know the details. But like they say, favor ain't fair. What are the chances somebody with her past would end up with that kind of pull on her side without it being miraculous?"

"Good point. What the heck was he involved in?" Neil asked curiously.

"I will never ask," Nigel said seriously as he maneuvered Hunter's tiny fingers from his chain.

Neil chuckled. "You're right. We will let him handle that and mind our own business."

"Exactly. Now, her mom is foul and double crossed her."

Neil scowled. "What? How?"

Nigel told him of the alliance between Fuller's mom and Lucca. He shook his head.

"That's messed up, but not shocking."

"Lucca has to go; I personally don't care how he exits the scene just as long as it's permanent. Life in prison or a dirt nap, makes no difference to me. Chelle may feel some type of way about how her mom is handled, so we should be cautionary. She has a lot to deal with. We need not add one more emotional bomb if it's not necessary."

"Noted," Neil said taking mental note of his brother's affectionate nickname for their niece.

"She and Eva are on really good terms."

Neil raised a brow. "Really?"

"Yeah, you need to catch up with your best friend. She misses you." Neil nodded. "When Chelle found out she was pregnant, she went to Eva. Apparently, Eva embraced her, told her what went down on our end, at least the spiritual stuff. They're not besties but have a mutual respect for one another's journey."

Neil sat back as he digested everything he'd apparently missed.

"Okay, what else," he asked.

"Sam is worried though because she can't really get medical care for her and the baby with her criminal notoriety at the moment."

Neil nodded. "Who do we know?"

"Stephan's boy, but he's on the West Coast."

Neil nodded. "We could have Genevieve check her out."

"That's a thought," Nigel agreed. "But first, we gotta get her here."

"Where is she?"

"Just out there. She says, she wants to settle down with Sam, but she's not going to bring the drama of the organization to his front door. I don't know what she's up to. I warned her about her mother, but only to put her on alert so she didn't walk into a trap. Still praying that baby is motivation enough to keep her from doing something stupid."

"And Sam?"

"Oh, he will drop both Lucca and her moms without a second thought, but he doesn't want to."

"Makes their relationship too complicated if he did."

"Exactly," Nigel said.

"Well, like Grey said last night, her uncles are unified, and Satan better watch out because he will not have our brother's daughter. It's time to do what I should've done from the very beginning."

Nigel nodded and stood up. He put Hunter on his shoulder. Neil grabbed his brother's hand when he stood up. Their angels surrounded them and glorified.

"Father, we come to you together and on one accord. You said if I forgive her and love her through this, she will understand the depth of the love you have for her. I come to you contrite and broken with an obedient heart. Father use me as you see fit. We serve the enemy notice here and now that he cannot and will not have our brother's daughter nor his grandchild. We welcome them both into our family with open arms to share in the spiritual legacy you have entrusted to us. Now Father, equip us with insight, strategy and a mindset that's three steps ahead."

Kadijah and Grey heard Neil's voice getting louder as they approached the throne. They came out of the room and stood in the living room. Each one carrying one of the twins, they each placed a hand on their husband's backs to stand with them as they warred in the spirit for the family they married into.

"Father release your angelic alliance to tear down the plans of the enemy and annihilate this adversary once and for all. I plead the blood of Jesus over Michelle, her child and Sam. Now order our steps Father and lead us to her. Give us the means, intellect, and resources to bring her home. We don't know how you are going to work this out, but we're willing to stand on the front lines to bring her back to where she was stolen from. Today we take back everything the enemy has stolen from this family and we declare that we are blessed and favored of the Most High God. We know that you have ordered our steps. Now Father, expand our hearts to show your love in the darkest of places. Let your light shine through us and guide her back to where she was always meant to be. We thank you; we praise you and we love you. In Jesus name, I pray. Amen."

"Amen."

"Hallelujah, Jesus. Amen."

"Amen."

"Yes, God, amen!"

Neil and Nigel locked eyes.

"Let's do this for Niles," Nigel said.

"And for Pops," Neil said.

Nigel nodded knowing that was a big step for his brother.

"And your mother because she was about to get with y'all about her grand," Kadijah said.

They all fell out laughing.

Chapter 87: Accepting the Assignment

Genevieve stood at the podium, quite nervously. Her ever present warrior Arthfael was standing behind her with his wings spread and a big grin on his face. He was very proud of how far she had come.

Here she was standing before the people about to preach her first sermon. Not only had she been immediately obedient in accepting her new assignment, but she also faced all her fears and insecurities and let God use her to warn the people, in her husband's stead.

"Good morning," she said to the congregation.

There was a collective "good morning" in reply. Her spirit was so in tuned. She could hear the dissent, the judgments, and the naysayers.

"Oh, this about to be some foolishness."

"Um, marrying a preacher don't make you one."

"This my last Sunday at this church if this is the new norm."

"Girl, bye!"

From the middle of the front row, David saw the slight frown on his wife's face. He could tell, she was hesitant. He mouthed, "You got this," when her eyes locked with his. She nodded. Arthfael placed a hand on her shoulder and sent her peace.

She began, "I know you are all shocked to see me standing up here. But trust, you are not as shocked as I am. I can hear your negative comments because my Holy Ghost is real. However, if you take your eyes off me and put them on God, you'll hear the message He has for His people. This week, my husband got sick and didn't know if he would be able to bring the word. When he was praying about who should preach on Sunday, apparently God told him me. When he passed on this message, I looked at him like he had lost his mind."

The congregation laughed. Someone was petty enough to say, "Amen."

Genevieve ignored them and continued. "I never doubted what God told him before, so why start now just because it made me uncomfortable. And it was only confirming what had been in my spirit. They always say, the message comes to the messenger first. On

Tuesday morning, God woke me up earlier than usual and began to speak with me about my next assignment. To be honest, it was overwhelming and truly blew my mind. The sheer magnitude of what He was asking me to do made me immediately want to say nol, I think you should pass this one on to someone else. When I resisted, a gentle nudge from the Holy Spirit directed me to the book of Jonah. Truthfully, I rolled my eyes, but I picked up my Bible and began to read. There is a word from the Lord for His people today. I will not be before you long, but we are going to dig into the word today. Take out your Bibles and turn to the Book of Jonah."

People began to pull out their phones. Some pulled out their physical Bibles, a rarity in today's tech savvy society.

"I'm going to do something a little different. I am going to read the whole book from the New International Version. It's only four chapters, but I want you to see and understand what really happened in the life of the Prophet Jonah. Most people only know he spent three days in the belly of a whale, but there is so much more to glean from these four short chapters. I promise it won't take long, I timed myself," she said as she winked.

The crowd laughed. She began to read; it took all of six minutes. When she finished, she said, "Today's message is entitled, 'Accepting the Assignment.'"

"Amen."

"Alright now!"

"Let's start with Nineveh. This was a ruthless place known for their violence and war crimes. I'm talking beheadings, eye gouging, skinning, and impaling. These folks were thugged out on a whole other level."

The crowd laughed.

"Jonah probably was scared, but the Israelites had no love for the people of Nineveh. They were another culture, another people. To put it in perspective. Imagine God sending a black man to a city fortified by the KKK during the Civil Rights Era to warn them and preach and the gospel."

The crowd reacted.

"Yeah, that part. So, let's not be so quick to judge Jonah like we are immediately obedient to the assignments God puts in front of us. In our finite humanity though, we can miss the bigger picture. The first thing I want to point out is that Jonah had to spend money to flee to Tarshish. My first point is disobedience is going to cost you something. So, you need to ask yourself, can your spiritual or natural bank account afford that loss?"

The audience pondered.

"The storm God sent caused the other passengers on the boat to call out to their gods. My second point, does your disobedience wrongly influence others?"

The audience was left to ponder that question as well.

"They were confused as to what was going on, so they had to throw away the cargo. Now think about this. What if your disobedience caused the UPS man to throw out all these Amazon prime packages people were waiting on to show up?"

The audience laughed.

"I probably need to be delivered from my Amazon prime membership."

"Amen," David said loudly.

They all laughed.

"My third point is disobedience will cause you to waste valuable resources."

"Amen."

"That's a word right there."

Genevieve continued, "I found this very interesting. Jonah got on the boat knowing he was dead wrong, but he went to sleep. He was very much self-involved. When we are focused on how the assignment affects us and not on what God is trying to do, we're spiritually asleep and oblivious to the chaos all around us."

"You better preach that Bible, girl!" David shouted.

Genevieve shook her head and tried not to laugh. "Oh, but idol worshippers or not, when that wind and rain really started to cut the monkey fool, they found Jonah and said call on *your* God!"

Genevieve stepped away from the podium.

"Let me tell y'all something. Don't get it twisted. The world knows who the one true living God is. They know when to call on Him. Don't believe me? Remember 911? Everybody was in church that following Sunday. After every mass shooting, it's a call to pray. We shoulda been praying all along. This is how you know they knew better even though they *chose* to worship other gods. When Jonah told them to throw him over, they were afraid because they knew Jonah's God was real and they did not want any backlash for touching God's anointed. They did not want to incur God's wrath. My next point. What is this number four?"

They laughed.

"Yeah, it's four, baby," David said from his amen corner. She grinned.

"Point number four is our disobedience will jeopardize the lives of others. Do you want that blood on your hands?"

"My God!" Someone shouted.

"Jonah spent three days in the belly of that fish. Can you imagine? The smell, the sounds, the darkness? Why do we put ourselves in these precarious positions? I know people want to dismiss some biblical accounts as not real, but I watch the Discovery channel. You mean to tell me those whales out there the size of a bus can't swallow a man whole? The devil is a lie."

They laughed.

"Even when we know we're wrong, we still fight it. Jonah's hardheaded behind didn't get his life until the third day, then he wanted to pray. God moved immediately though and spit him out on dry land. Please understand that God knew what He was doing the whole time. Even in Jonah's disobedience he was redirecting his path so when he finally said yes, he was ready to roll. My fifth point. God will use your place of discomfort to move you into position. He wastes no time. Timing is important because lives are at stake."

That part pricked Monet's heart. She could relate all too well to this message.

"God repeated His instruction to Jonah. Never forget, He is the God of a second chance." Genevieve turned to face the choir. "As a matter of fact, during the altar call, can y'all please sing that song?"

Giselle nodded. "We got you."

"Thank you. When Jonah reached Nineveh, this massive city, God sent a warning, and the people were receptive. The King decreed a fast and instructed them to turn from their evil and violent ways. God did not bring the destruction he threatened because they had a heart transformation."

She moved away from the podium again.

"I'm not a parent yet, but y'all know how some parents, like my mother, can threaten to whip their child and they straighten up. That heart change prompts the parent to spare that rod. God is a Father. He wants the best for us. He doesn't want to send the punishment, but we are not always obedient people."

The congregation laughed knowing all too well the memories of their childhood rearing.

"I want to say this. Since we are in this election season and we are seeing some of the strangest behavior ever. Lord, have mercy. Listen, you can't legislate the departure of sin from the earth. Sin is eliminated by an internal transformation of the heart and that is due to a relationship with Jesus Christ, the one who bore the sin of the world and redeemed us through the shedding of His blood."

"Amen!"

"That's right."

"Sho' you right!"

"Now back to this word and I'm almost done. Jonah was hot with God. He was so mad because these evil people got a reprieve. He didn't want them forgiven, he wanted them punished. God showed love to people that Jonah deemed unworthy. Think about it. Who are we to tell God who is unworthy when we ourselves have never been worthy? Our righteousness is like filthy rags."

There were agreeable responses from the congregation. Neil, Grey and Nigel exchanged a knowing look.

"And don't make me break down what filthy rags actually is referring to." Those in the congregation who were familiar laughed. "You know what. I'm going to go there because some of us are so self-righteous. We forget to show grace and mercy to others. In that time, when women menstruated, they used rags to act as a sanitation apparatus. That's right, that is what your human righteousness looks like to God. So, put that in context the next time you want to toot your own 'I'm so saved horn,' that you want to determine who God's grace and mercy should cover. If that's what your righteous looks like, well what does the sin look like?"

"Oh my!" Someone shouted.

"But back to my message. So, then God asks Jonah the question, 'Have you any right to be angry?' Jonah felt like he did and said as much. God sent a vine that benefited Jonah and took it back the next day. Jonah was heated again. Again, God asked the same question. Jonah still in his stubbornness felt he had a right to be angry. God broke it down to him. He told him there were more than 120,000 people and cattle, which represents resources, who were lost. He asked, why wouldn't he be concerned about what He created and tended to? Now, we never got Jonah's answer. For all we know, he could be in heaven or hell, still pissed about it, but the point is, it is about God's sovereignty and His love for His creation. There are mass murderers sitting on death row right now. I can guarantee you their mother still loves them, evil though they may be."

The musicians began to play the chords for "Second Chance."

"You don't get to be the moral police. You don't get to insert your opinion. What you get is the privilege of being used by God to save a lost and dying world. Lives are at stake people. I know there are some of you in here that God has given specific assignments and you have refused. You can't know the consequences of your disobedience. If the assignment was given, it is necessary. The altar is open. If you're struggling with your yes to God, please come so we can pray with you. And for those of you who don't think you're worthy. I'm here to tell you, that's not your call to make. God chose you because He wanted to. He's not asking for your approval. He's not asking you to be someone you're not. He chose you, because of who He made you to be and that includes your entire life's journey. Jacked up past and all. He's asking for your faith and obedience. If you don't know Jesus as your personal Lord and Savior, come and we will pray with you. Altar workers come forth."

People began to flood the altar. Monet squirmed in her seat, but she did not budge. Kia was Genevieve's acting armor bearer. She went to the podium and grabbed her Bible and notes.

Darcy was so proud of the new First Lady. She had come such a long way. She also knew she was very much in the vein of what God was doing in this season. She wondered if the other two gatekeepers were in the building. Her spirit very much understood that Genevieve was one of them.

The altar was full. The altar workers began to pray with those in need of prayer or salvation. Angela sat with her family in the middle of the church. She had never been to the church her children attended, but she absolutely loved it. What a powerful word.

She knew God was definitely in the building as she had recently been assigned to be a gatekeeper. Cathal, one of her angels touched her shoulder. Something struck Angela in the gut. It couldn't have been a coincidence that she was here on this Sunday. She wondered if any of the other gatekeepers were here. She had a strange feeling that the First Lady of this house might just be one.

Though she didn't give detail to her assignment, something about the way she said it struck a chord with her. She leaned over to Neil.

"I want you to introduce me to your First Lady."

"Okay, no problem.

Chapter 88: The Gatekeepers

Angela was beside herself as she sat across the table from these three women for brunch at the Edison. It was a chic outpost of a restaurant that used to be a power station. It overlooked the beautiful Cascades park.

It was a very nice day, the perfect day for brunch outside. Not too hot, not too cold with a gentle breeze that caressed your face and made you grateful to be among the land of the living. The Edison was crowded with a diverse crowd of patrons that ranged in dress from fresh out of bed, to workout clothes to straight from church.

Angela would have been more beside herself if she could see all the angels that surrounded the area. Her four naval warriors were there, as well as Darcy's, which included the Captain of the Gulf of Mexico naval forces. Genevieve and Monet also had four naval warriors.

The sixteen angelic beings had weapons drawn and were not here for any foolishness the enemy may try to concoct. The Kingdom of Darkness did not want these four women bonding.

Angela had asked her son to introduce him to the First Lady after she heard her preach. There was something about what she said that pulled on Angela's spirit. As they were chatting, Monet came up and congratulated Genevieve on a job well done and Darcy followed.

They all got to chatting and Monet suggested the four of them go grab brunch. Angela knew none of these women, other than by name. *How was she here? Why was she comfortable?* This wasn't even her church.

No matter how odd, she felt deep within her spirit she was right where she needed to be, and God had indeed ordered her steps today. Anything out of her ordinary routine she made sure to pay extra attention just in case God was trying to tell her something.

Cathal, her Irish warrior, touched her shoulder igniting something in her spirit. Angela continued to listen as Darcy guided the conversation.

For whatever reason, she was drawn to Darcy's spirit the most. It was clear that Darcy was used to being in charge, but not in a dominant way. Her confidence was gentle and inclusive. Each of them joined in the conversation with ease, but Darcy kept the conversation focused on one topic at a time. She didn't let them stray too much.

Which was odd in a way because it wasn't a formal meeting. In a way that made Angela think she's the *point.* That's when it hit her. It was so clear she wanted to slap herself. The epiphany had so many layers. Darcy sat across from her and Monet and Genevieve sat across from each other. She had just met the other gatekeepers and she'd bet her life that Darcy was the North gatekeeper.

Etienne's letter said they would meet when they were made aware of their assignment. Cathal touched her again wanting her to find a deeper revelation. As she continued to listen to the conversation, she realized something. It didn't say when they all *accepted* the assignment, it said when they were all *aware* of their assignment.

She thought that was a very important detail. She knew she'd accepted hers and per Genevieve's sermon, she had accepted hers as well. She couldn't imagine that Darcy hadn't accepted hers, which only left Monet.

Angela took the last sip of her orange juice. When the waiter approached them with the check, Monet reached for it.

"I'll take that."

"Oh, that's so thoughtful," Angela said. "Thank you."

Monet waved her off.

"Thanks Monet," Darcy said.

"Thanks ma," Genevieve said.

"Ma?" Angela inquired.

"Oh, you didn't know. This is my daughter-in-love. You see my husband decided David was the son he never had, until he actually found the son he actually had." Darcy and Genevieve chuckled. "So, when David and Genevieve married, she was family," Monet admitted and winked at Genevieve.

She laughed thinking about their rocky start. Now they were as thick as thieves. They did lunch and spa days regularly. Monet was a wealth of knowledge. She kept it all the way real and Genevieve loved that they got past their issues and got to know each other.

"And of course, Monet is my daughter-in-law, but I guess you already knew that," Darcy interjected.

Angela nodded then said, "Ladies, I want to thank you for inviting me to have brunch with you all. I mean it was my first time visiting your church and now I'm surrounded by first ladies, even the first lady of our state. I'm honored."

Genevieve waved her off. "Miss Angela, if God didn't force that title on me, I wouldn't have it."

"Amen," Darcy said.

"And amen again," Monet rounded out the comments.

They all laughed. Angela just couldn't keep it to herself. She had to say something.

"I don't mean to be presumptuous or overstep my place, but random things don't just happen to me unless is God ordering my steps."

"You think the four of us meeting is Divine?" Monet inquired.

"I know it," Angela said boldly.

At the strength in her voice, Darcy tuned in. Then it hit her. She didn't speak, but let Angela continue.

"How do you know that?" Genevieve asked intrigued.

"Because we all have the same assignment."

"You're the southern gatekeeper, aren't you?" Darcy stated more than inquired.

No one saw Monet's hand freeze as she went to grab her drink.

"And you're the north one," Angela answered.

Darcy sat back and laughed.

"Whoa," Genevieve said. "Well, if I'm the east, then ma, that makes you the west."

Monet frowned. "Um, I don't think so."

The other three women frowned at her.

"You mean to tell me that God hasn't spoken to you about being a protector of this city?" Darcy asked.

Instead of answering, she responded, "I doubt very seriously God would use me in such a role. Sorry to disappoint you ladies. I'm not what you think I am."

Angela wanted to challenge Monet so badly, but she didn't know this woman. What she did know about her, she wasn't anybody's pushover.

"My mistake," she said politely then locked eyes with Darcy.

Darcy gave her a slight nod.

The devil is a lie, Angela thought to herself. It was time to fast and pray for their fellow gatekeeper. They needed to be unified. Something was coming. She could feel it in her spirit.

Chapter 89: Breaking Bread

Angela looked around her table, beyond grateful for her family. Though they were not quite whole yet, she was confident that God was working everything out in the background. She knew her children had found a home away from home with Jeremiah and Mia on Sundays, but they made sure to reserve one Sunday a month for Lawson family time. She was glad they went to the early service because she had time for brunch and still made it back in time to cook for her family.

She was so grateful to have daughters-in-love that she truly adored and a house full of grandbabies with a great-grand on the way. She didn't know her family would grow so fast, but she was not complaining. The sound of laughter, plates being scraped, and giggling babies brought unimaginable joy to her heart.

She studied her boys. They were so happy. She noted how Neil consistently found a reason to touch his wife. A casual hand on her thigh or his arm wrapped around her shoulders. Nigel on the other hand kept flirting with his wife. Throughout dinner he'd whispered stuff in her ear, making her blush and giggle. She smiled.

"So, ma," Kadijah began. "Grey and I were out shopping the other day and we met this very nice gentleman that would be perfect for you."

Neil stopped eating with his fork in mid-air. He frowned at Grey. She giggled as she held Hunter closer to her chest.

"Please tell me you are not a part of this nonsense Grey," Neil questioned.

Grey put her head down and chuckled.

"Hold up, why is it nonsense?" Kadijah asked.

"Don't y'all start this mess."

"What's his name?" Angela asked as she cut her eyes at her Neil.

Nigel fell out laughing.

"His name is Derrick," Grey said. Neil shot daggers at his wife with his eyes. "I'm sorry baby, but your mom deserves to have a companion in her life."

"I know that's right. I know you don't think I'm about to be around here lonely when all of y'all booed up."

Neil shook his head. "Ma, it's a lot of crazy dudes out there. I just want you to be careful. If you do start dating, I'm gon need a name and social security number," Neil said in all seriousness.

"Boy, if you don't sit down somewhere. I am grown. I know how to look out for myself."

"Well, ma, I'm with Neil on having old boy checked out. So, don't fight it. But I'm all for you having someone in your life," Nigel added.

"Thank you for your blessing, but y'all gon have to mind your own business."

"Now, ma, I'm not saying he gotta give up his social security number but having them look out for you isn't a bad idea," Grey said sincerely.

"It's not an option," Neil stated matter-of-factly. "It's bad enough I have to deal with my mother dating. I'm not about to deal with no shenanigans on top of it."

"Well, I tell you what, my prayer is that God does a quick work because your mama is long overdue for some good loving," Angela said with no shame whatsoever.

Nigel spit out his pineapple tea.

Neil just stared.

Grey had to hold on tight to her son as she laughed until she cried.

Kadijah hollered causing one of the twins to start fussing.

Neil dropped his fork. "Alright, so we're done with that conversation."

"Indeed, we are," Angela said smugly.

She knew exactly what she was doing. They needed to mind their own business and let her handle her own affairs. It took a minute to settle the table back down. Kadijah got up to put Gideon back in the bassinet. Her sides were hurting from laughing at them.

"Can we play spades or something. I need to do something to distract me from that rabbit hole y'all just forced me down," Neil pleaded.

Angela laughed. "Negro, how you think you got here?"

"Ma!" Neil yelled exasperated.

Nigel could not stop laughing. "Bruh, why you so starchy? Let mama get her groove back."

"Oh, y'all getting on my nerves," Neil said rubbing the bridge of his nose.

"Hey, y'all back up off my baby. What y'all not gon do is come for him while I'm sitting here."

Nigel chuckled. "Okay sis, I'm backing off."

"Thank you," Grey told him.

Angela laughed. "Y'all are silly. Now please clean up my kitchen while I go in here and love on my grands."

"Yes ma'am," they said collectively.

Nigel moved the bassinets in the living room, while Angela scooped up Hunter. The four of them began to clean up the kitchen as they clowned each other over nonsense.

When the dishes were done, Neil pulled his wife into him as he leaned against the kitchen counter. He kissed her neck.

"So, are we playing spades or what?"

"Oh, fa sho, y'all can come get this beat down," Nigel said cockily.

"Uh, I believe me and Dij are winning right now. Keep dreaming."

"Whatever, that's all about to change," Grey said pulling away from him.

"Oh, that's cold baby," Neil told her.

"Hey, it's time for spades, you know where my loyalties lie on the table."

Neil shook his head. "Go get the cards, sis," he said to Kadijah.

"Right, let's do this."

They played spades for the next few hours.

In the living room, Angela continued to ignore their loud and ruthless conversations as she enjoyed spending time with her three grandchildren. She inhaled Gideon's sweet baby scent and smiled.

"You are so precious baby girl."

A thought struck her as random as it could be.

What if she gave her children a night just for them?

She would offer to keep the babies tonight, so they could spend some quality time together. Kadijah and Nigel were definitely overdue. She saw how exhausted they looked as new parents of not one, but two babies.

She whispered, "You want to spend the night with granny?" Gideon gave a toothless grin. Angela laughed. "Okay."

The valiant naval warriors that guarded her gave each other a knowing smile. They didn't know what Jehovah had planned, but they knew how to order her steps.

In the kitchen, Kadijah stood up and slammed down the big joker.

"Run me my money, negro! I want it in all crisp bills."

Nigel stared at his wife. "Really, we're not even betting! But if we were, you'd get it all in pennies."

Neil and Grey fell out laughing. These two had yet to properly adjust to being married, but rivals on the spades table.

"Well, that's wise on y'all part seeing as how y'all can't get a book to save your life!"

Neil laughed harder, "You were saying, bro."

"I'm saying, I want my wife back and I'm ready to go home," Nigel said a little salty.

"I just bet you are," Neil said as he gathered up the cards.

Grey stood up and slid onto Neil's lap. "Nah, gone now. You wanted to ditch me for Nigel earlier. Don't come crawling back now."

Grey smirked and nibbled on his earlobe. He closed his eyes and shivered.

"A'ight, you can come back home."

Grey laughed. "Ah, the power of persuasion."

They laughed.

"So, who's going to tell your mother that we are leaving and taking her grandchildren with us?" Kadijah whispered.

"Not it."

"Not it."

"Not it."

Neil was left holding the bag. "Y'all a bunch of punks you know that."

He tapped Grey on her backside signaling for her to stand up.

They went into the living room to see Hunter having the time of his life on his favorite blanket surrounded by toys.

"Hey ma, your kitchen is clean, and your baby boy is a loser." Nigel walked by and popped Neil on the back of his head. "We are getting ready to head out. So, get in all your grandma kisses," Neil told her.

Angela frowned. "I am not ready for y'all to take them." Kadijah, Grey and Nigel suddenly got busy and left Neil alone in the living room. "I tell you what. Why don't y'all let the babies stay with me tonight? Couldn't you all use a quiet evening at home with your spouses?" She said laying it on thick.

"You don't have to ask me twice," Grey said coming into the living room. "Come on baby, let's go before she changes her mind."

Angela laughed. Neil scooped up his son and kissed his cheek.

"Be good for granny okay."

Hunter stared at him then started speaking his baby talk where only a few syllables were comprehendible. Neil laughed. "God, I love this kid." Neil kissed his chubby cheeks, then handed him to his mother. Grey kissed him several times then put him back down on the floor to play with his toys.

"What about you, Kadijah?"

Nigel looked at his wife's apprehensive expression. He was okay with them staying, but it was the first time she would be away from them since they were born three months ago. He trusted no one outside of him and his wife more than his mother. He looked at his wife.

"Baby, it's your decision. I want you to be comfortable."

Angela smiled and appreciated her son's thoughtfulness towards his wife's needs. It was moments like this that let her know, they'd done an okay job raising them.

"Um," was all Kadijah managed as all eyes went to her.

"There's no pressure baby," Angela told her. "I'm just not ready to say bye yet."

Kadijah looked at her husband. They so needed some quality time and some sleep. Their lives had been completely inundated with finding a house and being parents. There was no romance, no dating and very little sex. She knew her husband was overdue for some time alone with her and she wanted to give it to him, but she was not okay with leaving her children.

Grey gave Neil a knowing stare. He chuckled. She hit him. He knew exactly where his brother's head was, spending time alone with his wife. He wasn't mad at him.

"I need a minute y'all," Kadijah said and went back into the kitchen.

"Well, y'all work that out. We're off to get this party started," Grey said as she pulled Neil behind her.

Nigel shook his head. "Just selfish."

Grey chuckled. "Ma, Neil will bring Hunter's extra bag back in. I'll be by to get him around ten tomorrow morning."

Angela stood to hug and kiss Grey and Neil as they headed out. Nigel went in the kitchen to find Kadijah leaning against the counter biting her thumb nail. He went to her and wrapped her in his arms. He kissed the top of her head.

"Let's talk this through," he said.

"You're team spend a night alone with my spouse, huh?" she asked with a smirk on her face.

Nigel tried to play it off, she hit him playfully. "Well, you know it's been a minute," he told her laughing.

"I know baby and I'm sorry, I'm just freaking out a little bit."

"And that's completely understandable. I get it. I really do."

"I mean of course I trust your mom, but they're my babies and I've never been apart from them."

"If you're not okay with this, I won't be mad. But if you decide to let them stay then..."

He leaned down putting his lips to her ear. He whispered in great detail what he planned to do to her. The tingle that ran down her spine made her shiver. She remembered vividly how she got pregnant with those twins. She stared up into her husband's eyes. His yearning for her was crystal clear.

"I miss my wife," he said his eyes now a vivid green and full of desire. Her resistance was getting weaker. Nigel leaned down and softly pressed his lips to hers. She melted into the kiss and he took it deeper. The kiss stirred something in her she hadn't felt since she became a mother.

When he released her from the kiss, she looked up at him still hesitant. Cheveyo, her Native American angel touched her shoulder and nudged her to let them stay.

"You drive a hard bargain," she said breathlessly.

He grinned. "Come on, let me take you home beautiful. I promise, we will come and get them first thing in the morning."

Kadijah took her husband's hand and followed him into the living room.

Taking a deep breath, Kadijah said, "Okay, ma. I'm going to take advantage of this reprieve, but my nerves are shot. I trust my husband though."

Nigel had a wicked grin on his face.

Angela smirked. "I promise, I will take care of these babies."

"Please don't get aggravated with me if I call a million times," she said pleading.

Angela laughed. "I won't get upset."

Nigel mouthed behind Kadijah's head, "She will not be calling."

Angela chuckled. Kadijah leaned down and kissed both of her babies who were now sleeping.

"Ma, is there enough formula?" Kadijah asked in a panic.

"Yes, girl, I have my own stash and diapers. I got this. Go enjoy the alone time with your husband and come back and get them tomorrow morning since I know you're not going to let them stay longer than that."

"Okay, ma." Kadijah looked down at her babies and the panic hit her. "Okay, Nigel, you better take me home now before I change my mind."

"You ain't gotta tell me twice. We out ma," Nigel said as he threw up the deuces.

Angela laughed and hugged and kissed them both. Nigel kissed his babies quickly and hustled Kadijah out of the house. Angela shook her head and laughed. She was excited to have her grands all to herself. She scooped Hunter up off the floor.

"Let's get you a bath before your cousins wake up."

Hunter giggled as his grandmother put kisses all over his belly.

Chapter 90: Lurking

The demon sat lurking in the front yard of the house across the street. There were stone gargoyles that "guarded" the bright red front door.

The sniveling demon hid himself inside the gargoyle and watched waiting for any piece of information he could collect to bring back to Insidious. The light had thrown a deafening blow and the Kingdom of Darkness needed a win.

When Insidious found out that not only did the little girl survive, but she was accompanied by a shield in the form of a twin, he lost his evil mind. He ranted and raved and vowed to make the Angel of Death pay for what he'd done. He couldn't stand that angel and was determined to render him useless in this ongoing war.

They were searching and hoping for any type of slip ups. He watched as Angela left for church. He was there upon her return, patiently waiting. Studying her as best he could. She now had four naval angels guarding her.

Angela was a problem for many reasons. Not only was she the gatekeeper of the south gate to the city, but she was also the matriarch of a powerful family with many gifted warriors.

An hour after she arrived home her sons and their families showed up. The demon kept watch as they unloaded their families from their vehicles laughing, smiling, and hugging without a care in the world. He smiled. He couldn't wait to strike them and strike them hard.

Hours passed before he saw them again. Curiously, he perked up when he saw Neil and Grey hop into his truck all hugged up, but without the bundle of joy. Twenty minutes later, Nigel and Kadijah left without their new babies. How intriguing. They had left their children with their grandmother.

True, she had warriors and so did Grey and Neil's kid, but still this was an opportunity. He was off limits anyway and was of no concern to them.

If they came with enough demonic power surely, they could do some type of damage. At the very least, create a riff in the family making it appear the mother could not protect their children.

If Nigel and Grey were away from their children, the opportunity was too good not to strike. While Neil could shield them, only Grey and Nigel could sense darkness coming.

He grinned and waited. Satisfied there were no angelic warriors watching, he slipped out of the gargoyle, took flight, and headed straight for the train station. Insidious had to know about this.

Chapter 91: Quality Time

Neil and Grey arrived home. In the kitchen, Neil grabbed his wife and pulled her into him. Grey grinned as she surrendered to the kiss he planted on her lips.

"So, what are you in the mood for tonight?" she asked. "Lingerie, music, candles, wine, the whole nine?"

He grinned. "Honestly?"

"Of course," she replied.

"Um, I really don't need all the theatrics. But I am feeling freaky enough to take you in every room of the house."

Grey stared up at her husband's mischievous face.

"Oh, my."

He seductively bit his bottom lip, knowing it drove her crazy. She pulled off her blouse and threw it down the on the floor.

"Let's start in the kitchen then."

He grinned and scooped her up.

†††

When Nigel and Kadijah arrived home, they stared at the clutter that was everywhere.

"Not exactly romantic is it?" Kadijah asked scrunching up her nose.

He laughed. "I guess not." Kadijah frowned. "No worries though. Go pack a bag," he told her.

"Really?" she asked excitedly.

He nodded. "I'm taking you to a fancy hotel and we gon wild out!"

She laughed. "Okay."

She went in their room to pack an overnight bag.

†††

Neil and Grey lay on the living floor staring up at the ceiling.

"Where's the doggone cat?" Neil asked.

"I don't know, but my screaming probably scared the crap out of him."

Neil chuckled. "You were in rare form."

"As were you," she told him.

"What room is next?" he asked.

"You know the bed in the guest room is very firm."

He turned to face his wife. "The carpet is very plush too."

"First one there gets to pick the spot."

"Deal," he said.

She scrambled up to take off running. He let her win. It didn't matter to him; it was going down in both spots.

†††

Nigel and Kadijah arrived at Hotel Duval, a luxury hotel in Downtown Tallahassee. Their angels valiantly guarded them. Pulling up to the front of the establishment, Nigel opted for the valet. The worker opened the door for Kadijah as Nigel grabbed their bag off the backseat.

Coming around the car, Nigel placed a hand on the small of Kadijah's back as he led her through the automatic doors. The lobby was spacious and decorated with unique chandeliers, contemporary art, and fresh flowers.

While they waited for the patron in front of them to finish, Kadijah tugged off Nigel's tie that hung loose around the collar of his unbuttoned dress shirt. Still dressed in his church attire, Nigel felt most comfortable in dress clothes. He winked at her when the clerk signaled for them to come to the counter.

Nigel placed their bag on the floor when he approached the desk. Kadijah had changed into some distressed jeans and a tank top. It had a been a while since she was dressed in anything other than workout clothes. She felt girly and sexy.

Thankfully, she had bounced back pretty quickly to her prebaby body with just a little pudge left behind though she still couldn't get used to the breasts her children caused her to have. She clung to her husband as he booked the Diamond Suite for the night. He pulled out his black card and handed it over.

While the clerk worked on the transaction, he put an arm around his wife.

"I cannot wait to get you up to that room."

"I brought something special to put on for you."

He raised a curious brow. "Oh really."

"Yes indeed."

"Well, I hope it's skimpy."

She laughed. The clerk tried to suppress a chuckle as she handed him back his card and their room keys. She explained to them how to find the suite and wished them a good evening. Nigel picked up their bag and headed towards the elevators.

†††

Grey's breathing was labored.

"You sir are showing slap out!"

Neil grinned. "Freedom will do that to you."

"If I have rug burn tomorrow, we fighting," she told him.

He chuckled. "Well let me make it worth your while."

He scooped her up and put her over his shoulder. She giggled.

"Where are we going now baby?"

"Our bed. Suddenly, I want to make love to you."

She had no protest.

†††

"I know you want to call my mother so go ahead. It will give me some time to set the mood in the room," Nigel told his wife.

She kissed his cheek, "Thank you for understanding."

"Don't thank me yet, because after this you are mine woman!"

Kadijah took the phone Nigel handed her then plopped down on the sofa in the living quarters of the suite.

Angela answered on the third ring. "Nigel, I thought it would be Kadijah calling me."

Kadijah laughed. "It is, I'm just using his phone."

"Oh, hey baby."

"How are they?"

"They are good.

Gideon is asleep, and her brother is sitting here staring at me, while Hunter is fighting his sleep."

Kadijah laughed. "You must've given Hunter his bath already."

"Yep," Angela laughed. "Now he doesn't know what to do with himself."

"You don't feel overwhelmed with three babies do you ma?"

"Girl, no. I got this. Now, I am about to feed your baby boy and put him to sleep."

"Call us if you need anything, we'll be there."

"Girl go enjoy your night. I'm not going to tell you again."

"Yes ma'am. Good night."

When Kadijah hung up the phone, she realized her husband had been very busy. In the room, he had rose petals spread on the plush king-sized bed.

"Negro, where did you get rose petals from?"

"A magician never reveals his secrets."

She smirked. There was a large spa tub across from the bed. The water was running. She could see the steam coming from the water. The tub was surrounded by candles.

"You want to find some mood music while I light these candles?" he asked snagging a kiss as he passed her.

"Sure thing, sexy," she said as she ran her hands down his abs that were on display now that he'd unbuttoned his dress shirt. Kadijah pulled out her phone.

"How about the Calvin Richardson Pandora Station?"

"Sounds perfect."

Kadijah set the station then connected her phone to the Bluetooth speaker in the suite.

"We Gon' Love Tonite" began playing through the speaker.

Nigel began to bob his head. "Oh, yeah, turn that up."

Kadijah obliged.

Nigel turned the water off. He went to his wife and pressed her up against the wall she was standing next to.

"I've missed you like crazy."

"I missed you too, baby."

He leaned down and kissed her. Nigel undressed his wife slowly and methodically. Carrying her over to the tub, he gently placed her into the warm water. After undressing, he joined her.

"Reminiscent of our first night, isn't it?" she asked.

"It is," he said pulling her to him.

"You better not get me pregnant negro," she said half serious.

"No promises," he said laughing as he kissed her again.

When he joined their bodies, he took his time savoring the mother of his children. He couldn't believe he was a father. Seeing her with his children and what she went through to bring them into this world made him love her even more. He wanted her to feel what he felt for her.

Kadijah was lost in the moment and took full advantage of their quality time together. She greedily took advantage of the moment making sure to show her man just how much she'd missed him.

Nigel drowned in the pleasure his wife delivered until he just couldn't take it anymore. Their finish was poetic. Kadijah held on to her husband as her body shivered with the aftershocks of their love making.

†††

Neil stared down at his wife.

"Your eyes are green baby," Grey commented. "What are you thinking about?"

"I don't think you understand how much I truly love you," he told his wife.

"Why do you say that?"

"Because I don't know how to put it into words, so I can't really tell you. When I say you're my light in darkness, I don't think I really understood what that meant until you helped bring me back from the darkest place I'd ever been in. I understand that loving a man like me isn't easy, but you do it with grace and patience so for that, I'm grateful."

Her eyes filled with tears. "If you can't tell me, then show me," she said softly.

He kissed her passionately and ignited something deep down in her soul. He took his time and tortured them both. Grey wrapped her arms around her man and held on as he led them down a memorable trip to a place only they shared.

They had made love countless times, but something about tonight struck her in a different way. The tears ran down her face as she sank deep into the ocean of their love. His name danced off her lips in a sensual whisper that ripped away his control. He was powerless to stop what she demanded, so he surrendered.

They lay wrapped around each other in silence for a while.

"What are you thinking about?" Grey asked him.

"Hunter."

She grinned. "Me too. Isn't it crazy how our whole lives have shifted to revolve around him?"

"Yeah, but I wouldn't have it any other way."

"Neither would I," she confessed.

"He can't stay away from home more than one night at a time. I don't care what my mama says," Neil told her.

Grey laughed. "I agree. I want to kiss his fat cheeks."

Neil pulled his wife closer to him. "I really want to know where that doggone cat is," Neil said curiously.

"Go to sleep. He's somewhere lurking."

"Before we go to sleep, I have something for you," Neil told her.

Grey turned over to look at him. "What?" she asked with a curious look on her face.

He chuckled. "This infamous push gift you been harassing me about."

Grey sat up as Neil climbed out of bed. "You must be want another baby," she said smirking.

He laughed and headed to his closet. He came back and placed a large box on the bed. Grey sat up, pulling the covers over her as she yanked the top off the all-white box.

Rummaging through the tissue paper, she found three boxes.

"I got three boxes?" she inquired excitedly.

He shrugged, "For your three stretch marks."

Grey fell out laughing.

She pulled out the first one and opened it. She gasped. It was a Tiffany blue Glock 43.

"Oh my God! I love it!" she screamed.

He laughed, tickled to no end. Only his wife would get excited about a firearm. She opened the next box to find another pistol, this one also Tiffany blue, but this one was a Ruger LCP .380. She already had one, but he knew it was her favorite compact carry, so he figured she'd like some options. One for fancy occasions. Grey did a little dance then opened her final box. This one was a Charter Arms .38 Special in Tiffany blue high gloss. It also had her name engraved on the barrel of the gun.

"Oh, I love it. I didn't have a revolver of my own."

Neil laughed. "I know. You're always stealing mine at the range."

"Baby, thank you. I love it."

He chuckled then leaned down and kissed her. "You're welcome."

"We can work on baby number two tomorrow because your girl is worn out!"

Neil laughed as he grabbed his wife and tumbled back onto the bed.

†††

Nigel and Kadijah had finally made it to the bed.

"So much for my lingerie," Kadijah said with a smirk.

Nigel laughed. "You didn't need it anyways."

"You didn't give me a chance to need it."

"Hey, I was focused on the main event."

She laughed. "Speaking of, can I get an encore performance?"

He stared at his wife. She grinned. He pulled her beneath him and kissed her letting her know her wish his command.

Chapter 92: The Attack

Fuller had followed Lucca for two days. She knew he was up to something, but she was about to end this once and for all. She believed Lucca was lying about what was left of the organization. He seemed to be working with her mother exclusively.

When they ended up back in Tallahassee, she knew he was going after her niece and nephew. She wasn't having it. Tailing him for two days, he always seemed to go to this old, abandoned train station. She desperately wanted to get a peek inside but could never find the opportunity. Usually a risk taker, the child she carried put a halt to much of that.

Sam would kill her if something happened to their child. When your lover was a professional assassin, one couldn't assume that expression was only figurative.

On day two, his behavior seemed erratic. At about 8:00 on Sunday evening, he went into the train station and didn't come out until about an hour later. There was something about his demeanor. He was definitely up to something and it was not good.

She tailed him like a professional which led them to a single-family home in a quaint neighborhood. She had no idea whose house it was, but she watched from two blocks down to see what he would do. They had been sitting on the street since around 9:30 PM.

The house was too basic to be Nigel's. She didn't think it was Neil's but wasn't sure. Either way if it belonged to them it would have much better security. Her plotting and scheming hadn't gone the way she planned, so the reconnaissance she would have gotten was now a deferred strategy. It could be her grandmother's, but she wasn't sure. She waited and waited and waited.

After midnight, Lucca got out of the car, dressed in all black. He lurked in the shadows and crept toward the house across the street. Lucca was surrounded by five ferocious demons ready and salivating. They wanted Nigel's baby girl and they were coming for her.

As far as they were concerned, she was left unguarded. What they couldn't see was Death in all his glory, except his skin had transitioned to clear diamonds as he stood with his massive wings spread in front of the house. As the demons excitedly approached the house, he came into his full black beauty. His diamond eyes firing the colors of the rainbow.

They screeched. They scrambled. They screamed, but it was too late. Death began to snatch demons left and right. In the spirit realm all that could be heard was their cries. In the house, all the angels were alerted by their screams to get into position.

Fuller frowned as she watched Lucca. She slipped on her black hoodie and quietly exited her car. By the time she made it to the house she thought he went into, she could no longer see him.

Something wasn't right. She could feel it in her gut. She rubbed the tiny bump of her belly, then pulled out the silencer for her pistol and attached it. She studied the house and decided to go around the back. She moved like a shadow making no sound as she went through the back gate.

A few steps into the backyard and she was momentarily blinded by the motion activated light. She cursed as she slammed up against the wall. She waited a full minute as she counted in her head. Nothing and no one moved.

Moving along the wall, she headed to the back door. She was about to pull her lock picking tools out of her pocket when something occurred to her. She turned the knob and found it open. Her heart sank. That meant Lucca was already in the house. She opened the door and slipped into the house.

Everything was quiet. There was a low light illuminating what she assumed was the kitchen. She tiptoed to the entrance then stopped to listen. She didn't hear anything, but her gut told her, he was here. She moved through the kitchen swiftly with her silenced pistol leading the way.

When she got into the living room, she knew where she was. There was a night light on that illuminated one wall. The wall with pictures. There they were, her family. She saw her father, her grandfather, her grandmother and Neil and Nigel along with Grey and Nigel's wife and their children.

She knew where she was, but why would Lucca attack their mother? Was he there to kill her? Why? Then she heard her answer. There was the whimper of a child. Something fierce rose up in her. She moved quickly toward the sound.

Lucca was evil, but she didn't think he would kill a baby, which meant only one thing. He was there to take the baby. She knew he wanted the girl but didn't know if he knew about the boy. Not if she had anything to do with it.

The door was open, and she saw the silhouette of a man over the bassinet. What she couldn't see was the huge white wings that canopied the bassinets.

Lucca, who was there to kidnap Nigel's daughter, thought his demonic protection was still in play. He didn't know that Death and his Shadow had taken them out.

Aiming her pistol at him, Fuller shot twice. Once to the head, once to the chest. He grunted and dropped to the floor never knowing what hit him. Quickly, she moved over to him to remove the firearm she knew he had on him, her instinct and thoroughness in full affect. Pulling off her gloves, she reached down to check his pulse and found none. She heard movement coming behind her.

"I don't know who you are, but you came for the wrong babies."

BOOM was all she heard, before she could utter a word. Angela was grateful she'd listened to the nudge in her spirit to let the babies sleep in her room, which was in the back of the house. The Angel of Death had cast his shadow over them as they remained sleep through it all. She turned on the light and stared in absolute horror.

"Oh my God! Oh my God!" she screamed.

"Don't," Fuller begged. "Don't shoot."

Angela couldn't make heads or tails of what was going on. She saw the dead body and she saw her granddaughter bleeding out on her floor.

"I shot you."

Fuller was holding her hand against the wound that was burning. She breathed through clinch teeth.

"I have to call 911!" Angela yelled.

"No, don't! Don't!"

Realization hit. Angela ran to get her phone. Her angels had never left her side. Cathal, her Gaelic warrior touched her shoulder.

"Call the police. She's losing too much blood. Trust in the Lord your God."

Angela made the decision then and there to call the authorities.

†††

Grey sat up clutching her chest. She gasped like she was drowning.

"Neil!" she screamed. He jumped up. "Something's wrong. Something is wrong."

Disoriented, he grabbed her.

"What happened?"

"I don't know. Call your mom. Call her now!"

†††

Nigel stirred in his sleep. He awoke with a start causing Kadijah to fall off his chest.

"Baby, what's wrong?" she asked confused.

"I don't know. Something doesn't feel right. Get up and get dressed."

She came to full alert.

"The babies," she said in a panic.

"Get dressed now!" he demanded. He was already pulling on his pants.

Chapter 93: Chaos

Before Neil could call his mother, his phone rang.

"Ma! What's wrong?"

She was crying. His heart stopped.

"Baby get over here. I don't. I need. Help."

"Ma! Calm down. Are the babies okay?"

He didn't hear any noise in the background.

"Yes, they are fine, just. Get here. I shot her. Neil, I shot her."

"Shot who?"

"Michelle."

By the time he got off the phone, Grey had thrown on jeans and a t-shirt, she was sliding into her sneakers. Neil threw on a pair of sweats and t-shirt, while jumping into his boots. He grabbed his badge and gun as they hurried out.

†††

"Something isn't right," Nigel said as they were heading out of the hotel. He was extremely irritated they had to wait for the valet. Restless, he was about to call Neil when his phone rang.

"Bro! What the hell is going on?"

"I don't know. Mama just called me crying saying she shot Michelle."

"What? Did she come there for our kids? For mama?"

"Bro, I don't know."

"The babies?"

"They're okay."

"We're on the way."

"What happened Nigel?" Kadijah demanded.

"My mom shot our niece."

She shrieked. "What?"

"I don't know what's going on baby. Let's get over there."

†††

Neil and Grey arrived in a disturbingly short amount of time. They both hopped out of the truck. Grey broke out in a full run. Neil looked around the neighborhood. It didn't look like anyone had heard the gun shots.

As Grey approached the house, she felt a familiar presence. Her eyes flamed, only visible to spiritual beings. She stared at Death blocking her mother-in-law's house. He nodded at her.

Neil turned, "Grey! Come on!"

Grey blinked and followed her husband in the house.

"Ma!" he yelled as soon as they got inside.

"Back here!" she yelled.

Grey ran past Neil to get to her son. She stared horrified at the man on the floor, clearly no longer alive and Angela covered in Fuller's blood as she held on to her.

"Grey the babies are in my room."

Grey nodded and went to check on them. Neil stared down.

"Neil, she's losing a lot of blood. Help her. She told me not to call 911, but I had to. She was losing too much blood. The baby."

He nodded. "Keep pressure on the wound."

Fuller kept her eyes closed, but he could see she was still breathing. The bullet had struck her just above her heart. Neil assessed the situation. He thought he understood what was happening, but now was not the time. He had to think.

They could hear sirens blaring and approaching. Nigel came rushing in. Neil took off his belt and made a tourniquet to staunch the blood flow by looping it around her shoulder and under arm.

"What the hell happened? The police and EMS are arriving."

Kadijah was clutching her chest. "The babies."

"In my mom's room with Grey," Neil told her.

She disappeared.

Fuller tried to speak. "Lucca, kidnap."

"Shhh sweetie," Angela cooed. "You're going to be okay. Just hold on."

Tears ran down Angela's face as she looked up at her sons.

"Whoever he is, I think he was here to take the babies. Michelle shot him, but when I heard the noise, I grabbed my gun and came in. I saw her shadow and I just shot. I didn't know it was her," Angela cried.

"It's okay, ma. It's gonna be okay," Neil said trying desperately to calm his mother down.

"What's the plan?" Nigel asked Neil.

Neil cussed. This was quite the jacked-up situation.

"Mama called 911. It is what it is."

"They are going to arrest her," Nigel said.

"I know, but we gotta figure that out later. Right now, we need to get her medical attention. The baby, Nigel."

Nigel shook his head.

"I need to call Sam."

"Yeah, you do."

The police and paramedics arrived on the scene. Chaos ensued. There were police officers taking notes, interviewing Angela and Neil, and crime scene investigators marking evidence. Nigel kept them away from their wives and children.

Angela had a fit when she couldn't accompany Fuller to the hospital because they needed her statement. Grey agreed to go with her. It took six hours for the whole ordeal to come to an end.

After the first hour, Nigel and Kadijah took the babies away from all the crazy. Sam was on his way to Tallahassee and Neil watched as they wheeled Lucca's body out of his mother's house. He closed the door and took a minute to just breathe.

His phone vibrated. It was an update on Fuller from Grey. He read it, his heart sank. After another deep breath, he headed into the kitchen where his mother sat at the kitchen table staring into space not drinking the chamomile tea, he'd made for her.

He took a seat next to her and grabbed her hand. She blinked and stared at him.

"Ma, Grey just text me."

She squeezed his hand. "Just tell me."

"She made it out of surgery and the baby is okay."

Relieved, Angela broke.

Neil pulled his mother into his chest and let her release all the anxiety of the night. He was trying to wrap his mind around it, but it was difficult. When she finally stopped crying, he gave her some tissue to clean her face.

"Ma, they know who she is. She's been arrested."

Angela stared. "Oh my God, what have I done?"

"I know it's hard ma, but you did the right thing."

"She's going to hate me. She told me not to call the police."

"She's going to be grateful for you because you saved her life and the life of her unborn child."

Angela shook her head. Then she remembered. She stared at Neil.

"What?" he asked.

"At first, I hesitated to call, but I swear I felt this conviction that if I didn't call, she would lose the baby. I promise you I heard, trust the Lord your God."

Neil stared then blinked. "Well then that's what we're gonna do. Trust God."

"Will they let me see her?"

"I don't know, but ma, you need to get some rest. It's too much for one day. They have to keep her in the hospital for a couple more days. You can see her later today, okay."

"You're right. I just want to take a hot shower and lay down."

"Okay. I'm staying. Plus, I need to get a cleaning crew in here first thing in the morning. Or you could finally move."

"Boy, I'm not moving out of my house."

He shook his head, "But you are getting an alarm first thing in the morning. I do not want to hear any objections."

"Neil, you don't have to stay. You need to go be with Grey."

"My wife is a very capable woman, mama. I'm staying."

Angela smirked. "She already told you to stay here, huh?"

Neil laughed. She did too. It felt good to find humor in the most chaotic night of their lives.

Chapter 94: The Seer

Grey sat next to the hospital bed holding on to Fuller's hand. She'd confessed she was afraid, so Grey did what she could to comfort her. The woman was four months pregnant, had just been shot by her grandmother, survived surgery for a gunshot wound to her chest all while handcuffed to her hospital bed.

Grey took a look at the officer that was outside that guarded the room. She prayed for peace, comfort, and favor. This situation was so bizarre she didn't know how to pray for it. She finally concluded that she'd just pray for God's will to be done in this situation.

Clearly, God's favor was already in play. She was able to stay with Fuller because Genevieve was working a double shift and was assigned to the emergency room that night. Etienne's words floated into her memory. *Nothing is coincidence, and everything is connected.*

"Why don't you get some rest?" Grey suggested.

"I'm afraid to close my eyes."

"I won't leave your side, okay."

"Has anyone talked to Sam?" she asked.

"Of course. Nigel said he's on his way."

"I'm going to jail, Grey." Grey saw the fear and pain in her eyes. "I know I deserve it and if it was just me, I would take it like a champ, but my baby. I don't want my precious baby born behind bars."

Grey squeezed her hand. "The people who love you will do everything in their power to make sure that doesn't happen."

Fuller shook her head. "I need a miracle."

"Well, the God I serve is able. I'm praying for you."

"I don't know Him," Fuller admitted.

"Do you want to?"

"I'm not sure."

Grey nodded. She didn't push. This was a lot to take in.

"Get some rest. Just close your eyes. I will not let you be here alone."

Fuller nodded and tried to get comfortable. The pain was severe. They gave her something topical for it, but she couldn't and wouldn't take any oral pain medication. She closed her eyes.

Grey began to pray for her and the baby. Mostly for her heart to surrender and she give her life to Christ. It would be a shame to survive all this and then lead a life that led to eternal damnation.

Outside, Insidious lurked in front of the hospital room. Grey's warriors wouldn't let him inside. He wasn't one to unnecessarily engage in battle. He had other means at his disposal. He was seething that they had not only forgiven their niece but continued to show her unconditional love. It was absurd after everything she'd done. He was so sure Neil's hatred of her would be forever. He couldn't get in the room, but he would use the power of the air. He began to speak contrary words and thoughts into the atmosphere. After all, his master was the prince of the power of the air.

The angelic beings didn't engage with him because he wasn't violating anything. The saints had the same power he did, to speak into the atmosphere and change things. They would not intervene. Grey felt resistance in the atmosphere. She began to travail in tongues. As she did, the gift of her spiritual sight ignited. The majestic blue flames were in her eyes.

Suddenly Grey opened her eyes and gasped. She stared as she saw a golden key dangling from Fuller's neck just like the ones she, Neil and Hope possessed.

"Oh my God," she mouthed in shock. She guessed it made sense somehow. After all, she was their brother's daughter. All she could do was shake her head.

The revelation ignited a fire in her. She continued to pray for God to deliver her from having to go to jail. She didn't know how or if, but the Bible said you had not because you ask not. She wasn't going to let her finite human mind assume it was higher than God's.

Chapter 95: Shut It Down

Sampson walked through the front doors of the emergency room. Dressed in army green BDUs, a matching t-shirt, boots, and his dog tags. His gait exuded quiet authority. In his hand, he carried a thin manila envelope and nothing else.

With him, was the angel that delivered the message to move God had promised He would send him, the incomparable Archangel Gabriel. His frame was 18-feet in height. His two sets of brilliant pearl colored wings were expanded and stretched 22-feet. His skin was the color of alabaster, and his golden mane flowed freely to his shoulders.

There was a qama dagger tucked securely in a golden sheath at his waist. The emerald cuffs on his wrist sparkled with otherworldly splendor. The demons that always lurked in places where sickness abounded came to full alert in sheer panic that he was there to take them out.

They looked on in fear to see what the angel would do. Gabriel's four wings were spread out as he followed Sampson. He made no effort to address the demons that surrounded the place. That was not his current assignment.

Regardless of how the patients in the waiting room were feeling, they noticed Sampson and wondered about him. When he approached the front desk, the young woman couldn't even hide her shameless stare nor the blush on her buttercream skin.

Wide-eyed, she smiled and showed every single one of her perfect white teeth. Sampson was used to the attention, especially when he was in military apparel. He ignored her flirtatious behavior.

"I'm here to see the patient that was escorted in by law enforcement," he said in his melodically deep voice.

"Oh," she blinked. "I'm not sure how that..."

Genevieve walked up. "Excuse me." Sampson turned toward the voice. "I will escort him up. He's expected."

"Oh, okay," the young girl said.

Sampson was confused, but whatever got him to Nyla was fine by him.

Genevieve said, "Follow me." Sampson obliged.

When they were through the doors and alone, Sampson stopped. Genevieve, put her hands up in surrender.

"I'm a friend of Neil's wife. She told me to make sure you were able to get through. I've been waiting for you."

He nodded. "Thank you."

"It's no problem. Now please don't come up in my hospital acting a plum fool. Grey and them stay with some shenanigans going on."

Sampson chuckled. "It's not my intention, but..."

Genevieve shook her head and laughed.

When they got off the elevator, Sampson saw the officer guarding her room door.

"If you don't mind, I'll take it from here," he told Genevieve.

She nodded and made her way to the nurse's station. She knew enough about anything connected to the Lawson's to ask zero questions, keep your mouth shut and just pray!

As she approached the nurse's station her coworkers were staring hard as he walked past them to the room at the end of the corridor. Even one of the patients stared with admiration.

"Girl, who is that?" one of the nurses asked.

"Not your husband," Genevieve said sarcastically.

The nurse rolled her eyes. "Nah, but that's the kind of man that's worth repenting for."

"Oooh you ratchet," Genevieve said frowning. "Trust me when I say. You don't want those type of problems. He is spoken for by that patient in the last room."

"Um, she's about to go to jail so he's about to be lonely. I can help with that."

"What you can do is help yourself to a cold shower. You are very married, and that woman down there is on some other stuff. I caution you to remain professional at all times and keep your little crush on her man to yourself."

"So, you holy now because you a first lady?" the nurse asked.

"No, I have common sense," Genevieve said shaking her head.

Hard heads always made a soft behind. She for one was grateful Fuller was handcuffed to her bed, but she still had one hand free. She hoped the nurse had sense enough to not do or say anything inappropriate.

Sampson approached the officer. The large burly man that looked tired put his large, meaty palm up.

"I'm sorry sir. No unauthorized access to the patient."

Sampson remained unbothered. "My name is Sampson Steele. I was a naval special warfare officer in SEAL Team 7."

"Well that's admirable, but...," the officer cut Sampson off.

"As I was saying. I don't want to get in her room. I want you to call whoever is in charge and can make life changing decisions and tell them I need to speak to them immediately."

The officer chuckled at the audacity. Sampson raised a brow. He handed the officer the envelope. The officer frowned then undid the tiny red string, opened it and peeked inside. He pulled out the all black piece of paper that appeared to be blank save for the official stamp of the CIA.

The officer looked up at Sampson and frowned.

"I'm not asking you. I'm telling you," Sam said with a dangerous edge to his tone.

The officer nodded and pulled out his phone.

Chapter 96: A Past That Haunts

Sampson sat in the chapel of the hospital. Genevieve had pulled some strings and agreed to give him 30 minutes of uninterrupted access, so he could meet with the high-ranking CIA official.

Sampson was playing no games. This room had no windows and one door. He wished he could have Neil and Nigel in there watching his back, but the information was too sensitive. He didn't want them carrying the burden of what he knew. He would just have to depend on God to watch his back. After all, he was only alive today because of divine intervention.

Sampson couldn't know that Gabriel was right there with him, his expansive wings covering the entire chapel. Either they met on his terms or he flexed the political and military muscle he had that would take decades to recover from.

He wasn't meeting in any open space. He wasn't meeting anywhere where a sniper could take him out through a window. He knew the game. He was the game.

When the official entered the chapel, he paused. "Well, this is new."

"I have my reasons," Sampson said as he stood up.

The man reached to shake Sampson's hand. Sampson slid his hands into his pocket.

"I'd rather not."

"Paranoid much?" the official asked smirking.

He was a non-descript man that could blend in with any crowd and go unnoticed. Average height, brown and brown, with skin slightly tanned that would cause people to not assume his ethnicity was white, but not able to rule it out.

"I was told you have something of importance you want to exchange for Michelle Fuller's freedom."

"I do. Indeed."

"I assure you there's nothing you can offer that would..."

Sampson cut him off. "Miss me with the bargaining and intimidation. You know who I am, and you know what I know. It's real simple. Michelle took down one of the most notorious psychopaths to ever exist. She will hand over any information she has on the rest of the organization. Y'all have been searching for Lucca Prescott since the drama in Florida and California last year. She did what y'all couldn't do. Find him and stop him. Here's the deal. Agent Michelle Fuller no longer exists. Records of who she worked for and what she did, disappear. She's allowed to go on with her life under her new identity. If she is not allowed to do this, I will release the documents which exposes levels of corruption that reach far and wide. I was meant to be taken out in the raid to ensure my silence like the rest of my team, but I'm still breathing, and my memory is sharp. I'm not a killer anymore, but don't push me."

"You're bluffing," the man said not ready to concede.

He had been instructed by his superiors, but his ego didn't want to bow down to this self-righteous, love-struck, soldier.

"You're lucky we're in a church, otherwise I'd show you, I don't bluff. I'm not asking you all to do anything you haven't done before. Hell, I've escorted your people with cases full of cash to drop-offs to trade information for clean slates. Ain't nothing new under the sun. We both know this deal has already been signed off on at the highest levels of government. Oh, and tell your boy that I check in every 48 hours. The minute I miss a check in, it all goes public. Not just the smoking gun, but all of it. To every credible news source and every noncredible one."

"Blackmail is beneath such an exemplary soldier who was awarded the nation's highest military honor."

"That was a bribe that didn't work and we both know it. Besides, fair exchange is no robbery. The government has taken enough from me. Now, I'm taking my life back and I'm disappearing to live out my life with my woman and my child. Do not make me come out of retirement or I promise you, I will unleash all my suppressed rage without mercy or conscience starting with you. I'm done with all this. Leave me and mine alone."

The man reached for the file.

"Is this the only copy?" he asked.

Sampson smirked. "That's a sworn statement from me. What I give you is my word none of this will see the light of day at my hands as long as you all continue to respect our agreement. You have my word which you and your boy know is bond."

The man sighed. "You're treading on thin ice, Sampson."

"No worries, I'm a SEAL, I know how swim. Call me when it's handled, and I'll give you the location to some of the hardcopies as a gesture of faith. The rest will remain in my possession."

With that Sampson dropped the envelope on the seat next to him and walked out of the chapel. The man picked up the envelope and took a seat. He sighed. Loose ends always come back unraveled.

Chapter 97: The Arms of the One That Loves You

When Sampson returned to Fuller's room there was no officer standing in front of her door. He walked in to find Neil, Nigel, Grey and their mother inside her room. There was an officer uncuffing her.

His lips were tight when he said, "The charges against you are being dropped."

Everyone in the room gasped, but they all had sense enough not to ask any questions. Fuller rubbed her wrist at a complete loss for words. Then she felt him enter the room. When she looked up, she smiled. His heart skipped a beat.

Everyone stared at him, but his eyes were focused on one person, his woman.

He asked, "Could you all give us a few minutes?"

They all nodded. Angela walked up to him and placed her hands on his cheeks.

"I don't know what you did, and I do not care. I just want to say thank you. Make sure you come by my house before you leave town."

"Yes ma'am," he said.

She leaned up to kiss his cheek then hugged him tight. He squeezed her back as he closed his eyes. It did his weary heart good to have the embrace that only a mother could give. He hadn't had his parents around to guide him in many years. The open affection she showed him was so needed.

Angela reached down and grabbed Sampson's hand. He frowned when he felt her place something in it. She smiled. He discreetly looked at the ring she placed in his hand.

She whispered, "You were going to ask, right?" He grinned. "Well, do you have one?" He shook his head. "You do now," she said with a wink. Angela pulled away and looked at Michelle. "I'll see you soon, baby."

Oblivious, Fuller nodded, "Yes ma'am."

Neil and Nigel exchanged a look. Grey just shook her head as they exited the room giving them their privacy.

When they got outside the room, Nigel asked, "Ma, what was all that whispering about?"

"Mind your business, son," she said laughing.

When the door closed, Sampson sat on the side of her bed. He leaned down and kissed her forehead then he kissed her belly.

"I missed you," he confessed.

"I missed you too," she said as tears brimmed in her eyes.

"How did you..."

He placed a finger on her lips and shook his head.

"No questions. No worries. It's over. Just trust your man. I will always look out for you and our baby."

She nodded. He grabbed her hand.

"Marry me."

"Okay," she said smiling.

"Before you leave the hospital. In the little chapel."

"Okay," she said.

He leaned down and kissed her.

"I have something for you," he said.

She looked down at what was in his hand. She gasped.

"That's my grandmother's ring."

"Well, I didn't steal it," he laughed.

"She gave you that? For me?" He nodded, with a huge grin on his face. Her eyes misted. "They really do love me, like actually love me, don't they?"

"Yeah, they do," he told her sincerely. "You have a family of your own that no one is going to ever take from you."

He slid the three-carat halo engagement ring on her finger. The tears ran down her face and for the first time in her life, she was not ashamed to show her true emotions.

Chapter 98: The Greatest Love of All

Sampson had called Nigel and told him he wanted to marry their niece as soon as humanly possible and he wanted to do it in the chapel at the hospital. Grey, being a notary public, offered to do the honors when the discussion of where to find an officiant came up. It all seemed to effortlessly fall in place.

Now they were all in the small chapel with silly grins, all of them feeling the surrealness of the moment. There was a fierce contingent of angels that surrounded this wedding. Gabriel stood behind Grey while the Angel of Death stood blocking the doorway from anything that might try to hinder this divine moment.

Sampson's guardian angel could not stop the grin that was on his face. He was so proud of his charge that he had followed the steps that were ordered for him to get to this moment.

Angela could not stop crying. Genevieve feared they would have to treat her for dehydration if the woman didn't stop bawling. Nigel stood as attendant for Sampson, while Kadijah stood for Fuller. Neil walked her down the aisle.

When Grey asked, "Who gives this woman away?"

Neil said, "I do." He leaned over and kissed Nyla's cheek.

Grey winked at her husband.

Genevieve sat at the back of the chapel holding a giggling Hunter and keeping a close eye on the twins as they slept peacefully in their car seats.

Sampson, in his fatigues stood with a smile on his face as he never took his eyes off of Nyla. Nyla stood in a simple red dress Grey had given her. They were the perfect picture of love and war. The precious bump that was their child stuck out in the bold colored, fitted dress. Nyla put a hand on her belly and grinned.

"Nyla, do you take Sampson to be your lawfully wedded husband from this day forward to have and to hold, in sickness and health, for richer or poorer until death do you part?"

"I do."

"Sampson, do you take Nyla to be your lawfully wedded wife to have and to hold from this day forward in sickness and in health, for richer or poorer, until death do you part?"

"I do."

"Then, by the power vested in me by the State of Florida, I now pronounce you man and wife. Sam you may kiss your bride!" Grey said with the biggest grin on her face.

Sampson pulled Nyla into his arms.

"I love you. Thank you for choosing us."

She smiled. "I love you, too."

He leaned in and kissed her softly. She wrapped her arms around his neck and indulged herself. The crowd cheered and woke up the babies. When they were done, they both wore silly grins.

"There's something else, we want to do with all of you here," Sampson told the crowd.

"What's that?" Grey asked curiously.

"If you could lead us in the prayer of salvation, we'd really appreciate it," Nyla told Grey.

Grey's eyes misted as she clutched at her chest. "Really?" They both nodded. "It would be my absolute pleasure to do so."

When these two assassins accepted the free gift of salvation and let the love of the Creator of all things surround them while the Blood of the Lamb washed away their pasts, there wasn't a dry eye in the house.

Genevieve had to remember she was responsible for the babies because she wanted to tear up the carpet in that little chapel shouting. What a mighty God they served.

All the angels in Heaven and on Earth rejoiced as two more souls were snatched from the pit of hell and two more soldiers had been added to the light to fight the good fight of faith. Their testimony would be earth shifting.

Death walked up to Nigel and placed a golden key around his neck. He had earned the full activation of his discernment for the part he played in his niece's salvation. Gabriel and Death nodded at each other. Their work was done. They took off in a brilliant swirl of emerald and navy-blue light!

There were lots of hugs and tears. Neil grabbed Nyla's hand and led her to a corner of the chapel away from everyone. They sat.

"I'm sorry it took us so long to find you and all that you had to endure. Family is the most important thing to us and you're a part of that now. That means you, Sam and this little one will always be welcome, and we will always have your back. Trust may take some time, but my loyalty and my love are in full effect."

Nyla was speechless. She leaned in and hugged him. The last bits of uncertainty fell from Neil's heart and soul. He embraced her. Grey had to look away or she would just bawl all over the place.

Nigel smiled as he pulled his mother in for a hug. Angela's heart was overwhelmed, she thought it would simply burst. God had kept His promise to her to watch over her seeds if she watched over His city.

"Thank you, Father," she said as she raised her hand in worship.

Chapter 99: 8:00

Nyla Steele
Ocho Rios, Jamaica

A week later, after all was said and done, Sam whisked me away to a spectacular resort. I had been medically cleared, our baby was healthy, the charges had been dropped and now it was time to get on with our brand-new lives. I felt like I had shed two hundred pounds of emotional weight. Basically, a whole person.

I couldn't wait to get to our hotel room. Between all the plotting, scheming, killing, redeeming, and forgiving, who had time to get their freak on. Priorities, you know. But now, I was focused on one thing and one thing only.

My man.

My husband.

My future.

My baby daddy.

My lover.

I was sitting in one of the big comfy red chairs in the living room area of our suite as I watched my husband put our things away. It was weird to say *my husband.* I looked down at my grandmother's ring. Yep, it was real. No fairy tales here. I was in awe of the type of feelings and freedom that were found when you were truly loved and truly knew you were forgiven.

I felt weightless, as if I were simply floating through my current existence. I wasn't naïve enough to think that life couldn't get crazy again, but the moment I was in now, was picture perfect and I refused to dwell on anything other than our child, our love and what I wanted to do to this man as soon as possible. He'd told me to relax and so that's exactly what I did while he got ready.

After he'd showered, he walked over to me with that sexy stride of his wearing a pair of sleek black pajama pants and no shirt. I made a mental note of the three bullet wounds he had on his chest, something else we had in common, battle scars. He reached for my hand.

"Come with me."

Those three words sent fire down to my toes. I took his hand with no hesitation. He led me to the spacious bathroom with the enormous jacuzzi tub. Slowly he undressed me and helped me get into the frothy water that smelled of lavender. I leaned back into the warm water, closed my eyes, and exhaled.

"How you feeling beautiful?"

"Relaxed. Free," I confessed.

"Funny, that's how I feel too."

I opened my eyes and stared into his sincere brown ones. "How did we get here?" I asked sincerely.

"Faith and favor are my guess."

I smiled. "Right. We don't deserve this, so we have to protect this at all costs," I said as I reached down and placed my hand on my protruding belly.

He placed his hand on top of mine and said, "I agree. Always grateful. Always humbled."

I touched his dimpled cheek with my hand. He leaned down and gently placed a kiss on my lips. It was innocent and sweet, but still lit a fire in me.

"You stir me in new ways."

He grinned cockily. "If I had a collar, I'd pop it."

I laughed. "Are you scared?"

"Of what?"

"Being a father. Being married. Being a *Christian*."

He laughed. "Yep to all of it." I laughed. "You scared?"

"Terrified," I said laughing.

"We are highly trained soldiers, and we choose to fear domestication and faith," he said shaking his head.

"Better the devil you know," I shrugged.

"You think the madness is done?" he asked with a little trepidation in his voice.

"I know it's not, but our battlefield is going to be different from now on," I warned.

"You mean a spiritual one."

I nodded. "He chose us for a reason. It's like spiritual insider trading. Let's be valuable to the team we now choose to serve."

He nodded. "That's a bet." I smiled. "Now, let's get on with consummating this marriage."

I laughed. Sam took his time pampering me. When he was done, he wrapped a plush white robe around me and led me to the bedroom. The pristine plush white down comforter somehow looked like the beginning of a second chance. A clean slate.

"I'm just gonna put this out there," I told him.

His eyebrow went up. "What's up?"

"I'm not sure if this belly is going to alter my skills."

He laughed. "I'm so not worried about that."

He leaned down and kissed me. I was lost in the language of our tongues as he laid me back on the bed.

His touch was gentle.

His caress was sweet.

His words were soul-stirring.

His lips were soft.

His timing was patient.

His hands were possessive.

His love was exquisite.

His thoroughness was epic.

His kiss was therapeutic.

His arms were safety.

His heart was *mine*.

It felt like a dream that I never wanted to wake from. His love made all the ugliness that came before him worth it. There is no way I could appreciate the light in him without the darkness I had once existed in. I now understood my journey with crystal clarity. The bitterness I carried for so long began to dissipate.

That revelation sent peace through my entire being. The tears ran down my cheeks. I gave up the ghosts of my past and everything that haunted me with my release. Minutes later he followed, and I prayed he did the same.

Silence enveloped us as we lay tangled in the sheets. Sam placed his hand on my stomach. I interlocked my fingers with his.

"This is a gift," he said.

"I know."

Silence took over again. I looked up and saw the clock read 8:00.

"Sam."

"Huh?"

"You sleep?"

"Not yet, but I plan to be."

"Why is 8:00 so special to you?"

He was silent for a few moments, but he did draw me in closer.

"The night of the raid in Afghanistan, I died." I gasped. "My time of death of 8:00 PM. They brought me back to life two minutes later, but I coded."

I sat up and looked at him.

"Every time I see those numbers hit the clock, I'm grateful. I researched the number. Did you know in the Bible, the number eight means new beginnings?" I shook my head. "Needless to say, there is no greater new beginning than a rebirth. It was the beginning of my path to Christ. I understand that now, but then I was just grateful and clueless as to why. Now I know why it wasn't yet my time. I still had or should I say *have* work to do."

I wiped the tears that slipped past my guard. I was so over all these emotions. I wrapped my arms around him. I had no words. I closed my eyes thankful that God saw fit to give his life another chance.

"I love you Sampson Steele," I finally said.

"I love you too, Nyla Steele."

With that, I closed my eyes and waited for sleep to come.

Chapter 100: Full House

They all sat around waiting for the new family members to arrive. The house was full of fierce angelic warriors. Angela's four naval warriors stood guard around the house. Grey's warriors valiantly stood near her as the others stood near their charges. Cheveyo, Quan, Ern, Koldo, Bomani, Lajos, Ranj and Alvise all stood surrounding them. The twins did not yet have warriors specifically assigned to them. They knew this meeting was divine. Cathal, Angela's Gaelic warrior, threw up a shield to protect this meeting from spiritual eavesdroppers.

Kadijah was kicked back in Angela's comfortable recliner with Gideon covered under a blanket as she was breastfed. She was completely at ease with the new additions, but then again, she had no direct contact with their niece prior to her redemption.

Nigel held his son on his shoulder as he burped him. He'd just finished a bottle. He wasn't nervous, but just a tad leery. This was the first time they were "hanging out" as a family. He wondered if it would be organic or forced. He didn't have any issues with his niece, and even though Neil loved her, trust was going to take time. He was excited about getting to know Sampson. He really liked him.

Grey was cautious. She was ready to snatch Fuller or hug her. It didn't really matter to her. She matched energy. If she was rowdy, she could go there. If she was cool, she could be that too.

Neil glanced over at his wife. He could read her mind. He shook his head. Grey chuckled. Neil kissed the top of Hunter's head as he sat on his lap watching *Super Why* on his phone. For Neil, he was cool. He was ready to put the works with his faith. He trusted that God knew what He was doing.

Determined not to go back to that dark place, he kept his eyes on forward movement only. He knew he needed to deal with this because there was a spiritual reason they were all brought together. Of that he was thoroughly convinced. Their mother was a gatekeeper for the city. Grey said she'd seen a golden key around Fuller's neck, and he needed to work on his relationship with Eva.

He nodded. He was ready to get this show on the road. Grey winked at him.

Angela was excited. She couldn't wait to meet her great grandchild. She couldn't wait to bond with her grandchild, and she couldn't wait to get to know her new grandson-in-love. The smile she wore on her face felt like it would be permanently etched there.

"Y'all good?" she asked.

"I'm good," Kadijah said.

"I'm a'ight," Grey said.

"I'm cautious," Nigel said.

"I'm good," Neil rounded out the replies.

"Do we need to pray?" Angela asked.

"It couldn't hurt," Nigel said laughing.

They all laughed, but it was cut off by the ringing of the doorbell.

"Looks like y'all better say, 'Jesus wept' and keep it moving," Nigel quipped.

They fell out.

"Boy hush!" Angela said as she stood to open the door. "Hey!" she greeted Nyla and Sampson with huge hugs. She could tell that Nyla was nervous and Sampson was cautious. "Well come on in," she shooed them in.

"Thank you for having us," Sampson said as he offered her a bouquet of bright colored flowers.

"Oh, that's so sweet. Thank you. And what is this nonsense, thanks for having us. I done told you, y'all are family. You're welcome here."

Nigel stood up handing his son to Grey. He shook Sampson's hand and gave Nyla a one-armed hug.

"Welcome. Man, she always got something good on the stove and wait until y'all taste that pineapple tea."

They laughed and some of the tension left the room. Everyone greeted each other.

"How was the honeymoon?" Grey asked.

"It was great," Nyla said as she rubbed her belly nervously.

"Relaxing," Sampson added.

An awkward moment rested in the atmosphere.

"Well, let's head into the kitchen for dinner," Angela suggested.

Neil had bought his mother a new table for her expanding family. This one sat eight comfortably. They all sat around as the food was placed in the middle of the table by Grey and Angela. Dinner consisted of a spiral ham, fried chicken, macaroni and cheese, yams, fried corn, and collard greens. Angela figured you could never go wrong with soul food. Neil sat at one end of the table, while Nigel sat at the other.

"Let's pray," Neil said commanding everyone's attention.

Everyone grabbed hands on either side of them unless a baby prevented it. Neil blessed the food and thanked God for bringing them all together.

"Dig in," Angela said when he finished.

They all fixed their plates. For the first few minutes, it was quiet.

"Soooo, do y'all play spades?" Nigel asked.

"I do," Sampson said.

"What's that?" Nyla asked.

Everyone stopped eating and stared at her.

"Please tell me you're not serious?" Nigel inquired.

"What is it?" she asked again clueless.

"Um, the blackest card game ever," Sampson told her.

"Oh, sorry. I'm not familiar," she confessed completely oblivious to her proximity to having her black card revoked.

Everybody shook their heads. Angela patted Nyla's hand.

"I'll teach you baby."

"Thanks, grandma. They act like I violated something precious."

"I'm sure these nuts will be playing sometime this afternoon. It's quite entertaining."

"Wait a minute, I thought the rule was you can't play with your own significant other?" Kadijah pointed out.

"That's true, but we gon have to make an exception because I am not partnering up with the newbie," Neil said. "Not when I finally started winning."

Nyla frowned. "I might not know what it is, but I know you just threw major shade my way."

They laughed. Sampson leaned over and kissed her cheek.

"I'll be your partner baby."

"Ahh, that's cute, but we show no mercy," Grey said.

"Zero," Nigel confirmed as he reached across and bumped fists with Grey.

"So, you and Grey against Neil and Kadijah?" Nyla inquired. They nodded. "Oh, that has to be pure comedy."

"It's actually more ratchet than comedic," Kadijah added. They laughed.

"So, have you guys decided when you're heading back to Central Florida?" Angela asked shifting the subject.

"In about a week," Sampson told them. "I need to get her setup with a doctor and get her on regular checkups. We're getting closer to the finish line."

"Well, please keep us posted. I so want to be there for the birth. I mean if that's okay," Angela said.

"I would love to have you there," Nyla reassured her. "I'm so scared about labor and delivery. I've tried to read books, but I just panic and throw the book across the room."

The women laughed.

"Well, don't listen to Grey. She was a certified mean girl. Oh, she was awful." Grey gave her husband a severe evil eye. "You can look at me crazy all you want. You know you were hell on wheels."

"Hey, until you have firsthand knowledge of that kinda pain, there is no judgment, you hear me?" Neil laughed. "Since you got me my push gift, I guess we can have another one."

Everybody laughed.

"What was your push gift?" Sam asked.

"Three Tiffany blue pistols for my three stretch marks."

Everybody fell out laughing. Angela shook her head.

"Are you serious?" Sampson asked.

Grey nodded. He looked at Neil.

He shrugged. "I know my wife."

"How long did your labor last?" Nyla asked.

"Girl! Twenty-two pain filled hours."

Nyla dropped her fork. "Are you serious?"

"As serious as my three stretch marks!" Nyla stared. Kadijah laughed. "Sam, prepare your mind and your pocket now. She needs a push gift. Do you hear me?"

Sampson laughed. "I know just the thing."

"Are you sure you're just having one baby? You know we had a whole baby hiding in there," Kadijah said.

Nyla's eyes got huge. "You didn't know you were having twins?"

"Nope, not until the doctor pulled them out of her during an emergency c-section. We thought she was giving birth to one stillborn and instead we got two fully healthy babies. God is good," Nigel told them.

"Wow," Sampson said.

"Let's just say the delivery rooms in our family tend to be interesting," Neil warned.

"Duly noted," Sampson said.

He understood that this was his seed their niece was carrying, and he didn't possess the same spiritual legacy they did, but still he wondered if their child would possess something special as well. His life was spared for a reason. Why?

"I will be there for as long as you need me," Angela told Nyla.

Neil and Nigel exchanged a look at their mother's confession. Grey was the only one who caught it.

"There's still so much to do. We gotta find a place down there because living at a hotel is no longer an option. It's going to be pretty crazy for the next few months."

"Yeah, but it will be fun. New beginnings are always fun," Angela said.

At the phrase "new beginnings" Sampson and Nyla shared a look.

"What?" Neil asked.

Nyla looked at her husband to see if it was okay. Sampson's guardian angel nudged him to share his story. He nodded.

"Um, Sampson had some pretty crazy spiritual activity before we met."

"Oh really?" Grey asked. "Do tell."

Sampson put his fork down and leaned back.

"I can't give any details about my assignment, but my last mission, my entire squad was wiped out and I was left for dead..."

When he finished the story about his encounter with the angel and the hand of God, they were speechless. Hunter let out a scream when he couldn't get the food off his father's plate and broke the silence. They laughed.

"Whoa, I got goosebumps," Kadijah confessed.

"I knew it was something about you that I liked," Nigel told him.

"Well, since y'all aren't completely strangers to the game and we're spilling spiritual tea," Grey interjected, "Nyla, there's something you should know." Nyla and Sampson stared wide-eyed. "That night you were shot, and I watched over you I was praying for you. I saw you wore a golden key around your neck, just like Neil and I have."

"Are you serious?" Nigel asked.

Grey nodded.

Sampson frowned. "Wait, you actually saw a golden key around her neck?" Grey nodded. "How?"

"That's a long story, but we'll exchange war stories one day."

"What does it mean?" Nyla asked.

"It means you have a spiritual gift and something on your journey to redemption activated it."

Nyla frowned. *How was that possible?* She barely grasped deserving to be forgiven. Now she was gifted on top of it.

"Well, what's my gift?"

Grey shrugged. "I don't know sweetie. You're going to have to seek God. He'll reveal it in His time. Two things you better learn now when dealing with our Heavenly Father is patience and blind faith."

"So, what is your gift, Grey?" Sampson asked.

"I'm a seer. I can see things in the spirit realm. Angels, demons. The past, the present, the future. It's interesting."

"Like on demand?" he asked.

She laughed. "No, God very much controls what I see and when I see it."

"What about you?" he asked Neil.

"I'm a shield. My spiritual gift allows me to protect and conceal others during spiritual battles."

"Seriously?" Sampson asked.

Neil nodded.

"And yours?" he asked Nigel.

"Mine is discernment. I know things before I *know* them. I'm not sure if I have a key or not, but it has gotten stronger during all this family drama. Like for instance, I knew we could trust you right away and so from there I was able to back off my pursuit of Nyla pretty easily. I also knew she was pregnant before I *knew* she was pregnant."

"And you?" he asked Kadijah.

"As far I know, I was just chosen to be their mother. Gideon is a prophet and Griffon is a shield."

Sam frowned.

"So is Hunter," Neil added.

Nyla had yet to say a word. She was overwhelmed with all this information. Grey could sense her hesitation.

"Listen, it's okay. I know it's a lot to take in, but trust me, it will become second nature. Don't fret. Your gift will reveal itself."

One of Grey's angels, Savas, touched her shoulder. She felt her Holy Ghost kick in.

She said, "Sometimes the war has to begin in order for your gifts to be revealed. They will manifest themselves the minute you're under attack because their function is to protect you. Only a powerful adversary can release a powerful gift. So, patience is a virtue. Not all things need to be asked for. Sometimes you're not waiting for God to show you, you're waiting on the threat to reveal itself, so God can show it!"

There was silence as everyone absorbed the words she'd just uttered. Neil reached for his wife's hand. He silently prayed for her. He knew in this moment; God was using her. Grey felt her husband's silent prayers strengthening her.

"Whew," she said. "I wasn't expecting that. Listen y'all there are more battles ahead. Ma, we know you've been called to be a gatekeeper for the City of Tallahassee. We also know that Nigel and Neil are your watchman, your sword and shield. Kadijah, just so you know, your babies are also a sword a shield. If Gideon is God's mouthpiece, then her brother is her shield. They go hand-in-hand."

Nigel frowned. "Wait, so that makes me the sword, right?"

Grey nodded. "I was wondering when you were going to clue in. That call is coming bro."

Immediately his discernment tuned in to what Grey was saying and something that was always there began to make a strange kind of sense. For the first time ever, he resisted what his gift was telling him.

"What call?" he asked as the panic set in.

"To preach the Word of God."

Neil stared. "I did not see that coming."

"I did," Kadijah and Angela said at the same time.

"How?" Nigel asked sincerely traumatized.

"How did you not?" Angela asked. "Well, maybe it's our fault. We didn't tell you guys your grandfather was a preacher and your father never surrendered to his call to minister. I figured it would hit one of y'all. Nigel because you were so wayward, I felt that was a clear indication it was you."

Nigel frowned. "Wife... you can't be keeping these kinds of bombshells from me," he said to Kadijah.

"It was just speculation on my part, baby."

"Based off what?"

"The way you went to war for your family. When Neil couldn't, and your mom's heart was torn between our daughter and your niece. I watched you cover this family in prayer and spend time in your Word. There was something there. You began to speak differently about this situation. You began to let God order your steps. Oh, there was something there indeed."

Nigel shook his head.

Neil added, "Didn't Etienne tell you that your daughter would need to see it from you. He said it had to come from you. You had to watch over, nurture and direct her calling. He said it had to flow from the head down."

Nigel sat there sincerely baffled.

"Whoa, this is a lot," Nyla said as she rubbed her belly.

"You have no idea baby girl, no idea," Angela said.

"Bro don't trip. Don't think you have to run out and do anything crazy or drastic. What I've learned is this. When God speaks, He will bring His Word to pass and He doesn't need your help to do it. All you have to do is say yes to whatever assignment He puts in front of you. They're like little breadcrumbs. Each yes will get you closer to your destiny and one day you will walk right into it without even trying. But now that you know you are called, it's your job to study the Word and be ready so *when* He calls, there is no delay," Grey told him.

He nodded but chose to remain silent.

"Alrighty then. That was fun," Angela said trying to lighten the mood. "Looks like this dinner was divinely inspired. Let's have some cheesecake and put all the heavy stuff aside for another day."

They all nodded though they were deep in their thoughts about what was on the horizon and what part did each of them play. Sampson pulled Nyla into him. He kissed her forehead. Like she said, they were already soldiers, now they were fighting for a different team. He *never* backed down from a fight. If the Kingdom of Darkness wanted this smoke, they could get it.

Chapter 101: Mending Fences

Supai, Arizona

He knocked and waited. Two minutes later the door opened and all he saw was her hand up over her eyes to block the bright morning sun. Eva pulled her robe around her tank top and boxer shorts.

"Neil? What are you doing here?" she asked confused and shocked.

"We need to talk."

"At seven o'clock on a Saturday morning with an unannounced arrival?" she questioned sincerely baffled.

He shrugged, "I miss your coffee."

Eva smirked and opened the door wider. This was his white flag. She missed him terribly and was grateful he finally was giving them a chance.

Neil stepped into their small, but cozy living room, wearing jeans, a t-shirt, and his Timberland boots. The girls were sitting at the table eating breakfast. They screamed to supersonic levels when they saw him. They abandoned their bowls of cereal leaving the processed sugar to get soggy and ran towards him full force.

Neil knelt down to prepare for the embrace so he wouldn't fall. They rushed into his arms screaming and kissing his cheeks. His heart melted. He missed his goddaughters so much. He couldn't imagine what they had been through with all the crazy.

Eva smiled and wiped a tear from her eye as she headed to go make their coffee. The girls were excitedly telling him about everything that was going on. They were growing up so fast looking like three mini Eva's with random features of Juan sprinkled in.

Neil made himself comfortable on the floor as they continued to give random hugs and tell him everything about their lives. He pulled out pictures of Hunter for each of them to keep.

"He's so cute!" Maria, the middle daughter, said. "Does he have teeth yet?" she asked. "It took Erica forever to get teeth."

He laughed. "Yes, he's got a few pegs and a few more trying to come through," he told them.

"Are you going to have another baby?" Erica the baby girl asked.

"Well we haven't ruled it out. We just want Hunter to get a little older first."

"Uncle Neil, please don't wait this long to come and see us again," Sylvia, the eldest pleaded with tears brimming in her eyes. His heart ached. He pulled her in and kissed her forehead.

"I promise."

Eva came over with two mugs of steaming coffee, one black and one with sugar and cream.

"Okay girls, Uncle Neil and I are going out to the porch to catch up." They protested. "You guys still have chores to do. Your dad will be back in a couple of hours and if your chores are not finished, you can't go."

They exchanged looks, reluctantly gave Neil a parting hug and headed to do what their mother told them. Eva stared after her three stair steps and grinned.

Neil took his black coffee and opened the door. They took a seat on the comfortable rocking chairs Eva and Juan were infamous for. The desert air was dry, but there was a gentle March morning breeze that wafted through every few minutes.

"Why are you here, Neil?" Eva got straight to the point.

"It's time we mended what's broken between us."

She nodded and sipped her coffee. He did the same.

"Can this be mended?" she asked.

"I walked Fuller down the aisle, gave her away to an assassin who's going to raise my niece or nephew and confessed my loyalty and love to her. *This* is possible."

Eva fell out laughing and spilled some of her coffee. She chuckled as he grabbed her cup to keep her from burning herself.

"I missed you so much Neil."

"I missed you too."

"I'm sorry I betrayed you and everything we believed in. I'm sorry, but I tried to make it right, but everything just got screwed up."

"I've learned where there is a web of lies, there will always be something screwed up. You just have to be willing to sort through the layers and find out if what's left at the core is worth fighting for."

"You think our core is worth fighting for?"

"I do, because at our core are my precious goddaughters and I want to be in their lives. They are growing up."

"They are indeed and scaring the crap out of me as they do it."

Neil laughed. "I got a while before I do the teenager thing, but watching Nigel do the daughter thing is pure comedy!" Neil chuckled then sipped more of his coffee.

"I want weekly videos," Eva demanded.

"Done," Neil said still laughing.

For the next two hours they laughed, caught up, broke down, forgave, and mended.

Juan pulled up in their truck. He hopped out and was shocked to see Neil on his porch. Neil stood up when Juan came up the steps and extended his hand.

"You're back?" Juan inquired as he shook Neil's hand.

Neil nodded. "I'm back."

Juan grinned. He leaned down and kissed his wife's cheek then went in the house.

"Well that was uncomplicated," Neil commented.

"Juan's a very uncomplicated guy."

Neil laughed and took his seat again.

†††

His angels had never left his side. They stood valiantly at the corners of the quaint home not really expecting for much spiritual activity, but prepared, nonetheless. What they didn't expect to see was the Angel of Death heading their way.

His slow methodical steps were infamous. He was never in a rush. They didn't know if he was there to take a spirit to the Great Judgment Hall or if he was there for another reason. Lately, he had been extremely unpredictable in his assignments.

His black diamond skin sparkled magnificently in the desert sun. His notorious shadow was behind him. The faces of Neil's angels were apprehensive. Death nodded at them and approached the porch. He reached down to touch Eva's neck as he removed the piece of his shadow and revealed her golden key.

Ern and Koldo stared at the key, then at Death. He nodded and kept strolling completely unbothered.

Chapter 102: The Meeting

They all gathered in the old, abandoned church on the outskirts of Tallahassee, Florida. Every angelic being - military, naval, messenger, and minister - that was involved in the protection of these local saints stood around the sanctuary waiting for the conversation to begin.

Normally, whoever was specifically assigned to a post would not leave their charge unattended or split the duty, but todays debrief was different. The sovereign Lord God had done some amazing things to ensure the survival of one family's spiritual legacy. Chattering about what had gone down in the different battles had spread throughout the angels and Captain Valter wanted them all to be there to discuss so they could be sharper for whatever came next.

The Angel of Death lent his special talents to his brethren to ensure they could all attend. He duplicated himself to everywhere they should have been. Even the gatekeepers at Kingdom Builders Worship Center, Ahiga and Kamau, were in attendance. Now they could focus on the task at hand with full confidence in Death's ability to keep watch.

They were about to begin, then a sonic boom interrupted their meeting as it reverberated throughout the spirit realm. Every angel in attendance looked up. It didn't take long for God's chief messenger, Gabriel, to drop down in all his emerald splendor. He landed down on one knee with his massive wings covering his form.

When he stood up, he acknowledged his fellow angels with a nod. "I didn't want to miss this one either."

Captain Valter laughed and exchanged a warrior's handshake as they clasped forearms.

"We are here today," Valter began, "To assess these unique battles and get a plan for what's to come. The Great I AM went to extraordinary lengths to redeem these souls which we know means they are integral parts of what's ahead. We will be ready when that time comes. Lieutenant Nero will assign warriors to guard Sampson, Nyla, and their child. Your first assignment is to order their steps to move to Tallahassee before the birth of their child. They are new believers, and they are hot targets for the enemy. They need to be under the spiritual protection of their family. It is important they figure that out and soon. Guide them to Kingdom Builders as their church home."

Death raised his massive black diamond hand. "I'd like to volunteer to watch over the child, if the Lieutenant has no objections."

Nero eyed the Captain and then looked back at Death. "I have no objections. The child belongs to you."

"Wait, wait, wait a minute. I'm sorry to interrupt, but I must inquire," Koldo, one of Neil's warriors said.

His partner Ern chuckled. They had discussed on many occasions, Death's unique abilities. Prior to Hope being attacked only a handful of angels had seen him in action. He did not get involved in warfare and now he was always involved with a proclivity for protecting God's littlest soldiers.

"What's up with you and kids man?"

Death smiled, which caused everyone to pause and stare.

"They are under attack by the Kingdom of Darkness. Not just any attack, but the most vicious and the cruelest. Their world is running rampant with predators taking advantage of their innocence, naivete and small stature. The world has become such an abysmal place for them, they are not even protected behind the walls of the church. In some instances, they are preyed on even harder in what is supposed to be the House of the Lord. As Jehovah will reveal, it's not just men they are not safe in the presence of, but even women. The Spirit of Death is chasing them with a vengeance. Why not let me, the Angel of Death counteract those plans? Their innocence makes their faith unshakeable if they are molded and trained in the ways of the Great I AM. For those who are destined to break cycles, shift atmospheres and the change the world, I want to make sure nothing can touch or taint their anointing. There is no defense against me. I can be more than one place at a time. No demonic weapon can take me down and I don't require the prayers of the saints for added strength. Father fashioned me to do His sovereign will. There are some things Satan and his minions will never be allowed to interfere with. He allows them to think they can because it is an exercise in the faith of his children. Such as with Nigel's second born. I know I'm not usually the angel sent to engage in these battles, however, we are in the generation where Father's word, specifically about the children, is being revealed."

Gabriel replied, "And it shall come to pass in the last days, saith God, I will pour out of my Spirit upon all flesh: and your sons and your daughters shall prophesy, and your young men shall see visions, and your old men shall dream dreams."

The Angel of Death nodded.

"And woe unto them that are with child, and to them that give suck in those days!" Lieutenant Nero added.

Again, Death nodded.

"This generation will face spiritual wickedness in ways their ancestors never did. While there is nothing new under the sun, the tools used to accomplish the same old evil have evolved. The church and the saints must evolve as well. Their strategies must reflect the times that they live in."

The angels nodded.

"What are the spiritual gifts of Eva and Nyla?" Gabriel asked.

"Father has not yet revealed that even to me," Death admitted. "We must trust His sovereignty in regard to how they will be used."

"It's like what Grey said when the Holy Spirit led her to speak to all of them. Sometimes you're waiting on the adversary to reveal itself before your gift is activated," Savas, one of her warriors said.

Death nodded.

"Does Sampson have a gift as well?" Captain Valter inquired.

In reply, Death just grinned. The Captain understood, this conversation was done. It was time to get down to business.

"Next up is the gatekeepers moving into position. Everyone but Monet has accepted her assignment. Insidious is highly upset at the blow that was given to him and I have no doubt in my mind that he will extend his time here and insert himself into the fray. It's a personal vendetta for him now. He knows he can't challenge Death, but he will do his best to find a workaround. Monet's disobedience has left a gap in the hedge around the city. Unfortunately, we cannot fill it. If Insidious or any of his minions, especially Draven, get wind of the gap, they will take full advantage. They are bitter and egos are bruised so the attack will be vicious, and it will be strategic. Prepare your charges to think on a higher level. Ministers and messengers stir up their desire to get heavily involved in their Word. Guide them to the Old Testament where Joshua relied on God's strategies to win his battles. Guide them to Psalms to ready themselves for all their emotions and their frustrations. Most importantly, make sure they are understanding the generational curses that coursed through the Children of Israel because they didn't deal with the cancerous behavior in their families, but swept it under the rug."

The ministers and messengers nodded. David's angels took special note. They knew some of this would have to be incorporated in his messages to his congregation.

"We must fortify this city and these gatekeepers must be on post. We continue to be in a season where men have refused to take their place. So, God has called women to the front lines to rally for this city. Once they get on one accord, it will be time for the Watchman to be revealed. Insidious is wise enough to figure that out. Let's be alert and let's think ahead of all the ways he could possibly infiltrate these assignments."

They all nodded. Righteous indignation stirred in them all. Their eyes flamed blue and gold depending on their rank and position.

"We dealt a mighty blow to Nyla's mother," Bojan, one of Grey's warriors, added.

"We did indeed. Which means witchcraft is going to be in full effect," Captain Valter told them.

"Should we summon for naval warriors?" Ranj, Hunter's Hindu naval warrior inquired.

"Yes, you two go now. Ranj you go to the Atlantic Ocean and summon Captain Abrafo. Alvise, you head to the Pacific Ocean and let Captain Nacalli know what we're up against and to hand select warriors to stand with us."

Alvise, was Hunter's Italian warrior, he nodded at the instructions.

The Captain turned to Andronicus, the Latin Captain of the naval forces in the Gulf of Mexico, who had been sent to guard Darcy.

"We also need warriors from your region. I want to make sure we are familiar with any type of witchcraft they may operate in."

Andronicus nodded. He turned to Moray, a Scottish warrior, another of Darcy's guardians.

"You go." Moray nodded.

"Death, I want you to accompany each of them on their journey to ensure there's no interruptions."

Death nodded. He duplicated himself three times. All six of them snapped their massive wings and took flight in a tangle of midnight blue and golden lights. The Captain looked at his army of angels.

"We are here to stand with Father's so beloved humans. We will stand by their side, we will protect them, we will guide them, and we will challenge them. See the Lieutenant for your next assignments. We do this for the precious Blood of the Lamb!"

They all raised their fists in agreement and yelled, "For the Blood of the Lamb!"

Chapter 103: The Reconvening

Insidious paced back and forth in the abandoned train station as he rubbed his scaly chin with his clawed fingers. The other demons stood around waiting for him to speak. He had a decision to make whether he would stay or go. He rarely failed at his operations.

Normally, he would at least have a foothold in the situation, but this was a complete mess. Not only did he not take out Nigel's daughter, he was not successful in Neil and Nigel being the hand of God and taking out their niece. He gambled on the blackness of Fuller's heart and it didn't pan out. Not only was it light there, but a contrite spirit when all was said and done. Now she was married to another light bearer which made her ten times stronger in the spirit and they had received salvation. He couldn't' rely on her new-found knowledge and naivete as a disadvantage because she was surrounded by seasoned warriors.

His biggest devastation was without question, the Angel of Death. No one told him about this warrior's decision to join the warfare, nor did they tell of his unique abilities. He wondered why Lucifer didn't inform him of all he'd be up against when he gave him this assignment.

He shook his head in frustration. He needed to focus.

He asked, "I need an update on what's going on out there."

Draven stepped forward. "I've received reports from all witnesses, scanners and listeners. The angelic army has met up. All were present, even Gabriel made the meeting."

Insidious stared. "Well that's interesting. Their charges were left unguarded and we didn't receive word to attack?" he inquired irritated.

"No, they were all protected by the Angel of Death."

Insidious' eyes slit. "Oh, he is becoming a serious inconvenience that must be dealt with."

"But how?" One of the demons asked. "What defense do we have against him?"

Insidious pondered. "I'm working on it. There's always a way. We just need to find out what that is. Continue Draven."

"According to my most trusted imp, Eva and their niece are sporting golden keys."

Insidious stopped pacing and stared. His face slowly became angry and he let out a scream that shook the room.

"Are you serious?" Draven was hesitant but nodded. "Where is this imp? I want him to tell me this to my face?"

"He's back out on surveillance. I will have him come and speak with you when he returns."

"What about Natasha?" a demon asked.

"What about her?" Draven questioned.

"No, he's right," Insidious said as he began to pace again. "She isn't turning to the light and her level of vengefulness is perfect for what I need. What's the word on the gatekeepers?" he asked.

"All have accepted their assignment except for Monet," Draven informed him.

Insidious looked up. "Why are you just now telling me this?"

"Uh..."

"You idiot! Shut up! I cannot work with this kind of incompetence."

"Well what can you work with?" an unmistakable voice boomed and took the attention of the room.

As they turned toward the voice, all but Insidious bowed before their leader - Satan himself. He barely acknowledged their reverence and stared at Insidious. When they gazed upon him, they saw an angelic being that stood 18-feet tall. He had four wings that were expanded behind him. His wings were white and shimmered. He was still a beautiful creature as his black eyes gazed at each and every demon present.

"Is bowing beneath you?"

"Of course not," Insidious said with faux humility and a slight bow.

Lucifer decided to pick this fight would be petty and take away the focus from his overall agenda. In all his beauty, he stepped to Insidious.

"I can tell by your frustration you've been made aware of the light's secret angelic weapon."

Insidious scowled. "Why did you not warn me? I could have been better prepared."

Satan wasn't even aware of all the Angel of Death could do, but he would never admit that to his minions.

"Perhaps, but he did not stand in the way of you keeping the niece on our side. He didn't stand in the way of she and Sampson meeting. He cannot be blamed for all your failures. However, it was on the job training so you could understand that as skilled as you are, you need to think outside the box. You need to get out of your comfort zone and expand that sinister mind of yours."

Insidious scowled. "I do not have time for games."

"You have time for whatever I deem so," Lucifer said with a hiss.

Insidious kept his mouth closed. Lucifer gestured for him to continue.

Insidious began, "I will personally pay a visit to Natasha, get her to activate her coven."

"May I suggest," Satan interrupted.

Insidious cut him off, "I'm already there. I will make sure *she* is a part of the coven. She will be an asset, no doubt." Satan nodded. "Until Monet accepts her calling, there is a breach in the hedge. We must move quickly to get in before she accepts her assignment."

"So, I take it you're staying?" Lucifer inquired.

Insidious nodded. "It's personal now."

Chapter 104: Family Fun Day

Miami, Florida

Nigel sat outside at the poolside bar dressed in a black suit, crisp white shirt, and no tie. His collar was unbuttoned. His expensive sunglasses framed his handsome face well. Several scantily clad women in various bikinis had hit on him. He simply flashed his ring, ignored them, and continued to sip on his faux alcoholic beverage.

His intel said she would be at the bar between the hours of three and five PM. He checked his watch. It was 4:30 PM. He hoped they didn't have to go to their contingency plan and force her out of the room.

A woman slid on the barstool next to him. "I've been watching you from across the pool," she told him. "I've seen you turn countless women away." Nigel had yet to acknowledge her. "When you see a unicorn, you have to engage."

He turned to look at her. She was a beautiful redhead with full lips and green eyes. Her skin was smooth and alabaster.

"Oh, I'm not about to be added to the bunch. I just wanted to say thank you. It's been a long time since I've seen a married man respect his vows in this city."

Nigel nodded. "I married my wife because I love her."

She smiled. "Thank you for giving me hope that good men still exist."

He took off his glasses. His discernment was picking up something. He said, "I'm sorry he hurt you. Please don't make a good man pay for his mistakes."

She dropped her head. It took a moment to get herself together. He saw her blink back the tears.

"Thank you," she said as she slipped off the stool and returned to her chair across the pool. His heart ached for her. When he turned back around, she was heading his way.

A perfect blend of her two daughters, she sashayed over to the bar wearing an electric blue bikini and matching sarong. She had aged well. Nigel picked up his phone and dialed.

"Make your move," he said when the caller answered. When he heard the call end, he hung up and covered his ear with his hand.

"Do your thing," he said in a low voice, though he was quite confident the man on the wireless radio heard him.

It was confirmed by, "Ten-four."

On the other end of the bar Neil and Grey sat posing as a couple on vacation. They both wore dark sunglasses as they flirted with each other. They also wore tiny wireless earpieces. Neil had a hand on Grey's thigh. He leaned in like he was going to kiss her neck.

"She's here, baby," he whispered.

Grey adjusted her body, so she could get a look. She squeezed his leg to let him know she saw her. Neil's two angels were glorified as were Nigel's. Grey's were not there for strategic purposes. Koldo touched Grey's shoulder. Her eyes flamed. She saw there were four demons that guarded the woman. The demons saw the angels, Neil and Nigel, but they couldn't see Grey because Neil's gift concealed her. They had no idea she was on the scene. If they did, they would have known this was a setup.

Natasha frowned at her ringing phone when she saw that it was a private number. It could be Lucca finally getting in touch with her, so she answered.

"Hello."

"Hi mom." Silence. "Cat got your tongue."

"Michelle is that you? I'm so glad to..."

"Let's cut the bull mommy dearest. This isn't a social call, it's a warning. Lucca's dead." Natasha gasped. "Yeah, I finished that job for you. I have to give it to you, you're a great actress. You had me convinced I was loved, and you loved my father."

"And you're ungrateful. Squandering your skills and for what? A family that will never love you."

"Ungrateful, huh? That's laughable. I'm going to tell you this one time. Back off from me and Eva and leave us the hell alone. You go live your life and let us live ours free of your interference. I don't know what you and Lucca had planned for me, but I'm canceling those plans."

Nigel studied Natasha's face. He could tell whatever Nyla was telling her, it was pissing her off.

"You listen here..." Natasha said with venom.

"No, you listen!" Nyla snapped. "As a matter of fact, look at your chest." Natasha panicked as she looked down and saw the red dot from a laser over her heart. "I can tell by your silence you've seen my little light display. Now that I have your undivided attention know that I am no longer alone. I have my *real* family now watching out for me."

Natasha swallowed. She did not want to deal with Niles' family without Lucca by her side.

"I'm trying to turn over a new leaf. So, I'm showing you mercy. Take it."

"I don't take threats, I make them."

"I don't make threats, I keep promises," Nyla quipped back. "This is your only warning."

She hung up.

Natasha slammed the phone down. Nigel, Neil, and Grey kept a close watch on her. She looked back down at the laser still over her heart. She knew not to make any sudden moves or any phone calls while she had a sniper rifle zeroed in on her heart. She sat for a full minute stewing. Finally, she jumped up and hurried back into the hotel.

Nigel stood up, slid a few bills onto the bar and walked away. Grey and Neil finished the drinks they were nursing and then headed away from the bar.

From one of the high-rise rooms in the adjacent hotel, Sampson dismantled his sniper rifle and packed it in a small case then put the case in his backpack.

"Do you think she'll back off?" Nyla asked him.

"I hope she does," he said sincerely.

She stood up and rubbed her five-month belly. He pulled her into him and kissed her lips.

"We did what we needed to do. Now it's time to live our lives. If she comes with any foolishness, she'll get dealt with. Plain and simple."

There was a knock on the door they recognized. Sampson went to open the door as Nigel, Neil, and Grey walked in.

"So, Grey, what did you see?" Sampson asked fascinated by her gift.

"She's guarded by four demons. One was really ancient. He was part canine, part reptile. Gave me the creeps. She's definitely on team darkness."

They nodded. "What do we do?" Nyla asked.

"We live our lives, and should some shenanigans arise deal with it accordingly," Nigel told them.

"Sounds good to me. Now can we go eat?" Nyla begged.

They laughed.

"Not in this city. Can you wait an hour?" Sampson asked.

"Ugh," she pouted.

Chapter 105: Dabbling in Darkness

Miami, Florida

Natasha sat in her hotel room crying. Her lover and partner in crime was dead and gone and at the hands of her child no less. She was seething with rage. She had to pay for taking him from her. In a fiery rage, she threw things across the room. She cursed. She screamed. She wept.

Insidious watched the tantrum with boredom. He was beyond pissed that those feckless saints had bested him and managed to overcome all his well laid manipulations. It was degrading to say the least.

Now, it was time to take the gloves off. He knew it was only a matter of time before Natasha summoned the darkness. He'd wait her out, then give her an earful.

†††

After a while, Natasha calmed. She placed tea light candles in the shape of a pentagram on the floor of her hotel suite. Once they were lit, she sat in front of them. She began her séance to try and reach Lucca.

As she performed the ritual to commune with the spirits and the dead, Insidious began to whisper to her in Lucca's voice.

"She is with child. You want revenge, take the baby for your own. Gather your coven and launch an attack. Take out her uncles first. Then you can get to her grandmother. Once you get her out of the way, then she'll be unprotected and all yours."

Natasha smiled at the instructions. She was coming to avenge the death of her lover and to take her grandchild. With that kind of sacrifice her power would be unmatched. She smiled. Yes, it was indeed time to gather her coven. Insidious grinned.

Chapter 106: The North Gate

Darcy was washing dishes while Jessica sat at the table doing homework. Their angels surrounded them and their home as they had been since they were assigned. It was an ordinary weekday, but the extraordinary was about to occur.

There was this immense feeling that passed over Darcy. She gasped and dropped the glass she held in her hand. It fell to the tile floor and shattered.

Jessica screamed, "Mama! Are you okay?"

She stared wide eyed waiting for a response. Darcy hadn't moved and seemingly didn't acknowledge the glass she'd just broke.

"Ma! Are you okay?" Jessica asked again, this time standing.

Darcy put her hand out for Jessica to stay put. She clutched her chest and then said, "I'm fine. Don't come any closer until I get this glass up. You're not wearing any shoes."

"Ma! What's wrong? You look like you saw a ghost."

Darcy leaned against the kitchen counter. "You know, it's funny you say that because honestly, it just felt like someone walked over my grave."

Jessica frowned. "Say what now?"

Darcy shook her head. She didn't know any other way to describe what she felt. Since God had revealed she was the North Gatekeeper she had begun to see many things, mostly in dreams. She knew God was trying to tell her something, but what she had no idea. Whatever it was, it was big.

"It's okay sweetie. It's okay."

Jessica stared at her mother not at all believing it was okay. Darcy stepped around the glass and went to get the broom and dustpan. When she returned and began to sweep, she felt something evil vexing her spirit.

"Jesus!" she cried out.

When she looked up, the vision played out right before her. There were four hooded dark figures standing behind a massive black wrought iron gate. The one in front threw her hand out and the gate opened. They hesitated, but only a second or two and then walked through the gate.

Darcy blinked rapidly as the vision fell away. Andronicus, the Latin Captain of the Gulf of Mexico, reached out and touched her shoulder. He glorified to give her insight and revelation.

Darcy gasped.

"Ma, you are really starting to scare me," Jessica interjected.

"I'm okay, baby. God is just trying to tell me something. What is it Father?" Darcy asked aloud. Then it hit her. "Oh my God, there are four of them and only three of us. Is that why the gate opened? Jesus! I need to call Angela right now. We have to close that gate!"

Chapter 107: A Message from Beyond

It was five o'clock in the morning. Nigel was up sitting on the porch of their new four-bedroom home being grateful. He'd wanted to build a house, but Cynthia had found one at a great price that he couldn't resist, especially since they had outgrown their apartment. Plus, it was near Neil and Grey's neighborhood, a definite bonus.

He'd taken off a few days to get them moved. Today they had to go buy Kadijah a new car because he wanted more reliable and larger transportation for her to move around with the twins. His family had grown by leaps and bounds in a short period of time.

He chuckled about all the plans he had and how one move of God shifted it all. They said, if you wanted to make God laugh, tell Him your plans. Truer words had never been spoken. For the last month life had been insanely crazy and moving at a pace he could not keep up with.

His last day of work before the move, he had an unexpected visitor. Etienne's nurse came to hand deliver one of his infamous letters from beyond the grave. He was not shocked because his discernment had told him to expect one. Honestly, he was afraid to open it. He hadn't told his wife or Neil about it. Today he felt a press to open it. He stared at the beautifully addressed stationary, still resistant to opening it and finding out what Etienne had to say.

Personally, he'd had enough bombs dropped on him to last for at least the next year. He wasn't ready for any more spiritual responsibility. He really and truly wanted to focus on raising his children. He had plans to decrease his hours at his company soon. He was definitely getting off the front lines of dignitary protection, unless God informed him otherwise. He had children now and being there to raise them was his top priority. He fumbled with the letter then sipped his coffee.

The sun wouldn't be up for another couple of hours. He enjoyed the stillness and quiet. He loved when it was just him and God. His screened in porch was immaculate. He couldn't wait to go and buy rocking chairs so they could enjoy the serenity of the nature around them. He could see his children running and playing on the lawn. It brought a smile to his face.

Lajos, his Hungarian angel, touched his shoulder, nudging him to read the letter. Nigel sighed. He knew once he read it, he would be accountable to it. He sat his coffee mug down next to his pistol and carefully opened the pristine stationary. His penmanship was beautiful and looked like a font. Nigel sighed and began to read:

Nigel,

Congratulations on the birth of your twins. I know it was a shock, nor was it easy, but I knew Jehovah held them in His bosom their whole journey to get here. Gideon and Griffon, what strong names.

"What the... How did he know their names?" Nigel asked out loud and confused. He just shook his head. This letter was already too much. He continued:

These weapons have been entrusted to you because everything you need to raise them is already inside of you. Do not doubt yourself or think it strange as your new spiritual identity is revealed to you. I'm sure Grey has already clued you in, if she hasn't, there is a call on your life to preach the Word of God. Your path to the pulpit will be unorthodox, but don't doubt for one second that you have been chosen by God to do just what He's going to have you do. You're such a unique vessel, one that can fit in anywhere. Those who you are called to preach to won't be the kind that sit up in church in their Sunday best. Don't let traditional ways of thinking limit what God wants to do with your life. So many people are searching for something that only God can provide, but they have no desire to come to anybody's church to find Him for many reasons. It's time for the church to come out of the four walls to reach people where they are. Through you, your children will learn how to love all people and how to show the love of God to anybody in need. Continue to study the Word of God. You are the sword of the sword and shield sent to protect your mother until God sends her new covering. As the sword, the Bible will be your spiritual weapon. Study it to show yourself approved. The Word of God is alive and breathing. Let it be an experience. Immerse yourself in it so you can get the divine revelations He has for you. By the way, don't let that wife of yours be deterred from her pursuit of that law degree. God placed that desire in her heart and He wants a return on His investment. Her assignment doesn't change because she's a mother, just like yours doesn't change because you're a father. Work together as a team to be the powerful unit He created you two to be. I'm so very proud of you son. By the way, there's a reason you feel what you feel about Sampson. Seek God, He will reveal all. He can't replace Niles, but your brotherhood was always meant to be a three-strand cord. The word says, "Though one may be overpowered, two can defend themselves. A cord of three strands is not quickly broken." Neil struggled until you came to help him with his assignment. The two of you had your hands full fighting for your niece. Don't think for one moment a man with his skill sent to be a part of your family was a coincidence. Embrace him. All of him. He needs family just as much as your niece does. There's a great man inside of him. Help him find it. Well, I so wish I could have been there to meet your children, but Jehovah lets me peek down every now and then to get a glimpse. Neville and I will keep watch from here. Down there, you keep watch, remain sober and vigilant. A great warrior resides in you. Don't be afraid to unleash him.

Eternally,
Etienne

"Wow," was all Nigel managed to say when he finished the letter. He held the letter to his chest, laid back and closed his eyes. "Okay Father, I hear you." His angelic warriors grinned as the golden key around his neck glowed brightly in the spirit realm.

Epilogue: The Breach

Dawn had yet to settle on the City of Tallahassee, Florida. In April of 2016, the fog hovered on the grounds of the Sleepy Hollow Cemetery, creating a very creepy picture that would make any horror movie proud. It was too early for visitors, but the groundskeeper, Ulysses was there.

Per his usual modus operandi, he was intoxicated, but functional. In the early mornings, he liked to sit in his wooden rocker outside the tiny building for the groundskeeper sipping his Irish coffee. This morning was no different. At least not until he looked up and saw them.

Four figures all hooded in plush velvet black robes with hoods that covered most of their faces entered the cemetery. He almost fell out of the chair but managed to right himself. He blinked. It looked like they were floating, but he convinced himself their robes simply covered their feet.

They walked with one in front, two on the side and one bringing up the rear. He didn't know if it was the dense fog that protected them from seeing him. He was grateful the sun had yet to come out.

As they passed by him, his skin prickled. He felt a sense of evil wash over him. He trembled as he watched them float towards the back of the cemetery. He squinted and gasped when he realized they stopped at the grave of his Angel's family.

He quietly sat his coffee down and decided to get a closer look. He pulled out his cell phone and began to record them. He tried his best to be quiet. He saw one of them bend down and scoop up some dirt with a small shovel and put it in a Ziploc bag.

He scratched his head completely traumatized. *Was he really looking at witches?* He took a step back and felt the twig snap beneath his clumsy foot. All four of them turned towards the noise. He gasped in fear and dropped his phone. Losing his balance, he stumbled a bit.

They ran toward him, but he couldn't manage to get his feet to cooperate.

"What are you doing in my cemetery?" he asked as they approached. "I won't let you hurt that family," he blustered.

The woman that stood in front of him removed her hood. She was beautiful. Her red lips broke into a grin.

"Too bad you won't live long enough to tell."

He didn't see the ancient athame at her side. She swiped so fast, it never even registered to him what happened. He grabbed at his throat as he stumbled back and fell on top of his phone. His eyes rolled in the back of his head as he bled out.

One of them said, "Let's take some of his blood, just in case."

They nodded. "Good idea," another said.

The killer smiled.

†††

Hours later, a family came to visit the grave of their loved one.

"Hey what's that on the ground?" the man asked.

"Looks like someone fell asleep in the middle of the cemetery," his wife said. "That's creepy."

She was about to walk closer. Her husband stopped her and shook his head.

"I'll go," he said. He slowly approached the figure on the ground. "Oh God! Call 911 now!"

Letter to the Reader

Hello Reader,

I hope you enjoyed reading this book as much as I enjoyed writing it. When I started this "new war" I had no idea what to expect. I knew who the "villain" was, and I had no plans of redeeming her, but God did. Hey, who am I to argue with His sovereignty, even if it was for a fictional character, LOL.

I know this story is wild and it may make some church folks uncomfortable having killers redeemed, but Paul was an assassin, and he went on to write two-thirds of the New Testament. Also, God changed Jacob's name to reflect his destiny and not who he'd been in his old trickster days. However, whenever God reminded other saints of who He was He said He was the God of Abraham, Isaac, and Jacob. Let *that* marinate. God changed his name, but often referred to him by his birth name to remind us of His redeeming power.

In this season, realize the choice of who should and should not be redeemed, who should and should not be blessed was never yours to make. It is the sovereign will of God that is for us all. No one sin is greater than another. Be the vessel that God can use to recruit new soldiers into the Kingdom in these last and evil days! You never know which vessel is carrying God's most powerful gifts.

I also hope, in addition to entertaining you, you realize that no matter who you are or where you come from, God loves you. He has a plan for your life. *You are so important to God that angels and demons are fighting over you every single day!*

If this book in any way, shape, or form made you want to know Jesus Christ as your personal Lord and Savior, then I want to extend to you the free gift of salvation. It doesn't matter who you are, where you are, or what you've done. You can stop right now and ask Jesus to come into your heart. It's as easy as your ABC's.

A = Admit you are a sinner, ask for forgiveness
B = Believe in Jesus Christ, that he died and rose again
C = Confess, I accept Jesus as my personal Lord and Savior

Romans 10:9-10 (NASB) –That if you confess with your mouth Jesus as Lord and believe in your heart that God raised Him from the dead, you will be saved; for with the heart a person believes, resulting in righteousness, and with the mouth he confesses, resulting in salvation.

Sincerely,

Melinda Michelle

Discussion Questions

1. Do you agree with Fuller being redeemed? Why or why not?
2. Have you ever judged someone who got pregnant out of wedlock? Did it ever occur to you that only God can give life?
3. Do you believe that spiritual gatekeepers are a real thing? Why or why not?
4. Why do you think Monet resisted her assignment?
5. Have you ever deliberately disobeyed an assignment given to you by God? Why?
6. What were your thoughts on Genevieve giving a sermon?
7. How do you feel about Sampson Steele?
8. Who do you think is the witch Satan and Insidious want Natasha to reach out to?
9. What do you think about the Angel of Death and all his "special" skills?
10. Were you shocked by the new soldiers that earned keys?
11. What do you think their gifts are?

12. How did you feel about the Angel of Death's strategy for Nigel's children? Have you ever known a baby that didn't have a heartbeat, but still was born healthy? Did this storyline add perspective?

13. Did you realize Nigel prayed to "blind" his enemies and that's exactly what Death did?

14. When trying to hear from God, have you ever searched the Bible for your answer? Why or why not?

15. What new things did you learn about having a relationship with God from what the characters experienced?

About the Author

Gwendolyn Melinda Michelle Evans (GMME) is a Florida native - born in Jacksonville, raised in Sanford and currently resides in Tallahassee. Tallahassee became her home when she graduated from the renowned HBCU, Florida Agricultural and Mechanical University, with a Bachelor of Science in Accounting. After the completion of her bachelors, Melinda received an MBA with a concentration in Finance and Accounting from American Intercontinental University. After enjoying a career in business for a decade, she stepped out on faith to fulfill the purpose inside of her - writing. Melinda is currently pursuing her Doctor of Philosophy in Social Psychology from Walden University.

Melinda Michelle is the author of 22 published works. Her titles include both fiction and nonfiction. Although the genres vary, spiritual warfare is her signature subject. She remains true to a theme in all her books - the love and power of the Almighty God. Her work has won awards and brought her before many audiences as a speaker. She has served as a panelist, keynote speaker and conference orator tackling the subject of spiritual warfare for women's groups, prisons, and churches. Her publishing company, Global Multi Media Enterprises (GMME), currently has 12 authors with over 40 published books.

When you pick up a book by Melinda Michelle you should expect for your eyes to be opened, your heart to race, your emotions to rise and your faith to be taken up a notch. Purpose is her passion and with that passion, she weaves a story about the matchless power of the Almighty God through the written Word by the guidance of the Holy Spirit. It is her desire to awaken the Body of Christ to not only the power that they have but the knowledge that they truly wrestle not against flesh and blood. Melinda's stories are designed to connect with Christians, but it is her desire to connect with readers from all walks of life. Her stories are designed to captivate the reader with powerful testimonies about God.

Melinda received the Author of the Year award by Divas on Fire Magazine in 2016. Her Chronicles of Warfare series won the Redemptive Fiction Award of Excellence by Radiax Press and "Saturday Showdown" was a nominee for Indie Book 2016 by Metamorph Publishing. For more information visit her website @ www.melindamichelle21.com.

Appendix

Character Appendix

Character	Description	Nickname	Other Details Revealed	From
Aliaksana Novik	Girl in captivity that Neil secretly passed info to		High tolerance for the drugs used on her	Belarus
Alonzo Casales	Republican Congressman running for Governor		Marcus's father; Untouchable	
Angela Lawson	Mother of Neil and Nigel		Knew about family's generational curse	Tallahassee, FL
Aunt Miriam Walker	Naomi's Aunt		Her sister abandoned Naomi	Fort Lauderdale, FL
Barrington Scottsdale	Grey's Cat		Left to her in her neighbor's will	
Beau	Grey's bodyguard		Receives salvation (Thursday)	
Blake	Guest appearance from Color Me Blind			Jacksonville, FL
Brooklyn	Grey's Friend		Church Administrator	
Captain Neilson	Captain of the Homicide Division of TPD			Tallahassee, FL
Cassia Reynolds	Monet's Best Friend			Las Vegas, NV
Charles Wesley	Given up for adoption by Darcy, falsely imprisoned	C	Lived in FL for 7 years before imprisoned	Hattiesburg, MS
Constance	One of Kadijah's friends			
Cynthia	Nigel's assistant		Came with him from California	California
Dallas Easton	Monet's Son/Architect		Tattoo, Triplet	Las Vegas, NV
Daniel Richards	Seth and Sheridan's son			
Darcy Stone	First Lady of Kingdom Builders Worship Center			Georgia
David Michael King	Youngest to be Ordained/Appears in Charles' Dreams		Senior Pastor of KBWC	Miami, FL
Desmond Blackwell	Brother to Pearl and Miriam Blackwell		Afraid of Black Pearl	
Dr. Lucca Preston	Sheridan's Partner		Untouchable	
Ebony	Church Gossip			
Emma Lee Ellis	Sheridan's Mother			Jacksonville, FL
Erica Galarza	Eva's youngest daughter		Goddaughter to Neil	
Etienne	Great prophet		105 years old	New Orleans, LA
Eva Galarza	Neil's Partner		Untouchable	
Genevieve Lewison	Third watch intercessor brought to KBWC		In Witness Protection	Miami, FL
Grey Elise Lawson	Banker/Accountant; Neil's wife		Godmother to Hope; Seer	Orlando, FL
Gyselle	Praise & Worship Leader @ KBWC			
Hope Elizabeth Parker	Jamal and Lindsey's daughter		Healer; Guarded by Angel of Death	Tallahassee
Isaiah Justice	Jeremiah and Mia's youngest son			
Jacob Parker	Stacy's son		Jamal's previously unknown son	Tallahassee, FL
Jamal Parker	Lindsey's Husband		Lindsey's Attacker	Chicago, IL
Janine Stone	Middle Daughter of Josiah and Darcy Stone			Tallahassee, FL
Jasmine	Guest appearance from Color Me Blind	Jaz, Jazzy	Co-Owner Diversified Styles	Jacksonville, FL
Jeremiah Justice	Seth's Best Friend		PJ's armor bearer	
Jeremiah Justice, Jr.	Jeremiah and Mia's son	Lil Jay		
Jessica Stone	Youngest daughter of Josiah and Darcy Stone		Spiritually gifted; received father's mantle	Tallahassee, FL
Jewel Stone	Oldest Daughter of Josiah and Darcy Stone		Married with child	Tallahassee, FL
Jocelyn Stone	Middle Daughter of Josiah and Darcy Stone			Tallahassee, FL
Jody	Charles' best friend and cell mate		Gave his life to save Charles'	
Josiah Stone	Pastor of Kingdom Builders Worship Center (KBWC)	PJ	Deceased	Mississippi Delta
Juan Galarza	Eva's husband			
Julian Black	Assistant to Chief of Staff for Alonzo Casales		Kadijah's best friend	
Kadijah Lawrence	Student (Poli Sci)		Works for Alonzo Casales' Campaign	Miami, FL
Kane Kennison	Leader of Miami cell of the Untouchables		Real Name is Dexter Kingsley	Miami, FL
Kelly	Hotel Clerk that spotted Sheridan		Prayer warrior	
Kia	Genevieve's best friend since 3rd Grade		Speaks Spanish, Creole and French	Miami, FL
Lamont Blackwell	Genevieve's ex-boyfriend		Mason; Dabbles in Witchcraft	Miami, FL
Lawrence	Grey's Neighbor		Neil's Cousin	
Lewis	Monet's trusted private investigator		Monitored Seth most of his life	

Character	Description	Nickname	Other Details Revealed	From
Lindsey Parker	Woman who falsely accused Charles of Rape		Formerly known as Charlotte Brown	Chicago, IL
Logan Randall	Cassia's Brother/Defense Attorney		Responsible for Seth's Adoption	Dallas, TX
Lucy	Guest appearance from Color Me Blind		Co-Owner Diversified Styles	Jacksonville, FL
Madison Justice	Jeremiah and Mia's daughter			
Maksim Novik	Works as a runner for Untouchables		Helped Grey when she was kidnapped	Belarus
Marcus Williams	Sarah's teenage son		Neil's mentee; Doesn't know Alonzo is father	Unknown
Margaret Lawrence	Kadijah's step mother/Tiara's mother		Black Pearl's half sister	
Marie Galarza	Eva's middle daughter		Goddaughter to Neil	
Martin Adams	Cassia's Husband		Financially supports Cassia's endeavors	Miami, FL
Melissa	Monet's Assistant			
Meredith Sutton	Journalist		Usually gets exclusive interviews with Charles	Tallahassee, FL
Mia Justice	Jeremiah's Wife			
Michelle Fuller	FBI Agent		Neil's undercover partner	
Miriam Blackwell	Sister to Pearl and Desmond Blackwell		Mentally ill; Paralyzed in a wheelchair	
Miss Essie Mae	Midwife who delivered Darcy's son		Close to Jessica before deceased	Jacksonville, FL
Monet Grayson	Madam (Seth's Biological Mother)	Monie	Assisted Neil with undercover operations	Las Vegas, NV
Monroe	Kane's driver		Having an affair with Kane's wife	Miami, FL
Ms. Ruth	Nurse that Helped Kadijah		Prayer Warrior for the city of Tallahassee	Tallahassee, FL
Naomi Walker	Choir Member		Accused Seth of Fathering her child	Fort Lauderdale, FL
Nathanial Justice	Jeremiah's Nephew			
Neil Lawson	Homicide detective, Grey's husband		God requires his natural abilities in the war	Tallahassee, FL
Nigel Sims	Neil's Younger Brother		Works in Security (Executive Protection); Different last name than his brother for security	Tallahassee, FL
Niles Lawson	Neil and Nigel's Older Brother		Killed as a teenager; Unsolved Murder	Tallahassee, FL
Orlando Grayson	Monet's Son/Computer Engineer		Tattoo, Triplet	Las Vegas, NV
Parker Easton	Pimp (Deceased)		Triplets Biological Father	Las Vegas, NV
Pearl Blackwell	Lamont's Mother	Black Pearl	High Priestess (Witch)	
Percival James	Pastor/Tiara's/Simone's Father	Percy		
Phoenix	Alonzo's chief of staff		Julian's boss	
Randall Livingston	Pastor trying to hire Seth away		Untouchable	
Reece Richards	Seth's Adopted Father		Caucasian; Habit in common w/Naomi	Deland, FL
Regina	Genevieve's old roommate		Delivered from Demonic Possession	
Remington	Kane's right hand man		Killed by Eva	Miami, FL
Renet Richards	Seth's Adopted Sister		Caucasian	Deland, FL
Samantha Kennison	Daughter of Kane		Neil saved her life while undercover	Miami, FL
Sarah Williams	Mother to Marcus, fled her home		True identity unknown	Unknown
Seth Richards	Minister of Music @ KBWC		Triplet (previously unknown)	Deland, FL
Shayla Richards	Seth's Adopted Mother		Caucasian	Deland, FL
Sheree	Grey's Friend			
Sheridan Richards	Psychologist, Seth's Wife	Sheri	Ministry of Deliverance	Jacksonville, FL
Sierra	Lawrence's wife			
Stacy Legend	Sheridan's assistant	Stace	Has a son with Jamal, previously unknown	Tallahassee, FL
Sydney	Grey's Friend			
Sylvia Galarza	Eva's oldest daughter		Goddaughter to Neil	
Tameka Monroe	Naomi's Best Friend		Cousin to Jasmine Jessup (Color Me Blind)	
Tiara/Janet/Simone	Girl that tried to kill Kadijah		Is Kadijah's stepmom's real daughter	
Timothy Kennison	Son of Kane			Miami, FL
Troy Waters	Killer of Lillian Powers			Hattiesburg, MS
Vanessa Kennison	Wife of Kane		Having an affair with husband's driver	Miami, FL
Viviana	Grey's friend who works for the IRS	Viv	Requested Grey's Help in a Fed Investigation	Fort Lauderdale, FL
Yvonne	Woman in car accidents with both Seth & Grey		Red and Blonde Afro/Married Orlando	Haiti

Spirit Appendix

Name	Assigned To	Color Aura	Type	Height	Heritage	Weapon	Position	Function	Book
Cibor	Charles Wesley	White	Military	8 Feet	Polish	Battle Axe		To Fight In Warfare	Monday
Hondo	Charles Wesley	White	Military	8 Feet	Egyptian	War Hammer		To Fight In Warfare	Monday
Mardig	Charles Wesley	White	Military	8 Feet	Armenian	Sabre Sword		To Fight In Warfare	Monday
Andrej	Charles Wesley	White	Military	8 Feet	Czech			To Fight In Warfare	Monday
Merek	Charles Wesley/(Joseph)	Blue Sapphire	Minister	6 Feet				To Fight In Warfare	Monday
Ragnar	Essie/Jessica	White	Military	8 Feet	Scandinavian	Falchion		To Fight In Warfare	Monday
Thane	Essie/Jessica	White	Military	8 Feet	English	Bec de Corbin		To Fight In Warfare	Monday
Ifor	Essie/Jessica	White	Military	8 Feet	Welsh	Lochaber Axe		To Fight In Warfare	Monday
Jalmari	Essie/Jessica	White	Military	8 Feet	Finnish	Flail		To Fight In Warfare	Monday
Arthfael	Genevieve	White	Military	8 Feet	Welsh	Broad Sword		To Fight In Warfare	Tuesday
Murtagh	Genevieve (Temporary)	Gold	Naval	13 Feet	Scottish	Zweihander		To Fight In Warfare	Tuesday
Savas	Grey	White	Military	8 Feet	Turkish	Two Broad Swords		To Fight In Warfare	Sunday
Bojan	Grey	White	Military	8 Feet	Serbian	Long Sword		To Fight In Warfare	Sunday
Abrafo	**Grey**	**Gold**	**Naval**	**13 Feet**	**African**	**Scimitar Sword**	**Atlantic Naval Captain**	**To Fight In Warfare**	**Tuesday**
Alvise	Grey	Gold	Naval	13 Feet	Italian	Arming Sword		To Fight In Warfare	Wednesday
Arluin	**Grey/Neil**	**White**	**Military**	**8 Feet**	**French**		**Captain in New Orleans**	**To Fight in Warfare**	**Tuesday**
Death	Hope	Midnight Blue	Military	16 Feet	Made of Black Diamonds	Scythe		Escort spirits to Great Throne of Judgment/Fight in Warfare	Tuesday
Agro	Hope/Jamal	White	Military	8 Feet	Celtic	Spatha		To Fight In Warfare	Wednesday
Hilde	Hope/Jamal	White	Military	8 Feet	Swedish	Flail		To Fight In Warfare	Wednesday
Cerdic	Hope/Jamal	White	Military	8 Feet	Anglo Saxon	Claymore Sword		To Fight In Warfare	Wednesday
Lutz	Hope/Lindsey	White	Military	8 Feet	German	Horseman's Pick		To Fight In Warfare	Wednesday
Orion	Josiah	Blue Sapphire	Minister	6 Feet				Usher in God's Anointing	Sunday
Roman	Josiah	Blue Sapphire	Minister	6 Feet				Usher in God's Anointing	Sunday
Cheveyo	Khadijah	White	Military	8 Feet	Native American	War Scythe		To Fight In Warfare	Sunday
Quan	Khadijah	White	Military	8 Feet	Japanese	Arming Sword		To Fight In Warfare	Sunday
Kamau	Kingdom Builders	White	Military	8 Feet	African	Crossbow	Gate Guardian (KBWC)	To Fight In Warfare	Sunday

Name	Assigned To	Color Aura	Type	Height	Heritage	Weapon	Position	Function	Book
Ahiga	Kingdom Builders	White	Military	8 Feet	Native American	Pike	Gate Guardian (KBWC)	To Fight In Warfare	Sunday
Takeshi	Lindsey	White	Military	8 Feet	Japanese	Claymore Sword		To Fight In Warfare	Monday
Nolan	Lindsey	White	Military	8 Feet	Irish	Flamberge Sword		To Fight In Warfare	Monday
Koldo	Neil	White	Military	8 Feet	Basque	Pike		To Fight In Warfare	Tuesday
Ern	Neil	White	Military	8 Feet	English	Morning Star		To Fight In Warfare	Tuesday
Bahadur	Neil	Gold	Naval	13 Feet	Persian			To Fight in Warfare	Saturday
Ranj	Neil	Gold	Naval	13 Feet	Hindu			To Fight in Warfare	Saturday
Aidan	Seth	Blue Sapphire	Minister	6 Feet				Usher in God's Anointing	Sunday
Tero	Sheridan	White	Military	8 Feet	Finnish	Scimitar Sword		To Fight In Warfare	Monday
Wayland	Sheridan	White	Military	8 Feet	English	Horseman's Pick		To Fight In Warfare	Monday
Valter	**Sheridan**	**White**	**Military**	**8 Feet**	**Scandinavian**	**Sabre/Shoulder/Baldric**	**Captain of the Host**	**To Fight In Warfare**	**Sunday**
Gage	Sheridan	Blue Sapphire	Minister	6 Feet				Usher in God's Anointing	Sunday
Nero	**Varies**	**White**	**Military**	**8 Feet**	**Italian**	**Spatha**	**Lieutenant to Valter**	**To Fight In Warfare**	**Sunday**
Michael	**Varies**	**Gold**	**Military**	**Unknown**	**African**	**Long Sword**	**Archangel**	**To Fight In Warfare**	**Tuesday**
Gabriel	**Varies**	**Emerald**	**Messenger**	**18-Feet**	**Anglo Saxon**	**Qama Dagger**	**Archangel**	**To Deliver Msgs/Fight**	**Thursday**
Cree	Varies	Emerald	Messenger	7 Feet		Stiletto		To Deliver Msgs/Fight	Sunday
Lance	Varies	Emerald	Messenger	7 Feet		Anelace		To Deliver Msgs/Fight	Sunday
Rowan	Varies	Emerald	Messenger	7 Feet		Poniard		To Deliver Msgs/Fight	Tuesday
Darrow	Varies	Emerald	Messenger	7 Feet		Cinquedea		To Deliver Msgs/Fight	Sunday
Tallis	Varies	Emerald	Messenger	7 Feet		Baselard		To Deliver Msgs/Fight	Sunday
Saban	Varies	Emerald	Messenger	7 Feet		Katara		To Deliver Msgs/Fight	Sunday
Cassius	Varies	Emerald	Messenger	7 Feet		Rondel		To Deliver Msgs/Fight	Monday
Asher	Varies	Blue Sapphire	Minister	6 Feet				Usher in God's Anointing	Monday
Bomani	Nigel	Gold	Military	8 Feet	Egyptian	Takoba		To Fight In Warfare	Friday
Lajos	Nigel	Gold	Military	8 Feet	Hungarian	Viking Sword		To Fight in Warfare	Friday
Nacalli	**Varies**	**Gold**	**Naval**	**13 Feet**	**Aztec**		**Pacific Naval Captain**	**To Fight in Warfare**	**Saturday**
Powers Angels	Varies	Pinkish White	Military	12 Feet				To Fight In Warfare/Guard	Monday
Corruption	1st Ruling Demon in charge of Tallahassee (vanquished back to the underworld)								Sunday
Destroyer	2nd Ruling Demon placed in charge of Tallahassee (replaced Corruption(Monday); vanquished by Lucifer for failing (Thursday))								Sunday
Naamah	Marine Kingdom ranking siren								Tuesday
Strongman	Ruling Demon over a territory								Sunday
Rege	Drugs of sorcery: weed, hashish, cocaine, speed, LSD, peyote, mescaline							Principality	Friday
Larz	Sexual Lust: homosexuality, adultery, sexual pleasures							Principality	Friday
Bachus	Addictions: drugs, smoking, alcohol							Principality	Friday
Pan	The Mind: Mental illness, depression, suicide, nerves, rejection							Principality	Friday
Medit	Hate, murder, killing, war, jealousy, envy, gossip							Principality	Friday
Set	Death: Wars, terrorism							Principality	Friday
No Name	Strife in the church and among the brethren							Principality	Friday

Chess Board

(Sheridan) Rook
(Neil) Knight
(Josiah) Bishop
(Grey) Queen
(Charles) King
(David) Bishop
(Monet) Knight
(Kadijah) Rook
(Seth) Pawn
(Jessica) Pawn
(Jasmine) Pawn
(Genevieve) Pawn
(Hope) Pawn
(Lindsey) Pawn
(Cassia) Pawn
(Marcus) Pawn
(Simone) Pawn
(Kane) Pawn
(Troy) Pawn
(Miriam) Pawn
(Margaret) Pawn
(Lamont) Pawn
(Desmond) Pawn
(Tiara) Pawn
(Lucca) Rook
(Michelle) Knight
(Percy) Bishop
(Pearl) Queen
(Alonzo) King
(Randall) Bishop
(Eva) Knight
(Vanessa) Rook

Connect with Me

Instagram: @TheMelindaMichelle
Twitter: @MelindaMichell
FB Fan Page: Melinda Michelle
Email: gmme@melindmichelle21.com
Web: www.melindamichelle21.com

Works by Melinda Michelle

Novels
Surviving Sunday (Book 1)
Monday Madness (Book 2)
Temptation Tuesday (Book 3)
Watchful Wednesday (Book 4)
Tumultuous Thursday (Book 5)
Finally Friday (Book 6)
Saturday Showdown (Book 7)
The Unexpected Gift (Book 8)
Deleted Scenes: A Behind the Scenes Look at the Chronicles of Warfare (Book 9)
My Brother's Daughter (Book 10)
Color Me Blind: A Divine Love Story (Book I)
Breach of Faith: A Divine Love Story (Book II)
A Christmas Wedding: A Divine Love Story (Novella)

Short Stories
You Can Never Leave
Guilty of the Body and the Blood

Novellas
7 Days and 7 Nights
A Date with Death

Non-Fiction
It's Complicated but Not Really: A Compilation of my Facebook Shenanigans

Misery Loves Company: The Truth About Sexual Strongholds & How to Break Them
The Chronicles of Warfare Handbook: Volume I (Website ONLY)
The Chronicles of Warfare Handbook Volume II (Website ONLY)
Soul Work: How to Wage War on Your Sinful Nature (Website ONLY)

Anthologies
The 21 Lives of Lisette Donovan (You Can Never Leave)
Truth Awaits You on the Other Side (Guilty of the Body and the Blood)

Audio Books
Color Me Blind: A Divine Love Story
Breach of Faith: A Divine Love Story
A Christmas Wedding: A Divine Love Story Novella
Surviving Sunday
Monday Madness
Tumultuous Thursday
7 Days and 7 Nights
A Date with Death
It's Complicated but Not Really: A Compilation of my Facebook Shenanigans

Made in the USA
Columbia, SC
04 July 2022

62782977R00297